MW01199920

PROMISE ME FOREVER

MANHATTAN RUTHLESS

SADIE KINCAID

RED HOUSE PRESS LTD

CONTENT WARNING

This book deals with mature themes including parental death, kidnapping and assault. It also contains scenes of a sexual nature, including but not limited to, bondage.

To all of my readers who have ever fantasized about being railed over a desk, this one's for you.

Love Sadie xx

PROLOGUE

I always loved the sound of ice clinking against glass. It reminds me of summers when I was a kid. As an adult, it comes with the promise of a good Scotch. Which is exactly what my father is pouring into six tumblers. He hands a glass of the fifty-year-old Macallan to each of my brothers and me. My two older brothers stare absentmindedly out the window, watching the fireworks that herald the new year.

Maddox stares blankly at his drink, keeping up the pretense that he has no idea what to do with it. He might be the youngest of us, but I know for sure that he's capable of telling a single malt from an Irish blend.

Mason is the first to say what I suspect we're all thinking. "Does anybody else feel like it's weird that it's just us?"

New Year's Eve was always a big deal in our house. It was a time for dancing and drinking, for family and friends. Tonight, the place feels empty, apart from all the memories. Just five miserable brothers who miss their mom and a dad who can't see past his own pain.

Elijah suggests putting on the TV to watch the ball drop, probably just to fill the silence, but I object straight away.

1

"Nah," I say, shaking my head. "She used to hate that, remember? Was always convinced the time was off by a few seconds." I smile as I say it, but it's a smile that doesn't reach my heart. It's too soon for that.

Mason laughs though, taking up the story. "Remember how she'd always insist on using Great-Grandad's old Navy diving watch to determine when it was midnight instead?"

This is all we have left of her now. Memories and nostalgia, and in my case, a great big dollop of guilt.

"Where the hell is that thing?" Nathan says, frowning. Maddox pulls the watch out of his jeans pocket and holds it up to show us, tears making his eyes shiny.

"Jesus, it feels so weird without her here." Mason downs his Scotch and gets to his feet. "Like this house has no fucking soul anymore. Let's get the fuck out of here and go somewhere."

That's Mason for you. Always in motion.

"Like where, jerkwad?" I ask, rolling my eyes. He's acting like he has a plan, but I know better.

"I dunno. A club or something. A place where there's life."

Life. I think we've all forgotten what that is. I know I have. All I've done since I lost her is focus on my studies and work my ass off. I still feel like shit, but it's helped distract me from how much I miss her. How much I regret.

Maddox pulls a face. He's big—football-star big—but he's still only sixteen, and he won't get into any clubs. "And what about me, dickface?"

"Nobody is going anywhere," Dad snaps, shutting down our bickering in the way only he can. "So quit your whining and drink your Scotch."

"Sorry, Pop." Mason drops back down onto the couch.

We all watch our father down the rest of his drink, his silhouette outlined by the streaks and flashes of color coming from the window behind him. Dalton James is a big man. A tough man. He built his business empire into one of the most successful in the world and made his first billion by the time he was thirty-five. He's impressive in every way—but to us, he's Dad. A dad who was always strict but also fair; a dad who adored all five of us boys but worshipped the very ground his wife walked on. He hasn't been the same since she died, but I guess none of us have. We hoard our grief, him most of all, because that's all we have left of her.

"I have a piece of advice for all you boys," he announces. It's clear that he's serious, and not even Mason rolls his eyes. "You live by this, and I promise that you'll never know a day's heartache in your life."

Too damn late for that, I think.

Elijah looks up at him. "And what's that, Dad?"

Dad pauses, and we all wait to hear what he wants to share with us. His eyes swim with tears I know he will never let fall. He's too hard for that, at least on the outside.

He clears his throat and says, "Never fall in love."

ONE

AMELIA

Weddings suck.

At least they suck if you're single and too scared to mingle. Or if your confidence is blown after discovering your husband was giving more than dictation to his twenty-three-year-old secretary. Or if you're so low on funds that your credit card screams for mercy when you buy the cheapest thing from the couple's Bloomingdale's gift registry.

And if you happen to check off all of the above? Then weddings suck even more. I would have skipped it if I could have and stayed home with a bowl of ramen and the latest season of *Bridgerton*. But this isn't just any wedding—this is the wedding of my best friend, Emily Gregor. It's hard to skip out on a wedding when you're the maid of honor, and besides, I love Emily to pieces.

We've been best friends for the past fourteen years despite the fact that we're as different as two people can possibly be. She's a beautiful, outgoing society heiress who dated a string of rich and successful men before finally settling down with her brand-new husband, Tucker. I, on the other hand, am almost penniless and married my high school sweetheart straight out of college.

He was my first and only love, and I expected to be at his side forever. Until the secretary thing happened. That took some of the shine off things after fifteen years of loyalty, I have to admit. I followed him around the country to support him in his career, but it turned out I was supporting him into the arms of an ambitious blond with enormous boobs and a ring finger begging for a diamond.

Still, I will not be cynical, especially not today. I refuse to put that kind of negative energy out into my best friend's wedding reception, and I can't let one bad experience sour me for love forever. That would mean he really has won.

Anyway, what I lost in a husband, I more than made up for in friendship. Emily and I have always been close, but she really stepped up for me during the breakdown of my marriage. Along with my mom and my childhood friend Kimmy, it was girl power all the way. They were like the Spice Girls on steroids, supporting me through it all, providing me with everything from giant tubs of ice cream to offers to hire a hit man. If wearing this horribly uncomfortable lilac dress and watching other people smooch at a wedding is the price I have to pay for Emily's friendship, then it's a bargain. Deal of the century.

I pick up the glass of champagne in front of me and down it in one as I watch the happy couples mingling around the room and on the dance floor. Well, they look happy, but if there's one thing I've learned over the last year, it's that appearances can be deceptive.

When I spot Emily and Tucker, though, I have to smile. They're gorgeous together—both tall and blond and dressed in white. But the most gorgeous thing of all is the way he looks at her as he twirls her in his arms. Like she's the only girl in the whole universe. It's the way every woman wants to be looked at, and I don't think I've ever seen her so content. She's finally found her true love, and despite my recent man trouble, I am genuinely delighted for her. If anyone deserves to find their Prince Charming, it's Emily. She had to kiss a lot of frogs to find him—hot, rich frogs, sure, but a frog is a frog no matter how much money he has in the bank.

We've reached that stage of the evening when everyone is either drunk, very drunk, or passed out under a table. The children have all crashed after hours of sliding around the dance floor in their fancy clothes, and Emily and Tucker will soon be leaving for their honeymoon in Italy. The once-structured seating plan has gone to hell, and the young singles are all involved in some kind of dance-based mating ritual. It's a lot like a game of musical chairs, only you kiss whoever you end up sitting on.

I'm keeping my distance from the whole thing as I have no desire to lock lips with a stranger tonight. I don't have the energy or the confidence to play that particular game. Being cheated on takes quite a toll on your self-image, it seems, and I've fallen into the very bad habit of rejecting myself before any man can do it for me.

If only Kimmy had been able to make it. My childhood best friend would have ensured I had the time of my life. At least until she found the person she'd give the time of their life to for the rest of the night. Alas, being the head of legal for a worldwide investment firm means that work emergencies can't be fobbed off on anyone else.

But I'm making the best of my solitude and have snuck off to a table at the back of the room. We were all given name tags at the start of the reception because Emily knows a million people from different walks of life, and she wanted them all to get to know each other. It was a fun idea, even if it did give some of the men an excuse to stare at the women's boobs for a bit too long. I've taken mine off now and am busy doodling on it with some crayons that were left in pots to amuse younger guests. And apparently, the maid of honor.

The table shakes lightly as someone sits beside me, and the sudden jarring movement makes my hand slip. When I turn in my seat, ready to slap on a smile and say whatever necessary to get rid of my new tablemate, my mind goes blank. I forget all about the crayons and the dancing and the fact that my feet are killing me. I forget about my mom's health problems and my financial issues and my cheating bastard of an ex-husband. I forget about everything because the man sitting next to me is so damn hot that he erases all other thoughts.

I suck in a breath and wish I had some champagne left. Seriously, if I did, I'd raise a toast to this guy and whatever god created him. Congratulations are very much in order. He's tall even sitting down, his shoulders broad and bulky, and his face ... wow. His face belongs on one of those post-Renaissance statues of a fallen angel, all hard angles softened only by the sinful curve of his lips. His hair is dark and lush, and his strong jawline is coated in a thick but neat beard. I love a beard, especially one as well-groomed as his.

Like most of the male guests, he's dressed in a tux, but this man wears it like he was born in it. He doesn't only look incredible; he smells it too. It's like a full assault on the senses. Maybe he has a voice like Mickey Mouse to make up for everything else being so perfect. I'm staring at him so intensely, he's probably wondering if I should be here with a caregiver, and when he smiles, I drown in the warmth of his deep brown eyes. Dear lord, this guy is hotter than a New York sidewalk under the July sun. It's a shame I seem to have lost the power of speech. I can only hope I'm not drooling.

"Apologies, I didn't mean to disturb you when you were so busy." His voice is pitched low and is smoother than chocolate.

Damn. He officially has the complete set of hot qualities. He gestures to the table, and I flush when I see what he's talking about. Wonderful. This fine-ass man caught me drawing roses on the back of my abandoned name tag with a fricking crayon. I'm so sophisticated.

"Oh! Well, that's okay. It's not like I was jotting down a cure for cancer or a memo to the presiding officer of the UN. I was just, uh, coloring."

"Coloring? I'm told that's good for you. Mindful or whatever they call it." He looks deeply amused, and who can blame him? This guy is off-the-charts handsome, wearing a tux that screams class, and he looks as comfortable in this environment as I feel out of place. I'm guessing he doesn't have the time or the need for mindfulness activities in his life.

"Maybe," I mumble. "Do you want to give it a try?"

His response is a rumbling laugh, and I consider smacking myself in the face. So cool, Amelia. What a smooth operator.

"Thanks, but I'm okay. Just looking for a quiet place to people watch."

"Me too. I like watching people at these kinds of things more than I like mixing with them."

He quirks an eyebrow at me, and I feel even more stupid. Where the hell did that come from? I'm not normally the sort of person who speaks without thinking, but something about this man seems to have taken a sledgehammer to my usual filters.

"Look," I say in an attempt to distract him. "The happy couple." He follows my pointing finger, and we look on as Tucker and Emily swirl by in a blur of white.

"Yeah," he replies, shaking his head. "The happy couple." There's a bite to his tone that contradicts his words, and I look at him sharply.

"What's that supposed to mean? They *are* happy," I insist, feeling very protective of them on their special day. Who comes to a wedding and talks crap about the bride and groom? I don't care how hot he is, that's just rude.

He laughs softly, the corners of his eyes crinkling in a way that makes him look even sexier. "I mean, they do look very happy—at least right now. But ..."

"But?" I ask, annoyed but a little intrigued by his lack of etiquette. "You don't believe in marriage?"

He sucks on his top lip and thinks about it. "I suppose I just don't believe in happily ever afters ... of any kind," he finally replies with a shrug. "How can you promise someone forever? Nothing lasts forever."

I blink at him. Is he for real? We've spent the whole day celebrating two people committing the rest of their lives to each other. He could at least pretend to believe in true love for a few hours. Even I'm not that cynical, and I have every reason to be. "I take it you've never been married, then?"

"No, but I was close once. A million years ago." His gaze travels to my now-bare left hand. I'm only just getting used to the feel of it, even though that ring has been gone for almost a year. It's like those stories about people who have amputations; it left behind phantom pain. "You?" he asks.

I swallow nervously. Do I want to open this can of worms right now? Or do I want to politely make my excuses and sneak away to be alone again?

He looks genuinely interested in what I'm about to say, and I remind myself that I need to start living again. I need to start engaging with the outside world and accepting that what I had in my old life is no more. I have to build a new one, one that has a solid foundation.

Running scared the first time an attractive man speaks to me wouldn't be a good start. Plus, what the hell—I'm four glasses of champagne in, and I have nothing better to do this evening. I have zero interest in joining the mating frenzy on the dance floor, and I can't leave until Emily and Tucker are gone. Maid of honor rule.

"Yes, I have, actually," I say, not meeting his eyes.

He tilts his head. "But you're not married now?"

"No." The word comes out in a harsh whisper, and the swell of emotion in my chest takes me by surprise. It's been a long time since I found out Chad was cheating on me, and our divorce was finalized two weeks ago. We've been living apart for eleven months, and our once-joined worlds are now very much separate. I should be over this by now, shouldn't I? I promised myself that I wouldn't give any more of myself to that man. That I wouldn't waste any more tears or energy thinking about him and his new fiancée. Now, here I am, talking to a hot stranger and blinking away the hurt.

He notices even though I try to look away. I get the feeling he's the kind of man who notices everything. "I'm sorry," he says, sounding sincere. "But I suppose you've also proven my point."

"No, I haven't. Plenty of marriages go the distance," I say defensively. "Just because my ex-husband was a cheating asshole doesn't mean that all men are."

"Or all women," he counters with a cock of one eyebrow and a grin that lightens the mood. It also makes my ovaries ache, which wasn't a thing I thought could happen. "Men haven't cornered the market on infidelity, though I grant you, they have the bulk of it. What's your name, *rosa*?" He taps his pointer finger on the flowers decorating my now brightly patterned name tag. "I'd like to know who I'm debating."

Debating? Is that what we're doing? I kind of like the sound of that. It makes me feel more like a grown-up and less like an emotional wreck. Maybe I haven't handled this encounter quite as disastrously as I thought.

I flip my tag over, ensuring my actual name remains covered

up. "It was Amelia," I announce firmly. "But now I'm considering changing it. Tonight, I feel like being someone entirely different. What do you think?"

I hear the purr in my own voice, and it takes me by surprise. I'm not usually flirty at all. I was with my husband from the age of sixteen onward, so it's something I never really learned how to do. I'm totally winging it here.

"I think it's always fun to try something new for size. See how you like the fit. What's the new name going to be?"

I give it some thought. "I'm torn between Scarlet and Portia. Something deeply glamorous."

"Hmmm ... I prefer Scarlet, I think." He leans forward across the table and smiles in a way that makes my heart flutter.

"Scarlet it is, then. She's quite the catch, you know. An independently wealthy business magnate with her own jet and a home in the Hamptons. She's confident and sassy, and she can have any man she wants." I'm quite carried away with my vision of Scarlet and wish I could have even a fraction of her self-assurance.

"I'm sure she could," he replies, giving me a lopsided grin that goes straight to my core. "And I totally get the appeal of being someone else for the night. Letting go of everything else, all the things you're expected to be, and just recreating yourself."

"Exactly! I'm ... Well, I'm not normally that person. The one who throws caution to the wind. But Scarlet is. She's a minx."

"I see that," he says, laughing. "I think Scarlet and I are going to really hit it off."

"Maybe so. I notice you don't have a name tag on, though. What should I call you?"

He reaches into his pocket and pulls out a crumpled badge. He lays it flat on the table, and I see the name "Charlie" written in Sharpie.

"I warn you, though, Scarlet," he says, his dark eyes pinned on mine. "That might not be my real name either. Maybe I saw you from across the room and decided to come talk to you. Maybe I'm not even a guest at this wedding."

My lips tremble at the intensity of his look, and I find myself staring at his mouth, imagining it closing over mine. No. He must be joking. Men like this don't look twice at women like me, never mind crash a wedding just to get close. But I decide to go with the flow. That's what Scarlet would do, after all.

"Nice to meet you, *Charlie*," I say, holding out my hand for him to shake.

"The feeling's mutual, Scarlet," he replies smoothly as he takes my fingers in his. His skin is warm, and I can't help but notice that his hand is huge, his palm practically swallowing mine whole. The touch of his flesh, along with those intense eyes, sends a thrill of excitement shooting through me. This man is pure sex in a suit, and my whole body is tingling in response.

He releases me from his grip, and I sit back against my chair, studying him as his gaze rakes over my face. His attention flickers to my breasts for a few seconds, but like a gentleman, he doesn't linger there. He opens his mouth as if about to speak, but before he can utter a word, we're disturbed by someone dropping heavily into the chair on the other side of me.

The strong smell of Scotch fills my nose, and a heavy arm drapes over my shoulder, his hand pawing my bare skin. I roll my eyes because I know exactly who our new table companion is, and I'm not thrilled about it. Charlie arches one eyebrow at me in amusement before I turn in my seat to face our new friend.

"You know if the best man and the maid of honor are both single, it's tradition for them to get together, right?" he slurs in my ear.

"Hey AJ," I say with a sigh to Tucker's very annoying younger brother. "I don't think that's how it works."

"Sure it is." He peers down at my cleavage as he leans closer, puckering his lips for a kiss. He's harmless enough, I'm sure, but I recoil from the stink of his breath and the reckless expression on his face. Why do men always think this kind of behavior is acceptable? I know he's drunk, but still. If we weren't at a wedding, I'd be tempted to slap him.

We are at a wedding, though, so I shrink back from him, wanting to avoid his touch without causing a scene. He's about to shuffle forward to make another attempt when Charlie grabs his arm and removes it from my shoulder.

"I'm sorry, AJ," he says smoothly. "But Scarlet isn't single right now. She's with me this evening."

AJ looks momentarily confused, probably wondering who the hell Scarlet is, but he has a goofy grin on his face and a glassy-eyed expression that tells me he won't remember a word of this conversation tomorrow. He might, however, be in dire need of a sick bag and a handful of Advil.

Charlie towers over us both, holding his hand out to me. I look at the waiting hand, then up at the rest of him. God, he is so damn tall. I could climb him like a tree.

I smile and slip my fingers into his, letting him lead me to the crowded dance floor. The band is playing something slow and sultry, and before I have time to think, he slides his arms around my waist.

"Thank you," I say to him, a blush creeping over my cheeks as we move to the music. This is dancing, but it feels like so much more. My hips are crushed up against his, and his thick thighs are warm and solid against mine. "For the rescue."

"No problem. I'm sure Scarlet could have dealt with him anyway. We can go and sit back down as soon as you're safe from your would-be suitor. If you want to, that is."

The heat of his firm body radiates through the silky fabric of my dress, and that plus the touch of his fingers on my waist wreak havoc on my brain function. How is a girl supposed to think clearly when a man like this is holding her so close? My hands rest on his wide shoulders, and I flex my fingertips, feeling the hardness of the muscle that lies beneath the perfectly tailored tux.

"Actually, I quite like dancing. I don't think I've danced like this for years. Or maybe ever." I blush again and scold myself for being so open with a complete stranger. We're playing a game, this man and I, and it's not a game that involves me revealing intimate details about my pathetic life.

"Oh?" He narrows his eyes at me. "Your husband didn't take you dancing?"

"He wasn't much of a dancer." I shrug. "Not like you."

Shit! Just shut the hell up, Amelia. Remember, you're Scarlet. Be Scarlet.

He laughs softly again, and I feel the sound deep in my bones. "Well, I had lessons when I was younger. My mother insisted."

"I'm glad she did," I reply, leaning into him. I'm hyperaware of his warm hand moving to the small of my back. He tugs me a bit closer, his eyes on mine, and the intensity of his gaze makes it impossible to look away. Not that I want to look away. All I want to do is dance, to lose myself in his eyes, to enjoy the touch of his breath against my skin as we sway together in our own world. My fingers curl into the thick hair at the back of his head, and I wonder what the hell has gotten into me. But as I relax into his chest, inhaling the scent of his mouthwatering cologne, I realize that I don't care what's gotten into me. I'm simply glad that it has.

TWO

AMELIA

The music has stopped and the band is packing up to go home. Most of the guests have left, and Tucker and Emily are long gone. The dance floor is strewn with multicolored streamers, discarded name tags, and a solitary red stiletto. A Cinderella mystery that may never be solved. The weary staff is clearing up, but my friend and I have grabbed a bottle of champagne and moved outside. I don't want the night to end, and he seems to feel the same.

Charlie and I are sitting at a small patio table in one of the hotel's luxuriously landscaped gardens, and he's placed his tuxedo jacket around my shoulders in a chivalrous attempt to keep me warm in the cool night air. We talk and laugh and flirt beneath the dark blanket of sky and the shining lights of New York City. He's funny and charming and has listened to me ramble on about my mom and my cheating husband. He must be bored by it all—I know I am—but he shows no sign of being fed up.

In return, he tells me about his childhood, about growing up in a loving family as one of five boys. I'm an only child and was raised by a hardworking single mom, so our early years couldn't have been more different. Still, it's fun listening to his stories and sharing mine. I can't remember the last time I felt so comfortable with someone I just met.

"How did you two meet?" he asks after I get done telling him about the time I lost a bet to Emily and had to wear a Mets jersey to a Yankees game.

"We met on our first day of college. We've been best friends ever since."

"That kind of enduring friendship is rare. Where did you go to college?"

I know he'll be surprised by my answer. Everyone always is. "Harvard." His eyebrows shoot up, and I have to grin. "You look shocked. Is that so hard to believe?"

"I never said that." He laughs, the sound so deep and sexy and genuine that my heart jumps in my chest. "You talked earlier about doing temp jobs, and I assumed ..." He takes another sip of his champagne. "Well, I assumed, and we all know what they say about that. I'm trying to make a good impression, so I'd hate for you to think I'm an ass. And you are far too lovely to be compared to a donkey."

He is so damn charming. I roll back my shoulders and pretend like I'm not about to melt into a puddle in this chair. "That's okay. I'm used to it. There's this pervasive belief that everyone who went to Harvard has some high-flying corporate job, like most of those stiffs we just spent the evening with."

"Ouch!" He places a hand over his heart and grins at me. "That hurt."

"I'm sure you'll survive." I chuckle at his wounded expression. Talking to him feels so easy and natural, like we've known each other a lot longer than a few hours. I consider giving him the sanitized version I tell during job interviews when asked about my unconventional career path, but that half-truth doesn't seem appropriate when we're both being so candid. "I did have plans, but I put them on hold while we moved around the States. Then, somehow ... well, I suppose I kinda got lost along the way. I started seeing work as a job rather than a career, and there is a difference, isn't there? It felt like there was only room for one of us to reach the stars, and that was my husband."

"Isn't there always room for two? Success is better when it's shared, or so I'm told."

He's right, of course, and I see that now. But Chad had the charm and smarm of a good snake oil salesman, and he convinced me that we would both be better off if we focused on getting him to the top first. That there would be time for me later, maybe after we started a family.

Looking back, it was a mistake—at least for me. But we'd been together since high school, and it seemed like our relationship was worth the investment. It's only recently that I realized how much I bent and gave and made it so he didn't have to. During college, I was the one who always made the trip home to see him at Columbia. In fact, our biggest point of contention back then was his unwillingness to come to Boston for even a single weekend. I shake my head and take a long sip from my glass. That's all in the past, and even now, I'm not sure it was my choices that were wrong so much as the person I was making those choices for. "Well, relationships are complicated beasts, aren't they? You do odd things when you're in love."

"If you say so."

"You've never been in love?" I ask. "I don't believe that for a second."

He shakes his head and smiles, but it's a smile that doesn't reach his eyes. "I was, yeah. But that was a long time ago, and I'm not keen to repeat that particular experience."

I reach for his hand and twine my fingers with his. "I'm sorry, Charlie."

"You do know that's not actually my name, don't you?"

I squeeze his fingers and flash him a devilish smile. "Hush now. Tonight it is. Tonight, you're Charlie, a gorgeous stranger who's new to town."

"I actually am kind of new here. I just moved back after years away."

"Really? Why'd you leave? It sounds like you have a great family here."

He sucks his upper lip and is quiet for a long moment. I wonder if he's about to lie to me, if I've accidentally touched a nerve.

"I moved away because I needed to be me," he finally says, shrugging. "I needed to be independent, not part of a whole, you know? My family *is* great. My dad is a force of nature, and my brothers … Well, we're close, and they're amazing. Sometimes so amazing that I don't feel quite good enough, like I don't match their high standards. It's nothing they've ever said or done, it's all on me. And moving halfway across the country felt like a way to escape that. After we lost our mom, I found it even harder to stick around. I managed it for a while, and I kept busy with work, but I never felt settled. It was almost a relief to get away from the home we all shared."

It feels like a confession, and I can sense his discomfort. I also wonder what the rest of his family is like if this impeccable man feels like he isn't up to par. They must all be superheroes. "Why did you come back now?" I ask.

"It just felt like the right time. And who knows, maybe it was fate. Maybe I was meant to be here for this wedding. Maybe I was meant to meet you, Amelia."

"Oh no," I say, playfully swatting his arm. "You were meant to meet Scarlet, the super-hot chick who is far more likely to be Emily's friend than plain old Amelia."

"There is nothing plain about Amelia." He lifts my hand and

drops a kiss onto my palm. My heart stutters and then sends some highly excited messages to somewhere much lower. "But you and Emily do seem very different. She works in finance, right? Comes from old money?"

"Yep. And I work in admin with no money. But opposites attract, as they say. Sometimes, though, I do wish I was more like her. For more than just a night."

"And why is that?"

"I suppose I'd love to have her confidence. Her self-assurance. Her ability to have fun without second guessing herself."

"Oh?" He sits up straighter. His eyes narrow as he stares at me, and I wonder why I said that out loud. "And what would you do with that self-assurance? Right now? What would be fun?"

I could give him some vague and noncommittal answer to that question. In fact, I definitely should, because all my genuine answers could land me in a world of trouble. But his gaze is every bit as intoxicating as the champagne, and I figure I'm never going to see him again. We are wedding guests passing in the night. What's the harm in telling him the truth? "Sometimes, I'd like to be able to let loose and do whatever I want. Just go wild. Make rash decisions, live for the moment, and have no regrets. You know what I mean?"

Staring down into his glass, he swirls the last drop around the bottom. "Tell me more."

"I'd like to try being someone else entirely. Like Scarlet. She has no worries, no insecurities. No responsibilities. It would be nice to live like that for a while."

"Yeah. I understand that."

"You do?" Why on earth would this incredibly sexy, charming, obviously rich man ever want to be anyone other than who he is? He seems to have everything a person could possibly want in life.

"Of course. The chance to be selfish? To cast aside what people expect of you? To act on nothing but your own desires without worrying that you're going to hurt someone or let them down? Hell yeah, I get that."

When I look into his eyes, they're no longer chocolate brown; they're almost black. His voice is raw with emotion, and goosebumps prickle along my skin at the sound. We're just playing a game here, aren't we?

A game we're both enjoying and that could allow us both to be winners. That thought urges me to speak. "What if we both agreed to abandon our real lives for the night? What would that look like? If you got the chance ... What would you be looking for?"

His lips quirk up, and his head tilts to one side as he assesses me. I might be bad at flirting, but I'm also not a complete idiot. Unlikely as it may seem, this gorgeous man is interested in me. But now that I've basically propositioned him, a flurry of nerves erupts in my belly.

"I'd be looking for something a little ..."

"A little what?" My eyes stay locked with his, my heart beating so hard I swear he must be able to hear it.

"Casual?" He arches one eyebrow. "I'm the kind of guy who goes all in, Scarlet, but only for one night."

I can't help thinking that all in with this man for one night would be better than half-assed with Chad for more than a decade. In fact, it's perfect. My life is busy and complicated, and I don't have space in it for a relationship.

But I do have space for one awesome night.

I process his offer, trying to stay calm and think it through properly. No matter which way I look at it, though, I can't find the downside. I'm a little drunk, but not so drunk that I don't know my own mind, my own body. Both are floored by the incredibly sexy and charismatic guy right in front of me. I'm most definitely Scarlet now, and I'm thrilled about it. I deserve to be a little bit naughty just once, don't I? And it's not like anyone will ever find out.

"I can do casual," I whisper.

His Adam's apple bobs, and he stares at me for a few seconds. The electricity crackling between us is palpable, like fireflies sparkling in the air around us. Surely he feels it too, this magic?

"I'm at the hotel next door," he offers.

I take a deep breath and nod. "Okay."

Holy shit. Am I really going to do this? He could be a serial killer for all I know. An incredibly hot serial killer, but his looks won't matter so much when he's burying me in a ditch. Emily wouldn't invite a serial killer to her wedding, would she? God, my nerves are so shot that I'm babbling to myself. I've never done anything like this before, and I am completely outside my comfort zone.

He stands up and holds his hand out to me. To my surprise, I see my own reach out and take it. "Shall we, Scarlet?" He flashes me a wicked smile, and my insides melt like warm butter, washing away all doubt. If he is a serial killer, at least I'll die happy.

We walk arm in arm, quickly covering the short distance to his hotel. The Grand Regent is by far the fanciest hotel I've ever set foot in, and he gets polite nods from the staff as he leads me through the expansive lobby. He keeps walking past several banks of elevators until he reaches the private elevator for the penthouse and scans his keycard. The penthouse! This guy isn't only super hot, he's super rich as well. I wonder what it's like living in his universe. I'm overwhelmed enough only gate-crashing it for a few hours.

On the ride up, he stands silently beside me with his hand on my hip, dangerously close to my ass. My ass really doesn't mind, and my legs are trembling with anticipation. I'm a little worried they won't know what to do when the doors open and I'm expected to somehow walk again.

As if sensing my unease, he slips his hand down to skim the curve of my backside and turns, giving me a slow, sexy smile that almost finishes me off. "You okay, Scarlet?"

I smile back, nodding with a shaky jerk of my head. Yeah. Scarlet's just fine. Amelia, however, is absolutely terrified. Scarlet might be a woman of the world, but Amelia is a scared divorcée who has only ever slept with one man. I can't tell him that, obviously. It's outrageously unsexy, and I'm guessing he's used to dating women with a lot more skill and experience than I possess. I can fake this 'til I make it, and maybe he won't notice.

When the doors open, he gestures for me to go ahead, and I step out into a vast, exquisitely decorated living area. The man has a room that takes up the entire floor of the nicest hotel in the city, and that doesn't do much to calm my nerves. I am so far outside my comfort zone that I can't do anything but gape at the spectacular room. It's bigger than my whole apartment, with floor-to-ceiling windows and the most incredible view of the city. The drapes are open, the bright lights of Manhattan spread out beneath and around us, the whole world lit up like a Christmas tree.

I wander over, mesmerized by the sight. I wonder if one of those twinkling lights is my mom's place miles away. Mom would approve of me having a little fun, a little adventure. She always tells me I need to let loose.

"I don't think I'll ever get used to that view. There's nothing quite like the Manhattan skyline, is there?" he says, passing me a tumbler of Scotch. He's taken off his tie, and the top few buttons of his crisp white shirt are open, revealing a golden patch of skin that I immediately want to kiss.

"I guess it's a pretty awesome view," I reply breathlessly, admiring the way the material of his shirt molds to his muscular physique. "But I prefer the one from here."

He grins at me and slowly sips his drink, ice cubes clinking. The sight of his lips curving around the glass fascinates me, and now that we're alone together, my body is even more aware of his raw sexual energy. He may have been a perfect gentleman until now, but there's something dangerous and edgy beneath that suave exterior. Something reckless and wild and passionate, calling to me and making me melt inside. I have never had a one-night stand. I never plan to have a one-night stand again. This is something special, something outrageous—something that will make me smile when I'm a lonely old woman in my house full of cats.

As if trying to read my thoughts, he stares at me intently. Then he holds out his hand and beckons me closer. "Come here, Scarlet."

I'm so lost in the dark promise in his eyes that it takes me a moment to respond to the name. I obviously hesitate too long, and he narrows his eyes at me.

"Now," he commands in a low growl.

"Yes sir," I reply, closing the distance between us. I'm frightened, in the most delectable way I could ever imagine. I don't know what this man is going to do to me, but I know that I am going to enjoy it. Probably more than I've ever enjoyed anything in my whole damn life.

THREE

AMELIA

M y heart hammers as I stand there before him, and I take a sip of the Scotch to cover my nerves. Damn, that burns. He silently takes the glass from my hands, and places it down with his before he looks me up and down. Every touch of his eyes burns even hotter than the alcohol.

Charlie runs his hand through my hair, stroking it back from my face before winding it around his fist. He uses it to tug my head back and slides his other hand across my hip and onto my ass. He looks down at me, licking his lips, and it makes me sigh out loud. The way he stares at me is so possessive, like I belong to him and he's deciding exactly what to do with me. It's so sexy I start to shake inside, wet heat throbbing between my legs. Even though I'm wearing heels, he looms over my five-foot-six frame, and I feel completely overwhelmed by him.

I gaze up into those incredible brown eyes, and my entire body trembles with anticipation. He must feel it because he gives me a smug smile.

"It sure as hell feels like you're enjoying this, but are you sure? Are you sure you want this, Amelia?" he asks, his voice low and gruff with need.

"My name is Scarlet," I remind him with a wicked smile. "And yes, I'm sure."

"I need both of you to consent, mi rosa, because this isn't going to be a night that either of you will forget. Scarlet might have given you the courage to make it this far, but it's Amelia I'm going to be fucking. It's Amelia who will be screaming for more."

My eyes shoot wide open at his dirty talk, and my hips rub closer to him. "I want this. I'm sure."

As soon as the last word has left my mouth, he seals his lips over mine and flicks his tongue over the seam of my lips until I welcome him inside. He tastes of whisky and heat, and I want so much more. It feels like we've been building up to this first kiss all night, and now I'm desperate for him.

I moan into his mouth, and his fingers dig into my ass cheeks, pulling my body closer to his so his hard length is pressed against my stomach. Wow, he's ... *impressive*. Terrifying, in fact.

My hands burrow into his thick hair, and I pull him deeper into our kiss. He groans, his hand sliding to my back and searching for the zipper of my strapless dress. He finds it and slowly tugs it down, then lets my dress fall into a pool of fabric at my feet. It came with a built-in corset, which means I'm now standing here in only my panties. My nipples harden as he stares at me, and I fight the urge to cover myself. I didn't come here to hide. I came here to experience something new. Something amazing.

He takes a step back and looks me up and down, his eyes roaming over my body like he owns it. His appreciative growl makes me blush. I know I'm not disgusting, but I'm also not a supermodel. I carry a little extra in the places most women do, and Chad is the only man to have ever seen me naked before. In the end, he decided that I wasn't enough for him, and I didn't realize how much that affected me until now.

"You are fucking beautiful, Scarlet," he says, taking in my slight shudder. "I can't wait to claim every inch of you."

He guides me into the bedroom and gathers me up in his arms. I slide my hands to his chest and start to unfasten the buttons on his shirt, desperate to see more of what lies underneath. I don't make much progress because he scoops me up and lays me down on the enormous bed, then stands over me, his eyes full of fire and passion. I never thought I could make a man feel like that, and the knowledge empowers me. I trail my fingers between my breasts, keeping my gaze locked on his.

He growls again, the predatory sound making me even more needy. I expect him to start undressing, but he crawls on top of me instead, still fully clothed. His lips claim mine in another kiss before he gently catches my bottom lip between his teeth. I moan as he trails his mouth lower and lower, planting soft, delicious touches along my neck and throat, working his way to my breasts. He holds himself up on one powerful forearm, admiring the sight of my body. "So fucking beautiful ... I've been wanting to do this to you all damn night."

He sucks one of my already hard nipples into his mouth. His tongue licks and flicks the pebbled flesh, and I feel a rush of wet heat between my thighs. His hand slides to my panties, and one finger strokes along my folds, the soft fabric already soaked.

My pleasure-filled moans are loud and wanton as he continues sucking my nipple, his hand edging its way inside my underwear. He groans against my skin and slides his fingers through my slickness, quickly finding my swollen clit and massaging it. I whimper beneath him, flooded with pleasurable sensations. His name is a sigh on my lips, and he pauses and pulls his mouth away from my breast, his dark eyes aflame.

"When I make you come, I want to hear you cry out my real name. Drake."

I nod, so wild with need that I don't care who he is. I only care about the way he's making me feel.

"Drake ..." My back arches as he slides a finger inside me, skimming my clit with his thumb.

"You're fucking soaked, and I've barely even touched you yet," he growls.

This has never happened to me before. Embarrassment and shame wash over me. I should be more in control. I shouldn't just be lying here while he plays with me, helpless beneath his touch.

"No need to be shy about it, mi rosa. I love how wet you are, and the feeling is entirely mutual. My cock is so hard, I might come while I'm eating your pussy."

The dirty talk has me melting like chocolate in the sun, but it also provokes a moment of uncertainty. When I find my voice, it's most definitely Amelia speaking, not Scarlet. "Y-you're going to do that? Even though we've only just met? I mean, I haven't showered."

"Why would I give a single fuck about that? I already know you're going to taste amazing. Eating pussy is my favorite part of sex. I can't wait to feel you come on my face."

I swallow nervously. "Okay. If that's what you want to do ..."

How do I tell him that my ex-husband gave me such a complex about oral sex that I feel awkward and embarrassed? Again, I am so out of my depth with this man.

"If it's what I want to do?" Drake repeats as he looks up at me, concern flashing across his face. "This is about what you want too, Amelia. Do you want me to eat your pussy until you scream my name?"

Oh god. When he says it like that, it seems insane to refuse —but still, there is a part of me that's too self-conscious to let go. "I'm just not very experienced in that area, that's all. My ex … he didn't really like to. What if there's something wrong with me?"

"Scarlet," he says, sounding annoyed, "your ex was an asshole. I don't know why he left you feeling like this, but he was wrong. I can already smell your sweet pussy, and I can guarantee you it's going to taste fucking delicious. But if you don't want me to, it's not a problem."

"It's not that I don't want you to. It's just that I don't know why you want to. I mean, we hardly know each other."

He grins at me wickedly. "Well, let's see what we can do to change that, shall we?" He tugs my panties down and off my ankles, then gives his full attention to the space between my legs. He slides his hands up my inner thighs, then runs a finger through my folds. I moan as he slips a finger inside my opening, brushing my tingling clit with his thumb each time he thrusts in and out. His movements are perfection, building a steady pressure that chases all rational thought from my mind. When he stops, I feel like crying with disappointment. He licks each of his fingers clean, making a meal of it.

"There," he says, smiling at my reaction. "I've been inside you and I've tasted you. As predicted, fucking delicious. I'd say we know each other pretty well now, wouldn't you?"

He is still fully dressed while I'm now completely naked, but the look in his eyes leaves me in no doubt that he wants me. That he's hungry for me.

"Okay," I finally say.

"Okay what? I want your words, mi rosa."

"Okay, I want you to do it. I want you to …" My cheeks burn hot. "E-eat my p-pussy."

He smiles and dips his head low. "Have you ever come this way?" he asks, his face close enough to my center that I feel the warmth of his breath on my flesh.

"No. Never."

"I'm sure we're about to change that."

He spreads my thighs wider, opening me up to him. I inwardly cringe at being so exposed in front of this almost-stranger, but I remind myself that tonight, I am Scarlet, not Amelia. Scarlet would be proud of her beautiful lady parts, not ashamed.

He bends his head lower, and I quiver with anticipation. The moment his hot, thick tongue presses against me, I forget all about my embarrassment. I forget all about my ex and his damaging comments. Hell, I forget all about everything in the entire world apart from the way his tongue feels.

He licks the length of my wet center, and pleasure rockets through me. My response causes him to chuckle against my skin before he settles his mouth over my clit and swirls the sensitive bud of flesh with his tongue. My hips buck up to meet him. "Oh god!" I cry out, astonished that something so simple can feel so good.

I look down at him, and our eyes lock. He winks at me as he sucks my clit into his mouth, and I let my head fall back against the pillows. A delicious fluttering feeling starts to build in my core, and he seems to instinctively know what rhythm I need and how much pressure to apply. It's almost as though he's in my mind, in my body, feeling everything I'm feeling and dragging every last ounce of sensation out of me. My thighs tremble as he continues licking and sucking at my sensitive flesh, and I rake my fingers through his hair.

"Jesus, Drake!" I gasp, and that seems to spur him on. He wraps his hands around the back of my thighs and pulls me closer to his face, devouring my pussy like a starving man eating his final meal.

When my orgasm finally crashes through me, my blood thunders in my ears and my vision fades to black. Every cell in my body is on fire, and the ecstasy rolls over me in pulsating waves. My inner walls contract and clench, a rush of arousal seeping out of me. I lie back, gasping for breath, my fists clutching the sheets and my entire being turned to molten lava.

Drake moves back up the bed until he's lying over me again, his beard glistening with my juices. "Your ex must be a fucking idiot, because that is one of the sweetest pussies I have ever tasted in my life." With that, he seals his mouth over mine and slips his tongue inside, giving me a brief kiss before he pulls back. "You see, Scarlet? You taste like absolute fucking heaven."

He climbs off the bed, leaving me weak and breathless and confused. What the hell just happened? I've had orgasms before, but never one like that. That was ... wow. That was life-changing.

"There are condoms in the nightstand," he says as he starts to unbutton his shirt.

I'm finally going to get to see that gorgeous body of his. I roll over and find the foil wrappers in the drawer and wonder momentarily how many there were to start with, but I dismiss the thought immediately. What does it matter? The man just made me come harder than I ever have in my life with only his tongue. It's not like we're a couple or we've made any promises to each other, and at least I know he's practicing safe sex.

Any doubts I might have had disappear the second I turn my gaze back toward him. I knew he was toned and muscular from the way his body felt against mine and how he filled out his suit, but shirtless ... I hate to repeat myself, but wow. This man is a feast for the eyes. He looks like a Greek god with his broad shoulders and abs that appear to be carved from stone. His forearms are massive, and I love the way his muscles flex as his hands move to his belt. Dark hair trails down from his chest in an arrow to his waistband, and I sit up in anticipation, watching him unzip his pants.

He grins at me and takes his time pushing his boxers down over those thick thighs. His cock is huge, standing to attention and glistening with a bead of pre-cum.

"You like what you see, mi rosa?" he asks.

"I sure do."

He crawls back onto the bed and takes the condom from me before sitting back on his heels. I watch as he slides it expertly down his cock and wonder what it would feel like to take that smooth, hard shaft in my mouth and pleasure him the same way he just pleasured me. He gently pushes me back down so I'm lying flat on the bed and trails soft kisses along my collarbone and up my neck. I spread my legs wide, lifting my hips to try to capture him, but he keeps the tip of his cock paused right at my opening, teasing me.

"Is this what you want, Miss Scarlet? Do you want my dick inside you?"

"Yes! Drake, please."

He pushes in farther, and there's a rush of wet heat as I stretch to accommodate him. "You are so fucking tight," he murmurs against my neck. "It's taking every fucking bit of willpower I have not to fucking nail you to this bed."

"Don't hold back. Please. I want to feel you inside me, all of you, right now."

He growls and pushes himself deep inside me, and the initial shock of being invaded by a man this big makes my eyes fly wide open. But the shock is soon replaced by pleasure, and every nerve in my body feels like it's on fire as he drives into me over and over again. His thrusts are hitting a sweet spot deep inside me that has never been hit before, and it makes me whimper shamelessly. My inner walls squeeze around him, pulling him in deeper, my hands clasped onto his shoulders as he slams into me. He lifts his head and looks into my eyes, our gazes locking in a way that's almost as intense as the sex. This feels right on every single level, and I cling to him as he carries us both higher and higher.

His arms are solid pillars of muscle and sinew on either side of my head, and his beautiful face is coated with a light sheen of sweat as he pounds into me. I feel the pressure building again, a familiar tingling in my spread thighs, a relentless throbbing as he grinds into me. Screaming his name, I come once more, digging my nails into his skin and riding the crest of a blissful wave. I'm still riding it when he closes his mouth over mine and swallows my moans of delight, his pace increasing as he chases his own release.

"Fuck!" he bellows as he orgasms, his hips shuddering against me and his deep voice strained. I keep hold of him, shocked by the intensity of it all, my legs wrapped around his waist as he collapses on top of me. He rests his forehead against mine, and we both try to catch our breath. "What the hell was that?" he says, panting.

I stroke his hair and laugh gently, my brain still too fried from the mind-blowing orgasm to form a coherent sentence. And I figure it's a rhetorical question anyway. At least I hope so, because I have no logical answer. *That* was spectacular and life-altering, and I have no idea how the hell I'm supposed to live the rest of my life without having that kind of sex again.

CHAPTER
FOUR
DRAKE

She lies facing me in the king-sized bed, naked and looking completely sated after I fucked her for the second time. Despite making her come four times already, I'm still twitching to make her moan my name again.

She reaches out to stroke the hair on my chest and meets my gaze, but she seems different now. Hesitant even. It's as though Scarlet has left the building and Amelia is unsure of the rules of the game. I'm not entirely sure of the etiquette here myself. I have a healthy sexual appetite and I'm never short of companionship, but I don't usually find myself in situations like these. And I definitely don't lie in bed with my sexual partners afterward like this, leaving myself open to the precarious risk of cuddling. It's strange how having my face between her thighs and my cock inside her tight pussy somehow felt less intimate than whatever this is.

"What time is it?" she asks, then covers her mouth as she yawns.

I reach over her to grab my watch from the nightstand, pinning her to the bed as I do, and I don't miss the way her breath hitches or the way my cock twitches to life at the feel of her skin on mine. "Almost three," I say, grinning down at her.

She bites on her bottom lip, looking even more nervous now. And fuck me, but it's adorable. "Um, I've never done this before."

"What?" I tease, unable to resist making her blush. "Had sex? Because from the way you moaned and arched your back when I fucked you, I never would have guessed."

"No! Of course I've had sex. I mean ... this. Being with someone I've only just met. You're probably used to women a lot more sophisticated than I am. I doubt I'm your normal type."

I roll off her and prop myself up on one arm. I guess she's right about not being my normal type, but I can guarantee it's not in the way that she thinks. Beautiful women with sparkling eyes have always been my type. Her gaze drifts to my biceps, and she bites on her damn lip again before her eyes dart back to mine. Her blush deepens like she's embarrassed of the fact that she was clearly admiring my muscles. Yeah, adorable. "That's a bit presumptuous of you, Miss Scarlet. You have no clue what my normal type is. What is it that's bothering you?"

Groaning, she hides her face with her hands. "Everything! Like ... What happens now? Do I just get up and leave? How does this usually work? I mean, it's a bit late for the subway, but I'm sure I could get a cab."

How do I explain that this is new to me without her thinking I'm some kind of grade-A pervert who usually pays women to sleep with him? Yeah, there's definitely no way to have that conversation without it sounding creepy. "There is no 'usually' about this situation. And as for what happens next, that's up to you. I have no expectations of you. If you'd feel better leaving, go for it. I'll even call you a car. But if you don't want to leave, stay here."

"With you?"

With me? I'm as shocked as she is about this development, but still I find myself agreeing. "Well, I'm pretty exhausted because I've spent the last couple hours fucking the brains out of this sex-starved bridesmaid I met tonight, and I have no intentions of leaving this bed. So yes, with me."

I'm not used to this level of connection with a woman, and it isn't even about the incredible sex. At least not entirely. I've had plenty of great sex before. It's everything else that makes this different. We spent the entire night talking, and while I was very careful not to share or discover anything too identifying—no last name, no details about our jobs or where we go for coffee every morning—we shared things much more intimate and personal than I think either of us planned to. She's the kind of person who's just so incredibly easy to engage in conversation with. Sweet and warm and so vulnerably honest that it was hard not to open up to her. Ironically, she probably knows more about me than most people—outside of my family, at least.

So I allow myself the fantasy of being Charlie a little while longer. I pull her hands away from her face and drop a kiss on her lips. "It's perfectly acceptable to spend the night and even have breakfast with me in the morning. I am a gentleman, after all."

"You weren't behaving like a gentleman about ten minutes ago," she murmurs, and I can't help but smile.

No, I definitely was not. And I'd like to not be a gentleman again before she leaves. "Maybe not. But I think we have one condom left for the morning, and it would be a hell of a shame to waste it."

Her eyes sparkle mischievously. "I suppose it would."

I wink at her, convincing myself this is all still part of the game we're playing. And when she stares up at me expectantly, I find myself rolling onto my back and lifting my arm so she can snuggle into the crook of my shoulder. I can't remember the last time I did this, although I recall who I did it with. That was another lifetime and another version of me.

I rest my lips on the top of her head and try not to think too much about how good her soft body feels curled up against mine. This ends tomorrow when real life begins again.

But just for tonight, I can be Charlie. A guy who has normal relationships with women, who likes to cuddle and spoon after sex, rather than Drake James—workaholic kinky fucker with raging commitment issues.

FIVE

AMELIA

O h dear lord, how much did I drink last night? My temples throb with a dull ache, and my mouth is drier than sand. I yawn my way back to consciousness and stretch out on the cool sheets. They feel expensive and luxurious and nothing at all like the bedding in my apartment.

My eyes fly open as memories of last night flood back. Shit. I'm not in my apartment, am I? There was the wedding. There was an incredibly hot guy. There was even hotter sex. Oh. My. God.

My heart flutters in my ribcage, and I look around for signs of him. The room is empty, but the shower is running. I sit up and smooth back my hair, noticing all the tender spots in my body as I move. Wowzers. That really was some night, and now I have to do the walk of shame for the first time in my entire life. And I'll be doing it in a strapless bridesmaid's dress, which is extra shameful somehow—yes, I was that cliché. I put my head in my hands and groan.

"Feeling that bad?" I hear him say in his perfectly smooth voice, and I look up to see Drake walking out of the bathroom, wearing nothing but a white towel tucked around his waist. His skin is still damp, and he looks good enough to eat or, at the very least, lick.

When I was replaying last night, I wondered if the alcohol made him appear hotter than he really was, but no. Here he is, still hotter than the earth's core. I suddenly feel very self-conscious, lying naked in his bed with wild hair and breath untouched by toothpaste. I must look like a hot mess, especially when compared to him.

"I don't feel too bad, considering," I say with a faint smile. "I'm just pondering the trip back to my apartment in last night's dress."

"Hey, this is New York. Nobody will even notice. But don't worry about it. I'll get my driver to take you home."

His driver? Who the hell has a driver? It's an odd concept, and one I'm not entirely comfortable with. It's not like he handed me a wad of dollar bills, but being handed off to a member of staff still makes me feel a little cheap. What did I expect? For him to walk me home, for us to stroll hand in hand through Central Park like we're in some rom-com? This was a one-night stand, and we promised each other nothing.

He starts to get dressed after pulling clean boxers from a full drawer and a shirt from a crowded closet. "Wait," I say, frowning. "Do you actually, like, *live* here?"

He pulls on the white dress shirt but leaves it unbuttoned. Damn, the man is built. Amused, he quirks an eyebrow. "Like, uh, yeah? I told you last night, I've just moved back. I'm in the process of buying somewhere, but these things take forever to go through. Damn lawyers slow everything down." He grins at his own comment like he's just made a joke and carries on getting dressed.

Before I can reply, there's a knock on the door, and I tug the sheet right up to my neck. In case, you know, the person knocking has x-ray vision and can see through doors and walls.

"Relax," he says on his way out of the bedroom. "I promised you breakfast, and I thought we both might prefer to eat in private rather than in the restaurant."

Well, yes. Especially in last night's bridesmaid's dress. That wouldn't be a good look for either of us. Speaking of which, I realize that it's in the other room, along with breakfast. A sudden rumble in my tummy lets me know that my body needs sustenance, and I cast my eyes around, looking for something else to wear.

When he walks back into the bedroom, he catches me scrambling back under the covers. "Don't be coy." He smirks at the one bare leg that's still exposed. "It's not like I didn't kiss every inch of your body last night, is it, Scarlet?"

I feel myself blush brighter than my alter ego's name, and he seems to be trying to hide his amusement as he passes me a shirt. It's the one he had on last night, and it still smells of his cologne.

"Come on, let's eat. Get your caffeine fix. Whatever. I don't know about you, but I need to work."

I slip on the shirt, glad that it at least covers my ass, and follow him through to the other room. There's a tray laden with fresh fruit, pastries, and pancakes, and the dining table is set for two. He grabs himself food and a coffee and watches me as I hesitantly do the same. This feels beyond weird, and I'm kinda desperate to escape now. He seems different this morning. More distant, colder. Too polite.

He's still drop-dead gorgeous, but somehow less approachable. Last night, before all the mind-melting sex, we talked. Really talked. About our childhoods, our families, our moms. This morning, he seems more interested in his phone. I tell myself I'm being an idiot and pour myself a cup of coffee. The smoky aroma of top-quality coffee automatically makes me feel better.

"You're working on a Sunday?" I ask, grabbing a flaky croissant and sitting down opposite him. I bite into it, sending a shower of crumbs all over my cleavage.

He stares at my chest, and his jaw twitches. I suppress a smile at his reaction, but then a healthy dose of humility bites me in the ass. What if I've read this completely wrong? Maybe he's a neat freak and he's having a meltdown about the mess. "I am, yes. I work every day. What about you?"

I brush the crumbs away, noting his eyes following my fingers, and shrug. "I'm not important enough to work on a Sunday. I am starting that new job tomorrow, though."

"The one with the asshole boss?"

I cringe when I recall our conversation from last night. I gave him some scant information about my new job. Nothing about the kind of work I'd be doing or who I'd be working for— I am neither indiscreet nor an idiot—but I definitely told him stuff that I should have kept to myself. Scarlet was way too chatty.

"Well, I feel bad for saying that now. I mean, that's just repeating gossip. When I met him during my interview, he was okay. Nice even. And maybe it's not weird that he has this reputation—you don't get to be the boss of a huge firm without being a bit of a ball-buster, do you? People say he's a crazy perfectionist with super-high standards. But again, maybe not a bad thing given how many people work for him."

He nods and lays his phone down on the table. "No, it's not, and as long as he expects the same high standards from himself, it probably doesn't qualify him as an asshole either. But if he turns out to be one, you don't have to keep working for him."

I shake my head and sip my coffee, smiling at how simple

he seems to think it is. "What's so funny?" he asks, frowning slightly.

"That comment. Only a man like you could say something like that."

"A man like me?"

"Yeah, you know." I wave my hand, indicating the grand room. "Guys who live like Bruce Wayne."

"You think I'm Batman?"

"Frankly, I wouldn't be surprised. Is your driver's name Alfred?" I'm at risk of babbling now, and I need to shut up. It's only because I'm nervous.

"It's Constantine, actually."

"Oh. Okay. Well, ordinary people—people like me—can't just walk out on a good job because their boss is an asshole, you know? We need little things like healthcare and money for groceries and to make our rent."

He stares at me, and I feel a flush creeping over my neck. I suppose he might consider what I just said as rude, even if it is true. Since my split from Chad, cash has been tight, and my limited experience in the world of work has meant I've had to do a lot of temporary jobs. Nobody cares if you went to Harvard when they want someone to manage an office. I suppose it's made me more aware than ever of the importance of being self-sufficient, especially with my mom's health needs.

"I have heard of things like rent," he says slowly, his tone calm but also frosty. "Of course, up here in my ivory tower, I've never been concerned with such trivialities. My life is, naturally, completely perfect in every way and totally free of all stress and worry. How is your croissant?"

I blink at him. I guess being rich doesn't automatically mean you don't have problems, but men like Drake have no idea about the cruel hardships of the real world. And that isn't his fault; it's simply a fact of life. "It's good. Uh, I think I'd better go. Leave you to build your empire or buy Arizona, or whatever it is you have on your to-do list today."

He nods and gazes at me over the steam from his coffee mug. "Okay. But that's my favorite shirt you're wearing. I'd like it back before you go."

Seriously? Does this guy think I'm some kind of international shirt thief? "Of course you can have it back. I'm pretty sure walking out of here in nothing but your shirt and my panties will look even worse than me walking out in my brides-maid dress."

"Take it off, then."

"What? Right now? You can't wait like five minutes?"

"No. It's my favorite shirt. Take it off. Now, Scarlet," he demands. I'm about to call him out for being such a dick when I see the look in his dark eyes. It's not a look that says he gives a shit about a shirt. It's a look that says he gives a shit about what's underneath the shirt. My body immediately responds to both the fire in his eyes and the command in his voice, and my lips tremble as I lick the last crumb of my croissant from them.

My pulse speeds up, and I squeeze my thighs together in response to the soft throb that now lives between them. Fuck. What is it about this guy that makes me act so out of character?

He raises one eyebrow at me, looking cool and calm while I quiver before him.

"Why is it," I say quietly as I stand up, "that I behave like this when I'm with you? I'm usually a very respectable woman, you know."

I unbutton the shirt with unsteady fingers, and he follows every move I make. "I'm sure you are. But isn't this more fun?"

It's not only fun, it's scintillating. It's like being on vacation from my real life, from being myself. I'm not sure I even like this guy, with his mood swings from hot to cold, but I definitely want him. I slide the soft cotton over my shoulder blades and walk slowly around the table, completely naked. Ignoring every instinct that tells me to be embarrassed, I hand him the shirt. His fingers brush mine as he takes it from me, then he tosses it to the floor.

My mouth drops open in mock horror. "I thought that was your favorite shirt?"

"I lied." With a sharp jerk of my wrist, he pulls me onto his lap. Tugging my hair back with one hand, he slips the other straight between my thighs. I'd like to make him work for it, but my body has other ideas, and I'm already wet. I tip my head back, and he nips at my skin, running his teeth along my jawline and kissing my neck.

"Drake," I gasp as he slides his fingers between my slick folds.

"You know there is no way you're leaving this hotel room without getting fucked again, Scarlet, don't you?"

I'm thrilled when I wriggle on his lap and feel how hard his cock is. "I hope not," I moan as his fingers continue teasing me.

"So damn wet." He pumps them in and out of me, the obscene sucking sound filling the room. My orgasm building, I wrap my arms around his neck and suck my bottom lip between my teeth.

"That's it, mi rosa. Show me how much you want my fingers," he says into my ear. "I'm going to make you come, then I'm going to spread you open on this table and bury myself inside you."

His words make me clench against his probing fingers, and when he rubs the pad of his thumb over my swollen bud, my legs tremble.

"Oh, fu—Drake!" The orgasm washes over my body, drowning me in a wave of pleasure. He rubs the last of it from my body, then crushes his mouth possessively over mine. The man is a magician; I've never felt a physical response like this with anyone else. He breaks the kiss, and I melt as I look into those incredible deep brown eyes. I know I'm inexperienced, but surely it isn't possible to have this kind of connection without feeling something. Without it meaning something. Am I that naive, or do I see a flicker of emotion cross his perfect features as he gazes at me?

He stands up with my legs wrapped around his waist and holds me there with one hand firmly on my ass. With the other, he sweeps the table clear, sending cups and plates flying and obviously not giving a damn. He lays me on my back and pushes my thighs apart. "Jesus," he mutters, his eyes on fire as he inspects my body. "You are so damn fuckable."

He pulls that final condom from his pocket and unzips his pants. Within seconds, he's ready, and I'm wet and waiting. I squeal as he hoists my legs over his broad shoulders, almost bending me in two, and guides himself inside me.

His hands go to my breasts, and he teases my tight nipples as he slams into me, rolling them between his thumb and fingers in a way that perfectly straddles the delicious line between pleasure and pain. My hands scrabble for a grip on the smooth wood of the table, but he's fucking me so hard that I'm sliding backward and forward with each dynamic thrust.

"You're lucky I have to work," he growls, not slowing his pace for a moment, each stroke precise and deliberate. "Otherwise, I'd chain you to the bed and fuck you all day long."

The dirty talk pushes me over the edge, and as he leans down to nip at my neck, I scream his name yet again.

"Come for me, Scarlet," he commands as he drives into me. "Because if this is going to be the last time I ever fuck you, I'm going to make sure you feel it."

For some reason, a deep sadness settles in the pit of my

stomach and tears burn behind my eyes, but I quickly blink them away and focus instead on the pleasure this man's body wrings from mine. This was a one-time deal. I'll never see him again, and that's exactly the way I want it.

Isn't it?

CHAPTER
SIX
DRAKE

I press my lips to the top of my nephew's downy-soft head and inhale his unique scent. I had no idea how magical he would be or how the smell of tiny human plus baby powder would combine to turn me to mush. I've never had any interest in kids, either in producing my own or fawning over anybody else's, but I would give my last breath to make this chunky little guy laugh.

He curls his fingers in my beard and grins at me, a globule of drool rolling down his chin. I swipe it away with the tip of my thumb, and he squeals with delight. Maybe that's part of it—it's so damn easy to make them laugh, to make them happy. It's sad to think that he'll eventually be as fucked up as the rest of us.

Or maybe not, I think, as my sister-in-law walks over. Maybe he'll be the perfect blend of Melanie's selfless and sunny disposition and my older brother's drive and ambition. "Let me take him from you, Drake. He needs his nap," Mel says, giving me a warm smile. Her cheeks are flushed pink, her hair slightly mussed.

Nathan steps up behind her with a bottle of merlot in his hand. "Do you want me to take him, corazón?"

She smiles sweetly at him, and I swear he melts into a puddle before my eyes. It's like when the Wicked Witch of the West gets doused in water. He's so pussy-whipped these days—not that I blame him. Mel is great, and she makes him happier than I've ever seen him. That's no easy feat given the charmed life Nathan already led before he met her.

He's one of those guys that everything always came easy to —sports, school, work, women. He worked hard and played hard. Like the rest of us, he was devastated when we lost our mom, but he was the one who always seemed like he was treading a gilded path. I've always partially hero-worshipped him, even though he's only a few years older than me. He's the son our dad always saw as the one who would carry on the James family line, and I guess he was right. Luke is living proof of that.

"No," his wife assures him. "You go have a drink with your brothers. I've got him. I think maybe I need my nap too."

I'm pretty sure my older brother growls at that latter part, but I ignore him and reluctantly allow her to take the baby from my arms, but not without a final kiss on his head. "See you later, little guy." He gurgles and waves his chubby fists at me.

I spent the first four months of my nephew's life living in Chicago, but now I'm back in New York where I belong. I have a lot of uncle time to make up for, and I intend to enjoy every sweet minute of it.

THE NOISE in the den is comforting, reminding me of much happier times when we all lived here and Mom was still with us. For a while after she passed, our family home felt like a prison to me, every room a reminder of what we lost, the scent of her perfume still seeming to linger in every hallway. It was like the place was haunted, and we were all suffering. I'm glad to be back here, rebuilding, all the James boys together again— just like she would have wanted. As though he knows exactly what I'm thinking, Nathan gives my shoulder a comforting squeeze. "It's been a while since we were all here for Sunday dinner, huh?"

The past three months have been a whirlwind of tying up loose ends on my old life in Chicago, so this is the first time I've made it home since shortly after Luke was born. An unexpected lump balls in my throat, and I swallow it down. "Yeah. She would've loved this."

"She would have. I wish she'd been able to meet Mel, to hold Luke in her arms." I see a sudden shine of tears in his eyes, and it freaks me out. Nathan James is not the kind of man who cries, for fuck's sake.

He swipes the moisture away and gives me a sheepish grin. "Don't you dare tell a living soul you just saw me crying at Sunday dinner. I'll never hear the fucking end of it."

"So I can't tell everyone that becoming a dad has turned you into the kind of emotional sap you used to roll your eyes at, then?"

He punches me hard in the arm, turning it numb. I grunt, but I'm used to it. When you grow up with four brothers, someone is always walking around with a dead-arm. It's brutal.

He jerks his head in the direction of our other three siblings who are huddled around the large oak coffee table our parents brought from their very first house in Spain. "We'd better get in there before Mase and Elijah drink all the good Scotch."

I notice the familiar black label on the bottle. "Does Pop know they've nabbed some of his fifty-year-old Macallan?"

Nathan shrugs. "The old man is so happy to have us all under one roof, I'm sure he'd let us drink his cellar dry. Besides, he's too busy prepping for dinner to be interested in what we're doing right now."

I can picture him in his *I'm the boss* apron, the one our mom bought for him shortly before she died. It brings a smile to my face and very nearly a tear to my eye. Only the fact that I just mocked Nathan for being a wuss holds it back. "Can't believe he still hasn't gotten himself a cook."

"You know him. Too set in his ways. Besides, it keeps him out of trouble."

He's not wrong. Our dad built his tech company up into the multibillion-dollar global conglomerate that it is today, and he is an amazing man, but he hasn't been the same since Mom died. It hit us all hard, but for him, it was like losing half of himself. He had a heart attack a while ago, and although he's made a full recovery, it's a worry. Dalton James is no frail granddad—he's still a force to be reckoned with as he quickly approaches seventy—but he is one of the reasons I moved back. He won't be around forever, as he likes to remind us on a regular basis.

Nathan walks across the room, and I follow him. Feels like I've spent a lot of my life following Nathan, and to be fair, he's never steered me wrong. He persuaded me to go all in with him on the law firm, and that worked out—my work is the love of my life. My Melanie. He sits on one of the big, comfortable sofas, and I flop down next to him.

"So, what was her name?" Mason asks as soon as my ass touches the seat.

Should have known I could hide nothing from these four. "Whose name?" I feign ignorance anyway. It's worth a shot, plus it'll annoy the hell out of him.

Mason narrows his eyes, but they're filled with amusement. "The girl you blew me off for last night. It better have been a girl anyway. If I find out you canceled on me for work again, dude …" He doesn't finish the sentence, but the implicit threat hangs in the air. Another dead-arm lurks on the horizon.

It wouldn't be the first time I canceled on one of them for work. My priorities have been clear since I was in my early twenties and everything else in my life went to shit. Work never lets me down. It never dies or walks out on me or makes me feel like crap about myself. Work is the best wife I could ever have, and out of all the James brothers, I'm the one who would be described as a workaholic. That's saying something, considering how driven and ambitious they all are. Apart from Maddox, and he is a different story altogether. Our youngest brother is working his way through his own demons, and they would eat mine for breakfast.

My brothers are all looking at me, waiting for a reply. "Her name was, uh, Scarlet. It was a one-off. I won't be seeing her again."

"You blew me off for some girl you're never going to see again? Dude." Mason shakes his head. "It could at least have been someone special."

"Someone special?" Elijah says, arching an eyebrow at him. "Since when did you start believing in that kind of romantic stuff?"

"Fuck you, bro," Mason says. "I watch a lot of Netflix."

Elijah hands me a glass, and I gratefully accept and take a sip, enjoying the smoky liquor warming my throat almost as much as I do the banter between my brothers. "I don't do *special*," I say, "and I never see any of them again."

I wince because that's not entirely true. I've been in Chicago for a long time, and as much as I love my family, they don't really know an awful lot about my life there. They only see what I allow them to see, the curated version of my world. But now that I'm back in New York, maybe that needs to change. "Well, except for the girls I ..." I lick the residual whisky from my lips, suddenly nervous. "The girls I hire."

Elijah arches an eyebrow, surprise clear in his eyes. No judgment, though. "The girls you hire? Like hookers?"

I shake my head. "Not exactly. It's a bit more nuanced than that. These are professional women from an exclusive company in Chicago. Women I had an ongoing *arrangement* with that suited us all."

Elijah stares at me, bemused. "But why couldn't you just meet women the old-fashioned way? You're rich. You're successful. You keep yourself well-groomed."

I frown at him. "Well-groomed?"

Mason nudges Elijah in the ribs and smirks at me. "He means that, objectively, you're hot."

"I'm curious too, Drake," Nathan adds. "I can't imagine you're short on offers."

Damn. I've not only opened the whole can of worms; I've dumped them out in the middle of the room for everyone to poke at with a stick. It's hard to explain because they're right, I don't lack offers. But I simply don't have the time or patience for the sheer mundanity of dating. The mind-numbing small talk, the getting-to-know-you shit. The pretending-we're-not-just-here-to-scratch-an-itch falseness of it all.

It's all so fake, especially when I know that I'm not interested in an actual relationship. I like women, and I love sex, but I'm not the settling-down kind. Presenting myself as someone I'm not, only to get to the naked part of the evening? That's not for me. My special arrangements are far more honest, and it certainly saves time—time I can spend working. "It's just easier that way," I explain. "More efficient. They get the job done, don't ask questions or expect small talk. We all know how it works and what our roles are. Plus, they don't have any objections to the rope marks."

Nathan sputters, nearly spitting out his Scotch. "Rope marks? Just exactly what kind of kinky shit are you into?"

Maddox and I lock eyes. Although he's always been open-minded, my youngest brother's travels provided him with a depth that he didn't have before, and that's why he's the only one I've discussed any of this with. He gives me a knowing look and answers for me. "It's called Shibari. It's a Japanese art form involving the aesthetics of bondage. The way the ropes create patterns on the skin, the contrast of textures ... it's not merely sexual. For some, it's almost spiritual, and at the very least mindful."

Huh. Mindful. Like coloring. There was something unbearably cute about watching that grown-up and completely gorgeous woman playing with crayons last night.

Maddox grins at me and holds his coffee mug aloft in salute. I offer him a smile of appreciation for his description of my "kinky shit" and raise my glass in acknowledgment. He's right. There is something about the practice of shaping and tying the ropes that relaxes me and brings me to a calm place. I don't practice it often, but when I'm stressed or strung out, it's the quickest way to get out of my own head. The women I deal with are professional and experienced, and everybody benefits from the arrangement.

"Well, it sounds like a lot of work to me." Mason smirks. "What happened to good old-fashioned handcuffs?"

Maddox rolls his eyes. "It's like comparing apples and oranges, asshole. Shibari is actually quite sensual."

"I bet it's not the way Drake does it." Mason chuckles and takes a sip of his Scotch.

"Kinky fucker," Nathan mutters. "Spiritual, my ass. You're just a grade-A pervert, bro."

Elijah and Mason snort a laugh, and I shake my head. Every time the five of us get together, we revert back to teenagers, no matter how old we get. It's juvenile, but I love it. I've fucking missed this while living in Chicago, and I only recently realized how much.

I punch Nathan on the arm, partly because he's the one sitting closest to me, partly because I owe him one. Out of all my brothers, he's the one I've always had the biggest rivalry and the most in common with. Out of all of them, I expect him to have my back, or at least to try to understand. "Don't judge just because you're married now and don't get to do any kinky shit."

He tilts his head and grins at me, his dark eyes twinkling with mischief and the effects of the Scotch. "Pretty sure I get more action than anyone else sitting in this room."

"Yeah, right." Mason snorts. "Sure, bro. Whatever helps you sleep at night."

"Or keeps me up all night," Nathan replies smugly.

Mason leans back in his chair, a perplexed expression on his face. "There's no way you get more action than me. I mean, you're married with a kid, and I'm ..." Our younger brother licks his lips like he's searching for the appropriate word.

Nathan rests his forearms on his knees. "You're?"

"A man whore?" Elijah offers helpfully.

Mason arches an eyebrow, a cocky smile curving his lips. "I'm ... well, I'm a busy guy. I have at least three dates a week."

Nathan sits up straight, rolling up his sleeves. His expression turns serious, and I bite back a grin. I've seen this side of him plenty of times before, and it's a joy to watch. It's exactly the same way he looks in the courtroom when he's about to destroy the prosecution. Mason is set to be schooled by the Iceman himself. "Let's be generous, Mase, and say four dates a week. Even if you score every single time—"

"Which I do," Mason chimes in.

Nathan nods, sucking on his top lip and eyeing our brother

across the table. "Okay. Accepted. So, accounting for downtime and knowing what I do about you and how eager you are to get them out the door as soon as the deed is done ..."

"Harsh, bro," Mason says with a barking laugh. He doesn't argue, though, because we all know it's true.

"I'm gonna say maximum you get laid is eight times. On a good week."

Elijah whistles and leans back in his chair. "Lucky bastard. Some of us haven't been laid eight times in the last year." I wish I could say I was surprised by my oldest brother's admission, but unfortunately, his marriage looks nothing like Nathan's.

A cocksure grin spreads across Mason's face, and he's obviously delighted with his stats. It's adorable that he actually thinks he's won. Nathan shoots me a conspiratorial glance. "You want to close this one for me, counselor?"

I roll my eyes before fixing them on Mason's expectant face. "You must know why you get so much uncle time with Luke on a Sunday, right?" This is my first Sunday dinner in a while, but I've already figured out the score. One nephew and four doting uncles, not to mention a besotted grandfather.

Mason frowns. "Because we're the best fucking uncles in the world."

I can see Nathan smirking from the corner of my eye. I place my hand over Mason's and squeeze. "Surely you're not naive enough to believe it actually took Nathan and Mel a full twenty minutes to choose the wine for tonight's dinner, bro?"

It takes him a few seconds, but realization dawns on his face. His jaw drops, and he looks from me to Nathan. "You—" His attention comes back to me, then returns to the happiest fucker in the room. "In the fucking wine cellar? Really?"

Nathan offers him a casual shrug. "Like I didn't catch you and that pretentious soap actor down there the Thanksgiving before last?"

Mason scoffs. "Exactly! Now I'll never be able to go down there again."

"You mean go down *in* there again?" I can't help but tease him.

"Not that I like to brag"—Nathan makes a show of checking his watch—"but I've already had sex more times this weekend than you do in one of your good weeks, Mase. At home. In the car on the way over here. In my room upstairs. In the tub. And yeah, in the fucking wine cellar. Thanks for the childcare, by the way."

"Fucking married people," Mason mutters. "It's not a fair comparison."

"Not all of us are so fortunate." Elijah sighs and downs the rest of his Scotch. "I'm here to skew the averages back to normal."

"That's because you're married to Amber the Ice Queen," Mason replies, grimacing. "Man, that woman would freeze your dick off with a glance."

Elijah glares at him. "You don't have to like my wife, Mason, but you do have to respect her. I'm allowed to complain about my love life. You're not."

"Besides," I say, jumping in to head off this potential flare-up, "Amber isn't as icy as you think, Mase. Her not liking you doesn't make her a bitch. It just makes her a good judge of character."

Everyone laughs at that, even Mason. He's quick to rouse but equally quick to forgive.

Maddox pours himself a coffee from the cafetière on the table. "Anyway, let's not turn this into a dick-swinging competition. We all know I'd win."

Mason barks out another laugh. "Says the guy who gets laid even less than Elijah."

"My celibacy is a choice, nutsack," Maddox quips, dodging

the balled-up napkin Mason tosses at his head. "I never strike out, so therefore my stats are perfect."

I take another sip of my drink, savoring the warm buzz of alcohol and the even warmer feeling of being surrounded by my brothers again. It's been too long since we've all been in the same room, trading barbs and inside jokes like no time has passed at all. My relationships with these guys aren't perfect, but they're the best family a guy could ask for.

"So, Drake." Mason leans forward, a glint in his eye. "Let's get back to where we started. You blew me off last night. You at least owe me some of the details—tell us more. How did you meet her?"

I open my mouth to reply, then shut it again. Really, what's to tell? I don't even know her last name, where she lives, or any identifying information about her. She should be instantly forgettable, simply another pleasant night of mutually satisfying sex.

Truth is, I remember way too much about her. I remember how her pussy tastes and can still almost feel her silky cum on my tongue. How wet and tight she was as I slid my cock inside her and the sexy sounds she made when she came. How my name sounded on her lips, like she had no control over it at all.

Even worse, I remember other things—things from before I got her naked. Her laugh. The sorrow hidden behind her smile. The way her eyes sparkled when she talked about her friends and her mom. How she called me out over breakfast. She was the perfect combination of sweet and sassy, and even thinking about her is distracting. I should have gotten her number, should have asked to see her again. Except I'm me—I don't do relationships and I don't break my own rules. So instead, I went cold on her as soon as we finished fucking and bundled her off on her way. Handed her over to Constantine like she was nothing but a package I needed delivered. That's the other thing I remember. The way she looked at me as she left, draped in that creased bridesmaid's dress. She was disappointed in me, and I hated it.

My brothers stare at me, anticipating my response. And I guess it's my fault I didn't shut them down completely. I didn't tell Mason to go fuck himself. I allowed her into the conversation, into my mind. Maybe I actually want to talk about her. Hell, maybe it will chase her away if I do. "Well, if you really must know ..."

"Oh, we must," Nathan interjects, his grin widening.

I clear my throat. "I kind of stumbled into this wedding. Purely by accident, of course."

Mason shakes his head, amused. "How the fuck do you stumble into a wedding, bro?"

I lean back in my chair, a wry smile playing on my lips. "Well, it's a long story, but let's just say it involved the finest steak I've ever eaten, a good tux, and an open bar."

Elijah snorts. "Steak and top-shelf liquor, should have known."

"Anyway," I continue, ignoring his comment. "That's where I met her. I saw her from the doorway, sitting alone, and I just knew I had to go speak to her. Can't explain it, just felt the pull, you know? There was this reception table where guests were supposed to sign in and there were name tags, which I thought was weird because it was a wedding, not a corporate retreat. But I grabbed one and went right in."

"Who were you?" Maddox asks, immediately homing in on something I hoped to avoid.

I narrow my eyes at him. "Charlie."

"Yeah, but Charlie what?" He grins at me, and I wonder if he somehow learned to read minds at some Buddhist retreat in Nepal or whatever the fuck.

"Charlie Cockburn-Cummings, all right?"

Howls of laughter break out around the room, and I have to join in. It is, after all, fucking funny.

"I'm not surprised he wasn't there," Elijah says, his lips twitching in a smirk. "He was probably too embarrassed."

"Yeah, I think I met him once in line at the clap clinic!" Mason adds between guffaws. "He needed some cream for his cock burn."

Maddox tries to stay calm and maintain his zen, but eventually he cracks too. "Maybe he was English," he adds. "Nobody would bat an eyelid at that kind of name in England. When I was there, I met a dude called Nathaniel Gildenballs, I kid you not. Anyway, carry on, Drake. Charlie. Whoever. You crashed a wedding and picked up a one-night stand?"

That's about the size of it. "Yeah. I mean, I kind of knew the couple—Tucker McDaid, who I think works for the Attorney General's office, and Emily Gregor? She looked familiar too."

"I know Emily," Elijah says. "You've all kind of met her, or at least been in the same room as her. She sits on some of the same charity boards as Amber. She's one of those women I know without really knowing." He shrugs. "I'm guessing it was a pretty good wedding party?"

"It was, if you like that kind of thing. The main attraction for me was this girl, though. She was in the wedding party, still wearing this purple dress that was clearly uncomfortable. Seriously, it looked like she wanted to crawl out of her skin. So I took my Scotch and sat next to her, and ..." I find myself lost in the memory for a moment.

"And?" Maddox prompts, leaning forward, his interest piqued. I'm not surprised. I never talk like this. I never *feel* like this. What the fuck *is* this?

I shake my head, snapping myself back to the present. "And we ended up talking for hours. We danced a little. Then we found ourselves in one of the gardens behind the hotel. One thing led to another, and ..."

"And you tied her up with a conveniently placed garden hose?" Nathan suggests with a falsely innocent expression.

I roll my eyes. "Quit with the fucking rope jokes, asshole. Don't make me regret telling you about that. No, we just ... connected. And yeah, I know, I'm the one who sounds like I watch too much Netflix now. She came back to my room, and that's as much as you pervs are getting."

My brothers exchange glances, clearly taken aback by my uncharacteristic sentimentality. By my standards, that was like a declaration of love.

"So, you actually talked to her before you banged her?" Mason asks, his tone less teasing now and more genuinely curious instead. "Did she stay the night in your suite, or did you kick her out the minute you shot your load?"

Fuck. I probably should have done the latter. "Yeah, we talked, and yeah, she spent the night. And no, I'm not giving you any more details."

"Bro, she sounds great. Seriously, why didn't you get her number?" Mason asks, frowning.

"What makes you think I didn't?"

"Your fucking face, man. You're trying to play it cool, but the way you're talking about her ... It's like you know you'll never see her again."

I shrug, trying to act unconcerned even though he's one hundred percent right. "You know me. I don't do relationships. It was just a one-night deal, that's all." But even as I say the words, I can feel something gnawing at my gut. Regret, maybe? Something I don't recognize, anyway. Something I'm not sure I like.

How the hell did Amelia manage to get under my skin like

this after only one night? No other woman has ever had this effect on me, and I have no fucking idea what to do about it.

SEVEN

AMELIA

Kimmy Park and I have known each other since first grade. Back then, she was obsessed with a boy in our class named Jamie Jessop and followed him around like a puppy, trying to get him to kiss her. Being a seven-year-old who was more interested in collecting Pokémon cards than having a girlfriend, poor Jamie was horrified. The only way she could have gotten his attention was if she'd dressed up as Pikachu and yelled, "I choose you!"

We're both in our early thirties now, but Kimmy still has the exact same approach to sex—if she sees someone she likes, she goes for it. Although she's a lot more successful these days. Her whirlwind of a love life has always left me dizzy. It certainly helps that grown-up Kimmy is drop-dead gorgeous and ultra confident. She's the kind of woman that makes members of both sexes go cross-eyed when she talks to them. We should all be more like Kimmy, I think as I sit opposite her in the latest bar to open in my neighborhood. I don't fail to notice that only last night I was wishing I could be more like Emily, and now Kimmy —what is wrong with me? Why can't I be happy just being Amelia?

Well, one reason is that Amelia's no fun at all when compared with her alter ego. Scarlet has all the good times, all the orgasms. Amelia got stuck with a vague sense of discomfort as she was driven home by a stranger after spending the night with his boss. Amelia felt tacky and disappointed and a tiny bit cheap, even though she knew she had no reason to.

"Tell me everything," Kimmy says, her eyes twinkling at me from across the table crowded with empty cocktail glasses. "I missed the wedding of the century last night because of work, and for once, it sounds like you've got some top-shelf tea. If I have to sit in this shit heap, you're going to spill it all."

"This isn't a shit heap." As I say it, I take stock of my surroundings and have to admit that the place is a bit rough around the edges. Despite being new, it still shows signs of the dive bar it was in a past life, and the waiter looked horrified when we ordered cosmos. Nobody has been by to collect our glasses, and the music being pumped out of the speakers sounds like a suicide playlist. "Okay, fair point. It's not great. But it's good to support new businesses, and we can't all live in swanky apartments on the Upper East Side."

"Girl, I was just giving you shit. I don't care where we are. I grew up the same place you did, so you know I'm not a princess. And stop trying to change the subject. Time to tell me everything. You said there was a guy. I've been waiting years to hear there was a guy. Who was he, and how good was the sex? On a scale of one to ten?"

I sigh and bite back the huge grin that wants to take over my whole face. "On a scale of one to ten, it was like ... a million. Kimmy, he was so hot! I mean, I don't want to sound like—"

"Me?"

"Yeah. But he was so hot, he could blister your skin just with a look. So hot he makes Death Valley seem cool. So hot you could fry eggs on his abs."

"So hot he melted your panties off?" Clearly fascinated, she's leaning forward now, her chin balanced on her steepled fingers. This is, after all, her favorite subject.

"Exactly that hot. I was sitting at an empty table at the back of the reception, and he just ... appeared. Like some benevolent god decided to give me a break and sent Mr. Fire and Ice to seduce me. I still don't know what came over me. It's not like me at all."

She shrugs. "What came over you is called being a woman, Amelia—a woman with needs. You've ignored them for way too long, and you spent years married to that selfish asshole. I'm guessing he wouldn't recognize a clitoris if it was wearing a T-shirt that had 'here I am, clit this way' written on it in neon letters."

I open my mouth to object, to defend Chad and his bedroom skills. But she's absolutely right, and why the hell should I stick up for him? I owe him no loyalty at all, and besides, he was awful in bed. I never knew how awful until now because I had nothing to compare it to, but Chad does not come off well in that comparison. One night with Drake made me understand exactly how bad my married sex life was.

"Maybe you're right. But having a spectacular one-night stand doesn't mean I'm going to be living like that from now on."

"Well, that's disappointing." She tilts her head and pouts at me. "I was hoping we'd get to have some fun together. There are two guys behind you who are definitely checking us out. They look like they're in a band, which in my experience means they're probably self-obsessed and have a tenuous relationship with personal hygiene, but hey, I have a generous spirit when it comes to love. We could go chat with them. Expand your number of lovers to a staggering three?"

The fact that I made it to my thirties having only slept with

Chad is a source of constant amazement to her. "I don't think so. I'm just not made like you."

"More's the pity. I have no shame—I enjoy sex and plan to have it with as many people as I can before I reach the stage where I need hip replacements and adult diapers."

"Knowing you, you'll still be on the prowl. Nobody in that day center will be safe."

"This is true. But seriously, babe, didn't this one magnificent night with a world-class sex god change your mind? There are other men out there, you know. Men who might be just as good in the sack."

I blush, remembering exactly how good he was in the sack. And on the table. And the floor. He made me feel things I've never known before, and it seems crazy to think that I could win the sex jackpot like that again.

It's enticing, but it would be reckless, and I have other, more important things to concentrate on in my life right now. It's not all about chasing orgasms. I can give myself orgasms, even if they are tiny and kinda pathetic compared to the way Drake made me come. Gusts of wind as opposed to a hurricane. It has also occurred to me that I might not have the right temperament for this casual sex thing, because I haven't stopped thinking about him all day.

"I don't think so. I'm glad I met him and that I finally let go of some of my inhibitions and went a little wild. I'm glad he brought out that side of me, because it does seem ridiculous to have reached my age and never have had a one-night stand. But it's not something I'm going to keep repeating. I can't imagine it would be anything but a letdown with someone else, anyhow, and besides ... it wasn't entirely casual. There were feelings involved."

"Ugh," she says, shuddering. "Feelings? I hate those. They

get in the way. Tell your Auntie Kimmy all about them, though, sweetheart."

"I felt like ... like we connected. Before the sex, we talked for hours. It was kind of like a confessional, you know? Soul sharing?"

"I don't know, no, I'm glad to say. But I do know that stuff matters to most women. You're sure he wasn't just turning on the charm to get into your panties?"

I bite my lip and think about it. "You could be right, but I don't think so. This guy ... He's not the kind of guy who needs to work that hard. He could get into pretty much any panties he liked with nothing but a smile. No, I think it was real. And we, uh, cuddled. After the sex."

She finishes her drink, her eyes wide over the rim of the glass. "You cuddled? Girl, that is one of the saddest things I've ever heard."

"No it's not! And we only cuddled after we had super-hot animal sex, all right? And after I came four times." I whisper that last part, glancing nervously around the bar before I drop my voice even lower. "And then we did it again this morning, on the breakfast table."

"Oooh, now I'm interested. Did he do that hot thing where he swept everything off beforehand?"

I laugh, because that's exactly what he did. It was insanely hot at the time, and it still makes me throb a little down below when I think about it. "Yep. He did."

"So, how did you leave it? Did you swap numbers? Did you make him a friendship bracelet?"

I roll my eyes but don't take it personally. She takes nothing seriously unless she absolutely has to. "We didn't swap numbers, no. He was ... He was different by the time I left."

"Mr. Ice rather than Mr. Fire?"

"Exactly. He had to work, and he made it very clear that it

was time for me to leave, and he kind of, well, shut down. It was weird."

Kimmy shakes her head. "Babe, I think maybe you're over-thinking this. You had sex. It was a one-time thing. It was time to leave. This isn't a love story—it's a lust story."

She's right, I know. I shouldn't waste any more time thinking about him.

"I know. I enjoyed it, and it was new for me, but I don't think I'll do it again. Maybe I'm just too soft. Maybe I'll always want more. But hey, I've got it out of my system and now I need to concentrate on my real life. On my new job and my mom."

Kimmy's expression becomes instantly sympathetic. She's known my mom since she was a kid and had endless dinners, sleepovers, and burned-waffle breakfasts at our place. My mom was always a terrible cook, but she made up for it with enthusiasm. "How is Edith?"

"Not great, truthfully. She suddenly seems old, you know? And the good meds cost a fortune, hence the need to concentrate on the new job."

My mom is only in her mid-sixties, and she was diagnosed with COPD years ago. She never smoked a day in her life, but thanks to the time she spent working in a plastics factory when I was younger, her lungs look like those of someone with a three-pack-a-day unfiltered-cigarette habit.

Her health has declined a lot recently, and moving back here after my split from Chad was a no-brainer. I need to be close by so I can help her as much as possible—or at least as much as she'll let me. She hates having her daughter be her caretaker and insisted that I get my own place so she wouldn't drag me down—her words, not mine. I would be happy to live with her, but it's probably for the best that I have my own space. It allows me to hide how angry I get at the world for doing this to her. It just isn't fair.

"You know I can always lend a hand with that. The meds, the cashflow. I may be a shallow-ass freak when it comes to romance, but friends are different, and you and Edith mean the world to me. Please don't struggle when you don't need to."

Kimmy's own childhood was chaotic, and our home was a refuge for her. I might never have known my dad, but my mom more than made up for it. She was always so cool, so kind, so completely there for me. She gave Kimmy a safe haven, and my friend has never forgotten. These days, she's living her best boss life and has no shortage of financial resources. "I do know that, and thanks, Kimmy. If things get really bad, I'll let you know, I promise. For the time being, though, she wants to stay as independent as possible."

"Hmmm." Kimmy cocks an eyebrow at me. "Sounds familiar—you're exactly the same. Now, tell me more about your new job, then. Not as exciting as a man with a magic tongue, but I'll take what I can get. It's with a law firm, isn't it?"

"Yeah. James and James."

"Wow. Not just *a* law firm, *the* law firm! They're massive, and very well respected. It sounds like a great opportunity for you."

"It really does, doesn't it? I'm so excited, but I'm a little nervous too."

"You have nothing to be nervous about, babe. You're a clever, well-educated woman with the most incredible organizational skills in the known universe. They're lucky to have you."

I'm not sure I'd go that far, but thinking about my new job feels a whole lot safer than thinking about the sex god who rocked my world on its axis last night. And again this morning. My future beckons, and I need to banish all thoughts of men I'm never going to see again.

CHAPTER
EIGHT
AMELIA

A bead of sweat dribbles down my spine, making me shiver even in the climate-controlled reception area of James and James. I have no idea why I'm so nervous. It's not like I haven't had a job before. In the past year alone, I've had five, in fact. Only none of them felt as important as this one.

This one is real and permanent, and it comes with so many benefits it makes my head spin. Including, most importantly, health insurance for nominated next of kin—in my case, my mom. I'm sure the work will be hard and the hours will be long, but the staff here is treated fairly and well. That's a marked difference from my office temping gigs.

That, of course, is what's making me nervous. This matters. I can't afford to mess this up. I tell myself I'll be fine. That it'll be like riding a bike. Except maybe that's not a great comparison, because the last time I rode a bike, I did a spectacular face-plant into a flower bed.

Amelia Ryder, get a damn grip. You are a Harvard-educated business graduate, and you will not be face-planting anywhere.

The pep talk isn't entirely successful, and as I look around the beautifully decorated reception area, I can't help feeling like the gawky new kid on my first day of school. I bet there'll be mean girls and jocks and teachers who make me feel stupid. Still, I navigated high school, and I'll navigate this place as well. It's big and it's fancy, but at the end of the day, this is nothing I'm not capable of. I'm pretty sure I wouldn't have gotten the job otherwise. I should trust their judgment even if I don't trust my own.

People pass me as I sit and wait, some giving me a cursory glance and others too absorbed in their own workday to pay any attention to me. It's like a corporate fashion show—men in well-tailored suits and polished brogues, elegant women in pencil skirts, colorful blouses, and terrifyingly tall heels. They all look so stylish, so busy and confident, like they absolutely belong in this plush space.

I glance down at my own attire, which I felt good about when I left home. I opted for a simple black wrap dress and classic black pumps. Perhaps it's too plain. Too casual. Am I dressing for success or dressing for a funeral? I run my hands absentmindedly over the fabric. It's too late to worry about it now.

"Miss Ryder?" A familiar voice interrupts my musings, and I glance up to see Nathan James towering over me. My new boss. The one people warned me was an asshole but who comes off as anything but. Tough, yes, and possibly a little scary if you're on the wrong side of him, but an asshole? Not as far as I saw. I quickly close down that train of thought. It reminds me of discussing it with my one-night stand, and I don't have the brain space to think about him right now.

I stand, ready for him to show me my desk and eager to get started. The sooner I can dive into some work, the sooner I'll start to feel useful. Useful people don't have time to feel like the new kid.

"Mr. James. It's so lovely to see you again."

He smiles, his dark eyes crinkling at the corners. That's the smile that put me at ease in my interview, and the questions he asked and the way he asked them allowed me to overcome my nerves and present the best version of myself. He understood the gaps in my resume and didn't judge when I told him I'd been focusing on my family. He was interested in the different places I'd lived and how it felt to be back in New York. He had a way of drawing truths out of me, of reading me better than I'd ever been read in an interview.

I release the breath I was holding. The fact that he liked what he heard enough to offer me the job should be enough reassurance. He was certainly more pleasant than Linda, the poker-faced woman from HR who sat in with us. Even the memory of her scowl is enough to make me shudder and want to cross myself with holy water. Hopefully I'll have no run-ins with her any time soon.

Nathan gestures to the corridor on our left. "If you come with me, I'll show you where you'll be based."

I glance in the other direction. To the hallway that leads to his office. "Is it not ...?"

He frowns. "Not what?"

I clear my throat. "Isn't your office that way? I assumed I'd be sitting near you if I'm your secretary."

He winces, and my heart drops through my chest. I'm so nervous that the slightest sign of anything going wrong has me heading for a tailspin. Have I made a huge mistake on my first day?

"Ah. It appears there's been a misunderstanding, Miss Ryder. You see, I already have a secretary, and while I'm sure you would do a very good job ..." He looks around as though he's checking for witnesses, then leans in and whispers, "I'd be kind of lost without her. Plus, she'd kill me if I even considered replacing her. I mean that. I'm terrified of her."

His tone is light, and his body language says this isn't a big deal. That it's amusing, if anything. Maybe that's how it seems to him, but my cheeks flush with embarrassment. I feel like an idiot who doesn't even know what job she applied for. I was absolutely convinced that my role was as secretary to Mr. James, the man who interviewed me. I guess it doesn't really matter in the grand scheme of things, provided the pay and conditions are the same, but I'm humiliated. I came here thinking I was working for the man in charge, and instead I'm … well, who knows? I suppose there's only one way to find out.

"I see," I say calmly, amazed at how unflustered I sound. "Then whose secretary have I been hired to be?"

He laughs, revealing a perfect set of white teeth. There's something oddly familiar about him now. Something I didn't notice at my interview last week and that I can't quite put my finger on. "Please accept my apologies," he says, holding up his hands in a placating gesture. "This was all done in a bit of a rush. Perhaps we should have been clearer." He gestures toward the hallway again, and I walk with him. "You were hired to work for the other Mr. James. My brother."

"Oh?" I blink, taken aback. I was aware from my research that James and James is run by two brothers, but I was under the impression the other one ran their Chicago office—at least that's what it said on the website. As I wasn't applying for a job in Chicago, I didn't pay a great deal of attention to his name.

"Yeah, he's only recently returned to the city, and he's in desperate need of some help. I hope that's okay? The pay and position are exactly the same, and on the bright side, you don't have to work for me. I've heard I can be a bit of a grouch."

"I'm sure that's not true," I reply politely, even though that's exactly what I heard too. I'm relieved that the job is basically the same, and how different can the other Mr. James be? They are brothers, after all.

"So you're happy to stay and give us a shot?"

"Of course I am! I'm a bit surprised that you're doing this yourself though. Don't you have, um—"

"I think the word you're looking for is minions. And yes, ordinarily, I might have sent one of them to show you to your desk. Today, though, everyone's pretty busy with our annual staff HR training, and I really wanted to make sure you were given a proper welcome. I would have asked my brother to come and greet you at reception, but he's still trying to work out his new coffee machine. And that, to let you in on a little secret about my caffeine-addicted brother, takes top priority."

He stops outside an office that has the door propped open, and points to a desk with nothing but an iMac and a welcome basket of fruit on it. I smile at the neat and tidy workspace, looking forward to making it my own. "Thank you, Mr. James. This looks perfect."

"Let me tell him you're here." He knocks on the door of the adjoining office, then turns to face me, his eyes pleading. "Perhaps you can help him make an espresso before he has some kind of withdrawal-related seizure?"

"I'm sure I can," I reply, eager to appear capable. "Uncooperative coffee machines are a specialty of mine."

He pushes open the door, revealing his brother, who has his back turned to us and is wearing a charcoal-colored suit that I can tell cost more than my annual rent. He doesn't seem to notice we're there, mainly because he's too busy abusing a poor, innocent coffee machine. He slams his fist down on top of the expensive-looking device. "Useless piece of shit," he grumbles.

"Drake!"

The word doesn't even have time to register in my mind before he spins around. His eyes land first on Nathan, and then on me. My heart surges up into my throat, and the shock takes my breath away. My knees start to buckle, and I hold onto the door handle to stop myself from crumpling into a heap. How can this be? What have I done in a past life that was bad enough to earn me this kind of karma? And who do I need to pray to make this go away? I blink slowly, harboring a childish hope that I might have imagined it. That when I open my eyes again, I'll realize it was all an optical illusion or a stress-related hallucination.

No such luck. He's still there, standing before me. He's still Drake James, my new employer. Still the other half of James and James, the man I thought was based in Chicago.

More alarmingly, he is still the gorgeous sex god who made me scream using only his tongue. Still the man with the biggest dick I have ever seen. Still the one-night stand I spent the most insanely passionate time of my life with. My boss.

I close my eyes again and try to convince myself this is my mind playing tricks on me. This isn't some cheesy Hallmark movie where I play Cinderella and fall for the billionaire. This is my life, and I desperately need this job, not only for myself but for my mom.

"Miss Ryder?" Nathan's concerned voice penetrates my thoughts, dragging me back to the here and now.

I snap to and nod. I need to appear competent, even if I don't feel it. Nathan looks slightly worried, but there's no hint of recognition on his brother's face. No shock, no surprise, no horror. Has he forgotten me already? Was I really that unmemorable? Was he possibly that drunk? Or maybe these things happen to him so often that it meant nothing at all. I don't suppose the reason matters—if he's playing things this way, then I need to go along with it.

"It's a pleasure to meet you, Mr. James. I'm Amelia. Amelia Ryder." I force out the words because it seems like the ground isn't actually going to do me a solid and swallow me whole. Is this really happening? Am I going to lose a job before I've even started it?

"You too, Miss Ryder," Drake replies coolly.

"Perhaps she can work your coffee machine." Nathan claps his brother on his back. He either hasn't picked up on the tension or he's choosing to ignore it.

"Stupid thing is broken," Drake snaps, his mood much sourer than the last time I saw him. Which is unsurprising, as the last time I saw him involved nudity and orgasms. The memory unfurls in my mind's eye, and an unwelcome warmth spreads through my core.

Dammit, Amelia. Imagining the boss making you come is so unprofessional.

"I could take a look?" I offer cautiously, still entirely unsure how to navigate the incredible awkwardness of this entire situation. Coffee seems as good a place to start as any.

Frowning, Drake glances between his brother and me as though he's trying to decide what to say next.

He's saved from the moment by the arrival of Satan's handmaiden, or Linda from HR as some people know her. "The briefing is about to start," she announces as she walks toward us. Her nose is wrinkled like she smells something off, and she glares at me. Does she know I've already screwed the boss, or is this her default setting?

"There's no need for either Drake or I to attend, Linda. We're well aware of our HR policies," Nathan says dryly. Huh. I wonder if this situation right here is covered in those policies.

Linda purses her lips and looks me up and down, assessing me and finding me not quite up to par. "Actually, I was thinking our newest employee should attend. These policies are important, Mr. James."

Nathan runs a hand though his hair and laughs. "They are, I agree, but on her first day? We don't want to scare her off now, do we?"

I feel like I've walked into the twilight zone and have no idea what to say or how to behave. All my instincts are telling me to run, but I can't.

After a few tense moments, it's Drake who answers. "That sounds like a great idea, Linda."

I glance briefly in his direction, and he avoids my gaze. So he does remember me. Well enough to want to get rid of me, at least. Of course he does. He might have spent more time with his head between my thighs in twelve hours than my ex-husband did in twelve years, but I'm fairly sure he looked at my face as well, at least when we were getting to know each other before all the naked time started.

"You can follow me," Linda says. "And make sure you pay attention." I can't help pulling a little face at her back as she strides away. She reminds me of Miss Trunchbull from *Matilda*. I do as she says, though, because Drake isn't the only one who needs some respite. I feel like I haven't drawn a proper breath in the last five minutes, and getting away from him will give me time to pull myself together.

I leave my purse on my office chair as I pass, because it makes me feel like I've claimed it. Like Drake will walk out of his office and see it there and have second thoughts about firing me on my first day. It's only a purse and it's only a chair, but it's all I have to cling to right now.

~

After listening to the snoozefest that was the James and James HR policies briefing, I head back to my desk, wondering how long it will actually be my desk. I did pay particular attention to the policy regarding office relationships, and while they are not encouraged, they're not explicitly banned. However, the employees must disclose any relationship to HR in case it impacts the firm or its reputation in any way.

I suspect that having to reveal intimate details about your private life to Linda would be enough to nip any office romance in the bud. Hopefully, the policy doesn't count if it's retrospective, because I really don't want to have to write a memo about how many times Drake James made me come on our one night together.

There's a bright yellow Post-it Note on my desk, sitting right beside my welcome basket. I bite my lip when I see it, afraid it's a particularly slapdash way of giving me the boot. He wouldn't, would he? I mean, he was cold the next morning, sure, but nothing implied he was the kind of bastard who would destroy someone's career for accidentally sleeping with him. But what do I know? He is a stranger, after all. And that stranger now has an awful lot of power over my life.

He could fire me. He could refuse to give me a reference. He could make my professional world hell. Whatever is written on that Post-it Note might set the tone.

I'm flooded with relief when I actually pick it up and read it. No mention of me facing a firing squad—just a scrawled message giving me the password to his online calendar and a request for me to start organizing his schedule. I sink down onto my chair and fan myself with the flimsy paper. There will undoubtedly be tricky situations to work through, but this is a start.

I glance at the closed door behind me, wondering if he's in

there. Maybe he's brooding at his desk like some sort of angry demigod, wondering how he managed to screw his new secretary. Maybe he's wondering how long he needs to keep me around until it's acceptable to say it hasn't worked out. Or maybe I'm giving myself way too much credit. Hell, maybe he screws all of his assistants and I'm nothing special. It's possible that every woman he comes into contact with simply drops her panties at his feet and begs for his magic touch. That could be why Linda looks like she's permanently sucking a lemon and why he wasn't at all affected by me walking into his office.

Seeing him, realizing who he was, was one of the most jaw-droppingly awful moments of a life that has included quite a few awful moments. I wanted to faint, throw up, and run away —not necessarily in that order. It was a miracle I didn't crawl beneath my desk and start singing nursery rhymes.

He, however, barely reacted. He looked cool as a cucumber sandwich on a bed of iceberg lettuce. Only his coffee machine seemed to dredge up any kind of emotion from him. I'm definitely overreacting if the man is more emotional about a coffee machine than he is about me.

My stomach growls, reminding me that I'm starving. I was too nervous to eat breakfast this morning, even before discovering that Scarlet's guilty secrets had come back to haunt her. The HR briefing lasted three-and-a-half hours, and now my body is begging to be fed. I'm sure I'm allowed a lunch hour, but this has been a crazy day so far, and I don't want to make any assumptions. I better check and be ready to accept the possibility that I will be eating nothing but the contents of a fruit basket all afternoon.

I take a deep breath and stand outside his door, my hand poised to knock. What if he's in a meeting? What if he's on the phone? What if he has a woman in there with him? I blow out a breath, disgusted at my own nerves. If I'm going to keep this position, which it seems I am, for the time being at least, then I'm going to have to interact with him. I should know if he has a meeting or if he's on the phone. Hell, I should even know if he has a woman in there, and if he does, I guess I should also find out when her birthday is and whether she likes diamonds or pearls.

I shake my head, annoyed at my uncharacteristic pettiness. That's not a part of my job, and neither Drake nor Nathan strike me as the kind of men who'd ask such a thing of their secretaries. They're too professional. And I can be professional too. I *am* professional. What happened between Drake and me was a mistake. Had we known, I'm sure we both would have behaved very differently. That was the past, and I need to focus on the future. Would Kimmy be standing here trembling? Would Emily? No, they damn well wouldn't.

Pep talk administered, I roll my shoulders back and knock on his door. A second later, he calls out for me to come in, his voice still as deep and dark as rich melted chocolate. It's all good and well telling myself it was a mistake, that it was in the past, but why does he have to sound like that? Why does he have to look so good? It doesn't seem fair.

Gingerly, I push open his door and step inside. He sits behind his desk against the backdrop of the Manhattan skyline. I was too stunned to take in the sight earlier, but it is truly breathtaking. The floor-to-ceiling windows reveal a spectacular view, but even that doesn't stop my eyes from drifting to Drake. His tie is pulled loose and his hair isn't quite as neat as it was a few hours ago, as if he's been running his hands through it. I remember how thick and soft that hair is, what it felt like to run *my* hands through it ... Dammit. This is not good.

"Did you need something?" His clipped tone snaps me out of my torrid thoughts.

I tip my jaw up, determined not to look as bothered as I feel.

This is a normal business relationship, after all. "I just wondered if I had time to get some lunch before I started work on your calendar?"

He glances at his watch before returning his attention to his computer screen. "Of course."

And I guess I'm dismissed. Awkward. He doesn't look up again, and I turn around to head out.

"Actually, Miss Ryder, may I have a word?"

My heart sinks. This is it. He's going to fire me. I'm going to get the whole *it's not your fault, but you can't work for me after I made you scream my name in rapture* speech. There will be some offer of an extended notice period and the assurance that I'll be recommended and other nice words—but I'm on the chopping block. I feel it in my bones. Why oh why oh why did I have to meet this guy at a wedding? And of all the weddings in all the cities in all the world, he had to walk into Emily's?

I swallow and turn back around. He's standing behind his desk now and looking damn near edible. Could that suit be any more fitted to his body? The fact that I know exactly what he looks like out of it makes him even more sexy in it, and the serious cast to his face makes him even more handsome. This really isn't fair. I even find the man attractive when he's about to crap all over my life.

"Of course, Mr. James," I say as calmly as I'm able to, hoping he can't tell that my heart is racing like a runaway stallion.

He clears his throat. "Please take a seat."

I do as he asks, and he sits back down behind his desk and loosens his tie a bit more. Is he feeling as uncomfortable as I am? The skin on my back is sticky with perspiration, and I've chewed the inside of my lip so much that I taste blood.

He clears his throat once more. "I just wanted to get this out in the open and clear the air. If I'd had any idea you were starting work here, I never would have ..." He clears his throat yet again, and his strangled cough is matched by his pained expression. He really is feeling as uncomfortable about this as I am. This is like pulling teeth, and it will be better for both of us once it's done.

"I feel exactly the same, Mr. James, I assure you. If I'd known you were going to be my boss ..." I don't finish the thought. Neither of us need any further reminder of what we *wouldn't have done*. It's too late. We've already done it.

His dark eyes rake over my face the same way they did two nights ago, and I can't help wondering if I see something more than regret in them. That's probably wishful thinking on my part. It's possible that I am so desperate for him to have some fond memories of our night together that I'm imagining it. "I don't date my employees, Amelia. Ever."

Of course he doesn't. He's a billionaire and a founding partner of one of the most prestigious law firms in the country. He certainly wouldn't date his secretary. That makes sense. That's good. So what's with the wave of disappointment that washes over me?

"And I certainly don't ..." He coughs again before his eyes lock on mine, reminding me of the eye contact he made the other night when he was ...

I press my hand to my forehead as heat blooms beneath my skin. No. Don't go there, Amelia. "You don't what, Mr. James?"

He swipes his tongue over his lower lip. "Fuck them senseless, Miss Ryder."

Wow. What an arrogant douchebag. And I don't care if it is true—it isn't right to use it against me.

"I think you'll find I'm still in full control of all my senses, Mr. James," I reply, amazing myself at the calm and steady cadence of my voice, given that my legs are trembling. "This might come as a shock to you, but I'm not in the habit of dating my boss either, so you have absolutely nothing to worry about. I won't be harassing you for a repeat performance, and I guarantee I have no feelings toward you other than professional. I want this job, Mr. James. I need this job. I will also be good at this job, and I feel just as upset as you do about this awful ... coincidence. I'd suggest the best thing to do would be to stick to being Miss Ryder and Mr. James. Let's leave Charlie and Scarlet where they belong—in the past. Would that suit you, *sir*?" I add the last word purely for sarcasm, but the look that flashes across his face makes me immediately wish that I hadn't.

His expression is too complicated for me to read. He's pissed off and amused all at the same time, and none of this makes any sense. This is too much. I need to get out of here and away from his square jaw and intense brown gaze. Away from the sight of his hands on his desk, and the way my body still remembers what he can do with those long fingers. I need to lock myself in the restroom and calm the fuck down. "Is there anything else?"

His brow furrows with a frown. "No, that will be all, Miss Ryder."

Ugh. I suggested he call me that, but the way he says it is so cold. I pull back my shoulders and take a deep, restorative breath. I guess I should count myself lucky that I still have a job. I can cope with a little chill in the air. "Thank you, Mr. James," I say stiffly before I leave his office, my knees threatening to give way with each step. Just keep going, I tell myself. Don't look back, and don't let him see your weakness.

When I sink into my chair a few seconds later, my heart is hammering so hard in my chest, I'm worried it's going to beat its way right out of there and take off. I have no idea what Linda's HR policies would say about that, but I'm fairly sure she wouldn't be happy with a heart floating through the office. That would definitely be a health and safety risk.

It's okay, I tell myself. I did all right. Drake didn't find an excuse to fire me, and I didn't give him a reason to. We can work together and be professional despite what happened between us. I'm sure of it. That was Scarlet, and I am Amelia Ryder. Sensible and dependable, the same person I've always been. The same person I will always be. My heart has survived far worse than this.

CHAPTER
NINE

DRAKE

Nathan is shrugging on his jacket by the time I walk into his office. There was a time when he would have worked until at least seven, but now that he has Mel and Luke to rush home to, he's eager to leave after a mere ten-hour day. I can't blame him for that, even though I'm likely to be working until midnight. I want him to have that freedom. It's one of the reasons I agreed to come back from Chicago.

Glad I caught him, I hold up the bottle of Scotch. "You have time for a quick drink?"

His eyes scan the label, and he smirks. "You brought the good stuff, huh? You either had a great day or a really shitty one."

With a sigh, I take a seat on the sofa in the corner of his office while he grabs a couple of glasses. He hangs his jacket back up, and I appreciate the gesture. It means he has time for me, and that will never not matter.

"So which is it?" he asks, sitting opposite me and placing a pair of empty crystal tumblers on the table. I pour us each a generous measure while Nathan eyes me suspiciously. He doesn't push me any further, although I've obviously got something on my mind. Something that merits the good stuff. He knows me well enough to understand that I'll get there when I'm good and ready. He holds up his glass. "To new beginnings. May the best day of your past be the worst day of your future."

"Is that Irish?" I down the entire contents of my glass in one. "It sounds Irish. You been spending too much time with the Ryans?"

The Ryans are clients of James and James's New York office, and they keep us busy. Never a dull moment, in fact, between their business activities and their not-so-legitimate activities.

"Perhaps. So. What the hell is going on with you? Is it really so bad being back here?"

I realize too late that he must be worried about me wanting to leave. I've been in Chicago for a long time, and the decision to move home wasn't made lightly.

"No. It's going to take some time to adjust, and that coffee machine is a total bitch, but no—I don't have regrets, I promise you. I'm glad to be here with you guys again."

"Good. That's a fucking relief, in fact, because I'm glad to have you back. I've missed you. So, other than the coffee machine, what's the issue?"

I look him in the eye. Time to rip off the Band-Aid. "I fucked Amelia."

He blinks at me in surprise. "Already? Jesus fucking Christ, Drake. She's only been here a matter of hours."

"Not today, numbnuts."

He blows out a breath. "At least that's something. So when?"

"Saturday. And technically Sunday. She was the maid of honor from that wedding."

He shakes his head in confusion. "The one you spent the

night with? You said her name was Scarlet. What am I missing here?"

I drop my head back and rest it on the cushion. "It's a long story."

"Jesus fucking Christ," he mutters.

"You already said that."

He snorts. "Yeah, well, it's a classic for a reason. What were you thinking?"

"I wasn't thinking anything. I didn't plan this. I had no way of knowing that she'd waltz in here a couple days later and be all, 'surprise, I'm your new assistant!' It's a coincidence. A really shitty one. There are, what, eight million people in this fucking city, half of them female? And I end up screwing her. I swear, I couldn't make this shit up. It'd be funny if it was happening to somebody else. What the fuck am I gonna do?"

He pours more Scotch and frowns as he thinks it through. "It's not ideal, but we'll have to think of some way to fix this. I can't see how she can stay as your secretary after this. I thought she seemed a bit off earlier. Of course, it would be much fucking cleaner and simpler if we could just let her go."

"Let her go? Why? She did nothing wrong." In fact, the memory of how she did everything so damn right is eating away at my insides. When she walked into my office today, I almost had a seizure. Only my years of experience in the courtroom allowed me to keep a straight face while my brain imploded. And if it wasn't bad enough that it was her, she had to be wearing one of those wrap dresses. The kind that falls open with the correct pull on the correct string. The kind of dress that seems like it was made specifically to get my blood pumping. One little tug, and she would have been unwrapped. Knowing exactly what lies underneath it didn't help. Even her hair was in on the act, all neatly pinned up and begging to be liberated. I can't shake the image of how all those dark tresses looked spread over my pillow ...

"You can't fuck your secretary, Drake. It's a damn PR nightmare. Plus, it's just fucking wrong."

I grunt in frustration—at him, at myself, at the whole screwed-up situation. "I know that, jerkwad. I know it's wrong. I know it's exploitative, but is firing her any better?"

"Maybe not if we guarantee her another job. We can pull some strings and I'll write her a glowing reference."

I slam my fist down on the table, and he raises his eyebrows at me. I'm mad, and I don't get mad. Her mom is sick, and she was excited and nervous about starting her new job. She needs the pay and the benefits. I know way too much about her to be calm. The image of how disappointed she looked when I basically fucked her and kicked her out of my room is still seared into my mind, and I couldn't live with myself if I screwed her over like this. Just because she had the poor judgment to go for an asshole like me doesn't mean she should suffer for it.

"No. It's not right, Nathan. She needs this job, and besides, I'm not fucking her now. I *fucked* her. Emphasis on the past tense. She wasn't even an employee then. It's a mess, but I'm not gonna be the kind of asshole who fires her because we ..." I swallow the knot in my throat. Because we fucked like animals, yet it was the most intense connection I've felt with a woman in as long as I can remember?

"Okay. Playing devil's advocate here, bro, but what if she talks? Tells the whole goddamn firm about the two of you?"

I throw my hands into the air. "About what? We didn't do anything wrong. We were two *very* consenting adults who had a great time together, and now she just happens to be my secretary." I drop my head into my hands as reality hits home. "Shit, I'm so fucked."

Nathan hums softly before he speaks. "Yeah. That's a good

way of putting it. And from a legal standpoint, firing her opens us up to a lot more scrutiny. Accusations of wrongful termination."

I look up, incredulous. "That's because it would be wrongful termination."

His eyes narrow the way they do when he's trying to solve a problem. "We could swap her out with someone else. One of the junior partners. Tim Sullivan needs someone."

Fuck no. For some reason, the thought of her working for anyone else pisses me off, especially Tim fucking Sullivan. The man's a horndog. I'm not going to admit that to Nathan, though, because I don't really understand it myself. "That won't work," I say. "The position she applied for was secretary to a senior partner. It has a higher salary band. Moving her potentially causes the same issues as firing her, which we are absolutely *not* going to do."

I wait for his response, keenly aware of the fact that I'm back in our New York office to make his life easier, yet it's only day one and I'm already causing him headaches. Way to go, Drake.

"You two are done though, yeah?"

I nod, unable to bring myself to say it aloud. The reality of the situation is that we have to be done. I'm not the kind of guy who nails his secretary. I don't even like to associate with the other partners outside of business hours. I don't exploit people, and that's the end of it.

Nathan downs his Scotch and licks his lips. Then he brushes a nonexistent crease from his suit pants and stands. "Have you spoken to her about it?"

"Yeah," I reply, looking up at the ceiling. "I was a bit of a jackass, but she basically agrees that it's over, all in the past. One hundred percent finito."

"You sure about that, buddy? Because the way you talked

about her … It seemed like it was more than a one-night stand, honestly."

"No. It wasn't. You know me, Nathan. I don't do relationships. They're too damn messy. Look what happened after one night. This won't be going any further, and I promise we'll work through it. I just needed you to know."

I also needed to talk to someone about it, and Nathan is my go-to guy. He doesn't know everything about me—we all have our secrets—but our relationship has always been solid. This little incident obviously hasn't helped the way I often feel like I'm in his shadow, no matter how hard I work. Here I am, back in New York and busting my ass for our firm, and I still somehow manage to feel like a fuck-up.

"All right," he says, grabbing his jacket. "If you two think you can handle it, then do whatever you think is best."

I stare up at him, suspicious. "Well, that's a complete one-eighty. What happened to moving her?"

He glances at his watch. "You're right. It's the wrong way to go, both morally and legally. Look, you don't need me to tell you what to do, Drake. You don't need me to hold your hand. This is your firm as much as it is mine, and I know you wouldn't do anything to put it at risk."

That's true, but it's good to hear that he trusts me. Seeing Amelia again today dredged up a whole load of confusing emotions, but he's right. I wouldn't do anything to jeopardize what Nathan and I have built together. Work is everything to me; this firm is everything to me. I've had a much longer relationship with my work than I have with any woman, and that's always been fine by me. I don't see anything or anyone changing that, not even the woman who has occupied my thoughts since I first met her. That stops now. Amelia Ryder is my secretary and nothing more.

CHAPTER

TEN

AMELIA

"So, how was it?" Mom yells as soon as she hears me close her front door. I hang up my coat and plaster on a happy face. She doesn't need to know all the complications. She only needs to know that it was great.

It's not exactly a lie—some of it was great. Some of it was a roller coaster of anxiety and sexual tension, but that definitely falls into the don't-tell-Mom category. I can just imagine. *Oh yeah, it was fine—apart from the fact that my new boss is the guy I banged at Emily's wedding, and he makes me weak at the knees every time he looks at me.* Nope. I'm gonna stick with the sanitized version of events.

Our house is tiny, tucked away in a working-class neighborhood in Brooklyn. Mom always worked hard, sometimes holding down three jobs to make ends meet. Despite that, I never felt like I went without anything. There was always food on the table, clothes on my back, and a whole lot of love. We never had a lot of money, but I didn't feel deprived. My friends all loved coming to my house, and not once did I wish for a different childhood. When I was younger, I would have liked to have known my father, but she never talked about him, and I had to accept that. The only time she ever got upset with me was when I pushed to know more, and these days I'm at peace with it. She's loved me hard enough for two.

When I got my full ride to Harvard, I was full of dreams. I was going to work in finance or start my own business or find some way to make it to the top. And when I did, I vowed, I'd move her out of this tiny two-bedroom and into someplace grand.

"Don't be silly!" she always said, laughing. "I'm perfectly happy here. This is the home where I raised you. It's always been full of laughter and love, and I have great neighbors. Why would I want to leave?"

In the end, it was Chad who started his own business and me who supported him during those tough early days. When he was doing prestigious internships, I worked as an office temp to pay the bills. It all felt worth it once he began to succeed, but I discovered during the divorce that he wasn't quite as high-flying as he led people to believe. His investment company was in debt, and the house we bought together in Philadelphia was mortgaged to the hilt. I ended up leaving the marriage with very little, and I didn't even mind that. It felt like a fresh start, and I was relieved to have no tangible reminders of our years together.

Now I have my shiny new job at James and James, and things are looking up. I need to focus on that rather than the complications with my boss.

I head into the space that doubles as a living room and dining room and find her curled up on the couch. She's tiny, my mom, five-foot-nothing as opposed to my five-six. I get my dark hair and hazel eyes from her, though, although her locks are striped with silver these days.

I lean down and kiss her on the cheek. "It was great, Mom.

Really great. I've got such a good feeling about it. I stopped by Wanda's, picked us some cannoli to celebrate."

"Pistachio?" she says hopefully.

"Of course. Do you even know me?" I tease. "You want it now?"

"Maybe a little later, babe," she replies, and I can tell she's trying to hide how sick she feels. Her breathing problems are steadily getting worse, and she needs to use more medication every month. There's a little table next to the couch that's now full of pills and inhalers and the mask she uses to boost her oxygen levels. It all leaves her low on energy, which she tries desperately to keep from me.

"Are you feeling okay, Mom?" I ask, sitting next to her and taking her hand in mine. "You know you don't need to pretend for my sake, right?"

"I'm fine, Amelia—I'm more interested in your day. Did you figure out all the important stuff, like where the break room is and the nearest place that does great coffee? Were the people nice? Were there any snot-buckets?"

I laugh at the silly word. For as long as I can remember, she's used it to describe snobs, starting with some of the people she used to clean house for, then on to some of my Harvard acquaintances. The James brothers are clearly super rich, but does that make them snot-buckets? No, I don't think so. That particular title is reserved for the kind of stick-up-the-ass types who look down on others because they're less wealthy or have lower social standing, and I don't get the impression that either Nathan or Drake buys into that.

"There are probably a few lurking around somewhere," I say. "It's a big building, and it is a law firm, so it'd be strange if it was entirely snot-bucket free. But so far, so good."

"And your boss?" she asks, her eyes sparkling. "I looked him up on my phone, you know. Nathan James. Phew, he's a hottie." She makes a little fanning gesture with her hands, and I laugh.

"Actually, it turns out I'm working for his brother, the other Mr. James. His name is Drake if you want to look him up too."

"Oh, I will—is he just as good-looking?"

I pretend to think about it, then pull a face. "He's okay, I suppose. Not as classically handsome maybe. A bit bigger? Not my type at all, but I'm sure some women find him attractive."

I must be doing a good job of lying, because she seems to buy it hook, line, and sinker. Her fingers fly over her phone, and she makes a funny *oooh* noise and holds up the screen. Drake is right there in front of me at what looks like an actual film premiere. He's on the red carpet with a stunning blond, his dark eyes glaring at the photographer. Damn, he is sex on a stick.

"Personally, I think he's even better looking," Mom says. "He has that suave-on-the-surface-but-savage-just-beneath thing going on, you know?"

"No, I don't know. But I think you missed your calling. You should have been a romance writer."

She waggles her eyebrows at me. "It's never too late. Maybe I'll publish one. I'll use a really cool pen name like Francesca de la Croix or something."

I shake my head and laugh as she prattles on. I'm in no position to comment, having recently spent a whole night pretending to be called Scarlet.

I make my way into the kitchen, where I plate up our cannoli. She rarely has much of an appetite, and I love trying to tempt her with her favorites. I peek through the pass-through and see that she's still staring at her phone. Possibly conjuring up smutty scenes of passion that involve my boss. Hah. If she only knew.

Leaning back against the counter, I sigh. Okay. So today was a shocker of a debut at James and James. I don't think I've ever felt so many emotions in such a short time span, but here I am. Still gainfully employed and ready to fight another day. Now all I need to do is figure out how to work with Drake without remembering how his tongue felt on my most intimate parts or how his strong hands tangled up in my hair when he kissed me. Because those things are *so* easy to forget.

Nope, it's not going to be easy, and maybe if this was only about me, I'd go back to the temp agency. But it's not only about me—it's about that wonderful woman in there. The woman who raised me and loved me and nurtured me, and she deserves so much better than the shitty hand nature dealt her. I would do anything for my mom, and that includes working with Drake James.

"Honey," she says, her eyes still glued to her screen. "Could you bring me that cannoli? Something about your new boss makes me really like the idea of a sweet tube full of pistachio cream ..."

ELEVEN

AMELIA

The next day at work is a lot less intense, mainly because Drake—Mr. James, I remind myself—is in meetings all morning. He was double-booked for one and triple-booked for another, and one of my first tasks as his assistant was untangling his schedule. He's fresh from Chicago and seems to be in demand, with constant requests coming in from new and existing clients. I can tell I'm going to have my work cut out for me managing his schedule, but I enjoy a challenge.

Kimmy wasn't lying. I do love organizing things—anything from a spice rack to a busy managing partner—and more to the point, I'm good at it. It feels nice to be working somewhere that skill is valued.

I've been fielding calls for him all morning, and it will take me a while to catch up on who's who. I will eventually understand exactly which calls need to be put through immediately and which can wait. I'll know how he likes his coffee and what he enjoys for lunch and the numbers of his favorite restaurants. I'll know everything about him, because that's how a good secretary makes her boss's life run smoothly.

Of course, I already know a few extra things that a secretary typically wouldn't know about her boss. Like how big his cock is and the way his hands feel on my ass and how his tongue tastes against mine. None of that will help me with work, though, so I need to bury that knowledge so deep inside me that even Indiana Jones couldn't dig it up.

I make my way down to the break room, which is located in the basement of the building. There's a much fancier version on my level, where clients can wait for meetings and senior partners and their staff can access barista-quality coffee and artisan baked goods. It's swanky and beautifully decorated and makes me feel like I'm going to stain or break something.

Down here, the staff room is a little more real, and I feel a lot more comfortable spending my breaks with the guys from the mail room and the ladies who do payroll than I do the managing partners. For a start, it's a Drake James–free zone, which means it's a refuge from the man. I'm guessing I'll need that at some point.

I pour myself a coffee and decide to grab a snack. I've yet to master the art of eating at regular times, and my sugar levels will plummet sometime in the next hour. I join the small group of people milling around by the bakery bar and grin when I see one poppy-seed bagel left in the basket. My favorite. I reach out to take it at exactly the same time as the man standing next to me, and our hands bump.

We both pull back and do that awkward dance strangers do when they're trying to cover up being embarrassed. "Please," he says, gesturing at the bagel, "be my guest. I hate poppy seeds anyway."

"Really?" I ask, looking up at him. He's tall and lean, with a mop of sandy hair and sparkling blue eyes. "Why were you reaching for it then?"

"So I could throw it in the trash. Eliminate its evil from the world. Protect the universe from contamination. Usual stuff."

"You're carrying out a one-man war against poppy-seed bagels?"

"I am," he says, puffing up his chest like an action hero. "It's a tough job, but someone's gotta do it. I'm Jacob, by the way. I work in accounting. I always hate adding that bit, because now I know whenever you think of me, I'll be 'Jacob from accounting' in your head."

"What makes you think I'll be thinking of you at all?"

"Foolish hope? And please—do have the bagel."

I laugh and acquiesce. It's only a bagel. I add it to my plate along with a small tub of cream cheese, and he joins me at a table.

"Are you new here?" he asks, sipping his coffee and looking on as I spread the cream cheese.

"I am." I slice the bagel in half and offer it to him, and he accepts it with a warm smile. "I only started yesterday. I'm Mr. James's secretary."

"Oooh, fancy. So why are you down here with the plebs when you could be hobnobbing upstairs?"

I shrug. "I don't know. I guess I prefer the plebs."

Grinning, he holds his hand up for a high five. "Power to the people!"

I slap his hand and laugh.

"Which Mr. James do you work for? Not that I've met either of them, being a humble accounting clerk, but you do hear stuff. Like how much Nathan has mellowed since he got married and had a kid."

Ah, I think, chewing a delicious bite of my bagel. That explains a lot—like why he had the reputation for being an asshole but in reality seems like a tough but nice man. "I work for the other Mr. James. Drake."

"Right. Well, nobody really knows him very well yet, though the ladies all seem to agree he's a catch. If you like that kind of thing."

"What kind of thing?"

He leans closer and grins at me, looking like a naughty kid about to get caught doing something he shouldn't. "Oh, you know ... Tall, dark, handsome, and loaded. Disgusting, right?"

"Absolutely. But speaking of my boss, I really should get back to it. He's been in meetings all morning, and I probably have a pile of work waiting for me. It was nice meeting you, Jacob. Good luck in the Bagel Wars."

He gives me a military-style salute, and I'm still smiling as I ride the elevator back up to my floor. Hey, maybe I've made a friend, or at the very least someone to chat with over snacks.

I have a spring in my step as I stroll along the corridor toward our office. Everything feels brighter, a little more hopeful. A few people nod at me, and nobody seems quite as intimidating as they did yesterday.

I swapped out my black wrap dress for a sleek skirt that hugs my figure a little more closely and spent an age trying to see my own ass in the mirror this morning, concerned that it looked enormous. I've paired it with a cream silk pussybow blouse, and together they make me feel less dowdy and more like I belong here. Nobody needs to know that I got both from a really cool thrift store in Queens, and it's not like anyone can tell by looking. Maybe after I get my first paycheck, I can treat myself to something new.

"Miss Ryder." The deep voice from behind me interrupts my pleasant thoughts and brings me to a halt. The way he says my name reminds me of our night together and how he commanded me to walk toward him. I suck in a deep breath and transform my face into neutral as I turn to greet him.

"Mr. James. How did your morning go?"

"A lot better than it would have gone if I'd tried to be in three places at once, so thanks for untangling that mess. Do you have a few minutes?"

"Of course. Let me grab my notepad."

"You won't need it," he replies firmly, falling into step beside me and leading me to his office. "It's not that kind of meeting."

I nod and swallow down my nerves. I hate this crazy uncertainty, hate living in fear. Has he reconsidered? Is this all too messy? Is he going to fire me after all? Is that a different cologne, one that smells even better? Jeez, Amelia. Keep it together.

He opens the door and gestures for me to go in first. I'm aware that my skirt is form-fitting and wonder if his eyes are on my ass. Maybe I need to start coming to work in a caftan.

"Please, sit. I've finally figured out the damn coffee machine. Would you like one?"

Is he trying to butter me up before he gives me the bad news? "No, thank you. But I'm glad you've solved the mystery. Your brother implied that you'd be hell to work with if you didn't get your caffeine fix."

He snorts with laughter as the machine hisses into life. "He's not wrong. But I've had plenty of coffee already this morning, so don't worry, I'm not going to bite your head off."

He did a little biting on the night of the wedding. Nothing too rough—gentle nips and nuzzles. Enough for me to know I liked the feel of his teeth on my skin. I cross my legs and squeeze them together, trying to quell the sudden throbbing between my thighs. He sits down behind his desk, and as our eyes meet, I have the terrible feeling that he can read my mind and my body.

He sighs and runs his hands through his hair, leaving it in thick furrows. "Look, Miss Ryder, I just wanted to check in. Yesterday was a shock ... for both of us. If this all feels like too much, I completely understand."

"Are you going to fire me?" I blurt out, barely waiting for him to finish speaking. It's difficult enough being so attracted to him, but I can learn to deal with that; however, this constant yo-yo of emotions about my job security? That I can't deal with. Seeing him every day and wondering what his mood is, whether my position is safe, feeling like my future is at his mercy. It's too much.

"What?" he says, looking confused. "No! No, we're not going to fire you. You—we—did nothing wrong. I spoke to my brother about it—"

"You did *what*?"

"I told Nathan. I had to. This goes beyond you and me. It involves the firm. I needed him to know and to get his opinion."

"Right. And did you tell Linda from HR as well?"

"Christ, no. I'd rather pour acid on my dick than talk to her about my sex life."

I burst out laughing at the intensity in his voice, and it breaks the tension between us. "Yeah, I know what you mean. And of course you told Nathan. He's your brother and your colleague. I just ... I suppose I'm embarrassed. It doesn't feel great, knowing the bosses are discussing my sex life."

He places his coffee cup on his desk, his throat working as he swallows. "I assure you that we didn't discuss any of the intimate details."

Heat races up my chest and neck as I recall those details ... vividly. "I just don't want anyone thinking I'm some kind of"—I lower my voice to a whisper—"slut."

He shakes his head. "For a start, that's a terrible word for someone who is simply pursuing her sexual desires, and secondly, neither Nathan nor I would ever think of a woman that way. What happened between you and me doesn't make either of us see you like that. Nathan does not think any less highly of you than he did when he hired you. I assure you."

"What about you, though? Does he think less highly of you now?" I say, risking a joke. His eyes flash, and for a second I think I've gone too far.

He shrugs and says, "Well, he already knows I'm a slut. Always have been, always will be. But that's none of your business, in exactly the same way that what you do in your private life is none of mine. Can we at least agree on that?"

I nod firmly. "Yes. Definitely," I say, but I suspect I'm lying. Truthfully, I hate the thought of him being a slut with anybody but me, but that is so many layers of crazy that all I can do with it is pack it away and ignore it.

"Good. I want this to work. From what I've seen so far, you're good at this job, and I definitely need the help. I don't want you to worry about being fired, because that's not going to happen. I'm not quite at that level of asshole, whatever you might think of me."

I meet his eyes, and my core clenches hard at what I see there. So intense. So brooding. So ... hungry?

"I don't think you're an asshole, Mr. James. Like you said, it was a shock. It feels weird that you know so much about me—not just the, um, the bedroom stuff—but about my life. I told you things I probably wouldn't have told my boss, and I guess that makes me feel vulnerable."

He nods. "I understand. That goes both ways. I opened up to you too. We were both operating on the basis that we'd never see each other again. That didn't work out so well."

"It didn't. Fate was against us."

"Fate," he says, leaning back in his chair, his expression distant, "can be an absolute bitch. Now, could I ask you to call

Graham Swanson? I need to rearrange tomorrow's meeting with him."

I nod, eager to get the conversation back on a professional footing. I feel much more comfortable there, and maybe I'll stop imagining him bending me over his desk and telling me what a good girl I am.

CHAPTER
TWELVE

DRAKE

I meet Elijah for drinks at his favorite spot, an old-fashioned pub in the East Village. At least he claims it's his favorite spot, but as I look around at the rough-and-ready clientele and actual sawdust on the floor, I wonder if he's screwing with me. He knows I like the top-shelf life, and this may well be his way of jerking me around. Elijah is the oldest of us James brothers, so he's got the most experience yanking our chains.

He turns up twenty minutes late and waves at me from the bar as he grabs drinks. When he joins me, he's carrying two pints of Guinness and two surprisingly good-smelling glasses of whiskey. I pick up the chipped lowball and inhale.

"Nice, right?" He looks delighted with himself. "I know it looks like shit in here, but the Irish know their booze. That's top-quality Bushmills right there. Slainte!"

He raises his glass in a toast and downs it in one. "You okay, brother?" I ask, feeling a whisper of concern.

"Sure I am. Just been a heck of a day. Started with a giant fight with Amber over some bullshit charity dinner she wants me to host."

"What's the cause?"

He rolls his eyes and starts on the Guinness. I've never been a huge fan of the black stuff, but I'm told it's an acquired taste. It leaves a little cream mustache on Elijah's upper lip, which I'm definitely not going to tell him about.

"Retired clowns."

"What now?" I say, feeling a rumble of laughter build in my stomach.

"Retired clowns. No, to be fair, retired 'circus folk.' Apparently it's a thing. Turns out the carnies aren't so good at stocking their pension funds, and there's a residential home for them just outside Buffalo. I'm not kidding, bro—this is what my life has become."

I can't keep the laughter in anymore, and it bursts out of me in loud guffaws. I laugh so damn much I have tears in my eyes and a stitch in my side. Elijah merely nods and lets me get on with it. "Yeah, laugh it up pal," he says eventually. "But know this—Amber is talking about organizing a date auction to raise funds for the poor clowns, and you're on her list as lot number one."

"I don't mind. Anything to help Bozo." I clear my throat and wipe my eyes. "Why were you fighting about it?"

"Aw, fuck, Drake. Why do we fight about anything? Because we were in the same room? Because it's become a habit? Because we hate each other as much as we used to love each other? I don't fucking know anymore. It's exhausting. It's one of the reasons I like this place. Amber wouldn't be caught dead in here."

I look around at the battered tables and equally battered faces and nod. He's right. Amber would hate this. Her world is one of high society, exclusive parties, and the charity committees she sits on. She comes off as distant and aloof, and the rest of my family has no time for her at all. None of them under-stand why Elijah sticks with her, tortured by their loveless marriage. I know her a little better and understand that life isn't always as black and white as it appears on the surface.

"Maybe she'd surprise you, Elijah. Maybe you could give her a chance."

He sighs and drinks some more. "I've given her a thousand chances, and I'm pretty sure she'd say the same about me. No. It is what it is. Anyway, enough of my bullshit." He jerks his chin at me. "How's your bullshit?"

I understand his desire to change subjects. When a problem doesn't seem to have a solution, sometimes all you can do is switch off and give your mind a break, so I indulge him. "My bullshit is coming along just fine, thanks. Saw Maddox earlier. He came into the office and made all the women swoon."

"Was he modeling his Buddhist quarterback look?"

I laugh, because he's nailed it. Maddox was a football star in high school, until he was derailed by the combined trauma of losing our mom at sixteen and a fucked-up situation with a girlfriend who took her own life. His future was pretty much mapped out for him—football, college, family—until it wasn't.

He's spent years drifting around the world, and the world has rubbed off on him. The rest of us live in our suits and ties, but Maddox prefers baggy pants and tunics in colorful fabrics that were handwoven by monks. Probably using the hair of magical goats. He's still a big, good-looking bastard, though, and the mix of that and the spiritual vibe he gives off seems to be a hit with the ladies. Not that he notices or cares. Bro's still on his celibacy kick. Weirdo.

"Yep. Even Linda from HR did a double take, and believe me when I say she's not a woman who is easily swayed. He seems okay, glad to be here with us all, but this is the most time I've spent with him in years. And even though he's been back a year, he's still such a fucking free spirit. I'm never sure, you know, if he'll stay."

"I do know, yeah. It feels a bit like we're on borrowed time with him, doesn't it? He doesn't have a job or a partner or anything really anchoring him to New York. He could drift off again at any moment. And, you know, we'd all miss him. But Dad?"

"Right. Dad would be devastated. I suppose all we can do is hope Mad continues being happy enough to stay and be ready to pick up the pieces if he leaves." I sip my Guinness and make sure to lick my upper lip clean.

"I think I've found Dad a cook," Elijah says, grinning at me.

"Why? He doesn't want a cook."

"I know that. But want and need are two different things. This woman ... Well, she's something else. She's Luisa's mom."

Luisa is Elijah's assistant—a supremely smart, ultra-ambitious business grad whose family is originally from Venezuela. I've met her a couple times, and she's an impressive woman, hyper focused and even more efficient. Her parents moved here to build a better life for themselves and their children, and Luisa seems determined to prove their sacrifice wasn't wasted.

"Is Luisa's mom as, um, assertive as Luisa?" I ask carefully.

"You mean is Luisa's mom also a total ball-breaker? I have to say, yeah, she is, but with a little more charm. I mean, Luisa is great, but she's also terrifying. Luz is just as great, and she takes literally no shit from anyone, but she does it with a smile and the offer of a pastelito. Her husband died when Luisa was thirteen, and she's raised four kids on her own in a country that wasn't her own. Honestly? I think she can handle Dalton James being a temperamental asshat."

I'm not sure our dad will be on board with this idea. He and Mom never had a cook. The kitchen was Mom's domain, but he loved spending time in there with her when he could. She was from Spain and taught him everything he knows about food. He still wears that apron she bought him, for god's sake.

"Why do you think he'll go for it? And is this more than just domestic help?"

Despite—or maybe because of—his marital situation, my big brother is a romantic. He always wants a happy ending for people, and I wouldn't be shocked if he was trying to set Dad up. Our father is still a fit and active man, and he does not go short of female companionship, but since we lost our mom, there hasn't been anyone significant.

"Would that be so bad?" he asks. "Doesn't he deserve somebody other than us? It's not healthy for him to live his life through his kids."

"Maybe." I shrug. "And I get that your motives are pure, brother, but don't expect too much, all right? As far as Dad is concerned, he's had the great love of his life, and that will never be repeated."

"It was a great love, wasn't it?" he says, finishing off his Guinness.

As an adult, I know that no marriage is perfect. No relationship survives without its ups and downs. But my overwhelming memory of growing up is how happy my parents were together. Maybe that's one of the reasons that most of us have found it so hard to settle down. Having the example of a perfect couple as your mom and dad is a lot of live up to, and seeing how broken my father was when he lost her was a powerful deterrent against giving that kind power to anyone. The man warned us all against ever falling in love, for fuck's sake.

"What about you? You're new to town. I know you had your, uh, arrangements back in Chicago. Will you build similar arrangements here?"

"Are you asking me how I plan to get my rocks off, Elijah?"

He waves his hand at me. "No. I'm just curious. I mean, whatever works for you. It's just that when you spoke about that woman, the one you met at the wedding? That felt like a little more than an arrangement. I'm the last dude on earth who has the right to advise anybody on their love life, but what can I say? I want you to be happy."

"You know what would make me happy right now? More booze."

I stand up and head to the bar. This isn't the kind of place that stretches to table service, and right now I'm glad. I need to stretch my legs and give my mind a moment to settle. By the time I've ordered, paid, and brought everything back, I've decided that I don't need to hide this from him.

"So," I say, as I sit opposite him. "A funny thing happened."

"Did it involve a retired clown?"

"It did not. It involved the woman from the wedding."

"Scarlet, wasn't it?"

I grin at him. "No, not Scarlet actually. That was just a game we were playing. Her real name is Amelia Ryder, and guess what? Turns out she's my new secretary."

"Wait? What? The one Nathan hired for you? You fucked her? And she's named Amelia *Ryder*? Is she a Bond girl?"

There's a lot to unpack there, so I let him splutter over it for a few seconds longer. "Yes, her name is Ryder, and believe me, I have thought of all the puns already. And yes, the one Nathan hired for me—which is why I had no clue who she was the night I met her at the wedding."

"Are you sure she didn't know? I mean, I hate to be cynical, but you're a good-looking dude who comes from money. Is it at all possible she, I don't know, targeted you?"

I cast my mind back to the night we met. The sweet, sad look on her face as she sat there alone, coloring with crayons. The way she bit her plump lower lip, how surprised she was when she looked up and saw me. Jeez. Even thinking about that moment is going straight to my balls, and that is not an appropriate way to feel while sitting with your brother in a place like this. "No possible way. She thought I was Charlie for most of the night."

"Charlie Cockburn-Cummings? I'd forgotten about him." He laughs softly, and then he's distant again for a few seconds, and I wonder if he's thinking about how he and Amber used to laugh together in the good old days. Before ...

I clear my throat and, that seems to snap his attention back to the matter at hand. "Nathan knows, I guess? Did he give you chapter and verse about the HR implications?"

"To start with, yeah. He considered firing her, but thankfully realized that would be the worst thing we could do. But the fact he even considered it didn't seem fair. She needs this job. Her mom is sick, and she's gone through a bad divorce, and although I shouldn't know any of this personal shit about my new secretary, I do. And I can't just ignore it. I can't ignore her."

My mind springs back to earlier, when I found myself walking behind her. That skin-tight skirt made it impossible to take my eyes off her swaying backside, and the front view was even worse—or better. The day before was the wrap dress with its little strings, and today was a silky blouse with a great big bow at the neck. A great big bow just begging to be untied. It's like she's torturing me without even knowing it.

Elijah clears his throat, and I blink at him. I completely forgot he was there for a moment. I was lost in the image of tying Amelia up, of capturing her in a web of rope. Seeing her soft skin marked and patterned, her round breasts exposed to my touch ... fuck. This is not good at all.

"I lost you for a minute there, buddy. You thinking about Amelia?"

"No," I lie. "I was thinking about an especially tricky case I'm dealing with."

He regards me with suspicion. "You were thinking about Amelia."

I sigh and run my hands through my hair. I do that when I'm stressed, and these days I seem to live with my hands in my stupid hair. "Yeah, I was. I can't stop thinking about her, bro. I can't possibly talk to Nathan about it. We agreed that she could stay, but only if I promised it was over. I want her to stay—of course I do. And I can't be the asshole who bangs the help."

"To start, I wouldn't call her 'the help' to her face. At least not if you want to keep your balls attached. But yeah, of course I get it. We weren't raised to take advantage. We were raised to understand how privileged we were, and to never use that privilege against others. But ... Look, I'm just going to say this once and get it out there. If you actually have real feelings for this woman, little brother, then none of the rest matters. If you think you have a chance at finding love with her, then you should go for it. Figure the rest of the shit out as you go."

I bark out a bitter laugh. He might be older than me, but sometimes I feel like his dad. His bitter, twisted old dad. The kind who doesn't believe love exists, never mind being ready to give and receive it.

"What I feel for Amelia Ryder isn't anywhere near love, Elijah. It's more basic than that. Something about the woman screams 'fuck me' every single time I'm with her. I can't see her walking down the hallway without wanting to be balls-deep in her. I can't speak to her on the phone without my dick getting hard. I can't look at my desk without wanting to bend her over it and screw her brains out. I'm a fucking mess—but I'm not in love."

"You sure?" he says, cocking an eyebrow at me. "Nathan didn't expect love either, and look at him now."

"I'm sure. Love isn't for me. I'm not the kind of man who can ever promise a woman forever."

"Okay then," he murmurs, shrugging like he doesn't believe me.

And I guess I can't blame him. I'm not sure I believe me either.

THIRTEEN

AMELIA

"You look amazing!" I say, once Emily lets me out of her bear hug. "How was Italy?"

"It was gorgeous—totally bellissima! The weather, the history, the food ..."

"The husband?"

She giggles and blushes slightly, which is a new and fun look for Emily. She's always come across as a confident and experienced woman of the world, and it's so sweet to see that talking about Tucker makes her behave like a teenager. "Yeah, the husband part was pretty good too. I'm just so ... So happy! I knew I wanted to marry him, I knew I loved him, but I didn't expect it all to feel so damn different, you know? The way I feel when he looks at me, the way he looks at me. The simple stuff —the little gestures and the way he holds my hand. Him introducing me as his wife, sharing my life with him. It's all pretty mind-blowing to be honest."

She leans back against my kitchen counter, positively glowing with her new tan and her joy.

"Aw," I say, uncorking the bottle of wine she brought with her. "That is so great. I really love this for you."

"I know, right? Who knew that being in love and getting married could actually make me this happy? I thought I was a career girl all the way."

"Well, you don't have to be one or the other," I reply as we take our glasses over to the couch. My apartment is tiny, and I appreciate that she made the effort to come here rather than inviting me over to her and Tucker's much swankier place in Chelsea. As she said on the phone, though, how could we possibly discuss how awesome he is in front of him?

They were in Italy for a week, and this is the first time we've met up with each other in the flesh since the wedding. She sent me tons of pictures from their time in Tuscany and Rome, and I almost feel like I was there with her.

But nothing compares to this, sitting on the couch with my bestie and sipping the gorgeous Chianti she brought back with her. We talk about everything and nothing, falling into the familiar pattern that we've followed since we first met. It never seems to matter how much time we spend apart; we always pick up exactly where we left off. Emily once moved to Zurich for a year as part of her job, and as soon as she got home, we were back to doing exactly this—gossiping like we were never apart.

Emily and I have always told each other everything, and she's been the best friend I ever could have asked for. She didn't judge me when I decided to focus on supporting Chad in his career rather than building my own or when I found out he was cheating. Not once have I received anything other than support and love from this woman, not even the hint of an "I told you so" when I was forced to rebuild my entire life from scratch. I have never had any reason to doubt her.

So why do I feel ever-so-slightly nervous as our conversation moves away from the glories of Italy and onto the less glamorous subject of my life?

"How's your mom?" she asks. "I know you've been worried about her." Emily has known my mom for years now, and they adore each other.

Looking back, I'm still blown away by how gracious Emily was when we met. She grew up in New York too, but it was a very different New York from the one I knew. Her father is a retired supreme court justice, her mom an heiress to an art auction dynasty. Whenever we came home to visit during college, Emily would come to stay with us in Brooklyn as often as I stayed with her in their family's townhouse near the Met. She never seemed thrown by the differences in our backgrounds, never looked down her nose at our tiny house in a working-class neighborhood despite our very different lives. None of that stuff really matters anyway because, at heart, Emily and I are like sisters.

"She's doing okay." I lift my hand, crossing my fingers. "Holding her own, at least. She's still not leaving the house much, which bothers me. You know how active she used to be. She always loved going to the movies, so I've been trying to talk her into going to see one with me, but no dice."

"I remember. A giant screen with a tub of popcorn was her happy place. What's the issue, do you think?"

"Well, she's obviously not great physically, but I think it's mental as well. She's nervous about being out of the house when her breathing is so poor and unpredictable. There are new meds on the market now, new portable devices that might help, and we're meeting with her doctor soon to discuss what's covered on the new insurance."

Emily sips her wine and gives me a look I've seen a million times before. "I know, I know!" I hold up my hands, laughing. "I only need to ask. Kimmy's said the same, and believe me, I'm grateful. But getting Edith to accept financial help from you guys? That's not going to happen. I've considered simply not telling her and bleeding you both dry, and I definitely would have if the new job hadn't worked out, but it has—hurrah for me. I'm finally useful."

"Don't you dare say something like that," she responds, pointing her finger at me and looking genuinely annoyed.

"What, I'm not finally useful?"

"You know what I mean, Amelia. I've never weighed in on Chad, at least not out loud. He was your husband and it was your life, and I respected that—but please don't lose sight of the fact that you were always useful. You supported him when he was looking for work and doing his endless internships. You paid the bills without complaint. Even when things were going better for him, you were useful—you kept everything running smoothly in his life, you were always like his unpaid PA. Plus, you were always there for your mom, you volunteered at the hospital, and you were the best friend ever. I never want to hear you describe yourself as 'not useful' ever again, you hear me, woman?"

Tears sting my eyes, but I nod gratefully. I might have bombed on the husband front, but I definitely won the friend lottery.

"Good," she says firmly. "Now, is there any gossip from the wedding after we left? A few people posted on Insta afterward, and I caught a glimpse of you dancing with an extremely good-looking guy. Where did he come from? Planet Sex God? Please tell me you didn't waste him."

It's not too big of a surprise that she wouldn't know every single wedding guest. He was probably Tucker's guest, anyway. But I also now remember the name tag he had—Charlie. It was only later, much later, that he told me his real name. "Oh. Right. Well, that's a funny story ..."

I'm still not sure if I should tell her, because it's not only my secret to share, is it? Drake's done me a favor by being willing to sweep everything under the rug and letting me keep the job I so desperately need. But this is Emily. She's kept all my secrets and would never betray me. I feel uncomfortable telling her, but I'd feel even more uncomfortable hiding it from her.

"Okay. Let's hear it," she says, topping up our glasses.

"I'll tell you, but it's classified, okay?"

"Classified as in 'you can tell one other person,' or classified as in one hundred percent Nasty Death Accident?"

That was our silly girl code when we were younger, a riff on the legal term—nondisclosure agreement. It means complete confidentiality. "Very much NDA."

Her pretty blue eyes widen, and she makes a zipping up her lips gesture. I sigh and gulp down half a glass of Tuscany's finest Chianti in one go. The good stuff is wasted on me.

"The guy I was dancing with was someone I met at your wedding. I assume you didn't recognize him?"

"Well, it wasn't a great shot, and he did look familiar, but I couldn't put a name to the face. Or the ass, which was especially fine, I thought."

"I thought you only had eyes for Tucker's ass?"

"No, I only have *hands* for Tucker's ass. My eyes are still free agents. So, who was he?"

I have no idea if the name will mean anything to her. I still have no clue whether he was an actual wedding guest. Just because he pretended to be Charlie doesn't mean he was a gatecrasher. I pretended to be Scarlet, and I was the damn maid of honor.

"He was, and in fact still is, Drake James."

"Wait," she says, blinking in confusion. "Drake James as in James and James, the place where you work? As in Nathan James's brother, Dalton James's son, and Amber James's brother-in-law?"

"I have no idea about the last two, but it's a definite yes to the first. Do you know him? Did you invite him to the wedding?"

"Nope, sorry sweetie. I kinda know Amber, in a charity committee–lunch kind of way. She's married to the oldest brother, Elijah. And I'm sure I've been at functions at the same time as him. But no, he wasn't invited as far as I know. I mean, I'm not worried about that—he's not the kind of guy you'd object to turning up. It's not like he was going to steal the silver. It's odd, but in more of a funny-anecdote way than a call-the-cops way. Why is this an NDA, babes? What else happened?"

I bury my face in my hands and don't know whether to laugh or cry. Am I pissed at him for lying about being a wedding guest? No, I'm not. He never actually said he was. In fact, he told me he was only pretending to be Charlie. I don't feel like he was being malicious. I do, however, feel completely bewildered. When I emerge from my hand cave, my cheeks are on fire, and the look on Emily's face pushes me over the edge into laughter.

"No!" she exclaims, her eyes huge. "You didn't? Did you? Drake fucking James? At my wedding? Oh my god, Amelia. I couldn't be more proud. Tell me everything, right now. No, wait —we need more wine. This is definitely a two-bottle conversation." She pulls out her phone and within seconds has ordered pizza and extra booze to be delivered. Looks like we're having a party.

"Right. Go," she instructs. "Leave out nothing. I'm a boring married woman now. I have to live vicariously through my girl friends' sex lives."

"That's not true—I can tell from the way you're glowing. You're getting plenty of first-class bedroom action."

"Okay, I am. But still ... Spill it."

It feels so good to talk to her about all of this and to laugh about it. She's not only my friend, she's also a creature from Drake's world. She bridges the gap between us.

"Well, I didn't ..." I clear my throat and continue. "We didn't you-know-what, actually *at* your wedding. We danced and talked, and then we went back to his hotel. He lives in the penthouse at the Grand Regent." Emily doesn't even blink an eye at this, which kind of proves my point about the world she comes from.

"And?" she asks, making a get-on-with-it gesture with her hands. "That can't be all I get. What happened?"

"Everything happened. Nudity happened. Kissing happened. Orgasms happened. Absolutely mind-blowingly awesome sex happened. The best I've ever had. It was ... pretty freaking amazing."

We both giggle, and for a moment it feels like we're eighteen again, lying awake in our dorm room and talking about boys. Or in my case, just the one boy. "I've always found the James brothers insanely hot," she says, draining the last of her red and staring at the empty glass in disappointment. "Every single one of 'em. Heck, even the dad is hot. One of my sister's friends had a fling with Nathan years ago, but that isn't saying much—a lot of people had a fling with Nathan before he settled down. Drake, though? From what I hear, he's always been a bit of a mystery. More of an enigma, living away and all. He was with someone years ago—one of the Gallagher girls, I think. Maybe Mimi or Tiffy ..."

"Mimi? Tiffy? Are they actual women or characters in a fifties sitcom?"

"Don't judge—they can't help it if they're the waspiest wasps in the waspdom. It was Tiffy, I think. Yeah. They were, like, pre-engaged, you know? Then after the mom died, there was some drama and they split. Later, he disappeared off to Chicago, and that's pretty much when my gossip ends. Wow. I just can't believe it. Drake James, hot damn. How have things been at work? Does your new boss know that you screwed his brother?"

"Ah. Well ... So. That's the thing." You'd think I would have come to grips with the situation by now, but the absurdity of it all continues to blow my mind. "As it turns out, Nathan isn't my new boss. Drake is."

She looks suitably horrified, and her hand flies up to cover her mouth as she gapes at me. "What? Noooooo! And you had no idea?"

"Not a clue. He was just this cute guy I met at a wedding. My first and only one-night stand. You can imagine my shock when I rolled up for work on Monday and there he was, still hot as sin, staring at me like I had two heads."

Emily makes sympathetic noises and asks a flurry of questions about what happened next. I tell her all about my fear that they would fire me and the deal Drake and I made to erase all memories of that night from our minds.

"But is that working?" she asks after checking her phone and telling me pizza is fifteen minutes away. "I mean, if your night together was as vagina-melting as you say it was, can you just forget all about it?"

"Well, it's been over a week now, and neither of us has mentioned it at all. But truthfully, Em, no, it's not working. At least not for me. Every time I see him, my vagina does indeed melt, and it reminds me of exactly what it's missing. But I just have to keep trying even harder to ignore it, because I can't risk everything by listening to my vagina. This job and my mom's health are a lot more important to me than sex."

"Even spectacularly good sex?"

"Even that. I don't ever want to be dependent on a man again, Emily. Not after what happened with Chad. I worked hard to get back into the working world, and this job was a real break for me. I'm not going to mess it up just because the man is ..."

"Irresistible?"

"No. I'm going to resist him, I swear. No matter how hard that is sometimes."

She looks at me with a perplexed expression on her face and shakes her head. "What?" I ask. "Are you horrified?"

"Well, I'm a bit horrified on your behalf at how it all worked out for you, but mainly I'm just ... surprised, I think? You, Amelia Ryder, having a one-night stand. Talking about sex like you finally understand what all the fuss is about. You're kind of lit up from the inside. It's like a completely different version of you than the one I know."

I suppose Emily's right—I am different around him. I've felt different since meeting him.

Different in a way that makes everything better, in a way that makes me better. No matter the awkwardness of the whole Drake situation, I will always be one hundred percent grateful that our night together happened. It might have meant little to him, but it's already changed me in ways he can't imagine.

FOURTEEN

AMELIA

"Dammit! Shit." Drake's frustrated curses drift through the crack in his office door. He sounds even more exasperated than he does when the coffee machine acts up. I shrug my purse onto my shoulder and pop my head inside to see what the problem is. He's leaning over his desk, a whirlwind of paperwork all over the room. There are stacks of it on the desk, on the floor, and on his chair.

"Is everything okay, Mr. James?"

He glances up at the sound of my voice, looking surprised to see me standing there. His usually styled hair is ruffled in a way that makes him look more human, and his plain navy tie is crooked. For a man who usually looks immaculate, this is the equivalent of walking naked through Central Park. It's kind of cute, not that he'd appreciate that word being pointed in his direction. We've worked well together so far, dealing with tasks efficiently and calmly. Both of us have done a good job channeling our inner robot, and whatever feelings either of us might have about the other have been kept firmly buttoned up. Not that I assume for a minute that he has any feelings at all about me.

Now, though, seeing him like this—unkempt, frustrated, ever-so-slightly vulnerable—I experience a rush of affection along with the usual rush of desire. I shift from one foot to the other, rubbing the sides of my pumps together. I'm suddenly nervous, and I probably should have just headed home. "It sounded like something was wrong," I mutter, unsettled by his silence. He's staring at me like he's never seen me before, and I quickly glance down at my outfit. It's my wrap dress again, but this time glammed up with some pearls. All perfectly acceptable, surely?

Even from across the room, I see his Adam's apple bob under the force of his swallow. He glances at the clock on the wall. "I thought you'd left for the day. Don't you normally finish at five?"

Drake, I know, puts in insane hours. He's always here when I arrive in the morning and still here when I leave. I suspect he's even here on weekends, and even if he's not in the office, he's definitely working. But he's also made it clear that he doesn't expect me to match that or to be at his beck and call.

Clearing my throat, I step farther into the room. His jacket is slung on the floor, and his white shirt clings to the muscular shape of his broad shoulders. Why does business attire have to be so damn sexy? It doesn't seem fair. I ignore my racing heart and cast my eyes over the chaos of the room.

"I worked late because I took an extra-long lunch. I had to pop over to check on my mom."

"Is she all right? You know you can take time whenever you need. Some things are more important than work," he says, looking genuinely concerned. Again, I'm reminded of how much we unwittingly shared with each other on the night of the wedding. He knows all about her health condition, and I know how much he misses his own mother, who died when he was only twenty-three. I suspect moms are a touchy subject for this man, and it moves me that he cares.

"She's okay," I assure him quickly. "I don't know if you remember, but she has COPD, and sometimes her oxygen levels get a little low. She called me upset, and I ..." I shake my head and stop myself from babbling. He doesn't need to know the finer details. "But she's okay now."

"Of course I remember. If you need any recommendations for doctors, just ask. My sister-in-law makes sure we all donate staggering amounts of money to local hospitals." Pausing, he tilts his head. "Uh-oh. Does that make me sound like Bruce Wayne?"

A smile creeps over my face as I recall that conversation. "Thanks, that's very kind of you. But right now it looks like Batman is the one who could do with some help."

He winces, his eyes dropping back to the pile of papers on his desk. He has a huge case starting tomorrow, and from the tight lines of his shoulders and the scowl on his face, I'd say he's incredibly stressed. He stares at the mess, mumbling something unintelligible as he absentmindedly winds and unwinds a thick length of cord around his fist. It looks therapeutic and strangely erotic. Then again, I'd probably find it erotic if he was crushing a tomato.

"Please let me help, Mr. James."

He looks up again, his eyes wide like he forgot I was here. He twists and turns the cord in his fingers, and his dark gaze holds mine for a few silent seconds. Heat blooms beneath my skin, and I wonder what is going through his mind. For a moment, I think he's actually going to tell me, but then he abruptly shakes his head. "No, thank you. Goodnight, Miss Ryder."

If this is a work thing, and it certainly looks like one, then he should let me help. It's not like I haven't signed a confidentiality agreement, and I have full access to his emails. I might not be a lawyer myself, but I know the intimate details of the case he's working on. I've arranged several meetings about it and taken notes during them. Next to him, I'm probably the person who knows the most about it.

With a deep breath, I take another cautious step closer, like I'm approaching a dog that might bite. "This is the Callaghan case, yes?"

He nods, not even looking up, lost in his world of paper.

"Right. Well, I think I'm going to stay and help you. What kind of a secretary would I be if I abandoned you to this?"

"There's really no need for that, Miss Ryder. I'm perfectly capable of dealing with this myself."

"I don't doubt how capable you are, Mr. James," I say, realizing as the words leave my mouth how flirtatious they sound. Or maybe I'm being paranoid. I decide to quickly move on, just in case. "But I'm capable too. You might be Batman, but my superpower is organization. I could at least help you get these papers into some kind of order."

I try not to show it, but I'm pretty desperate for him to say yes. So far, our working relationship has been fine. Certainly a lot better than I expected it to be on that first day. He seems pleased with my performance, and there have been no issues. But I've also yet to feel ... essential, I guess is the word for it. Like I, Amelia Ryder, am personally needed for the job. I know that's pathetic and that employees really shouldn't be so desperate, but I do like to feel useful. I like working here, like working for Drake. Not because he's a demigod with supernatural skills in the sack, but because behind his cocksure charm and surface confidence, he's actually sweet and a little vulnerable, and well, just a good person.

He works so damn hard and seems to take on so much responsibility. I remember him telling me he never quite felt good enough for his family—something I will never, ever remind him that he revealed—and I wonder if his workaholic tendencies are all tied in to that. Sometimes, like now, he looks like he has the weight of the world on those gorgeous shoulders and nobody to help him carry the load.

He glances up again, running his hand through his thick hair. His eyes narrow, and he sucks on his upper lip. "It's late."

I shrug, dropping my purse to the floor. "It's not even seven, and I don't like to brag, but all I have waiting for me at home is some leftover roast beef and *Sex and the City* reruns."

The corners of his lips twitch with the hint of a smile. "Which season?"

"I watched the end of season one last night. Carrie dumps Mr. Big for the first time. Are you a fan?"

"That would be telling, wouldn't it? Well, as much as I hate to deprive you of your exciting night in, Miss Ryder, I have to admit that I actually could use your help."

"Then I'm all yours for as long as you need me." I drop into the empty chair opposite his desk, and before I can regret my poor choice of words, I move on. "So, what are we doing here? Was there some kind of explosion?"

Drake sighs. "Opposing counsel just delivered me a whole new box of evidence to go through. They left it until the very last minute, but I'm used to those tactics and expected to spend the night going through it. But then the damn ass fell out of the box when I picked it up, and now I have two thousand pages all out of order. I could ask for more time, but he knows this case has already dragged on for longer than it should have. Fucker."

"Total fucker," I agree. "Bet he weakened the cardboard with nail scissors before he sent it over." I nod at the mass of scattered papers. "So, what are we looking for?"

Drake gives me a brief summary of the new evidence and hands me an index sheet that lists the contents. It's mainly hundreds of call logs detailing numbers that were dialed to and from office and home phones, along with dates, times, and duration of the calls. "Most of it is probably irrelevant," he explains, "but when you ask for information like this, they're perfectly within their rights to provide too much detail. Sometimes it's because there actually is pertinent information in there waiting to be found and they want to bury it in a pile of pointless dross in the hope that you miss it. Sometimes they do it just to be assholes."

"What do you think it is this time?" I ask, picking up the first stack of sheets.

"I have no clue. But the first thing to do is get the logs back in time and date order. Only then will I be able to go through them and really check."

James and James is one of the biggest law firms in the country, and Drake is one of its managing partners. He has a team of literally hundreds working for him and access to some of the best legal minds around. I've already learned, though, that he is a perfectionist or a control freak—possibly both. He goes through every scrap of paperwork on every case he works himself rather than passing it on to one of the many paralegals who are specifically employed to do exactly that kind of task.

It sounds crazy, but it seems to work for him. He never lost a single case when he was in Chicago, and he's renowned for his well-researched ruthlessness in the court room. He's a shark, but a shark who combines his killer instinct with hours of painstaking attention to detail. He wins because he puts the work in, and the fact that he is trusting me to help him gives me a little warm glow of pride. I have no doubt that the trust is partly borne of desperation, but it's a big deal to me.

"Okay," I say, standing up. "We need to relocate. At the moment, you have too many piles too close together, and I suspect you're losing track of which one is which."

"You're not wrong," he says, sounding annoyed with

himself. "I messed them up just before you came in and had to start all over again."

That explains the cursing. "Well, don't worry. We'll sort it. I'm going to set up a workstation over here by the window, and I'm going to make a stack for each day. I'll work left to right, earliest date first, and then beneath each, we'll add them in time order. We'll end up with a grid pattern, and that will make it easier to cross reference."

He stares at me for a long moment, then nods. "Have at it. How about I go through the papers and shout out the details, and you can add them to the right pile?"

"Sounds like a plan. I'll stay down here on the ground." I kick off my heels, and my dress rides up over my thighs as I fall to my knees. It can't be helped, and it's not like I'm flashing my stocking tops, but I feel the first hint of a blush as I catch him looking. It's been three weeks since I started working here, and after the initial super-intense awkwardness, things have settled down. I'm starting to think everything has been made easier by the fact that we managed to find a way to work together without ever actually being *together*. At least not alone, and not for any longer than a few minutes at a time. This is different. More intimate.

"Okay, I've got February Fourth here," he says, holding up a handful of pages.

"Great. Pass it over, and let's get started." Following his lead, I concentrate on the job at hand.

This is the kind of work I enjoy most, and time passes quickly once we get going. Having two of us plus a new and, frankly, more logical system in place means that the task doesn't feel anywhere near as daunting. Once all the call logs are in chronological order, Drake begins to check through his notes and look for the dates when his client claimed she was contacted by the man they're suing, Franklin Callaghan. So far, either her dates have been off or he used a different phone, one that he didn't disclose.

Drake rubs his eyes and continues flicking through the pages of his various notepads while I wait for him to call out dates and times. Again, it's a labor-intensive way to work—he could have had those notes digitized into a searchable database —but it seems to be the way he prefers. Old school. Maybe writing stuff down longhand helps him process it all. I get that, but I also make a mental note to suggest digital backup as well. There are so many great software programs out there now that would really help with things like this.

After what feels like forever, we finally catch a break. He calls out a date and time and tells me the call lasted approximately five minutes. Sure enough, when I check in the relevant pile, I find the page. "It's here!" I cry. "A call made from his office landline to hers, at exactly that time on exactly that date —call duration logged as five minutes, thirty seconds! Let me check his schedule ..."

I crawl across the floor to the small heap of loose sheets that provide a record of Callaghan's whereabouts during the relevant time period. "Bingo!" I cry, holding one in the air. "He was there that day—signed out twenty minutes later!"

Drake has pulled his tie completely loose, and his hair is still in those thick furrows. His face lights up when I pass him the sheet, though, and it's like all the weight lifts from his shoulders. He transforms before my eyes, and I can't help smiling. I don't know exactly what any of this means for the case, but I do know I helped him. I know he's pleased. And I know that it feels way too good. I climb to my stockinged feet.

He looks like a little kid on Christmas, waving the printout in the air. "This is great, Amelia. Perfect, in fact."

These days, he sticks to Miss Ryder, and it feels good to hear my name on his lips again, even though he doesn't seem to have noticed. He's lost in his work, grinning down at the call log.

"How does it help?" I ask, genuinely interested.

"Well, it doesn't prove anything by itself because there's no recording of the call—we only have our client's word against his. But he has consistently denied ever speaking to her, and this proves he lied about that. And proving that he lied about one thing, no matter how small, makes it way easier to show he's a liar about the big things too. Thank you—so much! I couldn't have done it without you."

He's standing close to me, the elation of the moment seeming to override his usual reserve. He normally keeps his distance, physically and emotionally, making sure everything stays on a purely professional level. But now, as he looms over me, so close I swear I can feel the heat of his body through the thin fabric of his shirt, I feel weak. My legs are unsteady beneath me, and my hands are desperate to reach out and touch him.

Our eyes lock, and his tongue flicks out to lick his lips. Oh lord. His tongue. His magical, mystical tongue. The way it can make me beg for mercy, scream for more …

"Amelia," he says simply, his voice a deep growl that echoes the way I feel inside. I gulp in air, knowing a blush is rising up over my chest. His eyes travel down to my breasts, and he reaches out, one big hand taking hold of the little cord that secures my wrap dress in place. All he has to do is tug it in the right way, and the whole thing will fall open. I will be standing before him in my bra, stockings, panties, and pearls, and I can't think of anything I want more. He tilts his head, dark eyes intense, one eyebrow quirked in a question. It feels like the rest of the world has disappeared, the whole of New York has fallen away, and all that's left is us two. This moment. What might come next.

I sigh and am just about to murmur his name when my stomach decides to speak for me. It rumbles, so loud and insistent that it can't be ignored by either of us. In fact, it probably can't be ignored by passing satellites in outer space. I let out an embarrassed "Oh!" and my hand flies up to cover my mouth. He snatches his fingers away and takes a few very deliberate steps back, putting some distance between us. It's certainly for the best, but part of me wants to cry from disappointment.

"Sorry." I wince. "I didn't manage to actually eat any lunch on my break today."

Concern colors his expression. "How long has it been since you ate?"

"I had a bagel at about ten," I say with a dismissive wave of my hand. "I'm good."

"That was like what, eleven hours ago? You need to eat, Amelia."

He's still calling me Amelia, I notice, but now he sounds borderline annoyed with me. Or maybe with himself—who knows? I definitely wasn't the only one feeling the intensity of that moment, and it isn't outside the realm of possibility that he's pissed at himself for his reaction.

"It's really no big deal," I reply. "It's not like I'm wasting away. I could stand to miss a few meals." It's meant to be a lighthearted comment, but his expression darkens, and I wonder what the hell I've done wrong now. His moods are exhausting, and it's been a long enough day. I'm about to make my excuses when he speaks, his tone firm.

"You could not stand to miss a few meals. You need to look after yourself if you're going to look after your mom."

"What?" I splutter. "I've looked after my mom for years, and we're perfectly fine. I'm not a child, and you're not my father. I can decide for myself when I eat and when I don't, thank you very much." Right on cue, my stomach pipes up again.

His lips quirk up in a lopsided grin, and I can't help but see the humor of it all. I want to stay angry with him, but the twinkle in his eyes is such a joyous thing to witness that it's impossible. "Okay!" I throw my hands up in surrender. "You're right, *Dad*. I need to eat. I'll go straight home and get started on that roast beef."

"No, that won't do. I'll order some food in. There's still work to be finished off here, and we both need to eat."

I want to say no—sharing a meal feels too intimate somehow. Last time we shared a meal, it was breakfast, and that ended up with me getting fucked on the dining table. That desk of his is looking awfully inviting right about now.

"I don't think so, Mr. James. I should really be going. I'm sure you can finish up here."

"Are you scared?" he asks, watching as I slip my shoes back on.

Absolutely petrified, if I'm telling the truth. The way I react to this man is so unpredictable, I have whiplash from jerking myself around. It's like I don't even know who I am anymore. "Am I scared of food? No."

"Are you scared of me?"

I narrow my eyes at him, angry that he's nailed it but even more angry that I feel it. It might be true, but he has no right to make it real by speaking the actual words. "Why would I be scared of you, Mr. James? You're just my boss, and I've had far scarier bosses than you."

I put some sass into my voice, channeling a little inner Scarlet to help me out. Sometimes, I really don't recognize myself when I'm with this man. He brings out sides of me that I never knew existed, and as much as it confuses me, I must admit that I kinda like it.

"Good. Well, you're not scared of me, so you won't mind

staying a little longer, will you, Miss Ryder? Now, what do you like?"

I blink at him, my mind immediately spinning off in an entirely inappropriate direction. I mean, him eating me was pretty amazing. But feeling his giant dick pushing inside me, his fingers on my clit? Also amazing. An impossible choice, really. What do I like? An unanswerable question.

"For dinner," he adds, the glint in his eyes suggesting he knows exactly where I disappeared off to.

"Right. I knew that. Uh, I like anything. I'm easy." Shit. I'm off-balance now, and my brain doesn't seem to want to cooperate. Probably because my libido is sucking all my energy down to the space between my thighs instead.

He arches an eyebrow. "Thai?"

For a second, my mind turns cartwheels. Tie? His necktie? The one that's dangling deliciously low on his shirt? Or the tie that holds my dress together, the one he was so close to tugging earlier?

"Do you like Thai food?" he clarifies. "And are you okay?"

"I'm fine." I nod quickly, my cheeks burning. "And yes, I love Thai!" I'm breathless and overenthusiastic, but he doesn't seem to notice as he flicks his finger across the screen of his phone.

"Then you're about to eat the best Thai food you've ever tasted."

Sitting back against my chair a little while later, I stifle a groan. "You were right, that is the best Thai food I've ever tasted." I rub a hand over my full stomach. "I couldn't eat another bite."

"I told you." His eyes scan the array of leftover food on his desk. I think he ordered half the menu. "You know you'll have to take some of this home with you though?"

I shake my head. "No way. I'm so full I'll literally burst if I eat any more."

He rubs a hand down his beard and tilts his head, still looking at the half-full containers. "Feels kind of criminal to let all this go to waste."

The aroma of the incredible Thai green curry I just devoured tickles my nostrils. He's right; there's enough here to feed another two people. "Good point. Actually, I will take it. My neighbor, Kris with a K, would love this stuff."

His brow furrows. "Kris? With a K?"

My heart rate spikes. Why is he frowning like that? Has he had a bad experience with a Kris in the past? Does he have beef with the letter K? Or could it be that he thinks Kris is a guy, and he's a tiny bit jealous? No. I'm definitely imagining that. He probably wants me to stay and work a bit longer, even though I think we've gotten everything straightened out.

"Yeah. That's how she introduced herself the first time we met, and it kinda stuck—Kris with a K. She has two teenage boys who both eat like they have hollow legs. This will be a welcome treat. If you really mean it about me taking some home, that is?"

His expression softens again. "Of course. I remember being one of those boys with the hollow legs."

"Yeah? What were you like as a teenager?"

"Hairy, hungry, and huge. Often also horny. Usual teenage boy stuff."

"And your house would have been fit to burst with all that, given there were five of you. Your poor mom."

He smiles, and the flicker of sadness in his eyes is quickly replaced by genuine pleasure. "Yeah. We were miscreants. A day never went by without incident. A broken window, thrown punches, playing football in the house. She pretended to be exasperated, but we all knew she kind of loved the chaos, you know? Being a mom was so natural to her. She always used to say that it was her career. She was the CEO of her boys."

"That's so sweet. And true—it's hard work being a mother. She sounds like an amazing woman."

"Yeah. She was. I think I'm only just reaching the stage where I can speak about her, think about her, and remember the good times too, you know? I spent so long shutting her out."

He's helping me pack away the leftovers, and our hands accidentally touch on the desk. I quickly move my fingers and hope he doesn't notice my reaction. "And I guess that meant you shut out the happy memories as well as the pain?"

"Exactly. So." He steps back and clears his throat. "Thank you for a productive night, Miss Ryder."

"You're very welcome, Mr. James. Thank you for the food. It really was fantastic. I love finding new places to eat."

"The Rice House makes the best food in the entire Tri-State area. I mean, it's no Waffle House, but I only ever got that once a year or so when I would drive back to visit from Chicago." His hangdog expression looks so genuine, I almost feel bad for him. "I guess that's a thing of the past now."

"I don't think so, Mr. James." I smirk, feeling mischievous again. "I mean I haven't sampled *all* the food on offer in the Tri-State area, and I have no idea what Waffle House is, but I don't have to. I already know the best of the best—*in the world*—comes from Mario's in Brooklyn."

His dark brown eyes narrow. "Mario's?"

"Mario's," I repeat firmly. "And his exploding donut balls."

Drake coughs like he's choking on fresh air. "His what now?" he finally manages to say.

His unguarded reaction makes me giggle. Between the banter about food and him opening up about his mom, I'm reminded of the first night we met, when we were Charlie and Scarlet and nothing was off-limits. "His exploding donut balls.

Trust me, you haven't lived until you've tried them. They are delicious." Closing my eyes, I kiss my fingertips as if I'm the chef of a Michelin-star restaurant declaring perfection. "Light and crispy on the outside, all sugary and hot, but when you pop them in your mouth and bite …" I lick my lips and moan. "It's like an explosion of sweet, heavenly cream in your mouth."

He stares at me, his Adam's apple bobbing as he swallows hard. The heat of his gaze blisters my skin, and a flush creeps over my cheeks.

"What?" I whisper.

The air in the room seems to shift, suddenly full of crackling electricity that buzzes over my skin and makes my pulse spike. Drake's eyes bore into mine for a few seconds longer before he looks away. "Nothing," he says. "Carry on."

Nothing? That wasn't nothing. The man looked at me like he wanted to throw me out of his office, and all I was doing was talking about donuts. But he said to carry on, so I do. "They're like heaven in pastry form. But you have to eat them straight away, while they're hot and fresh, and I'm pretty sure you don't travel to my neighborhood very often." My nerves cause me to retreat into the safe haven of blabbering about nothing at all important. "Which is probably a good thing, really."

"Oh? And why is that, Miss Ryder?" He's finished loading the takeout containers into the bag and is staring at me intensely. Jeez. This man is really passionate about donuts.

The heat from my cheeks races down my neck. I even feel like my internal organs are blushing. Nobody could withstand Drake James's laser eyes, and I almost feel sorry for the people who have to face him in court.

"B-because once you've tasted one of Mario's exploding donut balls, there's no going back. You'll have dreams about how good they are, they're that addictive. Even though you know they're bad for you, once you've tasted them, you can't get them out of your mind."

His jaw tics, his scowl murderous. The tension in the room is weird and supercharged, and I have no idea what's happening here. Boy, I could really do with an exploding donut ball right about now.

Drake sucks on his top lip for a few seconds, his eyes never leaving mine. Then, abruptly, he hands me the white takeout bag. "I think it's time I let you go home, Miss Ryder." His tone is cold and detached, his expression closed down.

What the actual fuck? I thought we were good, that we made progress. There were a few lusty glitches, sure, but we got through them. We worked together, ate together, and had a conversation like two normal colleagues. Only now, he's behaving like a total stranger, and there was a layer of frost in his voice with that last "Miss Ryder."

"Did I say something wrong, Mr. James?"

"No," he replies a little too quickly. "But it's late, and if you want your neighbors to enjoy this food, you'd better get it to them soon."

I accept the bag and turn to look for my coat. He's right, I'm sure. Except ... Except no. He's being weird and rude, and I don't like it.

"Are you mad that I think Mario's exploding donut balls are better than your fancy expensive Thai food? Have I offended your male pride in some way?" I blurt out.

He glares at me, nostrils flaring like he's trying to keep a lid on his temper. "You really think I'm that much of an asshole?"

"The jury's still out on that, Mr. James. If you'd asked me that half an hour ago, the answer would have been no. But now? Not so sure. Why are you so annoyed with me?"

"I'm not." His annoyed tone completely undermines his claim. He closes his eyes and rubs at his temples like he has a headache, then sucks in a deep breath, holds it for a second, and lets it out. "I'm not annoyed at you, Miss Ryder. I'm annoyed at myself."

"Why? What have you done wrong?"

He steps around the desk and stands so close to me that I can feel the heat from his body. My eyes are on a level with his chest, and it's almost impossible not to reach out and place my hand on it. I imagine myself undoing those buttons, one by one, revealing the gorgeous body I know lies underneath the civilized clothing. His cologne fills my nostrils and my head spins at the sparks flying between us.

"I think you should go," he says softly, the words at odds with the tone. Time seems to stretch into an endless moment as we stare at each other, his liquid brown eyes growing darker as he scrutinizes my face.

"I will, don't worry. But just so you know, you *are* being an asshole now. I'm going to go home and spend the rest of the night worrying about whatever the hell I did wrong and whether you'll still be pissed at me in the morning."

He shoves his hands through his hair and growls. "I'm not even pissed at you now, never mind in the morning. Look, you want to know if I've ever regretted tasting something so good that I can't stop thinking about it? Something that I'm addicted to even though I know it's bad for me?"

My knees tremble, and it feels like all the air is being sucked from the room. I manage to breathe out a single word. "Yes."

He dips his head until his mouth is dangerously close to my ear. "I have, Amelia." His warm breath dances over my skin, making me shiver even as my temperature skyrockets at having him so close. "You."

Then, without another word, he strides out of his office, leaving me a quivering mess in his wake. I stare after him, open-mouthed, my heart hammering in my chest. Forcing myself to inhale deeply, I will my pulse to stop racing and look down at the bag of food dangling from my hand. I should get home. He has more work to do, and he's clearly not going to get it done while I'm here.

Rolling my shoulders back, I walk out of Drake's office and stride down the empty hallways until I reach the elevators. I've never been here so late before. I'm sure there are people still here working, shut away in their offices, but it's silent and kind of eerie. A touch on the creepy side, especially for someone who already feels on the verge of a cardiac event.

Despite my anxiety, I feel a slow smile spreading across my face. I know Drake is my boss and that he's a billionaire lawyer with the world at his feet. I know that he's completely and totally off-limits and nothing can ever happen between us.

But in this moment, and only in this moment, none of that matters. Because he said it and he can't take it back, and I will always have this one sweet victory.

I am Drake James's exploding donut balls.

I say goodnight to the security guard at the front desk and step outside into the cool spring air, my bag of food clutched in one hand and my purse in the other. I recognize the sleek black SUV idling directly outside the lobby and Drake's driver standing beside it.

"Miss Ryder," Constantine calls. "Mr. James asked me to drive you home."

"Hi, Constantine," I say as he opens the car door for me. "How are you?"

I refuse to feel embarrassed about the last time we met, when I was bundled in the back of this very same car in the night-before's underwear and a crumpled dress. I felt ashamed and dirty after Drake basically asked me to leave and only agreed to the ride because I couldn't face the subway. And now, here I am again, confused by the way Drake blows hot and cold with no apparent concern for the way the rapid-fire climate change affects me. I have nothing to be embarrassed about, I tell myself.

"I'm doing quite well, Miss Ryder, thanks for asking."

"And the baby?" I add. I learned during our last drive that his wife gave birth to a little girl just a few months earlier, and he even showed me the most adorable photo of her. I so appreciated that simple act of kindness at the time, the reassurance that I didn't look like so much of a nasty tramp that he wouldn't risk giving me a glimpse of his precious daughter.

"She's fantastic. Now, how about you get in the car, and we can chat on the way back to your place?"

"I don't think so, Constantine. Not this time."

I glance through the open door, quashing the vague school-girl hope that Drake is actually sitting in there waiting for me.

"Please, miss. He didn't want you taking the subway alone so late at night."

It is late, and I am tired, but I always take the subway home. It's perfectly safe, and I don't need Drake's car. As if sensing my indecision, Constantine smiles at me. "My life won't be worth living if I don't take you home, Miss Ryder. And if I don't get home within the next hour, my wife will watch the next episode of *Bridgerton* without me. So cut me some slack here."

The plush leather seats will be comfortable and warm, and getting back to my apartment will be much quicker and easier if I say yes. But this feels off—like Drake is trying to apologize for ending our evening the way he did but doesn't have the decency to actually do it in person.

"How will Mr. James get home?"

"He expressed the desire to walk," Constantine replies, gesturing at the open car door once more. "He really will be upset with me if you don't get into this car, Miss Ryder."

I roll my eyes. "Yeah, you already told me that. Your life won't be worth living, right?"

"He'll make it absolute hell," he replies, grinning. I don't buy it for a second. I, of all people, know Drake can be a demanding boss, but Constantine doesn't strike me as the kind of guy who would allow anyone to make his life hell.

He arches an eyebrow, his gray eyes twinkling. "So?"

"Fine. But only for you," I say with a smile.

He places his hand over his heart. "Gracias, mademoiselle."

"You're such a charmer, and multilingual as well." I climb into the car with Constantine's low laugh in my ears. Sitting back against the supple leather seat, I rub my temples. It's been a long day, and I have to admit, this is a lot nicer than spending an hour on the subway. I get my phone out of my purse and go to my messages. There's one from my mom saying she's fine and turning in for the night and one from Kimmy asking how I'm doing. I tap out quick replies to both of them, then chew my lip as I stare at the screen. It's only polite to thank Drake for the use of his car.

Thank you for the ride. I'll see you tomorrow.

I contemplate putting a kiss at the end like I do for most of my text message conversations, even my dentist, but for Drake, that would be too much. He is my boss, after all. A boss I have history with. I stare at the screen, contemplating whether to press send or delete.

Without any more overthinking, I press send. My pulse spikes immediately, and I'm flooded with nerves as my message wings off into cyberspace. I see the little icon appear that tells me he's received the message and also read it. I hold my breath while I wait for a response with no idea what I'm hoping for, but I'm definitely hoping for something. No matter how hard I stare at the screen, willing him to reply, nothing lands. I don't suppose it was really the kind of message that needed a response, but it would have been nice. It would have stopped my worries about whether I crossed a line or not. But then he crossed a line tonight too, and we both know it.

After dropping my phone back into my purse, I lean back against the seat and look out the window. New York flies by in a blur of light, the river twinkling in the distance. So what if he hasn't replied? Maybe it's for the best.

I will choose to focus on the good stuff, not the anxiety-inducing stuff. We worked well together. We made a good team, and I helped him with his case. All of that is solidly placed in the win column.

That's not what I'll really remember about tonight, though, I know. What I'll really remember is the way his lips felt pressed against my ear and the words he whispered to me. Holy exploding donut balls, that man makes me melt.

FIFTEEN

DRAKE

"**F**uck!" I yell, throwing my glass of Scotch at the wall of the penthouse. The tumbler shatters, and amber liquid splashes all over the paint. It's a mess, but I don't give a shit right now. Everything else is a mess too.

What the hell was I thinking, agreeing to let her stay late and work with me? I never let anyone do that. I don't care how many law degrees they have or how much experience, I prefer to go it alone. Not even Nathan has been invited to help me prep for trial. I have a process, and it's never let me down.

And if I'm being reasonable about it, I have to admit that it didn't let me down this time. I adjusted my process to include Amelia, and without her, I might have been up all night getting those phone logs in order. I have faith that I would have gotten there in the end, but she certainly made it quicker and easier.

As she said, she's my secretary—the whole point of her job is to help me—so why do I feel so messed up about it all? How did I let it get to the stage it did, with the goddamn exploding donut balls and the way she described them like she was in a porno? I know she didn't mean it like that, that she was innocently discussing a dessert, but nobody told my dick that. In fact, the innocent look on her face as she went on about an "explosion of sweet heavenly cream in your mouth" only made my cock harder.

Jesus fuck. How am I going to get through this whole shit-storm without bending her over my desk and fucking her? From the minute she walked through my office door, it was all I could think about. She was wearing that damn wrap dress again, the one I always want to untie, and even worse, pearls. Pearls that were done in a little knot around her throat! The contrast between the demure look and the filthy thoughts running through my depraved mind was just too much. I should have followed my instincts and sent her straight home.

Except I didn't. And we worked well together. She has brains as well as beauty, and a big heart to complete the set. I don't talk about my mom to anybody outside the family, and even with them, I'm guarded. But Amelia seems to have this instinctive way of unraveling me. It's absolutely fucking terrifying.

Now, here I am, the night before the first day of trial on a major case, and all I can think about is her. The little sighing sounds she made when she was eating, how she giggled when I dropped a spring roll on my lap.

The stone-cold fury I felt when she mentioned her neighbor and I assumed Kris with a K was a guy. For fuck's sake, what is wrong with me? She's allowed to have neighbors who are men. She's allowed to have *men*, period. What do I want from the woman? I can't expect her to live the rest of her life as a born-again virgin just because I can't have her.

I walk over to the shattered glass and pick up the biggest shards. I'll have to apologize to housekeeping. And order a few bottles of Scotch. I've been hitting it pretty hard recently.

Sitting down behind my desk, I scrub my face with my hands and wish for clarity. I need to focus on work, and to do that, I need to chase her away, get her out of my head. It certainly doesn't help that I'm in the penthouse where I tasted her "explosion of heavenly cream." The quicker I'm in the loft in Tribeca that I'm buying, the better. It will be an Amelia Ryder–free zone. A Scarlet-free zone. A *her*-free zone.

This isn't easy for her either. I know I provoke her and that she feels weirded out by it all. I can sometimes see it happening, notice the little changes in her expression or her breathing. The way her eyes flash with temper or desire, often both. The times I see not only Miss Ryder, my very efficient secretary, but also Scarlet, the wanton sex goddess that lives inside her and only comes out to play every now and then. I'm obviously not good for either of them.

If I were in Chicago right now, I'd call the agency. I'd arrange for one of my regular ladies to visit my apartment and spend an hour or so with her and my ropes. It would soothe my mind and help me see everything more logically, and by the time she left, I'd feel better. Mentally and physically refreshed.

There must be similar establishments in New York, and it would be a simple enough process to find a willing and discreet companion for the evening. Yet it feels wrong somehow, and I can't bring myself to pick up the phone and do it.

Truthfully, I don't want to go anywhere near my phone right now. She sent me a message a little while ago, thanking me for the ride home. It was innocent, innocuous, thoughtful. It reassured me she was safe and not wandering the streets of New York looking like she does with her hands full of Thai food.

I didn't reply to her. Nothing good could come from anything I want to say to Amelia Ryder. My fingers hovered over the screen, itching to tell her not to go back to her place. To come here instead. I was overwhelmed with my desire to have her in my arms, in my bed, maybe in my whole damn life. I want her like no woman I've ever wanted before, and I have no clue what to do with this shit.

She's my secretary. I can't be the douche who screws his secretary—that's what her ex-husband did, for fuck's sake. But more than that, I can't be the douche who promises a woman something he can't deliver. I'm not a relationship guy, and she is very much a relationship woman. She deserves better than me. She deserves everything that I can't give her.

I can't believe I said what I did tonight, that I let her know how addicted I am to her.

The scent of her skin, how she bites her lower lip when she looks up at me with those big hazel eyes, the curves her stupid dress did nothing to hide—all of it drives me wild, and tonight I crossed a line. Tonight, I showed her that side of myself.

It sucks for me, but it's especially unfair to her. It's also completely unprofessional. I shouldn't be sitting here now thinking about this. I should be thinking about one thing and one thing only: the case. My work has always been my whole life. It has saved me in so many ways. Without my work, what am I? Merely an empty shell, I suspect.

Without my work, I am nothing. I can't allow myself to let my clients down or let my brother down. To let my family down.

This thing with Amelia has got to stop.

SIXTEEN

DRAKE

I don't see her again until late the next day. The hearing is going well thus far, and I have the feeling Callaghan's lawyers will be pushing him toward a settlement. They know there's blood in the water and that I've caught its scent. The rest is only a matter of time and money.

I'm pleased with the day's work, but I'm also aware that it easily could have gone the other way. Yes, Amelia's organizational skills and the extra pair of eyes helped me find a crucial piece of evidence. But Amelia's very existence meant I didn't get a wink of sleep all night, which caused me to start my day in the courtroom tired and distracted. Not her fault, but still not acceptable.

Part of me, the cowardly part, hoped that she wouldn't be here when I got back to the office. I wouldn't mind some time to decompress, maybe chat with Nathan and drink some decent Scotch. But no such luck. As I walk down the corridor toward my office, she jumps to her feet to greet me.

She doesn't have the wrap dress on today or that top with the big bow that drives me just as wild, but I realize that it doesn't matter. Even in the perfectly ordinary pantsuit she's wearing, I still want to unwrap her. The issue lies with the woman underneath the clothing, not with what she's wearing. She has her hair in a ponytail today, and as she trots toward me, her heels clacking across the marble floor, it swishes from side to side like a glossy horse's mane. I immediately imagine tugging on it, dragging her head back, and running my lips across her throat. I shift my briefcase in front of me. We're about to have a difficult conversation, and I don't want to have it while she's looking at my erection.

"How did it go?" she says, a bubbly smile on her face. "No, you don't need to tell me—it went great, didn't it? Callaghan's team has already been on the phone wanting to set up a meeting with you. I scheduled it for eight tomorrow morning. I hope that's okay. I mean, I don't want to presume, but if they're looking to cut a deal, it'd be good to get something on the table before court starts at ni ..."

She trails off and looks crestfallen as she takes in my grim expression. "Oh. Was I wrong? Didn't it go well? Or is it the meeting—have I done that wrong?"

I hate that I'm responsible for putting that look on her face. That I'm responsible for stealing her zest and banishing that gorgeous smile. But if I don't do this, I'll be responsible for a whole lot more—like wrecking her career and potentially breaking her heart. Never mind my own. Assuming I have one.

"It did go well, and an eight a.m. meeting is perfect, Miss Ryder. Could I see you in my office in a few minutes? Just give me time to make some calls."

She nods hesitantly. "Of course, Mr. James. Do you want anything to eat? There's fresh sushi in the executive break room."

I decline and go into my office, dismissing her. I haven't eaten all day, and by rights, I should be starving. Too bad all I can think about is Amelia and her goddamn exploding donut balls.

As soon as I close my office door behind me, I look for something to break. There's nothing in here I don't need, though, which is a situation that needs addressing. All offices should come equipped with something to break. I glance at the coffee cups and wonder if I actually need all of them.

Standing at the window, I stare out at the harsh lines and beautiful curves of the Manhattan skyline. Chicago was amazing, but damn, I love this city. I want to stay here. I want to see Luke grow up and be there for my dad as he gets older. I want to play a part in all my brothers' lives. I want to exorcise the ghosts of my pasts and help Nathan build his legacy. I want all of it so goddamn much.

But I also want to run. That small part of me that feels inadequate is perched on my shoulder like a devil, telling me I can't deal with everything that comes with me staying here: commitment, pain, obstacles to overcome. Fuck, I can't even deal with a sexy secretary.

I told her I had calls to make, but that was a bare-faced lie. I just needed a few moments to gather myself and to think. Not to mention let my cock recover its composure. As a man who prides myself on hiding my true feelings, I fucking hate that one part of my body insists on giving me away to her.

Except as I'm concentrating on taking deep breaths, I'm forced to admit that my feelings for Amelia go beyond a stiff dick and dirty thoughts. Otherwise, I'd just take both of those things and let them out to play somewhere else. The reason I'm struggling with all this, the reason I'm so disturbed by what I feel for her, is that she's different.

Unable to contain my churning emotions, I grab one of the colorful little espresso cups and hurl it at the metal filing cabinet, where it makes a satisfying cracking sound as it shatters.

Much better. I straighten my tie, go back to my desk, and pick up the phone. "Miss Ryder, I'm ready for you."

She walks into the room a few moments later and cautiously looks around. At the sight of the broken coffee cup, she raises an eyebrow.

"It slipped out of my hand," I say. "Please, take a seat."

Her mouth opens and closes a few times, and it's clear she doesn't believe me about the cup. Tough shit, that's all she's getting. Her fingers tremble slightly on her lap, and I curse myself for noticing and being bothered by it. I don't know why she's trembling—it could be because of this thing between us, or it could be because I started acting like a coldhearted asshole toward her as soon as things started to settle between us. It could even be, I realize, that she is once again sitting there with the thought that I'm going to fire her. I need to nip that one in the bud right away. She's a human being, and I have no right to mess with her head like this.

"First of all, Miss Ryder, I want to say that I am totally satisfied with your work. You are completely competent in every way."

"Uh ... okay. Thank you?"

"That said, I think we need to address a few issues. We've both tried extremely hard to navigate the situation we found ourselves in through no fault of our own. There is no blame on either side, but I think it's clear that it's becoming increasingly difficult to tolerate."

"Is it?" she says quietly, a shimmer of tears in her eyes. Fuck. Don't look at her, Drake. Don't see her cry. "It's not that clear to me. I thought ... well, I don't suppose it matters what I thought, does it? You're the boss, after all. Do you want me to leave today, or do I need to work a notice period?"

I glance away, giving her the time she needs to compose

herself. When I look back, she's clearly swiped at her eyes, leaving adorable little smudges of mascara beneath them.

"You won't be leaving, Miss Ryder. I have no intention of terminating your employment, please don't misinterpret me. You're good at your job, and nothing else that's happened should overshadow that. Your position at James and James is safe."

She tries to hide it, but I see her body sag slightly with relief and feel like a bastard for not getting there sooner. I knew she'd be worried, and "your job is safe" should have been the first words out of my mouth. Instead, I had to be all lawyerly and shit and build my way up to it. Fuck's sake, this is hard. Frankly, I'm not used to having to worry about anybody else's feelings, and that's always been exactly how I liked it. Which is good, because it turns out I'm pretty crap at it anyway.

"Oh. I see. So ... What exactly are you saying, Mr. James?"

I run my hands through my hair, over my face, and down my beard. The full no-water wash for stressed-out dudes.

"Look, Amelia. Can I be honest with you?"

"I don't know," she replies, her lower lip trembling even as she tries to be stoic. "Can you?"

I blow out a breath and decide to plunge right in. "Neither of us asked for this, did we? We didn't expect to ever see each other again, never mind end up working together. It's ... it's complicated. In all kinds of ways. When I first found out, I spoke to Nathan about it, and we discussed how best to proceed. I won't lie—letting you go was an option. But neither of us felt that was fair. I promised him that we could work it out and get through this without it blowing up in our faces. He was worried, obviously, about the HR implications ... not to mention the public image disaster it could potentially be."

Her eyes flash at me, and her hands ball up into fists. "And yeah, Amelia, before you go ballistic, I know. You're a human being, not a walking complication. I know you never had any intention of going public or making an official complaint or making life difficult for anyone. I know that, okay?"

"Good." She nods, her spine ramrod straight. "You saved me a speech."

I have to smile at her attitude, the way she's fighting so hard to keep herself together. I admire her as well as respect her, which only goes to show that I'm doing the right thing here. "This isn't on you, Amelia, but I'm struggling with the whole situation. I find you ... distracting."

"Distracting?" she echoes, her head tilted to one side and her shiny ponytail draped on her shoulder.

"Yes, I tend to get distracted by women I find attractive."

The blush that creeps over her cheekbones is so fucking cute. "You find me attractive?"

"Oh, come on. Of course I do. You already know that, surely?" Maybe she doesn't. She genuinely doesn't see herself as the knockout she is, which makes her even more adorable.

"Um, I suppose. But you have to understand ... that night at the wedding? That was ... well, that was the first time I ever had a one-night stand."

"I know. I was surprised, but you did mention it."

"Well, maybe what I didn't mention is that it was the first time I slept with anybody other than my husband."

I stare at her, taken aback at the fact that I'm only the second man she's ever had sex with.

A rogue voice pipes up in my mind. *I wish I was the first. And I damn well wish I could be the last.*

Fuck! What the hell is wrong with me?

"So, anyway, I only told you that so you'd know how inexperienced I am, Dra—um, sorry, Mr. James. I don't really have much to judge things by or compare them to, and I don't expect men to find me attractive. Especially not men like you."

Men like me? I let that one go. "But that night, you had to have noticed that I wanted you. I don't make a habit of fucking women who repulse me, Miss Ryder."

"No, I'm sure you don't, but ... Oh gosh, I don't know what I mean. I'm trying to tell you that I was different that night. I was Scarlet. And sometimes, I'm Scarlet around you even now. I behave in ways I wouldn't normally behave. I guess I'm trying to say that I get it. If we're both being honest, then I get it. I find it hard to be around you and not think about the things we did together. I find it hard not to ... imagine them happening again." She's staring at her hands, her cheeks blazing, and my dick is now so hard it's like having a metal bar between my legs. Jeez. This is exactly the problem.

"That's the issue right there, Miss Ryder. Those things can never happen again. Not only because of the company's image or the legal ramifications, but because I'm not a good man."

Her attention snaps back to my face. "Yes you are! You might not be a saint. You work too hard, and you talk like you've got a stick up your ass sometimes. And you definitely smashed that coffee cup and lied about it, but you *are* a good man. You care about your job and your clients, you love the shit out of your family, and you're ... well, you're a good listener. I get that you need to end this, whatever it is, but please don't do it that way. You are a good man."

I have no fucking clue how to respond to that. I'm doing what, dumping her? I'm not totally sure, but I'm not doing anything great to her. Yet she's still defending me. She has no fucking clue who I really am. "We'll have to agree to disagree on that, Miss Ryder," I say, keeping my voice calm and locking my emotions away. "And what kind of man I am is irrelevant. For the time being, you will continue to be my secretary, but as soon as a suitable alternative position opens up, you'll take it. I guarantee your salary and benefits will remain the same, and it will have no impact at all on your career prospects or your future with James and James. But you will be moving. Have I made myself clear?"

"Crystal clear, Mr. James," she says, her voice matching my ice but her eyes flashing with fire. "Do you have any idea of a timeline on that?"

"Not as yet, but I believe Mr. Darwin's assistant is due to go on maternity leave at some point in the next month or so."

Fred Darwin is in his sixties and married to a man named Pierre, so I feel reasonably confident that she'll be safe with him. I haven't even discussed this with Nathan, never mind Linda, but I can make it happen. Technically, it might not be the same salary band, but I'll damn well change the rules if I need to.

"Good," she says, standing up and smoothing down her jacket. "Well, let's hope for both our sakes that she doesn't go over her due date, shall we, Mr. James? Is there anything else I can do for you?"

"No, that will be all, Miss Ryder."

She nods and strides out of the room. Her ass looks phenomenal in those pants, and I bang my forehead on my desk as I feel my cock go hard yet again.

I hate that I've hurt her and that I have to freeze her out. But I have no other choice. It's the only way I'll be able to get her out of my head.

CHAPTER

SEVENTEEN

AMELIA

I'm smiling as I show Stu Parker into Drake's office. He's a new client, and this is his first time visiting us.

I always make an effort with clients, but on their first visit, I show them the executive lounge and ply them with food and drink as part of the charm offensive. Not that the firm needs me to win or keep clients—the place is thriving—but I see it as part of my job. I am a representative of James and James, and as such, my behavior matters.

Clients like Mr. Parker make it especially easy. He's a self-made millionaire in his sixties, a man who still wears jeans to work and has never forgotten his roots. He's so easy to talk to, I'd quite like him to adopt me. In the hour he's been in the building, he's learned all about my mom, I oohed and aahed over several dozen pictures of his granddaughters, and we discovered that he used to live three streets away from my mom's house in Brooklyn when he first started his plumbing business. He's absolutely adorable, the complete opposite of a snot-bucket, and the smile on my face as I knock on my boss's door is genuine.

It falters as soon as I hear his voice telling us to come in and almost disappears completely when I lead Mr. Parker through. Drake, as usual these days, completely ignores me apart from a curt nod. It's been over a week since he told me I'd have to go work for someone else, and I don't think we've exchanged more than a handful of words in all that time. He communicates more via email than by actually talking to me, and although I'm usually sitting right outside his office, I've barely seen him. I swear, he times his comings and goings to avoid having to interact with me. It sounds ridiculous, I know. He's a billionaire master of the universe; he has far better things to do than keep tabs on me.

I tell myself I'm fine with our new reality, that all I care about is my job, but I'm a big fat liar and my pants are on fire. I do care, and I die a little inside every time he snubs me. He's not rude, exactly. He's simply perfectly professional and devastatingly distant.

"Mr. Parker, it was lovely to meet you," I say, smiling up at him. "If you need anything, Mr. James will buzz through— make sure to say goodbye on your way out."

"I sure will, Amelia—and maybe I'll see you at Mario's one day. Man, those exploding donut balls are something else."

"I know, right?" I reply, ignoring the look of disgust on Drake's face. He really needs to learn to live with the fact that Mario's is the best.

"Thank you, Miss Ryder," my boss says sternly, gesturing toward the door with his head. "Mr. Parker is here for legal advice, not a roundup of New York's greatest food trucks. That will be all. Feel free to take your break."

Right. Well. He certainly told me.

He doesn't even meet my eyes when he dismisses me anymore, and I feel a little whoosh of pain as I obediently trot out of the room, my cheeks blazing with humiliation. When he first told me I'd be moving to work for someone else, I was hurt and upset. Now, after a week of getting the cold shoulder, I'm starting to look forward to it. Work shouldn't be this hard, especially when home isn't much better. My mom is still struggling despite her new medications, and I've ended up staying with her a few nights because I was so worried. None of which I've mentioned to Drake, of course, because he doesn't have the right to know anything about me other than what goes on within these walls during working hours.

I decide that I'll take him at face value and take my break. Before I head off, I quickly check my emails and see one from him marked "annual leave." It looks like he sent it a few minutes ago, before I saw him. In it, he informs me that I have already accumulated several days' worth of paid vacation time, and that I should consider booking it "at your earliest convenience." Wow. He really doesn't like having me around, does he?

Screw him. The man is an arrogant asshole. I just wish that he'd be consistent and always be an arrogant asshole. It's the flashes of humor and humanity that devastate me, the way that we sometimes seem to connect. Other times, he seems to wish he never met me. Given the opportunity to go back in time, I'd tell him to get lost the moment he sat down next to me at the wedding.

Except I wouldn't, I think as I grab myself a coffee in the break room. No matter how things have worked out long-term, I'd do it all again in a heartbeat. Even the memory of his mouth on my skin makes me squirm. The contrast between that and the way he behaves now is what's breaking me.

I pick up a bagel and sit down at an empty table, lost in thought. Every day feels like an endurance test right now, and my feelings for Drake James don't help. I want to hate him, I really do. Even better, I want to feel indifferent to him—that would be the best result. But the reality is that I can't stop thinking about him, not even when I'm alone. He's like a ghost, haunting my every waking moment and finding a way to get in on the action in my dreams too.

"Are you going to eat that bagel or stab it to death?"

I look up to see my friend Jacob standing next to my table with a wry smile on his face. He's right—all I've done with my snack is slice it and dice it.

"Definitely stab it to death," I reply as he sits down opposite me. "It's an evil bagel and deserves to suffer."

"Ouch! Is it a proxy bagel? A scapebagel, if you will? Does it look like your boss?"

"My boss? Why would you say that?" I snap back, immediately defensive.

"Easy tiger, it was just a joke. Are you okay?" He tilts his head and studies me closely. "You look a little upset."

"I'm okay, Jacob, thanks. And I'm sorry for biting your head off. Just ... life stuff, you know? Sometimes it's all a bit exhausting."

"Tell me about it," he says, reaching out to pat my hand comfortingly. "You know what you need?"

"A fresh bagel?"

"That"—he laughs—"and a night out. Let me take you to dinner, Amelia. Or the movies or dancing. Or all three. Whatever you like."

I look at his earnest face, his cute smile. He's a nice guy, and nice-looking too. He's kind and funny, and he's interested in me.

What he's not, though, is Drake James. And at the moment, I only have space in my head for one man—even if it is a man who infuriates me and has made clear that there will never be anything between us. Not even friendship.

"Maybe some other time, Jacob," I reply gently. I'm not in the business of hurting anybody's feelings if I can help it. "Things are a little hectic for me right now. I appreciate the thought, though."

I stand up, preparing to leave, and he gives me a warm smile. "Well, although I'm brokenhearted and unsure if I'll ever recover, you know where to find me if you change your mind."

I laugh and tell him I'll see him later, confident that his heart is made of far more resilient stuff. As I reach my desk on the upper floor, I bump into Mr. Parker exiting Drake's office.

"Mr. Parker," I say, frowning as he walks toward me. "Did something come up? Why are you leaving so soon?"

"Ah, honey, I just don't think it's going to work out with James and James. I think I'll be looking elsewhere for representation."

"Do you mind if I ask why? Did we not look after you?"

He gives me a reassuring smile and shakes his head. "You certainly did, Amelia. But to be honest with you, I just ..." He sighs and shakes his head. "I didn't like the way that man spoke to you. You can tell a lot about somebody's character from the way they treat their staff, and he was downright rude to you."

"Oh, Mr. Parker, please don't think that. Everybody has their off days, and Drake James is an amazing lawyer. He's completely dedicated to his clients. I guarantee you won't find anybody with a better legal mind or a stronger work ethic. Sure, he can sometimes come across as a bit of a snot-bucket, but that's not the real him, I promise you. He hides it well, but deep down, he's dependable and decent. Give him a chance. You won't regret it, I swear."

He frowns at me for a long second, then bursts out laughing. "Well, I have no clue what a snot-bucket is, but I can take an educated guess. I'll think on it, dear. I suppose he must have something going for him if a girl like you is fighting in his corner."

I force a smile, both happy and sad at the same time. Hopefully, Mr. Parker gives Drake a chance and discovers the million things he has going for him. I only wish that I was one of them.

EIGHTEEN

Amber has a way of looking at people so intensely that they usually do whatever she wants without noticing they've been manipulated. It's a combination of charm, insistence, and sheer force of personality. I've seen grown men come away from encounters with my sister-in-law shaking their heads, wondering why they just agreed to do something they had no intention of doing.

I've completed a study of the Amber Effect during the years I've known her, and recently, I realized what it is. She doesn't blink. Well, obviously she does—she's a human being, not a lizard—but she blinks less frequently than most of us, and when she does, it's a slow and sweeping gesture that makes you gaze at her long eyelashes in wonder. Personally, I think it's a type of hypnosis.

Right now, for example, she's telling me how much I should be wanting to help the retired clowns and carnies of the USA. I mean, it sounds ridiculous, right? Elijah and I sat in that gritty Irish pub and laughed about this exact thing. Yet here I am, finishing up lunch and finding myself deeply affected by the story of Ebenezer Daley, a ninety-two-year-old former trapeze artist who lost an arm in a terrible Big Top accident in Wichita.

"And then," she says, leaning forward and pinning me down with those huge brown eyes of hers, "after decades of entertaining the American people, he was left with nothing! Not even a trailer to call his own, Drake—can you imagine? He was a homeless, one-armed tightrope walker with no hope, no future, and nobody to help him!"

I'm caught up in her story and powerless beneath her unblinking gaze, but my lawyer brain kicks in just in time. "Hold on," I say, pointing a finger at her. "Didn't you say he was a trapeze artist? When did he morph into a tightrope walker?"

She tries to hold it together, but eventually she cracks and bursts out laughing. It's a joyous sound, Amber's laugh, and it always makes me sad that so few people in my family get to hear it. Even Nathan, who is one of the best judges of character I know, can't stand her. It's a long, complicated story with too many layers of misunderstanding and sadness to unpeel, but my brother's wife simply does not gel with most of the James family. Sadly, that includes Elijah, the man she's been married to for eighteen years.

She runs a hand through her thick caramel-colored bob and winks at me. "Damn, you're too good Drake. Yeah, I made it all up. I was going to make him a war veteran who used his circus skills to escape a POW camp, but the timeline didn't quite fit."

She sits back and turns serious. "But truly, it is a community that needs help. Not a lot of 401(k)s floating around in that world, and quite honestly, the lifestyle lends itself to a lot of injuries and ill health later in life. So, I can put you down for a table?" She balances her exquisite face on her steepled fingers and gazes at me. It's like sitting across from a sexy human version of Kaa from the Jungle Book—if Kaa had been interested in robbing you blind in the name of charity.

"Of course you can. Just don't necessarily expect me to sit at the table on the night of."

"Oh, don't be like that, you meanie." She pouts, pretending to be offended. My phone rings, and I see that it's a call from a man I never expected to hear from again: Stu Parker, the owner of the now-national Parker's Plumbing chain.

"Sorry, Amber, but I need to take this," I say, getting to my feet.

"That's fine, sweetie. I'll just carry on drinking while you're gone," she says, smiling and holding up her wine glass.

I head out of the dining room and find a quiet doorway before answering. "Mr. Parker. How nice to hear from you."

I'm intrigued as to why he's calling. It's been five days since our meeting, and I've been bothered by it ever since. He left abruptly, and all he said was that he didn't think we were "compatible." It's not like we're desperate for his business, but he would be a solid client, and I liked him. I like what he's done with his company, his ethics, and the way he carries himself with honesty and decency. To suddenly be told that he decided against signing with us, with me, came as an unpleasant surprise.

"Yeah, well, maybe," he says. "Look, Drake, I wondered if we could get a do-over? Maybe set up another meeting?"

"We could, Mr. Parker, if you think that would help. But first, I have to ask—what went wrong? If I don't ask, we're potentially wasting everyone's time, and we're both busy men."

I hear the sound of yelling and cheering in the background. "Sorry," he says, "I'm at my granddaughter's soccer game. It's a rough crowd. Right, yeah. The way you treated Amelia really bothered me."

I blink, not quite sure I heard right. "Could you repeat that, Mr. Parker?"

"For goodness' sake son, call me Stu, will you? And I think

you heard me the first time. Amelia. Your secretary. The lovely girl who showed me around the building and looked after me. I don't like the way you behaved toward her."

I have a completely illogical moment where I think he's talking about the night Amelia and I spent together. An unpleasant vision assaults me—her confessing all and complaining about how the big, bad boss had exploited her for a night of passion. No. That's absurd. She'd never do that.

"And how did I behave toward her?" I ask coldly. I might like him, but I certainly don't need his business badly enough to grovel or talk about my personal life.

"I can tell from your tone that you think it's none of my business, but if I partner up with someone, I want them to share my values. And one of my values is that I treat everyone with respect, no matter their pay grade or how fancy their job title is. You were downright rude to that girl when she was nothing but professional, pleasant, and completely damn charming."

Oh, fuck, I think, as I cast my mind back to the day of the meeting. It was an especially tough morning. She came into work wearing one of her plain-on-the-surface outfits that somehow managed to completely inflame me. The tight black skirt had a decorative lace-up section at the back that was just begging to be undone. I've never talked to Amelia about my interest in Shibari, but she seems to accidentally stumble across clothes that remind me of it all the damn time. I spent the whole morning trying not to think about sliding my hands over those laces, about untying that bow and sliding that skirt down her juicy ass ...

By the time she came back in with Mr. Parker, I was fit to burst and annoyed with myself for yet again allowing myself to get distracted. It's why I sent her the reminder that she needed to take her leave—I needed a few days off even if she didn't.

Then she breezed into my office, all smiles and sunshine, obviously having charmed the new client in exactly the right way—by talking about Mario's again. Am I the only guy on the planet who hates Mario and his fucking exploding donut balls?

Was I actually rude, though? Rude enough for someone else to pick up on it? Jesus, I obviously was. Uncomfortable heat floods me, and I realize that I'm ashamed of myself.

"Mr. Parker—Stu. I think you're right. I was, to use the proper legal jargon, an asshole. I'm not going to start making excuses or telling you stories, but I hope you believe me when I say I'm sorry you had to witness that. No, more to the point, I'm sorry I behaved that way. It's a complicated situation, but I accept full responsibility. I was wrong. Whatever you choose to do with your business, I wish you the best, and I thank you for your honesty."

"Rosalie, go! Yessssss!"

I can't help but smile at Stu's excitement. "Did she score?" I ask.

"She did! Off an incredible steal too. Anyway. I appreciate what you just said, and I can hear in your voice that you mean it. I asked around about you, and everything I heard was good. Plus, she really fought in your corner, and that says a lot."

"What do you mean?"

"Before I left your building the other day, she gave me a terrific speech about how you were a good man at heart. How I'd misunderstood, and how nobody would fight for me like you would fight for me. Not gonna lie, son, it moved me. Loyalty like that has to come from somewhere. I promised her I'd think about it, and I'm a man who keeps my promises. So, shall we meet next week?"

"I'd love to, Stu. Contact Amelia, and she'll set something up. Hope the rest of the game goes well."

I close down the call and stand still for a few moments,

gathering my thoughts. Fuck, shit piss, I eloquently rant within my mind. Sometimes those are the only words that do the job.

I treated Amelia like crap because I'm too much of a jerkwad to deal with her being around. And then, when a man like Stu Parker objected to that, she defended me. Persuaded him that I'm worth a second chance. That I'm a good man. Shit fuck. I have a lot of thinking to do.

I walk back into the dining room and see that Amber has not only finished her wine, but she's halfway through mine as well.

"I'm sorry," she says, shrugging cheekily with the glass at her mouth. "It jumped into my hand. What's a girl to do?"

"It's fine," I say, and even I can hear how absentminded I sound.

"Drake ... Are you okay?" she asks, all playfulness gone.

"I don't know. Do you—" I lean back and study her face for a long moment. "Do you think I'm a good man?"

"I absolutely do. One of the best I've ever known. Sometimes the fact that you seem to like me is the only assurance I have that I'm not a terrible person. And our friendship is sometimes the only thing that makes my life tolerable."

It's a bleak statement and completely at odds with the stylish, charming persona she projects to most of the world. Depending on her mood and who she's with, she can come across as an ice queen, a bitch, a charismatic hostess, or a tireless fundraiser. But so few people see this side of Amber James —the side that lives with constant pain.

"That's a terrible thing to say, Amber. Lots of people like you."

"Yeah, but it's not like they really know me." The husky sound she makes could be interpreted as a laugh if you weren't looking into her eyes. "Not like you do. And the irony is that I can't even tell Elijah the truth. I'm only sorry I dragged you into it."

I reach across the table and take her delicate hand in mine. "You didn't drag me into anything, and Elijah loves you and he always will, no matter what. Now, can I talk to you about a woman?"

Her gorgeous eyes widen, and her perfectly made-up lips curve into an O of surprise. "Oh darling, of course you can. I've been waiting years to hear those words come out of your mouth."

Steeling myself, I take a deep breath, then I pour my heart out to my sister-in-law, telling her all about the woman who haunts my every waking thought.

NINETEEN

AMELIA

I've been dreading today with an absolute passion. I considered calling in sick or resigning. I even considered sourcing a fake identity and moving to Costa Rica. But here I am, ready for the James and James New York office's annual team-building day. Hooray. Go team.

It's all being held at a swanky hotel in Long Beach, and everyone else seems thrilled about it. Free room, free food, free booze—I mean, what's not to like? Everything else, that's what. Like the fact that Linda from HR has given us all tasks to complete and we're all required to give presentations about our work. Worst of all, everyone is expected to take part in "trust workshops." What does that even mean?

I was complaining to Kimmy about it on the phone last night. "Come on," I said. "I can't be the only one who thinks it's crazy."

"I think you're being very cynical, Amelia," she replied, glasses clinking in the background. She was, unsurprisingly, at a bar. "It sounds to me like you're not being a team player."

"Maybe I'm not a team player. Maybe you wouldn't be

either if it involved spending a night in a hotel with Linda from HR."

"We all have a Linda from HR, my love, they come with the office space. Show her some love, she'll open up like a little flower."

I snorted in response to that. "Yeah. One of those carnivorous flowers that eats secretaries for breakfast."

"An Amelia flytrap?"

"Exactly," I replied, folding a pair of socks and adding them to my overnight bag.

"Will there be men there?" she asked. "Or women, of course, if I can persuade you to be a little more open-minded."

"It's not about being open-minded, and you very well know it. I'm just not sexually attracted to women."

"More's the pity. It doubles your dating pool. And you didn't answer my question."

"Yes, Kimmy, there will be men there. And no, Kimmy, I'm not planning on fucking any of them. And bye, Kimmy, I've got to go finish packing. Or get takeout from that place that gave us horrendous food poisoning last March. That might be less painful."

The last sound I heard was her laughter as I hung up, which did at least make me smile. I told myself Kimmy probably had the right attitude. I shouldn't be taking this too seriously. And anyway, it might be fun.

But now I'm here. And so far, it is not fun. The name tag I was given at registration only serves to remind me of Emily's wedding, thus tanking my already sour mood.

Our office has almost two hundred employees, and most of them seem to be milling around the bar, drinking the breakfast mimosas and chatting. The atmosphere is more like a high school reunion than a serious work event. We're all getting split up into different groups, and I'm nervous about what might come later. I don't enjoy public speaking or being the center of attention. Maybe it's not too late to pretend I've just come down with a mild case of the Bubonic plague.

Keeping to the edges of the crowd, I spot Jacob across the lobby and give him a cheery wave, then say hi to a couple women I recognize from the break room. I know there's an active social life among the staff, but it's not something I've ever thrown myself into, no matter where I worked. Lack of money, lack of time, and lack of inclination, I suppose. I prefer to hang out with Mom or meet up with Emily or Kimmy. Making new friends requires so much effort, but as I look at all the smiling faces around me, I wonder whether I should try harder. Everyone seems to be having a great time with one another.

Even at my temp jobs, I usually had a handful of friendly acquaintances that I could grab lunch with outside the office on occasion. Thanks to being so caught up in Drake, I haven't even managed that.

As though I've conjured him up ... "Miss Ryder," he says, "fancy seeing you here." I hate how his deep, rich voice still makes me melt no matter how mad I am at him. It is so unfair.

"Mr. James. I ... I didn't expect to see you," I say after I turn to face him. I blocked his calendar for this but assumed he'd stay back in the office and catch up on work. I certainly didn't anticipate him choosing to be anywhere near this—or me, for that matter. "Surely you don't have to take part in this, this, um ..."

"Vitally important morale-boosting corporate retreat?"

"Yeah. That."

"Well, I do actually. As does Nathan. Though he's brought his wife with him, so he'll probably be having a much better time. It wouldn't send a very good message if the named partners didn't turn up to their own retreat, would it? I can tell from your face that you don't have high expectations, but give it a chance. It can be fun."

"Fun?" I repeat, staring up at him. He's dressed in what is, for him, casual wear—a short-sleeved navy-blue shirt that makes his biceps pop and tailored black pants that hug his muscular thighs. He looks like sex would look if it had a body and walked around. "Since when have you been interested in fun?"

He lifts his eyebrows and points to his name badge. I'm surprised it only says *Drake James* and not *God*.

"Remind you of anything?" he asks, his tone neutral.

"No," I say firmly. "Nothing at all. What do you ... Look, why are you talking to me like this? Is it part of a trust exercise? Because if it is, you've failed."

A flicker of something crosses his face, but I can't quite decipher it. Most likely anger. I probably shouldn't have said any of that, but he caught me unaware, and my usual facade isn't in place. Besides, according to the HR memos, one of the whole points of holding this event on neutral territory is that it leads to "open and transparent communication" across departments. If he doesn't like me being open and transparent, he'll have to take it up with Linda.

"You don't trust me?" he says quietly, his eyes intense on mine. He's standing way too close for comfort, and he has way too much skin on display. I shove my hands into the pockets of my jeans because I don't want them to reach out and touch those powerful forearms. I don't even want to be in the same room as them.

"Look, Mr. James—"

"I'm Drake today, and you're Amelia. Unless you want to be Scarlet again?"

Oh sweet lord, what is he doing? His gaze rakes over my body and lingers on my hair, which is tied up in a tidy ribbon on the top of my head. I erred on the side of caution in case I was forced to bungee jump or abseil down the side of a building to prove my loyalty to the firm.

"I have no intention of *ever* being Scarlet again. At least not with you. You're flirting with me, Mr. James, and it's freaking me out. Because no, I don't trust you, not anymore. You've spent the last two weeks freezing me out and shutting me down. You've barely spoken ten words to me in person outside of 'that will be all, Miss Ryder.'" I lay down a real thick pompous accent for that part.

"Basically, you've been an asshole. And you know what? That's okay. I understand your reasons, and if it's possible for assholery to come from a good place, I get that yours is. I appreciate the fact that, as far as you're concerned, you are being fair by letting me keep my job while you keep your distance. But you can't suddenly expect me to not be confused when you go from that to this ... Whatever the hell *this* is." I realize that my voice has gone up a few decibels and glance around nervously. Luckily, the noise level in here is similar to an airplane runway, so nobody seems to have noticed.

He grabs hold of my elbow and guides me, not especially gently, toward a quiet spot in the hallway. He pushes open a door and reveals a storage room containing stacks of fold-up chairs.

"I'm sorry," I say hastily as he bundles me in front of him, his face like thunder. "I shouldn't have spoken to you like that."

Being alone with him makes me feel suddenly vulnerable. He's a big man, and his proximity has me scared and turned on at the same time, which is so screwed up. Why has he brought me here? What does he intend to do that he can't do in public? Strangle me, perhaps? Kiss me? Kick me out of his life?

He closes the door behind him, and I back away as far as I can, only stopping when my ass hits the wall.

"No, you should have spoken to me like that," he replies, looming over me, his eyes scanning my face like he's trying to memorize it. "I deserved it, and I'm the one who's sorry."

He places a hand flat against the wall next to my head and stares at the topknot of my hair. He's so close I can barely breathe, and it would be so easy to reach out, lay my palms on his hips, and pull him toward me. I can smell his cologne, and it goes straight to my core. Dammit, even when he's harassing me in a storage closet, this man makes my panties wet.

"Stu Parker called," he says, every touch of his eyes feeling intimate and erotic. "He told me what you said. And he told me what he thought of me. He was right. I've been acting like a dick to you, and I apologize. Nothing has changed—we still can't ..." His hand drifts to my hair, and his pupils dilate as he gently tugs on the ribbon I had it all tied up with. I gasp at the contact, and he groans as my hair tumbles down over my shoulders. His fingers run through a few strands, and I automatically lean into his touch. My hips rock forward as though they have a mind of their own, and my eyes go wide when I feel how hard he is.

He skims his fingers down my cheek to my jaw and tilts my face up. His almost-black eyes bore into me.

"I am sorry, Amelia. I've been a jackass. I ... I'm a mess when I'm around you, and I've been so busy trying to hide it that I forgot your feelings. But like I said, nothing has changed. This is still wrong. This is still a bad idea."

It might be a bad idea, but gosh do I want it. The feel of his erection pressing into me leaves me in no doubt that he does too. My nipples are ready to pop through my bra, my pussy is clenching and shaking, and my hands have somehow found their way to his ass. This doesn't feel very professional at all. It feels absolutely delicious, and I know I'd let him strip me down right now if he tried. I clearly have a lot more lust than I have self-respect.

A knock comes on the door, jolting us both out of the moment. "Mr. James?" a voice calls. "Are you in there?"

Shit. It's Linda. We both freeze, and I clamp my hand over my mouth to stop myself from laughing. A few seconds pass, and we hear her say, "I don't know where he is, Susan. Someone said they saw him going in here, which is obviously nonsense. I swear, that man drives me crazy. He might look good, but I wouldn't object if he went back to Chicago and ..."

Her voice fades as she moves away, and we finally give in to the laughter. He puts some distance between us, and I very deliberately don't look at his groin. "Linda fancies you," I say, straightening my hair.

"She does," he replies. "I'm a lucky man. Though a little heartbroken that she wants me to go back to Chicago."

"Well, personally, I think you should put in a complaint with HR. You shouldn't have to tolerate being objectified like that."

I'm arranging my hair back into its ties and ribbon, and he's watching every move I make. "Leave it down."

I raise my eyebrows at him and see that he means it. "Um, no. Thank you for the apology, Mr. James, but you don't get to tell me what to do. You may be the boss of me at work, but this is a team-building day, right? So, let me communicate with you, openly and transparently—I'll wear my hair however I like it."

His lips twitch with a hint of a smirk while his dark eyes narrow. He's both pissed and amused—a dangerous combination. I roll back my shoulders. This is going to be a long day.

IT TURNS out that Drake is hosting my group's first session, and predictably enough, he does a great job. We all made our way into a large meeting room, the atmosphere still lighthearted and jovial, and after yet another round of refreshments, he took to a small podium at the front. He made a few jokes about the corporate world, spoke with genuine passion about the company and its ethos, and then basically told everyone that they should forget who he is for the next several hours because this day isn't about him, it's about us.

It could have sounded corny, but the way he delivered it left the crowd in no doubt that he genuinely believes in what he's saying. He truly believes in James and James and that we are all an essential part of it. I know he's a lawyer and he's used to performing, but I still buy into it, and from the sound of the applause echoing around the room, so does everybody else.

He calls people up by name and invites them to take their spot at the podium and share a little information about themselves and their role in the firm. There's a huge variation in how everyone manages this part of the proceedings—some simply stutter their names and job titles and clearly can't wait to escape, and others come complete with PowerPoint presentations and slides. One guy —the never-to-be-forgotten Drew, executive manager of catering services—even had his own theme song. He shimmied up to the podium to the sound of Kelis singing "Milkshake," then told us all about how many tons of fruit and how many gallons of milk it takes to provide us all with our smoothies, shakes, and lattes each year. It made us all laugh, but it also caused me to consider how much work goes on behind the scenes to make the small things happen—which I suppose is part of the point of a day like today.

Eventually, Drake looks down at his notes and smiles. "Now," he says, "as most of you know, I've been running the Chicago office for several years. That means that today is the first opportunity I've had to meet a lot of you in person. Our final team member, though, is one I know well. Really well. Please put your hands together for my assistant, Amelia Ryder."

He makes eye contact with me as I shuffle along my row of

chairs and walk nervously toward the front of the room. He quirks one eyebrow, and to anybody else at all, it would mean nothing. Just a boss acknowledging his employee. But I am hypersensitive to everything this man does, and that simple quirk of an eyebrow, along with his mischievous smile, is enough to make my heart hammer harder. I was already nervous, and now I have him telling the whole room that he knows me "really well." Nobody else will suspect that he knows me so well he knows how my orgasms taste. But still ... I know. And he knows. And that's enough to knock me further off-balance.

He applauds as I walk toward him and gestures for me to take his spot. With every other guest, he's stood off to the side or behind them. With me, he changes it up, taking a seat in the front row so he can see me.

I stare down at him, my throat dry and my hands clammy, wondering what on earth to say. The room is packed with people looking up at me, but he's the only one I can see. He meets my eyes and actually winks. Damn him. He's messing with my head, and he knows it. Well, two can play at that game. It's definitely time to be more Scarlet. I take a deep breath. I can do this. Or at least she can.

"Hi!" I say brightly to the assembled group. "Can I get anyone a coffee? Would you like me to run to the deli for you? Should I order your wife some flowers or order your mistress some diamonds? Does your dry cleaning need picking up? Would it help if I answered your phone so I can blow off the people you can't be bothered talking to? And then can I get you some more coffee?"

There are chuckles around the room, and I see some people nodding. I'm guessing the ones who have similar roles to mine. Drake looks momentarily taken aback, especially at the word "mistress," but then he settles back in his chair with an amused look on his face.

"I'm guessing most of you don't have secretaries or assistants, or whatever you want to call them. Most of you probably learned long ago how to get your own coffee, buy your own lunch, and remember your own wife's birthday. As for the mistresses, I'll leave that well enough alone, it's none of my business. But one of the perks of being truly successful, not only at James and James but at most companies, is that you get to basically unlearn all that stuff. You get someone else to do it for you. You get a babysitter. Mr. James says he knows me really well, and to some extent that's true—but how well does he actually know me? Shall we see?"

There's a chorus of cheers and people yelling "Yeah!" and other words of encouragement. I put my hand on my hip and tilt my head as I look at Drake. "Are you up to the challenge, *sir*?"

He narrows his eyes at me, and I know I'm playing with fire here. But he started this. He cornered me in a storage room and messed with my hair. He *winked* at me, goddamn it!

"Sure," he shouts back up at me. "Go for it." That earns him a round of applause too, and I grin at him. He smiles back, and I'm glad nobody else can see that smile, because it is downright wicked.

"All right. Mr. James, what star sign am I?"

"I have no clue at all, but your birthday is September Ninth."

I'm genuinely surprised he knows that, but I suppose it is in my employee file. "Correct. That makes me a Virgo, by the way."

"Good to know. Make sure to order yourself some flowers from me. Or diamonds, if that's what you prefer."

The room erupts into wolf whistles and cheers at that one, and I join in with the laughter. I can't believe I'm standing up here in front of all these people, verbally jousting with Drake. He's kind of flirting but doing it so publicly that it almost doesn't count—the room full of witnesses makes it harmless banter. At least to them. His knowing smile almost melts my panties off, but they don't know that.

"Okay. Next question. Am I a dog person or a cat person?"

He chortles and says, "Trick question. You like dogs and cats, but when you were a kid, you kept rabbits."

Wow. He's totally right, but I genuinely don't remember telling him that. It's hardly sexy pillow talk, but I suppose it must have crept out at some point on the night of the wedding —it definitely wasn't on my job application. "Very good, Mr. James. You must have been paying attention in class."

"Well, you're an excellent teacher, Miss Ryder. Next question?"

"Right. Okay ... What's my middle name?"

This is also a trick question. My middle name is actually Amelia, which I've always been known as. My first name is Nora, after my long-gone grandmother. Mom gave me the name as a gesture of love toward her own mother, but she said it didn't really suit me and raised me very much as an Amelia. I have no clue if Drake is aware of this or not.

"Ah. Well, that one's easy," he replies, giving me that lopsided grin that always makes my tummy flutter. "Your middle name is Scarlet."

Without breaking eye contact, he runs his hands along his thick thighs and leans forward. He's undone the top button of his shirt, and even that tiny flash of exposed flesh is enough to make me lick my lips. I remember so vividly the first moment I laid eyes on him, sitting at that table at the wedding. He was so good-looking that I could barely speak, and although we've come a long way since then, he still takes my breath away.

"Close enough, Mr. James, close enough. Though I let you

off easy. I didn't get into any of the really tricky stuff, like what Hogwarts house I am or what my favorite karaoke song is."

He stands up and walks toward me. His eyes are on mine, and despite the chatter of the watching crowd, it still feels like we're the only two people in the room.

"Well, I look forward to finding out more about you, Miss Ryder. But for now, would you mind getting me a coffee?"

He earns some laughter and jeers for that, and I smile and wave to everyone as I walk back to my seat. Now that the adrenaline rush has passed, I feel weak at the knees and amazed at what I just did. I didn't only stand in front of a packed room and speak; I called Drake out in public. He played along, but he didn't really have much choice, and I wonder if he'll make me pay for that later. Part of me hopes he does. The idea of being punished by Drake is more than a little exciting. What the hell is wrong with me?

The rest of the morning passes in a blur of meetings, games, and a surprisingly amusing scavenger hunt around the hotel. I'm aware of Drake, of course, and our paths cross frequently throughout the day. He's polite each time, friendly and approachable—the polar opposite of the way he's been treating me recently.

My feelings for Drake are complicated, and I'm not sure I entirely understand them myself. I know I feel more physically drawn to him than I've ever felt to anyone and that when things are going well between us, I enjoy his company. And I know that he can be kind, funny, and easy to talk to. But I also know that he can be unpredictable, cold, and dismissive. It's the not knowing which one I'm going to encounter that makes him dangerous, this constant game of "will the real Drake James please stand up?"

Today has been good. I got a version of Drake James that I like and who seemed to like me back. Tomorrow? Who knows.

For now, though, I put him out of my mind for a few moments while I sit outside in the gardens. It's a beautiful summer day, and the blue sky and birdsong are the perfect accompaniment to my break-time coffee. I'm messaging my mom, trying to persuade her to come to the movies with me this weekend. One of the theaters in Times Square is showing a back-to-back Indiana Jones marathon, and Harrison Ford is her all-time favorite actor. So far she's a definite no, which is disappointing.

"Amelia? Are you okay?"

I look up and see Drake himself standing before me. I shield my eyes against the sunlight. "Yes, I'm fine, why?"

"You looked kind of sad. May I?" He gestures at the bench, and I nod. He sits next to me, and I shuffle away when I realize he's close enough for our thighs to touch.

"I've been trying to convince my mom to come out with me. To go see a movie. She used to love that, but now she's more or less housebound, says she finds it too overwhelming to be out and around too many people. So I suppose I am sad, yeah. I want her to enjoy life again, you know?"

"Of course you do. What kind of movies does she like?"

"Oh, all of them. She'll give anything a chance. Big block-busters, little art-house flicks, rom-coms, thrillers—she has very eclectic taste. But she especially loves Harrison Ford, so I was trying to tempt her with some *Raiders of the Lost Ark* action. No go, sadly."

"I'm sorry," he says, his tone sympathetic. "It's so hard to see them reduced, isn't it?"

"Reduced. That's a good way of putting it. And yeah, I hate it."

He gazes off into the distance, and I guess his mind is drifting back to his own past. "My mom fought like hell against the cancer that eventually claimed her. She had a warrior spirit, and she tried so damn hard not to let it defeat her. But near the end, she was in so much pain—and loaded up with so many drugs—that she just wasn't herself. This proud, magnificent woman was confused, saying things she never would have said normally. She was, well, reduced. Realizing she wasn't super-human after all came as a shock to all of us. I suppose with your mom, all you can do is what you are doing—keep trying and always be there for her. Make the most of every minute you have together."

He doesn't add "because you never know which might be your last." He doesn't have to. The thought is lurking there between us, and his eyes are full of pain and regret. I reach out and touch his hand. He gazes down at my consoling fingers and squeezes them briefly in his.

Then he stands up and gestures back to the hotel entrance. "Come on, Nora. We'd better get back in. We can't let Linda catch us holding hands. Plus, it's time for the trust exercises."

"Nora? You knew that all along?"

"Sure I did. I'm not the kind of guy to leave a personnel file unread."

I pull a face behind his back but follow him inside.

CHAPTER

TWENTY

AMELIA

W e've been split into groups again for the afternoon activities, and the first one involves blindfolds and an obstacle course. It's a lot more fun than I expected. One person has their eyes covered with a bandanna while the rest of the team provides verbal instructions to guide them over steps and around chairs. It's pretty hilarious, especially when it becomes clear that some people still haven't figured out their left from their right.

After that, we're put in a circle and have to hold hands in different shapes, forming something called a human knot, and then we are put into revolving pairs to practice eye contact. That one is a lot harder and a lot more fun than it sounds, depending on who you're paired with—sixty seconds can fly by or it can take forever. One of the girls I recognize from the mail room keeps sticking her pierced tongue out at me when none of the prison guards—sorry, facilitators—are watching, and it cracks me up every time. My final partner is Drake, and as he settles down across from me, both of us cross-legged on our bean bags, the thought of spending sixty seconds gazing into his eyes makes me so nervous I can't speak.

"Just breathe," he says quietly, obviously picking up on my reaction. "It'll all be over before you know it."

I nod, and the bell that tells us it's time rings out. He's sucking on his upper lip, and his gentle smile is uncertain. Is he as nervous as I am? Our eyes meet, and again that strange thing happens: the rest of the world just seems to drop away. It is me and it is him and it is us. Nothing else matters. Nothing else even exists.

Drake's dark, shining eyes have always held power over me. They have a way of pulling me in and keeping me close. Being given permission to stare into them is an exhilarating experience, especially as we're not allowed to talk. This is all about silent communication, about acknowledging the person opposite us and facing them without fear. Making ourselves vulnerable. I don't need a training exercise for that—Drake always makes me feel vulnerable. But he also makes me feel alive, awake to the potential of the world, and aware of my body and mind in a way that is beyond confusing.

We sit, eyes locked, and I completely lose myself in him. Although we're not physically touching, I feel the heat of the connection stretching between us, a live wire of sensation that threatens to overwhelm me. I can barely breathe by the end of it, and I wonder if he feels the same or if I'm being crazy. Am I deluded, or is his breathing coming a little faster too? What do I really see in his eyes, and what does he see in mine?

If I could send him a message, if I could cut through the white noise and tell him how I really feel, what would my eyes say to him? I want him so much that I ache with it. I respect him. I like him. I ... I love him? Could that be true? Or is this merely infatuation?

No, I realize, the shock of it like a slap across the face. I love him. I really do. I've been trying to deny it, even to myself, but something about this silly corporate game has stripped away my defenses, and I can't lie anymore. I love Drake James, even though he can never be mine.

We're both still sitting cross-legged on the floor when the bell rings again. Tears sting my eyes, and he looks just as intense as I feel. "Drake ..." I murmur, feeling the sweet torture of being so close to him and yet so far away.

"I know," he says on a sigh.

I don't have time to ask him what it is he knows because the world that didn't exist a few seconds ago is now coming back to life around us. The next exercise begins. He smiles slowly at me as people start to move about, and it's a smile that makes me bite my lower lip in anticipation. What exactly I'm anticipating, I have no idea.

He stands effortlessly and holds out his hand to help me up. I feel bewildered and bothered and completely bewitched, and the touch of his fingers on my palm isn't helping. I pull away, because if I don't, I won't be able to stop myself. I'll tug him down toward me, kiss him, hold him, let myself be swept away in those strong arms ...

I'll tell him that I love him. That I need him. That I've never felt like this about anyone.

"Ladies and gentlemen!" one of the instructors calls out. "Time to take a leap of faith."

I back away from Drake and lose myself in the crush of bodies. The excited hubbub of chatter swallows me up, background noise that I don't understand. Everything is too loud, too colorful, too much. It's like the world has turned into a cartoon acid trip, and I'm trapped in the middle of it. I stagger backward, unaware where I'm going but knowing I need to get away from Drake. I need to be alone to think, to feel. To be safe.

I bump into a wall that turns out to be a person. One of the facilitators, a guy with a shaved head and kind blue eyes. He takes my hand and holds my arm up in the air. "Our first volunteer." He looks down at my name badge. "Amelia Ryder, thank you for your trust."

What on earth is happening? I've somehow wandered all the way to the far side of the room where a small set of portable stairs have been placed next to a table. The facilitator takes my silence as agreement and leads me toward the steps. They're not terribly high, but they're not nothing either. I shake my head, trying to find the words to tell him this was a mistake, but I've been struck mute. Everyone is cheering and clapping, and someone has started a chant of my name. "A-me-li-a!" they shout in time. "A-me-li-a!"

I find myself standing on the table, looking around with dazed eyes. The chanting is getting louder, my name being yelled faster and faster, accompanied by the heavy thudding bass line of people stomping their feet. I feel like a gladiator about to be thrown to the lions. How the hell did I end up here?

I see Drake among the crowd, his lips pressed into a thin line of concern. He isn't chanting, he isn't stomping. Our eyes lock, and my heart flutters helplessly in my chest. The facilitator takes hold of my shoulders and turns me around so I'm facing him. He nods at me, smiles, and whispers words of encouragement.

I suck in a deep breath. Hear my name being called. Remember how I felt when I was looking into Drake's eyes.

I plunge backward. Falling, falling, falling ... falling into his arms. The scent of his cologne teases my nostrils, the soft swoop of his hair tickling my skin as he holds me tight. "I've got you, Amelia," he whispers into my ear. "I've got you."

TWENTY-ONE

AMELIA

I retreated to my room as soon as I could after watching half a dozen colleagues take the leap of faith themselves. I was unable to pay attention and felt like my brain was disconnected from my body, like someone pulled the cord. Drake made sure I was all right, which I faked well enough for him to let me go, but truthfully, I wasn't. I suspect he knew that, but when I took off early, there wasn't much he could do about it. He's the boss, so he had to see this thing through.

I took a long shower, ordered some room service sandwiches that I have yet to touch, and climbed into bed. The whole hotel has been booked out by James and James, and I can already hear the signs of it turning into party central. There's a low thump of music coming from the floor above, and the sound of a woman's laughter floats in through the window. It's still relatively early, but a lot of them have been drinking all day, starting with the mimosas. That's obviously part of the whole deal and maybe why people look forward to this every year instead of dreading it.

Me, though? I'm not in a party mood. Drake being a cold-hearted bastard toward me hurt, but I survived it. I told myself that he meant nothing to me. That I would do as he suggested and move across the building to work for Fred Darwin, and we would simply avoid each other. To be safe, I'd never have a one-night stand again, and that would be the end of the whole damn thing.

But Drake today? Drake apologizing? Flirting with me, touching me, holding me. That was too much. That and the stupid trust exercises have broken me in two and made me realize how deeply this thing runs between us. At least on my side.

I shiver a little in the air conditioning of the room and pull the duvet closer around me. I need to get up and get dressed, I know. I need to at least show my face downstairs, even if I don't throw myself into the social whirlwind.

I check in on Mom first and see that a message has come in from Kimmy.

Having fun yet?

I grimace, not at all sure what the answer to that is.

I jumped off a table and got caught in the arms of my super-hot boss.

As soon as it shows as read, my phone rings, and I have to smile. Kimmy never knowingly turns her back on gossip. I haven't told her that Drake is the guy I had my wedding sex with. It's not that I don't trust her. I do. It's just that I haven't seen her in person. The last time we met face-to-face was the night before I started work at James and James. I really need to be breathing the same air as her before I can tell her the whole story. Like I said, she loves to gossip. While I know she wouldn't tell anyone who shouldn't know, I still want to look her in the eyes and make her promise that before I breathe a word.

"You know you're my sister from another mister, right?" she says as soon as I pick up.

"Uh-huh, I do."

"Well, as your sister—your big sister by all of three months—I have some advice for you. Go and fuck the hot boss, right now!"

I laugh. She makes everything sound so simple. It must be glorious to live in Kimmy's world.

"I'm not drunk enough," I reply.

"Well, there's only one way to remedy that. Do you have a minibar?"

I took note of the minibar when I first checked in but had no intention of partaking. The prices in those things are usually through the roof, and a miniature vodka probably costs as much as a car, but this trip is all expenses paid. James and James doesn't stint when it comes to employee care. I open the door and see that it's fully stocked. "Okay, you're right. About the drinking bit, anyway. I think I'll go for a ... hmmm. Wine, beer, or spirits?"

"Yes."

I laugh again and decide to keep it simple with a bottle of Budweiser. I sit back on the bed, propped against the pillows with my beer and my pastrami on rye. A simple meal, but what else do I need? The last hotel I was in was the Grand Regent with Drake, and that was a night of champagne and fine Scotch—and a morning of gourmet breakfast. It was great, but I suspect I'm more a bottle of Bud kind of girl.

"So, are you going to fuck the boss?" Kimmy asks. "And if not, should I? If he's that hot, I could try him out for you, maybe write up a review on PrickAdvisor?"

"Thanks for the offer. That's so kind of you, but I think I'll pass. On fucking him myself and also on you doing it by proxy. He's my boss. That would be ... messy."

"Even better. What's life without a little mess?"

"Tidy?" I suggest. "Organized? Safe?"

"Oh, give me a break—isn't that what you had with Chad the Cad?"

I take a big bite of my sandwich to buy some time. And because damn, this sandwich is freaking delicious. She's right, I know. At the time, I thought I loved Chad, but part of me stuck with him because he was safe. We'd been together since we were kids, and he was all I knew. He was like a comfort blanket in human form—until he wasn't. But now, I know that what I felt for Chad was nothing. It was a puny spark compared to a forest fire. Physically, emotionally, intellectually even—Drake is ten times the man Chad ever was. He's made me feel more in the last few months than Chad did in a lifetime together.

"You know what, Kimmy, I think you might just be right."

"Of course I am. About what?"

"About everything. I need to live more, don't I?"

She doesn't answer straight away, but when she does, she sounds uncharacteristically serious. "Babe, you really do. I know things haven't been easy for you, especially recently, with your mom and your marriage and money. But you're way too young to hide yourself away. None of us have a clue how long we have on this glorious, fucked-up planet of ours, so maybe it's time for you to start really going for it. You might make mistakes. You might crash and burn. But guess what? We all do. And your sister will always be here waiting to pick up the pieces."

"Kimmy, stop it—you're making me cry."

She chuckles, and I can picture her mischievous expression. "All part of the service, ma'am. Now, stop talking to me and go fuck someone, will ya?"

After she hangs up on me, I finish my beer and look around my room, listening to the sounds coming from upstairs. I have no desire to join the party, to get wasted, or to find someone to fuck. Not just anyone, anyhow. There's only one man I want to be anywhere near, and although I know it's wrong, I can't help thinking that he feels the same way.

Kimmy's words still ringing in my ears, I throw on some clothes, brush my hair, and add some mascara. I don't look like a model headed to a fashion show, but as I study myself in the mirror, I realize that I look okay. Chad never complimented my appearance, and I never thought anything of it because I've never felt deserving of them. But now that I take the time to really look, it's easy to see some of what Drake sees when he looks at me the way he does. I have curves, and I'm not a size zero. But there is nothing wrong with me at all, and Chad can go fuck himself. Boy, that felt good to say—even if only in my own head.

I will go downstairs and see what happens. I will socialize. And I'll talk to Drake. I'm already in love with the man, so what do I have to lose? Apart from hope, self-respect, and dignity, that is. I'll leave it to fate.

I pass several rooms with open doors that each contain groups of people drinking and dancing and even spot Linda from HR in the hallway, sipping a clear drink with a wedge of lime on the rim. She nods at me as I go by, her mouth not quite smiling, but not set in her usual scowl either. It is indeed a time of miracles.

The elevator carries me down to the lobby, and as the doors open, I'm immediately confronted with the sight of Drake chatting with Nathan. I dart behind a huge potted plant that's almost as tall as I am. If they turn around now, they'll see my head perched on top of the greenery, like I've morphed into a giant yucca. Shit. I might have thought I wanted to leave things with Drake up to fate, but I didn't expect for him to be the first thing I laid eyes on. I need a second to recalibrate.

I watch sneakily as the two of them chat and am once again struck by what a good relationship they have. He speaks so fondly about his other brothers and his father too, and although I was blessed with a great mom and never felt lonely, I have wondered over the years what a bigger family would look like.

I'm not close enough to hear everything they're saying, but it seems like Drake is heading out. He's wearing a stylish blue suit and a navy-blue tie, the casual look from earlier banished in favor of his usual awesome tailoring. I swear, nobody fills out a suit better than Drake James. He laughs at something Nathan says, and then they hug in that manly way that involves chest bumps and a high five. Drake strides toward the door of the hotel lobby, and I frown as I see Constantine outside, leaning against the hood of the car. Huh. Is he leaving for good? Going back to the city? He didn't mention it earlier, but then again, he also didn't say anything like "I'll see you later" or "fancy some wild and passionate sex in your hotel room tonight?"

"Hey, Drake," Nathan shouts. Drake turns around. "Enjoy your date—don't do anything I wouldn't do."

Drake laughs and leaves.

Grinning, Nathan walks off toward the bar, where a pretty brunette waits for him, devouring him with her eyes. That must be Melanie. At least I hope she's his wife.

I lean back against the wall and catch my breath. Drake is going on a date. Drake is all gussied up in his Tom Ford–Superman suit and getting driven back to Manhattan. To go on a date. He spent the day flirting with me—or at the very least, being nice to me—and now he's leaving. To go on a date. Of course he is.

For an allegedly intelligent woman, I am a complete fucking idiot.

CHAPTER

TWENTY-TWO

DRAKE

"So, how is your sex life?" Sapphire asks, her dazzling blue eyes twinkling at me over the table. "Still tying up strangers and calling it art?"

"Fuck you, you hag. Still seducing married women at the tennis club and calling it fun?"

"Ouch," she says. "I'd call that deuce."

"I'd say more like love–all. Especially with us two."

She shrugs, and the movement makes her shiny curtain of dark hair shimmer on her bare shoulders. Amelia's hair shimmers like that. But fuck it, I'm not here with Amelia; I'm here with Sapphire Huntington. We had a long-standing date to meet for the premiere of a new Broadway show she wanted to see; I bagged the tickets, and she bagged the aftershow. Now we're sitting here in this pretentious showbiz basement bar, sipping cocktails and rubbing shoulders with the stars. Not the kind of thing that impresses either of us.

Sapphire went to college with Nathan and is from Chicago. For both reasons, she's become a friend of mine too.

"No," she says, pretending to be heartbroken. "We are

deeply unlovable people. But also"—she shrugs—"deeply fuckable too. It's a conundrum. Anyway, here's to us."

She raises her glass, and I clink mine against it. It's great to see her, even if it meant I had to duck out of the team-building event early. Actually, scratch that—it was probably for the best that I had to duck out of the team-building event early.

Things were getting away from me, and I was starting to build way too much team with one particular member of the staff. I probably should have told Amelia I was leaving, but then again, she snuck off early too, and we didn't make any plans. I could have found out which room she was in, but it wouldn't have looked good—the boss lurking outside his assistant's hotel room. There was also a high risk that I would have ended up fucking her brains out.

"I suspect," Sapphire says, twining a strand of hair around her fingers, "that I might see more of you now that you live in New York than I did when we lived in the same city. Do I sense a weakening of your type-A-for-asshole workaholic nature?"

"How dare you." I slap a hand to my chest, feigning offense. "I'm insulted. I'll be a type-A-for-asshole workaholic until the day I die."

"Fair enough, my handsome friend, fair enough. I am much the same myself, although I do find a lot more time for dating than you do. Isn't it a crying shame that we can't do each other?"

She raises her eyebrows at me outrageously, and I shake my head and grin. "Is this the part where you tell me you went through an experimental stage in college and kissed a few boys?"

"Eeeeuw, gross. Boys? No way—they stink. But I'd possibly make an exception for you, Drake." She bats her eyelashes in an exaggerated manner and pretends to swoon. "You have such pretty lips."

I scoop an olive out of my martini and ping it at her. It lands amusingly in her cleavage, and she levels me with a look. "It truly is a shock that a gentleman such as yourself is spending his Friday night with his lesbian bestie." The sharpness of her words is dulled completely when she picks the olive out from between her breasts, shrugs, and pops it in her mouth. "But seriously, no action on the romantic front?"

"There is someone ... It's a complicated situation, and it only happened once. It was basically over before it began. It's a bad idea for both of us, but ..."

"You can't quite kick the habit?"

That about sums it up. I was right to apologize to Amelia for the way I behaved and to try to build a sturdier bridge between us. But was I right to feel her up in a storage closet and hold her hand in the garden? Or to stare deep into her eyes and see her bare her beautiful soul to me? Probably not. I saw the look on her face when I caught her after that stupid leap of faith she accidentally took. The way she gazed up at me with trust and wonder. She sees something in me that nobody else does— certainly not something I see. Now, instead of simply apologizing to her, I've opened all kinds of doors that should remain firmly shut. For both our sakes.

"Wow," Sapphire says. "You've got it bad. You're a junkie."

I pull at the collar of my shirt, feeling hot all of a sudden. Sapphire rests her hand on my arm. "You want to get out of this place? I mean, I like watching these guys sing and dance on stage, but in reality, they're all way too short, and their egos are sucking all the oxygen from the room." She laughs, and I'm grateful that she knows me well enough that she can see I'm starting to spiral, but she's far too diplomatic to point it out.

"Yeah. Okay. One drink, though, and then I need to hit the sack. I'm—"

"Let me guess, you're working tomorrow, even though it's Saturday?"

"You know me so well," I reply, standing up and offering her my arm.

We stride out onto the red carpet that's been set up outside the venue. There are several paparazzi around, which makes sense as the aftershow was packed with celebrities and professionally beautiful people. Sapphire pauses, draws me into an embrace, and gives the photographer a cheeky wink over her shoulder.

"There," she says as we walk away. "Now you can be my beard. Nobody will ever know I'm gay now."

"Apart from those seven million women you've fucked."

"Apart from them, yes. Shall we get that last drink at your hotel, and then I can hit the clubs and find a playmate for the evening? Assuming you're still living at the hotel."

"I am," I confirm, hailing a cab to take us there since I sent Constantine home to his family for the night. "The contracts on my loft are taking forever."

"So you say. I reckon you just like living in a hotel. You're so much of a commitment-phobe that you don't even want to tie yourself down to owning a property."

"I don't see any ring on your finger either, Sapphire."

Our banter continues in a similar vein for the next hour or so. One drink turns to two, but after that I draw a line under the night. I'm tired, I do have to work tomorrow, and I'm distracted. I need to get up to my room so I can indulge in my guilty secret and cyber-stalk my secretary. Because no matter how hard I try, I can't stop thinking about Amelia Ryder, and it physically hurts when I'm away from her. But none of that matters. I don't own the woman, and I never will. As Sapphire pointed out tonight, commitment isn't my style, and Amelia is a woman who deserves it all.

TWENTY-THREE

AMELIA

I lie in bed and wait for the damn room to stop spinning. Since when did they make that a feature in hotels?

I giggle to myself and sip some water from the bottle I brought up with me. It's stupidly late—or stupidly early, depending on what end of the day you start from. I see now why James and James organizes these shindigs for a Friday night. At least nobody needs to be at work tomorrow. Except really important people like Drake, of course. Mr. High and Mighty. Mr. Pompous I-Work-So-Much-Harder-Than-Anyone-Else Asshole. Mr. Cum Face. Mr. Big Bastard McDouchebag.

I giggle some more, and realize I probably need some coffee. I'm still drunk, and I know from experience that there's no point in trying to go to sleep when I'm drunk. There's that spinning room thing going on, plus I need to pee and I feel a little nauseous.

And I can't stop thinking about Mr. Big Arms O'Shit-Heel.

I manage to use the coffee machine, which of course makes me superior to Drake in at least one way. I might not be rich or hot or be able to perform amazing cunnilingus—to be fair, I've never tried. Maybe I'd be great at it. But anyway, I can use a coffee machine. I hold my cup aloft in victory.

After I saw him leave for his date, I planned to go back to my room and sulk, but Jacob and a gang of his pals from accounting happened to walk past and scooped me up to go along with them. A gang of people from accounting were a lot more fun than they sound, and one drink led to another. I met so many people and danced to so many cheesy tunes. I even won three games of pool in a row. I am always sensational at pool when I'm drunk.

All things considered, it was a far better night than I expected when I was hiding behind that giant plant watching Drake "I've Got You" James stroll out of the building. Looking lush. Smelling great. Probably on his way to getting laid.

Aaaaaagh, why did I have to think that? It's not like I couldn't have gotten laid tonight if I'd wanted to. I could be getting laid right now, in fact. Why aren't I? Why am I alone in my hotel room at, uh, almost five in the morning? Could it be because I'm a sad and tragic figure who can't get her head out of her ass? Or stop thinking about her boss's ass? I think it might be.

My phone makes a little pinging noise. I pick it up and see a message from Emily.

Are you okay? Did you call me for a reason?

Oh dear. I check my history and see that I did in fact call her at 3:20.

Sorry! Butt dial! Love you xxx

She responds with a string of emojis that include a smiley face, several hearts, and an eggplant. Ah. Maybe that's why she's up so early. My girlfriend be getting herself some penis! Whoop whoop!

I slump back on the bed, wishing that I was also getting some penis. One specific penis, in fact. I blow out air so fast my lips vibrate like a horse's, which is extremely amusing, so I do it again.

I still have my phone in my hand, and without thinking about it, I google the name Drake James. I mean, yeah, it's foolish and desperate, but everyone does this shit. I'll just look at some pictures of him and try to convince myself he's ugly.

Obviously, that doesn't work. The man is incredibly fine. The shots of him from our company website are so hot, I'm amazed the screen doesn't melt. He has that whole stern master-of-the-universe thing going on in them. I come across some coverage of a charity event to raise money for an animal shelter his sister-in-law Melanie volunteers at. The picture of him cuddling two French bulldogs in his arms has me swooning. Lucky French bulldogs. And then I see a photo that seems to have been posted tonight. Or last night, to be precise. It's on some kind of gossipy showbiz website, and there's a digital gallery of pics from the premiere of a new Broadway musical and the "exclusive and glitzy" aftershow party.

I flick through random photos of actors and stars I vaguely know, and then I find Drake. He's standing on the red carpet, which of course is a thing that people like him do in the same way us mere mortals stand on the subway platform after work. He's accessorized for the night with a statuesque brunette with killer curves, her bright blue eyes sparkling like a cloudless winter sky filtered through ice. She has her arms wrapped around him, and he's smiling down at her indulgently as she poses for the camera. *Billionaire playboy Drake James and his mystery date!* the caption screams. Or is it me who screams? At least inside.

"Billionaire playboy"—who writes this crap? Yeah, okay, he technically comes from a family that could accurately be described as billionaires. And yes, he's a boy. But a playboy? Is that true? Have I given my poor battered heart away to a playboy?

I stare at his mystery date. The woman he's possibly right now performing amazing cunnilingus on in his hotel bed. The bed he fucked me in after only knowing me for a couple hours.

Shit. Of course he's a playboy. That shouldn't be a surprise. A man with his money, his looks, his charisma. If he wasn't a playboy, he'd be married, wouldn't he? And it's not like he ever pretended to be anything else. He sat there at Emily's wedding and told me to my face that he didn't believe in happy endings. That he could never promise someone forever. In my case, he couldn't promise me more than one night. Maybe his "mystery date" will fare better, but I doubt it.

Because Drake James isn't merely a playboy. He's a playboy workaholic who will put the professional before the personal every single time. If I factor in his family as well, I would never be at the top of his list of priorities. Even if he did want to be with me, it could never work. I'm no prima donna, and I've never been high maintenance, but even my under-developed ego couldn't stand being third best.

There is no future for me and Drake, not even a hint of one, and I need to accept that. I need to stop dreaming and start living in the real world. The world where Jacob—a perfectly nice, funny, attractive man—spent ten minutes last night once again begging me to go to dinner with him.

TWENTY-FOUR

"Have you tasted these? Phenomenal!" Dad passes us the latest in a long line of trays full of food, urging us to sample them. "They're called tequeños. Go on, try one."

I do as I'm told, and like everything else he's shared this evening, they are delicious.

"They're great, Dad, but is deep-fried pastry and cheese really the best diet for you?"

"You mean because I'm ancient and I had a heart attack? You think I'm a frail old man, son?"

I see Mason snigger behind his back and make a throat-slitting gesture, and Elijah backs him up by shooting an imaginary gun at his own forehead. Even the saintly Maddox gets in on the act, giving me a thumbs-down signal like he's a fucking Roman emperor.

"No, Dad, of course I don't think you're frail. But you did have a heart attack. That's just a fact."

"Also a fact, Drake, is that because of that heart attack, my health is more closely monitored than Kim Kardashian's ass."

I almost choke on my tequeño. Did he really just say that? A glance at my brothers' faces confirms that he did.

"Anyway," he adds, "these aren't as unhealthy as you'd think. Luz knows I'm keeping an eye on my cholesterol and my blood pressure. She used low-fat cheese and that damn air fryer thing Melanie bought me that I never managed to master. Plus I'm eating lots of fish, lean meat, and all the beans. I bet I have a healthier diet than you do."

I hold up my hands in surrender. "Okay, Pop, okay. I'm glad it's working out for you. I was just expressing concern like a good son."

"Yeah, well, go and be concerned about your own life. Mine is just fine."

He seems rather cranky for a man who's been eating like a king thanks to his new cook, and I remember Nathan telling me that he decided to quit his cigars. Elijah's been on his ass about it for ages, but he always refused to even discuss it.

Looks like a few things are changing in Dalton James's world, and I wonder how much of it can be credited to Luisa's mom. He only agreed to give her a trial because Elijah laid out some sob story about how she needed the work. Not true at all, at least not financially, but according to my big brother, Luz was bored of being "old enough to be a grandmother but with no grandbabies to look after."

The woman in question steps into the dining room wearing a brightly patterned apron that she must have brought with her. She smells of sugar and vanilla, and all four of us boys inhale as she approaches the table. She smells like childhood.

Her eyes are huge, brown, and kind, but her slight scowl as she surveys the uneaten food suggests she could very easily switch between kind and killer. She stands with her hands on her hips and glares at us all.

"What is wrong with you skinny boys? Eat, eat!" She brushes a silver-streaked black curl from her face.

None of us are skinny, but all of us respond to the tone of her voice, jumping up and doing as we're told. I catch her winking at Dad behind our backs, and he snorts in amusement.

A few minutes later, I take a couple plates of food back to Dad's old office, where Nathan has been making a few calls while Mel settles Luke down for the night. It's Friday night, and we all had to rearrange a few things to be here, but Dad asked us to come for dinner to discuss the party he's planning for his birthday later this year. We were all a little surprised that he agreed to have one, never mind put so much effort into it, and again, I suspect Luz's influence goes deeper than his love of her arepas.

Nathan is just finishing up a call when I walk in, and I hand him the plate. "For fuck's sake, eat this, will you? I'm stuffed, and she's still nagging me to try more."

He laughs and rolls his eyes. "I know. Luz is a force of nature, isn't she? I feel kind of weird saying this, but she reminds me of Mom. Does that make me disloyal?"

It's a fair question, and it deserves some thought. We're all touchy about Mom and our memories of her. Even though we all grew up in the same home and lost the same mother, we all have our own versions of her. It's not just Luz's appearance that's similar though—both she and our mom were petite with dark hair, wide brown eyes, and olive skin—she's also warm and kindhearted in that take-no-nonsense way our mom was.

"No, it doesn't," I reply after a few beats. "Mom was one of a kind, and nobody will ever replace her." I have no desire to get into this subject with him, so I leave it there.

Nathan is no fool. He knows I went off the deep end after she died. There are things he doesn't understand—and doesn't need to understand—that make talking about this stuff especially difficult for me. When Mom passed, I was a mess for all kinds of reasons. I turned to my long-term girlfriend for support through that but didn't find it. Tiff made all the right noises, and for a while was the very picture of a sympathetic partner. But after a few weeks passed, she seemed to expect me to be back to "normal" and didn't get the fact that I'd never be "normal" again. The old me was gone, he died with my mother, and Tiff didn't seem to particularly like the new me. I was still completely fucked up, and she was wanting to go to parties and plan trips to Bermuda with friends. When I called her out on it, she told me I needed to "snap out of it." That comment came precisely sixteen weeks after my mom's funeral.

Needless to say, the relationship didn't survive, and the pain of that has never left me. I don't blame her—she was only twenty-two herself, still a kid really—but I have also never forgotten it. Grief is a sneaky beast. It infiltrates every aspect of your life, sometimes without you even noticing. You can appear fine on the surface, but beneath that, the fault lines are spreading through your psyche, a spiderweb of cracks weakening your foundation until you're ready to collapse. That's how it was with me, anyway. We all suffered, and we all dealt with it in our own ways. My coping mechanism was work, which is still my great solace in times of stress. Since the team-building event, for example, I've been working twenty-hour days.

I've seen Amelia at work, of course, and I haven't fallen back into being the borderline abusive ass I was—but I'm also keeping my distance. For both our sakes. It hasn't been easy, but it's necessary.

"Everything okay with work?" I ask him, seeing the signs of worry on his face. They're subtle, but I know him well enough to spot them.

"Yeah, all good. Some shit going on with the Ryans that I need to deal with tomorrow."

"Shit with the Ryans" can range between sorting out a parking fine to explaining why a trash bag full of body parts was found in a dumpster behind one of their nightclubs. Like the Morettis in Chicago, they're basically good men and have their own code of ethics. But that code doesn't always perfectly align with law and order's code of ethics.

"Anything I can help with?" I ask. His specialty is criminal law, and they often need him for that, but I bring more to the table when it comes to business contracts, civil cases, and the myriad of lawsuits that tend to spring up whenever money is involved.

"Nah, it's fine. I'll let you know if I do. I was just speaking to Helen, getting her to sort out some meetings."

"Dude, it's nine o'clock on a Friday night. I know that means nothing to us, but she's got a life."

"No she doesn't. She lives for her job, just like you. She loves it when I make her feel useful."

Helen is a widow with three grown daughters, and it saddens me that she's home alone on a Friday night, working. Is that what my future holds too? I shake off the unease and focus on my brother once more.

"Anyway," he says, toying with a small round dessert I've been informed is a papitas de leche. "She tells me your girl is out on a date tonight. How are you feeling about that?"

"What do you mean *my girl*?" I feel a muscle in my jaw twitch and try to hide it. "And what do you mean *a date*?"

He tilts his head and smirks. "Well, by your girl, I was sarcastically referring to your assistant, Amelia. And by date, I mean a social arrangement usually made between two people who find each other sexually attractive. It often involves food, alcohol, and conversation."

"Right. And who is she on a date with? And where?"

"You're not mad, are you?" He frowns. "You're not going to do something macho and stupid, right? Because you told me it was over between you two."

"It is over, and I've never done anything macho and stupid in my entire life. I'm merely curious."

He tells me the name of the guy she's dating and mentions the place he's taken her. Apparently it's the talk of the secretarial pool, and they're all thrilled for her. Which is, you know, nice of them.

I carry on making small talk with Nathan for a little while longer, somehow managing to appear completely normal. Inside, I am like a fucking volcano waiting to erupt. I have no idea why. When I got back to my hotel last Friday night, I poured myself a Scotch and spent two hours stalking Amelia online. She isn't one of those people who lives her life on social media, thank god, but she does have a Facebook page which is woefully poor on the privacy-settings front. I should probably have a word with her about it, but the stuff she posts is harmless enough. Plus, then I'd have to explain why I was looking at her online presence in the first place. And if she tightens up those privacy settings, I won't be able to stalk her. Yeah. That all sounds totally aboveboard and reasonable. If you're a psycho.

I even put her ex-husband's name into google. Chad. The name of a dick if ever I heard one. Has the face of a dick too. He was much easier to find; there are pictures of him all over the website for his start-up investment firm. I can admit he's good-looking, in that slightly over-the-top way that some guys get as they age. Blinding white teeth, skin too tan, blond hair. Frankly I wouldn't even buy a used car from the guy, never mind invest with him.

I scrolled away from Chad, officially the biggest idiot in the universe for letting a woman like Amelia get away from him, and headed back to her Facebook. For the millionth time, I flicked through her photos and found one from our company retreat. Specifically a selfie, taken at that weird angle where her arm is stretched out in front and above her, showing a big group of people at the hotel bar. She had a big grin on her face, her hair wild and her eyes not much better, and she'd clearly had a lot to drink. It took every ounce of willpower I had not to drive over there and take her to fucking bed—I mean put her to bed, obviously.

So yeah, I'm painfully aware that she's gorgeous and that other men are going to want her. Logically, I don't even mind—why wouldn't I want her to be happy? Why wouldn't I want her to meet someone great? Why wouldn't I want her to have screaming orgasms with some *other fucking guy*?

I tell Nathan I'm going to rejoin our father and brothers in the dining room. I'm not doing that, of course.

I'm about to do something macho and stupid.

TWENTY-FIVE

I force a laugh, hoping he doesn't notice that I'm faking it. It's not that Jacob isn't funny or that he's not a great guy. He's just not Drake James, which really isn't his fault.

"So how are you liking New York?" he asks as he tops up our wine glasses.

"Well, I was born and raised here," I remind him. I told him only last week that I'd moved back here from Philly to be closer to my mom.

He coughs awkwardly. "Of course. I remember you mentioning that now. I'm sorry. I'm not usually so forgetful. But damn." He uses a napkin to mop his brow. "First dates make me nervous as hell. Especially with someone like you."

That makes me laugh for real. "Someone like me?"

He smiles, and the dimple in his chin pops. "Yeah. You know —drop-dead gorgeous, funny, intelligent. Did I already say drop-dead gorgeous?"

Before I can reply, my phone vibrates on the table, shocking us both into a nervous giggle. "I'm sorry, Jacob, it could be my mom."

"Of course. Go ahead."

I flip the phone over, and the mild hammering of my heart turns into a full-blown gallop as I read the text from Drake.

I need you. Now. Work emergency.

That's bizarre. I was super careful to make sure everything was up to speed before I left the office today. We've both been keeping our distance while being polite and professional and have put a lot of effort into maintaining whatever equilibrium we have left. So if Drake says there's a work emergency, I better not piss him off by ignoring him. The truce is fragile.

"Is everything okay?" Jacob asks.

"Yeah, don't worry. I do need to make a quick call though. If you'll excuse me? I'll just be a second."

"Of course, go for it."

Jacob might be a little forgetful and he might be cute rather than panty-melting, but the smile he gives me as I stand up is warm and genuine. This is a man who would have realistic expectations of what I could give him, unlike the demanding man who has just messaged me. Jacob is here, he's emotionally available, and he's way more in my league. Plus, he thinks I'm drop-dead gorgeous.

I walk to the ladies' room, figuring I'll freshen up while I contact Drake. I don't want to end my date and go to the office if I can avoid it.

I quickly tap out a message.

What's the problem? Can I fix it tomorrow? I don't mind coming in on a Saturday.

I stare at the screen and wait for a reply, annoyed that the man can exert so much power over me without being present. I'm imagining him as he texts, maybe with that slightly annoyed scowl he gets when things don't work out exactly how he wants them to. The one that says he's right and you know it. I chew my lip as I wait, looking at myself in the mirror.

I'm flushed and my eyes are bright and my hands tremble as I tidy my hair. None of that, unfortunately, is because of the man I'm here on a date with.

> No. It can't wait. Finish your date.

How the hell does he know I'm on a date? I mean, it's not like it's a state secret, but I also didn't advertise it. I didn't want it to appear like I was maybe rubbing his nose in it or taunting him. He's made it clear he doesn't want me in any serious way, but there's still a history between us, a tension, and I didn't want to poke the bear.

But if he does know I'm on a date, then why the hell is he harassing me like this? I start to entertain a sneaking suspicion that he's only demanding my attention because I *am* on a date. Which is ridiculous, but also maybe a tiny bit satisfying.

> What's the emergency, and how did you know I was on a date?

My phone vibrates again, signaling another message. A kaleidoscope of butterflies has taken up residence in the pit of my stomach, and I hold my breath as I glance at the screen.

> I know everything. Leave the restaurant. Now.

Is he stalking me? How does he know I'm in a restaurant? I look around nervously, then laugh at myself. It isn't like he's lurking here in the ladies' room.

> Are you serious?

I watch the little symbols that tell me he's typing a reply, and my anger starts to build. There is no damn work emergency! He just doesn't want me out having fun with another guy. He's a conceited, controlling jackass. Sadly, he's also a hot, possessive, makes-my-panties-want-to-self-combust jackass who I can't stop thinking about.

> Deadly. Finish your date, Amelia. Right now, or I'll end it for you.

My cheeks burn with heat, and I splash my face with water. Ignoring his message, I emerge back out into the restaurant and glance around, paranoid. Does he have spies? Is he here himself? What the actual fuck is going on? This is crazy. I look back at the screen. *I'll end it for you.* What does that even mean?

"Are you okay, Amelia?" I'm back at the table, and Jacob's voice snaps me from my thoughts about our asshole boss. I'm being rude, not giving him my whole attention, and that's not like me. But Drake has a way of making me act like a person I don't recognize and, in this case, don't especially like.

I tear my eyes from my phone and blink at him.

"You look a little upset. Is it your mom?" He nods toward my cell phone.

I press the backs of my hands to my cheeks, hoping to cool them, but it doesn't work. It's like my skin is on fire. I shake my head, my phone vibrating in my hand again. "Everything's fine. I just ..." I take a deep breath. "Um, you know what, I'm not feeling great. Would you mind giving me a few more minutes? I think I just need some fresh air."

"You want me to come with you?"

"No, no, I'm good. Why don't you order dessert for us both, if that's all right?"

He nods and assures me that it is. Turning around, I try not to make it obvious that I'm scanning the packed room, looking for Drake or maybe for a suspicious-looking dude wearing a T-shirt that says *Drake James's Minion.*

It's crowded in here, but I don't see any sign of him. That should be a relief, so why am I disappointed? What the hell is wrong with me?

He's Drake James. He's made it clear he's not interested in relationships, especially not with his employees, which I one hundred percent understand. So why is he bothered about my date? Or am I overthinking this? Maybe there really is a work emergency. It makes a lot more sense that Drake would be upset about that than he would about my social life.

I head to the stairs that lead to the ground floor. At this point, I really do need some fresh air. And possibly a brain transplant.

I'm so deep in my own thoughts that I don't notice the man in the suit standing near the fire escape until he opens the heavy metal door. The rest all happens quickly, an unreal blur. I look up at the sound of the door opening, then feel a warm hand on the small of my back, and a hot, sexy-as-hell mouth is at my ear. "Why did you ignore my instructions, Amelia?"

"Drake?"

"In the flesh," he says, his voice terse. "We need to talk."

He bundles me out onto the cold stairwell, letting the heavy fire door slam closed behind us. One second I was in a busy restaurant, and the next I'm trapped out here, alone with a very pissed-looking Drake. I want to be pissed right back, but I'm not doing a great job of it.

Still, I fold my arms over my chest, gathering all the indignation I can muster while staring up at his impossibly handsome face. "What the hell are you doing?"

He glares at me, his jaw twitching and his mouth tight. Goosebumps break out all over my flesh, and I know it's not from the temperature because it is perfectly balmy out here. "I think the more pertinent question is what the hell are you doing, Miss Ryder?"

"I'm on a date."

"Yes, I can fucking see that," he growls.

I shake my head in astonishment. "What does that even have to do with you?"

He draws a breath through his nose, his nostrils flaring. He inches closer, and I retreat until my back hits the cold metal door we just came out of. "It has everything to do with me. If he touches you again, I'm going to send him to the Chicago office. If he's lucky. I might open an office in Siberia to get rid of him."

"Touch me? He barely brushed my hand."

His tongue, his wickedly sinful tongue, darts out, and he runs it over his bottom lip. "I. Don't. Care."

Anger simmers beneath my skin. Just because he gave me the best orgasms of my life, the kind that usually only happen in movies and books, doesn't mean he gets to act like a psycho. "So you don't want me, but no one else can have me, is that it? You don't want to touch me, but nobody else can either?"

He steps forward until his body is barely a millimeter from mine. The slightest movement from either of us would have his chest flush against mine. "You think I don't want you?"

I tip my jaw and try my best to maintain a semblance of composure. "You made that very clear."

He bangs his fist on the steel door beside my head, making me jump. "Goddammit, Amelia, I wish that I didn't fucking want you. Life would be so much easier if that were true. But every second of every goddamn day, all I can think about is how badly I want to touch you. How I want to kiss you and taste you and bend you over my desk and fuck you!"

Oh sweet baby Jesus. I'm going to melt into this door. I'll be stuck to it forever. "You do?"

A low, dangerous growl rolls in his throat. "Every. Fucking. Second."

I need to get out of here. I need to get very far away. My body is too treacherous. There's no way I can resist him, especially not when he's looking at me like he is right now. "We can't do this," I whisper.

"You think I don't know that? You think that every time you walk into my office and I picture you naked in my bed and remember how fucking beautiful you looked when I made you come that I don't realize how completely fucking wrong it is?"

My body burns like my blood is on fire. He's still my boss, still a playboy. He's still a man who could destroy me in every possible way. It's still wrong. So why does it feel so right?

Or maybe it just feels good. And perhaps that's why my body instinctively leans into his and my hand curls around the back of his neck. Maybe that's why I don't stop him when he takes my mouth, claiming it in a hungry, bruising kiss. I moan, parting my lips. He tastes of bourbon and sugar and Drake. He kisses me like I'm the oxygen feeding his fire, like he'll die if he doesn't consume as much of me as possible.

I have never been kissed like this in my life, not even by him. It is all-consuming and intoxicating, and it might burn me to the ground. One hand fists in my hair as he tips my head back, giving him the perfect angle to dominate me. And all I can do is let him. He explores my mouth, all tongue and teeth and lips, brutal as he takes what he wants from me. I rock my hips forward, pressing against him. A surge of triumph hurtles through me when I feel how hard he is. He wants me as much as I want him.

He finally breaks our kiss, leaving me gasping for air and grinding himself into me. "That's all for you, Amelia. You have me walking around this city with a permanent fucking hard-on." He tilts his head, eyes narrowed as they rake over my face. "Is the feeling mutual?"

"W-what?"

His free hand skates over my ass and down the outside of my thigh. He tugs at the fabric of my dress, pulling it higher. "Are. You. Wet?" He punctuates each word with a kiss on my neck that has me squirming.

"N-no," I lie.

He smirks, his deep brown eyes twinkling as he pulls my dress higher. "Shall we see about that?"

I press my back flat to the door. I should say no. I should shove him away and run. I'm not the kind of woman who lets a man slide his hand between her legs on a fire escape outside of an upscale Manhattan restaurant while my date waits for me at our table. Except I don't say no. I don't slap him and I don't run, because my body is screaming yes. When his fingertips brush over the fabric of my panties, my body wins out and I whimper shamelessly.

I feel him smile against my skin. He knows he's won, but I'm too far gone to care. He tugs my panties to the side and runs a thick finger through my center. He groans. "You lied to me, Amelia. You're fucking soaked."

Embarrassment heats my cheeks. I close my eyes and drop my head back against the door with a soft thud. "Oh god."

He rests his lips against the shell of my ear, his warm breath dusting over my neck. "Is this all for me? Don't lie to me again."

I screw my eyes shut. "Yes, Drake. It's all for you."

He chuckles darkly before inching the tip of his finger inside me. "That's my good girl." My eyes fly open, and I grab onto his forearm, holding him still. We can't do this here. Someone could come out at any second and find us. He arches a dark eyebrow. "You want me to stop? Or do you want me to make you come while your date's checking out the dessert menu and wondering where you are?"

I swallow, loosening my grip on his arm, and he sinks a little deeper inside me. Oh god, why does everything he does to me feel so good? My legs tremble. He runs his nose over my neck, growling when he inhales. "What's it to be, Amelia?"

"D-don't stop," I murmur.

He groans and seals his lips over mine at the exact same time he sinks his finger all the way inside me. I moan into his mouth, and he swallows the sounds, stealing the breath from my lungs while pleasure coils deep in my abdomen.

My head is spinning, and I feel like I'm going to pass out, gulping for air when he eventually breaks our kiss. "W-wait, are there cameras out here? What if someone—"

"There are no cameras. Trust me." He adds a second finger and rubs his thumb knuckle over my clit, making my legs buckle as sensations swoops through me. Resting his forehead against mine, he says, "I'd never let anyone see you like this. So fucking desperate for me."

"Am not," I protest, even as I snake my arms around his neck and grind into his fingers.

"Yeah you are. But make no mistake—I'm just as fucking hungry for you, mi rosa. If I had any protection with me, I'd be balls-deep in your wet cunt right now."

Oh. My. God. That's it. My panties just melted. "You have the dirtiest mouth." I breathe out the words.

He buries his head into my neck and hums against my skin. "You remember what else this mouth can do though, right?"

Hell yes, I do. Euphoria shuttles through my body as he drives his fingers deeper inside me, all the time massaging my clit so expertly that I'm already hurtling toward oblivion. I fist my hands in his shirt, gripping tight as my climax builds to a crescendo, washing over me and threatening to take me under its swell. But he keeps me on the edge, never quite letting me tumble over it. He wraps a hand around the base of my throat, his forehead still pressed against mine as he talks me through it. "That's my girl. Let go for me. Soak my fingers."

"Drake, please," I whimper.

"I wish I could get my mouth on you right now." He sinks deeper, curling the tip of his finger and rubbing a spot deep inside me that has my orgasm slamming into me with the force of a freight train. My eyes squeeze closed. My chest heaves as I try to drag in a breath, and I bury my head in his shirt to muffle the sounds of pleasure that are coming from my mouth. My knees tremble and my body sags, trapped between him and the door.

Drake pulls back, his gaze still locked on mine. He lifts the fingers he just had inside me to his lips and places them in his mouth. My throat works nervously as I watch him suck them clean, murmuring carnal sounds of satisfaction as he does. He releases them with a wet pop and grins wickedly. "Best pussy I ever tasted."

The heat from my cheeks races down my neck. I can't believe we just did that. In a stairwell. I can't believe I let him take all my control.

"I h-have to get back to my ..." I press my lips together, not wanting to say the word because it makes this seem even more wrong.

Drake's brow furrows, and he quickly fixes my dress, all traces of humor now gone. He takes my purse from the ground and presses it into my hand. "Go tell your date you're leaving. My car is outside. Constantine will take you home."

I am a shaking wreck, and I don't especially want to go back inside that restaurant and carry on with my date anyway—but that's not the point. How dare he order me around. How dare he play with me like this. I am not a toy put on this planet for Drake James's amusement.

"You don't get to tell me who I can and can't date."

He wraps his hand around my throat, squeezing the sides just enough to restrict my blood flow. I should hate it, but of course I don't. "You have two options, Amelia. You can have my driver take you home, or you can sit back down with that jackass out there while your cum, the cum that *I* pulled from you, soaks your panties. And if he so much as grazes you with a fingertip, I will follow him home and break the hand he put on you. And *then* I'll send him to Chicago."

Surely he's not serious. Would he actually hurt Jacob just for daring to be my date? Why the hell does he even care so much?

There is nothing in his demeanor which suggests he's not serious, though, and I hate how good his possessiveness makes me feel. Not that I will admit that to him. "And what about you?"

He runs his tongue over his teeth, eyes burning into mine. "I'll take a cab."

My heart bottoms out of my chest. Of course he will. Heaven forbid he should get in the car with me. That we should spend some time together. Never mind talk and try to figure this mess out. It's yet another reminder that I'm nothing to him, nothing other than an itch he occasionally needs to scratch. He's right about one thing though. I do need to leave. I suck in a breath and roll back my shoulders, glancing at the keypad on the door beside us. "How do we get back inside?"

Drake bangs three times on the door with his fist, and a second later, a man on the other side opens it. "Mr. James," he says with a polite nod, not making eye contact with me. Huh. Money sure does talk. Has he been waiting there all this time just to open that door? Did he hear everything that happened between us?

My cheeks flame hotter than the sun, and I look to Drake, but his face is unreadable now. He is once again every inch the coldhearted lawyer, all traces of the passion he showed a moment ago now gone. Is he some kind of machine?

Swallowing down the thick knot of shame and anger in my throat, I stride back to the table. My date's face is a mask of confusion and understandable annoyance, and I feel so awful about what happened that tears spring to my eyes. He's a nice guy who doesn't deserve what just happened to him, even though he has no idea about it. Drake James has ruined me for nice guys like Jacob.

When he sees my teary-eyed state, he pushes back his chair and stands. "Amelia, what's wrong?"

I force a smile. "Nothing important, honestly. I really don't feel well is all. I think I'm going to head home."

"Let me get the check and I'll take you."

I place my hand on his arm. "That's really sweet, but I'd rather just grab a cab and go straight to bed."

His eyes fill with concern, and his genuine consideration makes me feel even worse. I fish in my purse, pull out a wad of twenty-dollar bills, and place them on the table. "I think this should cover the check."

He glances at the money. "That's not necessary, Amelia. This was meant to be my treat."

"Please, let me." I can't bear the thought of him not only sitting alone while I submitted to my boss but then also paying for the meal.

"Okay then," he says, nodding. "Next time it's on me, okay? Let me know you get home safe, and I'll see you in the office?"

Oh god. I'll have to see him every day at work. Tears are

burning behind my eyes now. Why did I think this would be a good idea? "Yeah, sure."

"I'll save you a bagel."

I mumble something that's half apology and half thanks before I rush out of the restaurant. Now I actually do feel sick. I just allowed my boss to finger-fuck me in a stairwell. What am I, sixteen? What if someone saw us? What if I lose my job? What if—

"Miss Ryder," Constantine says, interrupting my catastrophizing. He gestures toward the sleek black SUV.

I shake my head. I want nothing from Drake James. "I'll take a cab."

He places a hand over his heart. "My life won't be worth living if I let you leave here in a cab."

I glance behind him at the busy street. "That won't work on me this time, buddy."

I whistle for a passing cab, and one pulls to a halt.

"Miss Ryder, please?" Constantine implores.

I walk past him and pull open the taxi door, my chin held high. "Tell your boss he doesn't need to give me a ride home to make himself feel better about being a coldhearted asshole. I'm a big girl, and I can take care of myself."

Before he can reply, I jump into the cab and give the driver my address. Drake James can go straight to hell. That is the last time he'll play me.

Ever.

CHAPTER
TWENTY-SIX

DRAKE

"What the hell are you doing here?" I bark at Constantine as I emerge from the restaurant. I watched in satisfaction as she said goodnight to the schmuck she was with and gave her enough time to leave and get into the car.

I look past my driver, trying to peer through the tinted windows. "If you're still here, she'd better be in that damn car."

His lips press into a thin line. "She's not, sir."

Mild annoyance turns to the burn of anger. "Why not?"

He offers a small shrug. "She insisted on taking a cab."

The woman is fucking infuriating. "You should have made sure she got into the damn car. I told you to get her home safe."

"What would you have preferred I do, sir? Manhandle her into your car in the middle of the street? Maybe tase her and shove her in the trunk?"

Yes! "No, of course not." Sighing, I run my hand over my face and immediately regret it. Her smell, the intoxicatingly addictive scent of her cum, is still on my fingers, and now all I can taste is her. My heart pounds a staccato rhythm in my chest. "Did she say anything else?"

He clears his throat and looks at his feet.

"Constantine?"

He takes a deep breath. "She said that you did not need to make yourself feel better about being a"—he winces—"a cold-hearted asshole. She also said that she is a big girl who can take care of herself."

She thinks I'm coldhearted? If fucking only. That would make this whole goddamn thing a whole lot easier, wouldn't it? If only I didn't feel so fucking much of everything whenever she's around. I pull at the collar of my shirt, twisting my neck.

"Would you like to go home, sir?" Constantine asks, the question loaded with meaning. He opens my car door as he awaits my answer.

I step inside the car, but home is the last place I want to go.

THE SECURITY in this apartment building is abysmal. I buzzed the super, and he let me in without even asking for my fucking name. Not a single word of greeting, the door just swung open. I shake off the uneasy feeling as I look around me with a judgmental eye. I'm fully aware of how privileged I am to have the kind of money that buys security and safety and to have grown up knowing nothing else. But still, I don't like her living here when any psycho off the street could walk in and knock on her door.

Case in point, I hammer on her door with my fist. My anger festered on the car ride over here. I was angry at her for refusing the ride, sure, but mainly I'm angry with myself. How did I let myself lose control like that? And how the hell did I expect her to react when I treated her like a whore by offering her a ride home but nothing more? I bang again, and a few seconds later, I hear her footsteps. At least she has the sense to check her peephole, which doesn't work out in my favor. She yells at me to go to hell.

I pinch the bridge of my nose. "I just want to talk."

"And I just want you to go away and leave me the hell alone."

Dammit, does she have to be so infuriatingly stubborn? This is why I don't do dating and relationships. They're fucking torturous. Except here I am, on her doorstep. Ready to drop to my knees and beg if it will make her let me in. "I'm not going anywhere, Amelia."

"Then you'd better get comfy, because you're not coming in here, asswipe."

I suck in a deep, calming breath, unclench my fisted hand, and rest it on the door. "Asswipe? Really? I'm offended, but only by the subpar caliber of your insults, Miss Ryder."

As I expected, that pisses her off enough that the door opens a little. She folds her arms over her chest, her cheeks pink with rage. She's wearing pajamas, if they could be called that—barely there boy shorts and a shirt, the fabric so flimsy I can see the outline of her nipples. Dammit it all to hell, now all I want to do is pin her to the wall and fuck every bit of attitude out of her and every ounce of anger out of me. "Can I come in?"

She taps her foot impatiently. "No. Whatever you have to say, you can say right here."

I make a show of glancing up and down the hallway. "I'm pretty sure you don't want your neighbors hearing any of the things I'd like to say to you right now."

Her breath hitches and her pupils dilate, but she tips her jaw defiantly. "I'll take my chances."

I lick my lips and hold her gaze, wondering how far I can push her. Because as much as she likes to pretend she hates this back and forth between us, she loves it as much as I do. "I want to fuck you. No, I *need* to fuck you. But before I do that, I'd really like to spread you wide open and—"

She pulls me inside and slams the door closed behind me. "What the hell is wrong with you? Kris with a K has teenage boys!"

Fuck me, I love pushing her buttons. "Well, I did warn you."

She blows a strand of dark hair from her face. "I don't just mean that, Drake, I mean ..." She looks at the floor and takes a step back from me.

I follow her, tipping her chin up with my forefinger until she's looking at me once more. "You mean what, Amelia?"

The curve of her throat works as she swallows. "You ruined my date."

I grind my teeth together so hard my jaw aches, and then I shove my hands into the pockets of my suit pants so I don't wrap them around her slender neck. At least not yet. She obviously needs to talk some shit through first. "I'm not here to apologize for ruining your date, because you shouldn't have been on a fucking date in the first place." She opens her mouth to speak, but I cut her off. "And it seemed to me like you were enjoying your time with me in the stairwell a hell of a lot more than your dinner with that prick from accounting."

"His name is Jacob."

"His name will be Jacob from the Chicago office if you so much as smile at him again, Amelia."

She steps forward and raises up onto her tiptoes, her hands screwed up into little fists. "Are you listening to yourself? Can you actually hear this horseshit coming out of your mouth? Why shouldn't I have been on a date, Drake? Why?"

I'd like to tell her, but I barely understand it myself. I've been working off instinct all damn night, and all I manage is a frustrated growl.

"Why?" she yells, her face so close to mine that I could dip my head and kiss her.

I move without thinking, and in a flash, my hand is on her throat and she's pressed up against the wall of her apartment. Her pulse flutters beneath my palm, her nipples spiking through her thin pajama top.

"Because you're *mine*, Amelia. Don't you understand that yet? You don't get to drive me crazy every second of every fucking day and then go on a date with some jackass who works for me. In fact, you don't get to go on a date with anyone. Ever." Where the fuck did that come from? What has this woman done to me?

"You're insane," she whispers, but her pupils are blown wide, her hazel eyes the color of a forest at midnight. Her pink tongue darts out to moisten her lips, and I swear I feel the action as though she's swiping it over the head of my cock. Hot, pulsating need ripples down my spine.

I press my forehead against hers, drinking in the scent of her. "Yeah? Well maybe I am insane, because I am fucking obsessed with you. Believe me, Miss Ryder, I have tried very hard not to be. I can't stop thinking about you for more than five seconds. Whenever you're anywhere near me, all I can think about is how good you taste." I release a low growl, and she shivers, those hard nipples grazing my chest. "All I can think about is how good your tight cunt feels when I sink my cock into you, like we were made to fit each other. Your smile is the only goddamn thing I see when I close my eyes. You are the air that I breathe. You are everything and everywhere, and I can't go one more single fucking day without touching you."

Her chest heaves as she sucks in a shaky breath. "We already agreed that we can't do this. You're my boss, Drake."

My cock pulses, twitching against her belly. "Then I'll fucking quit."

She rolls her eyes. "That's not even within the realm of possibility. I don't want to be the secretary screwing her boss, and I definitely don't want to lose my job. I've given up my career for a man before, and I'm not doing it again, not even for you."

Not even for me? I tuck her hair behind her ear, my other hand still resting on her collarbone. I'm mesmerized by the rise and fall of her breathing, my fingers gently exploring the hollows and curves of her throat.

"Nobody has to know, and you won't lose your job. We'll figure it out." My tone is desperate, pleading. I have no clue how we're going to figure this out or how we can make it work, but right now it appears I'm only thinking with my dick. And my dick is only interested in one thing—being buried inside Amelia Ryder.

"Drake, no. It's impossible, and not only because of work. I don't want something casual, and you don't do relationships."

Fuck. I want to put my fist through the fucking wall. That used to be true. It's how I've been since I was twenty-three years old. But with her, those feel like empty words I used to say. Words that became empty when I met her. "I don't know about all that. I just know that I want to do you, Amelia."

It sounds like something a high schooler would say, and she presses her lips together like she's trying to suppress a giggle. She doesn't quite succeed, and at least it does something to ease the tension that is filling the cramped entryway of her small apartment.

I wince. "Yeah, I didn't mean that quite the way it sounded." Well, not completely anyway. I'd laugh too, but I'm too on edge to find any of this remotely funny.

She pulls her juicy bottom lip through her teeth, cocking her head up and looking into my eyes. "So you *don't* want to do me?" The words vibrate through my body, bypassing the logical part of my brain and traveling directly to my aching cock.

There's no going back now. If I do this with her, then I'm really doing this. All in. "Oh, I want to do you every single way there is, Miss Ryder, and then I'm going to invent some new ones. But I want to do this whole thing with you. Whatever this is. Whatever it looks like. We can keep it a secret or tell the whole fucking world, but just let me have you."

She blinks, and a tear rolls down her cheek. I'm pretty certain my heart actually stops beating while I wait for her response. I don't know how the fuck I'll go on if she turns me down. "You've already got me, Drake."

I waste no time in sealing my mouth over hers, lifting her so she can wrap her legs around my waist. Rocking my hips, I chase a little relief by grinding my aching dick against her, but it's not enough. I need so much more. Breaking our kiss, I groan my frustration. "I don't have any condoms with me."

Her eyes light up. "I have some. They're in my dresser."

I try not to let my completely irrational anger show on my face, but I guess I fail because she rolls her eyes. "Women are allowed condoms now, you know. It's not 1950."

I rub my nose along her jawline, and jealous heat coils in my chest. When the fuck did I become this guy? "I know that. But I hate the thought of you ever wanting to use them with anyone but me."

She wraps her arms around my neck, her lips twitching with a smirk. Looks like my girl enjoys it when I'm possessive. "Well, I didn't and I don't. The girls bought them for me after my divorce, and the box is still sealed. Satisfied?"

"Not even a little. But I'm gonna be." I find her bedroom on the other side of her tiny living area and kick the door open with my foot, not bothering to be gentle. Amelia's legs tighten around my waist as I carry her to the bed, my lips never leaving hers. I set her down on the edge of the mattress and finally break our kiss.

"Where are they?" I ask, already yanking open the top drawer of her dresser.

"Second drawer," she pants. Yeah. She wants this just as much as I do.

I rummage through the drawer, pushing aside neatly folded sweaters until my fingers close around the small box. When I turn back to Amelia, the sight of her nearly brings me to my knees.

She's lying back on the bed, her dark hair fanned out around her on the pillow. Her pajama top is pushed up, exposing a strip of creamy skin above the waistband of her shorts. Her lips are swollen from our kisses and her eyes rake over my body. I toss the box of condoms onto the nightstand and prowl toward her, a predator stalking its prey.

"You're wearing too many clothes," I growl, reaching for the hem of her pajama top.

She lifts her arms and allows me to pull the offending item over her head. Her breasts spill free, nipples pebbled and demanding my attention. I waste no time lowering my mouth to one peaked bud while palming the other, squeezing hard until she moans.

She arches into my touch, another breathy moan escaping her lips. "Drake, please ..."

I release her nipple with a wet pop and look up at her flushed face. The sound of her begging has me desperate to give her what she needs. "Please what, baby? Tell me what you want."

Her fingers tangle in my hair, and she tugs me close enough to kiss me again. "I want you," she breathes against my lips. "All of you. Right now."

I groan, my cock straining painfully against my zipper.

CHAPTER TWENTY-SIX

"Fuck, Amelia. Do you have any fucking clue what you do to me?"

My hands slide down her sides, coasting over her ribs before hooking into the waistband of her pajama shorts. I pull them down along with her panties, leaving her gloriously naked underneath me. Allowing myself time to appreciate the moment, I drink in the sight of her, all creamy skin and supple curves.

"You're so fucking beautiful," I murmur, trailing my fingers up the inside of her thigh.

She shivers beneath my touch, her legs spreading wider in invitation. "Drake, please. I need you. I've waited so long."

Oh, her need is fucking exquisite, and I decide I'm going to make her wait a little while longer. I'm going to enjoy teasing my little vixen so damn much. I dip my head and press a kiss to her inner thigh. "Patience, baby. I want to savor every goddamn inch of you."

She whimpers as I trail kisses over her flesh, the heady scent of her arousal already scrambling my senses. I deliberately avoid allowing my mouth where she wants me most, knowing it will be even sweeter for the wait. I brush my nose over her pussy instead and inhale deeply, as intoxicated by her scent as I am by every other thing about her. Where the hell has this woman been my entire life?

"Drake," she moans, fingers tangling impatiently in my hair. I chuckle, and even the touch of my warm breath on her skin makes her gasp. When I finally drag my tongue through her wet center, she cries out, her hips bucking against my face.

"Fuck, you taste even better than I remember, mi rosa," I groan, sucking her clit into my mouth. "So much better than having to taste you on my fingers."

A shudder runs through her, and her grip tightens in my hair. I reward her with my tongue, alternating between broad strokes and teasing flicks, driving her wild. Her taste floods my mouth, sweet and addictive and so incredibly delicious that I could do this every day for all eternity and never get bored. Her breathing grows increasingly rapid, and I can tell she's close. I slide two fingers inside her, curling them to hit the spot that makes her see stars. Her walls clench around me as I gently work my fingers in and out of her, my mouth never leaving her pulsing clit.

"Drake, I'm so close," she gasps, her thighs trembling against my ears. "Oh god, don't stop, please don't stop ..."

I have no intention of ever stopping. I am going to spend the rest of my goddamn days with my head buried between this woman's legs. I double down on my efforts, pulling her clit into my mouth and lashing it with my tongue while I sink my fingers deeper inside her. Her back arches off the bed as she unravels, a cry of ecstasy coming from somewhere deep inside her and tearing out of her throat. "That's my good girl," I say, my lips still pressed against her skin as I work her through her climax, gently coaxing every last tremor from her beautiful body.

Her fingers fall from my hair. "Come here now." She sounds utterly sated and completely perfect.

I growl, unused to being told what to do, but for her, I can make an exception. For her, I can do anything at all. I crawl up her body, trailing my tongue and teeth over her skin until I reach her lips, and I capture them in a bruising kiss that lets her taste herself on me. She moans into my mouth, her hands frantically working at my belt buckle.

"Already greedy for more, baby?"

"You're wearing too many clothes as well," she mumbles against my lips.

Laughing, I pull back to shrug off my jacket and unbutton my shirt. Amelia's hands join mine, her fingers trembling slightly as she helps me undress. When I'm finally naked, she lightly scrapes her fingernails down my chest and across my abs.

"You're so perfect. Are you even real, or were you made in a lab?"

I capture her wandering hands and pin them above her head. "Not even close to perfect, baby. But I am very real."

Leaning down, I drop kisses along her jaw and down her throat and nip gently at her collarbone. She arches into me, her breasts pressing against my chest.

"Drake, please," she whispers. "I need you inside me."

I reach for a condom from the nightstand and tear one open with my teeth before handing it to her. She bites her bottom lip as she takes it from me, eyelashes fluttering and her cheeks flushed bright pink. "Don't pretend to be coy. We both know you're a wicked temptress, Amelia Ryder." I wink at her, and she laughs. When she rolls the condom down my length, her expression is one of intense concentration and her hands shake. There's something about her uncertainty, her lack of experience with other men, that makes me burn with the possessive need to ensure that she will never do this with anyone else ever again. That, along with the sensation of her hand on my cock, nearly undoes me.

After positioning myself at her entrance, I make myself pause and search her eyes for any hint of hesitation. Because there's truly no going back after this. We're doing this in full knowledge of the fact that I'm her boss and she's my employee. We can't pretend we don't understand the power dynamic that's at play here. I find myself uttering the words "Are you sure about this?"

She wraps her legs around my waist, pulling me closer. "I've never been more sure of anything in my life, Drake."

Thank Christ for that, because I have no fucking idea how I

would have torn myself away from her if her answer was different. I slowly push into her with one long, smooth stroke, savoring every inch as her tight heat envelops me, squeezing me tight. "Jesus, fuck, you feel amazing," I groan, resting my forehead against hers. "So fucking wet for me. You're fucking perfect."

Amelia gasps and rolls her hips, urging me to move. "You feel amazing too."

I rock into her, setting a slow, deep rhythm that has her groaning. I start gentle, but then I pull all the way out and slam back inside her, hard. Her nails dig into my back, and she cries out as I hit that sweet spot inside her. "Oh, my! Drake," she moans.

I pick up my pace, driving into her harder with each stroke until the headboard slams against the wall on every thrust. I worry vaguely about the neighbors, but only for a split second. I don't give a shit about the neighbors or the rest of the world. All that matters is Amelia and this moment right here. The way her body feels against mine, the desperate little sounds she makes as I push her closer to the edge.

"That's it, baby," I say, nipping at her earlobe. "Let me hear you."

Her cries grow louder and more feral as I pound into her. I feel her walls squeezing me tighter as she gets closer to the edge. I'm almost there too, my head spinning and my heart booming as endorphins race through my body. Snaking a hand between us, I find her clit and circle it with my thumb. Her back bows, arching off the bed, and a keening cry escapes her lips.

"I know," I say, soothing her, feeling my own release near. "Come for me. I want to feel you fall apart for me."

Her nails rake down my spine as she shatters around me, crying out my name. The tight squeeze of her pussy is enough to trigger my own climax, and I bury myself deep inside her with a guttural cry.

For a moment, we're both still, panting heavily as we come down from our high. I rest my forehead against hers, not wanting to break our connection just yet. Maybe not ever. Amelia's hands come up to cup my face, her thumbs stroking my cheeks. It feels magical, this thing between us, and for the first time in as long as I remember, I feel safe.

"Drake," she breathes out. "That was incredible."

It was better than incredible. It was so good they need to invent new words to describe it. But right now, I don't want to talk. If I talk, I might fuck it up. And if I fuck this up, my heart will snap in two. Instead, I seal my lips over hers once more, pouring everything I'm feeling, everything I am, into this kiss and hoping that it's enough.

TWENTY-SEVEN

Fingertips skate over my stomach, rousing me from sleep. I open my eyes and decide that I must be dreaming. Drake is in my apartment. In my bed. And he's not just here, he's leaning on his elbow, staring down at me with an expression on his face that makes my breath stall in my throat. Not to mention his fingers are moving lower, which is really distracting. "Morning, baby."

I press my lips together. He sounds real enough and feels real enough, but it could still be a dream. "How long have you been watching me sleep?"

He scrunches his nose like he's deep in thought. "Not long. I mean you look pretty fucking adorable when you're sleeping, but it's kind of hard lying here next to you and having to keep my hands off your body." His fingers head farther south. "Actually it's *really* fucking hard."

I shift my hips, accidentally rubbing myself against him. Wow. Smirking, I run my hand down the length of his thick shaft. "I'd say it was rock solid, actually." A flush of satisfaction comes from the knowledge that I can make him feel like this, that I have this power over him. This is the first time in my life I've felt truly powerful, and I like it. A lot.

He slides his hand between my thighs, fingers teasing my sensitive flesh. "Yep. Totally irresistible," he murmurs, his voice huskier than usual. "Especially when you're all warm and soft like this."

I gasp as he slides a finger inside me, my body already responding to his touch. "Drake ..."

He claims my lips in a dominant kiss, already knowing my body so well it's like somebody drew him a map. He knows exactly what I like, exactly how I like it. He works me with his skilled fingers, and I arch up to meet him, my body craving more despite everything we did last night. Despite him waking me in the early hours to do it all over again.

"God, you get so fucking wet for me, Amelia," he groans against my neck, nipping at the sensitive skin there.

My cheeks flush with heat. He's not wrong. He works my body like he knows the cheat codes. Still, a girl has to play a little hard to get, right? "You're so sure of yourself, Drake James."

He laughs softly, his fingers slipping out of me. The loss of him makes me groan every single time. "I'll tell you what I am sure of." He rolls on top of me, pinning me to the bed with the weight of his body—not to mention his monster penis.

I raise an eyebrow in amusement. "And what's that?"

"I'm sure I'm going to eat your pussy until you scream this entire apartment building down." He presses a kiss at the base of my throat. "And when I'm done, you're going to ride me like my good fucking girl."

Sweet baby Jesus, yeah I am. I'm so used to lawyer Drake, office Drake, borderline-stern Drake, that this playfully domi-nant, filthy-mouthed god is leaving me dizzy. He's going to eat my pussy, and this time I have no hesitation at all about letting him do it. Not now that I know how it feels and how much he genuinely enjoys it.

"Aren't you, Amelia?" his growl is a low warning before his teeth pinch at my collarbone.

I gasp. "Yes sir." I didn't mean to call him sir, and I guess it could be a little weird given that he's actually my boss, but it also feels all kinds of right. He lets out a satisfied groan as he moves lower, suggesting that he thinks so too.

I curl my fingers in his hair, urging him down. He resists for a second, flashing me a smirk before he presses his palms flat to my inner thighs and pushes them wide apart. "Drake," I whimper.

He swipes his tongue firmly along the length of my wet center, and my back bows almost in half. He's a genius with that mouth. "So fucking sweet, baby," he groans. "I think I'm addicted to this pussy, have been since I very first tasted it. But I guess you already know that, huh?" His words vibrate through my flesh, making little tremors ripple through me.

Oh. Oh god, I hope he is addicted, because I never want him to stop. Every cell in my body is lighting up as he licks me.

"I asked you a question, Amelia," he mumbles, lips resting against my flesh.

He flicks his tongue over my clit, and my eyes roll back in my head. "S-sorry. W-what—what did you say again?"

He lies down sniper-style, long legs hanging off the end of my bed, still holding my thighs wide apart as he rubs his nose over my flesh. "I asked you if you know I'm addicted to the taste of this pussy. And I have no doubt you answered me in your head, Amelia, but I want to hear your words. What are you thinking?"

I press my lips together and draw a breath through my nose. I've never been especially vocal during sex. Chad used to like nothing more than the occasional light moan to let him know I hadn't fallen asleep, which was a very real risk on some nights. Shit. Why the hell am I thinking about Chad when the hottest man to ever don a suit has his face between my thighs? Drake deserves my full attention, and Chad deserves nothing at all.

"I ... I hope that you are addicted to it, Drake, because I want this all the time. Like every single day for the rest of my life."

He grunts, and I want to find a hole to curl up in. I took it too far and sounded crazy, like one of those women who chooses her wedding dress after one date. This is why I don't speak during sex. Impending orgasms make a girl say stupid shit. I'm about to take it back when Drake wraps his forearms around the backs of my thighs and pulls me even closer to his mouth, then he devours me. Over and over again, he brings me to the edge only to ease me back down.

My legs are trembling, my head spinning, heart racing. I'm going to pass out if he carries on like this. "Drake!"

"What is it?" The movement of his lips sends a series of delicious little vibrations through to my core. This man could get me off just by talking to my lady parts. If he weren't too busy torturing me, that is.

"Please let me come," I beg.

He hums while he eats, and those tiny vibrations grow stronger. I buck my hips, fingers digging into his scalp as I grind shamelessly against his face. Stars pepper my vision. Euphoria lights up my body. I am definitely going to pass out. He rims my clit with his tongue, then sucks on the hypersensitive bundle of nerves.

Blinding white light flashes behind my eyes, and my climax crashes over me in wave after wave of pure, unadulterated bliss. His name is dragged from my throat on a hoarse cry, and I gasp for breath. He gently licks and sucks, drawing out my pleasure until it slowly ebbs away, leaving behind a contented feeling that I could totally get used to. It's like my whole body has gone boneless, the most relaxed it's ever been.

Drake pushes himself up onto his forearms, his beard glistening with my arousal, but I'm way too happy to be embarrassed by how much of myself I've left on his face. With one sweep of his powerful hand, he wipes his jaw clean. Then he crawls over me again, his lips and fingers never leaving my skin. I love how tactile he is—it's like he literally can't keep his hands off me.

"You taste so fucking delicious, Amelia." With that, he seals his lips over mine and slides his tongue into my mouth.

I trail my hand between us, running my fingertips along the side of his thick shaft. He pulls back, a devilish grin spreading across his face. "Oh, you want that too, huh?"

"You did say I was going to get to ride you." I bite down on my lip, trying to look like a sex kitten but probably landing somewhere closer to beloved pet tabby. The sparkle in Drake's eyes tells me that might be good enough for him, though.

"I did, didn't I? I said you'd ride me like my good fucking girl." He tips his head back and groans at the touch of my fingers, then rolls onto his back, pulling me with him. I'm straddling him, my wet opening pressed against his rock-hard length. "Show me how much you want me, baby."

My heart beats an erratic rhythm in my chest. Surely if I show him exactly how much I want him, it will make him run as far and fast as he can to get away from me.

TWENTY-EIGHT

DRAKE

"I think you've broken me," I say, rolling onto my back and opening my arms wide. She scooches into them, her head on my chest, her soft laughter muffled against my skin. Her hair is draped across me, and I absentmindedly pick up a long strand. It's dark and straight and looks a little like a rope.

"I'm not sure I have," she says, nudging me with her thigh. "There's already movement down here—surely you can't be ready to go again. I mean, I know you have an amazing work ethic, but really?"

I slap her ass hard enough to make her squeal, and that sound, along with the image of using her hair to tie knots with, does indeed go straight to my cock. He's ready to go, but I'm not sure my heart is. I've gotten so much cardio over the last twenty-four hours that I might as well cancel my gym membership.

"This isn't work, Amelia. This is the best sex in the whole fucking world."

"You think?" She looks up at me and shrugs. "I suppose it's been okay ..."

I hoist her over my lap and slap her butt a few more times. I don't go easy on her, and her skin is bright red after only a couple of whacks. She's wriggling around and crying out, telling me to stop in between moans as she grinds herself on my thigh. When I finally let her up again, her hazel eyes are shining and her nipples are like pebbles. She glares at me, and I laugh.

"You liked that, huh?"

Her eyes blow wide. "No. Why would you think I liked it?"

Without a word, I run my hand up her silky-smooth inner thigh and slide a finger inside her. As I suspected, she's soaking wet. I pull my finger out and make her lick it clean.

"That," I say, watching her intently, "is how I know you liked it."

Her answering blush is absolutely adorable. We've been naked together since I first got her into this bed, and we've made each other come so many times I've lost count. Yet she is still so easily embarrassed. The big advantage of her being inexperienced is that I get to teach her so many new things.

"I kind of did, and that weirds me out," she says, biting on her plump lower lip. "Am I some kind of masochist? Will I be joining a sex club and needing a safe word next?"

I laugh and pull her back in for a cuddle. Jesus fuck. I'm not only cuddling, I'm loving every second of it. She really has broken me.

Or maybe, I think, she's fixed me.

"Not unless you want to, baby," I say, kissing her head. "In which case, yeah, of course. I happen to know a few places."

"I bet you do. You're the kind of man that knows places."

She sounds a little forlorn, and I tilt her chin up so she's looking me in the eyes. I want her to see me when I say this. "Amelia, I have a past. Like you say, I know places. But please don't let any of that make you feel worth less than you are."

"What am I worth?"

CHAPTER TWENTY-EIGHT

"Right now?" I stroke her cheek with my thumb. "Absolutely fucking everything."

Her smile reaches her eyes, and I realize I'm telling the absolute truth. I would pay a million bucks just to see that look on her face. She strokes my chest, tracing the shape of my pecs and grinning. My girl is insatiable, and I love that about her.

"Okay, so I have to talk to you about something," she says, and my stomach knots.

I hate conversations that start like that. "Go for it."

"Who was your mystery date?"

My mystery date? What is she talking about? She looks up at me, disappointed at my silence. "It's okay if you don't want to talk about it," she adds, though her tone implies it very much isn't.

"Baby, I'm happy to talk about it, but I genuinely don't have a clue who you're referring to."

She leans up on one arm, and her breasts beg me for attention. No. I need to concentrate. Amelia is an amazing woman, but she's still a woman, and I recognize a conversational minefield when I stumble into one. One false move and my nutsack could get blown off.

"The night of the team-building thing at the hotel."

I grin at her. "The night you got shit-faced with half of accounting and danced to Salt-N-Pepa on a pool table?"

"Yeah, that night. The same night you went out on a date. I'm asking you to tell me about it, but if you don't want to, that's fine." The way she says "fine" implies the exact opposite.

I cast my mind back to that particular day and grin when the lightbulb moment happens. "Oh! Right. That wasn't a date. That was Sapphire." She frowns and doesn't seem at all satisfied with my answer. "Sapphire is a friend, nothing more."

"But when you left, Nathan said to have a good date."

"Uh, first of all, creepy, but second, he was just joking.

Sapphire was his friend first, from college, and he always jokes that I stole his date. She really is just a friend, baby."

As much as I hate her doubting herself and doubting me, I like the fact that she's jealous. Compared to how I reacted when she went out for a meal with the asshole from accounting, she's downright restrained.

"I saw a picture of you with her online," she says, looking uncomfortable. "I wasn't stalking you or anything. Well, maybe a little. But you were with her after some premiere on Broadway, and she was all over you."

I press a kiss on her forehead. "I get my picture taken a lot, Amelia, you know that. I don't especially enjoy it, but it's part of my work and part of my life. And believe me when I tell you I wasn't going out on a date that night. All I could think about was you. Plus, I am very much not Sapphire's type."

"I don't believe that for a second. I mean, look at you—you're a walking sex god."

Her eyes rake over my body, and I enjoy the appreciation. "Thanks for that, but I'm definitely not Sapphire's type. You see, I don't have a vagina, and she likes vaginas. A lot."

I laugh as Amelia's eyes pop open and her hand flies up to cover her gaping mouth. "Oh! So Sapphire's a lesbian? Is she single? Because she's exactly my friend Kimmy's type."

"Is Kimmy a fan of vaginas too?"

"Kimmy's a fan of everything. She's great fun, you'll love her."

This is going to be one of those complicated situations we'll have to navigate. If we're keeping this a secret, can we meet each other's friends and family? Can we exist in each other's lives? I want nothing more than to show her off, to have her at my side every minute of every day, but how does that fit with maintaining discretion? I have no clue, but I have even less intention of dragging us both down right now. I finally got the woman into bed, and the only time I plan to let her out of it today is for food. She needs to keep her strength up.

As if she read my mind, she says, "You want to go get something to eat?"

"I don't really want to leave this bed, but much as I'm willing to try, man cannot live by pussy alone." Again, she blushes. No less adorable than last time.

"Don't you have to leave soon, though?" she asks. I frown because I haven't said anything at all about leaving. "I assumed you have work to do."

Right. Of course she did. And yeah, there's always something that needs doing. But I regularly put in hundred-hour or more weeks, so it won't kill me to take a weekend. "I thought I'd spend the day with my secretary instead. She's a sex maniac."

"She is? You lucky man. Okay, so we'll go out for food. Can you guess where I want to take you? What I want you to taste?"

I close my eyes and groan. I certainly can.

"Mario's exploding donut balls!" she yells, bouncing up and down on the mattress. It makes her gorgeous tits do some interesting things, and I grab hold of her and pull her onto my lap.

"All right, all right. But first, I need to make something else explode."

TWENTY-NINE

AMELIA

"What do you think?" I say, leaning forward and watching him closely. Wait for it, I think, wait for it, any moment now ... Boom! I see the moment he bites into the donut ball, and I laugh at his expression.

"Holy fucking shit!" he says, his eyes wide. He carries on chewing, and I grin at him. I would have been so disappointed if he hadn't reacted exactly like that.

"Wow, they really do explode, don't they? What's in these things, fucking cocaine?"

We're sitting on the benches that line the river, looking across the water. You get way better views from Brooklyn because you're looking at Manhattan, and I've really enjoyed showing Drake around my neighborhood. Obviously, he's been to Brooklyn many times before, but not *my* Brooklyn.

"I know, right?" I reply, delighted with his response. "I told you they were great."

"You did. In fact, this whole day has been great. I've got the sneaky feeling that's because ... you're great."

"Aw," I say, pulling a goofy face. "That's so sweet—and undoubtedly true. So, I showed you my old school, and I showed you Wanda's and O'Kelly's, the bar where I first got drunk."

"You did. I think I've had the complete Amelia-in-Brooklyn guided tour."

"More of a highlight reel. I wish ... I wish I could have shown you my mom's house. I mean, I did show you my mom's house, but I wish we could have gone in, you know? I'd love for you to meet her. I feel like I always talk about her when she's sick or when I'm stressed, and I skip over the fact that she's a lot of fun."

He smiles at me, his head tilted to one side and sunlight glinting from his dark hair. He's wearing the most un-Drake clothes I've ever seen him in—a pair of gray sweatpants and an I-heart-NY hoodie that he picked up from Mr. Aziz's Mini-mart. He was wearing his usual suit when he turned up at my place, and I think we were both surprised that he spent the night.

"I know." He raises my hand to his mouth for a kiss. "I'd love to meet her too. And maybe I will. I suppose we have a lot to figure out, don't we, Miss Ryder?"

"We sure do. Is it ... Is it too complicated for you, Drake?"

He pulls me into his arms and holds me so tight I can't breathe. It's the absolute best hug I've ever had. "It's complicated, yeah. But too complicated? No. You're worth a little complication. What about you? Any second thoughts?"

I wonder what he'd do if I told him I'd decided it wasn't worth the risk. Because I am taking a risk, more than he even knows. This isn't only about my job or my career or my reputation. It's about my heart. I haven't told him that I'm in love with him, but there's no getting away from it—I am hopelessly in love with Drake James.

"None," I say firmly, luxuriating in the simple pleasure of being with him. We've carried so much tension around with us for so long that this feels like paradise. To finally be able to relax, to enjoy each other's company, is bliss. That and all the orgasms, of course. "I don't care how messy it is. As you said, worth it. Like those exploding donut balls and the calories."

"I'd better be careful with those. I don't want to get fat. You'll find some new guy with a six-pack to take care of your insatiable appetite."

"Drake James, are you fishing for compliments? Because you are so not fat, and I can't imagine you ever will be. But even if you were ..."

"Even if I were?"

"Well, even if you were, you'd still have your magic tongue, wouldn't you?" I blush as I say it but force myself to meet his eyes.

His pupils flare, and he growls, "You're really becoming quite forward, Miss Ryder."

"I know," I say, laughing. "I'm different when I'm with you. It's not just a Scarlet or Amelia thing. It's all of it. The way you make me feel. The confidence you give me. I like the new me."

"So do I. Though I do think the new you is a little on the bratty side. I suspect she needs tying up and punishing." He arches an eyebrow at me, and his words go straight to my core.

I feel a familiar little throb between my legs, a pulsing heat that tells me I'm interested. "Hmmm. Maybe she does."

He takes hold of my face, one big hand on either side, and kisses me so thoroughly that I'm dizzy when he lets me go. It's lucky I'm sitting down. "There are so many things I want to do with you, Amelia."

"Like what?" I ask, looking up at him from beneath my eyelashes.

"Like tying you up and spanking your bratty little ass. Maybe doing something else with it too." He squeezes my ass cheek hard.

Does he mean ...? "Drake!" I say, shocked. Shocked but unexpectedly thrilled at the prospect.

"Have you ever been fucked in the ass, mi rosa?" he asks, his lips quirked up in a half-smile, his eyes blazing. He tugs his hoodie down over his groin, and I know what's going on in those sweatpants. An enormously hard cock is what's going on, and it's all for me.

"No," I reply quietly, forcing myself to meet his eyes even though I'm nervous.

His gaze runs over my lips. "You're trembling, Amelia. Don't worry, I'm not going to do it right now. I'm not going to do it at all if you don't want me to."

I suck on my teeth and snuggle closer into his embrace. Who am I kidding? Of course I want him to. "I want to try everything with you, Drake. Everything. I mean, you tried Mario's exploding donut balls for me."

"I don't think Mario's exploding donut balls are in quite the same category of experimentation as light bondage and anal, baby, but I like your spirit." He brushes his fingertips over my cheeks. "I can't fucking wait to explore it all with you. We just need to make sure we always communicate, okay? Let me know if you need something I'm not giving you."

I can't imagine ever needing anything that this man can't provide, but I nod. "I will." We spent too long apart because we weren't communicating properly, and I don't want that to happen again. In that vein, I should probably ask him what's been on my mind all morning. "Would you stay over again tonight? I mean you don't have to, it's just ... It would be really nice if you could." The thought of him leaving is already making me sad, and I can't bear the idea of saying goodbye when we've only just said hello.

He's silent for a few moments, and I think I've blown it already. I curl into myself, anticipating his rejection. "I can't bear the thought of being away from you tonight, mi rosa," he replies eventually. "I was just trying to figure out some logistics. I do have some work I need to do, and I'm not sure I want to buy more of my clothes from Mr. Aziz's Mini-mart."

"Why not? They suit you." He gives me a "yeah, right" look, and I carry on. "I'll come back to your hotel with you instead if you prefer. Or you could work from my apartment, and I'll take your shirt and suit to the laundromat."

The shocked look on his face is a picture. Suits like his require expert cleaning, but I enjoy pushing his buttons so much. "The laundromat?"

I swallow a laugh. "Uh, yeah. It's a place where normal people wash their clothes."

"I know what a damn laundromat is, you cheeky minx. But that suit is bespoke Armani. Dry-clean only."

Unable to contain my laughter any longer, I let out a very unattractive snort that makes him laugh too. "Some secretary I turned out to be, huh?" I say, my eyes wide with fake innocence.

He hums softly. "You have other skills. I especially liked that thing you did with your mouth this morning. Fuck, how the hell am I going to keep my damn hands off you now? It's going to be even harder at work."

I slip my hand along his thigh. "So far, it's been hard everywhere."

"Can't help it. I can't get enough of you, and neither can my cock. And that's fine everywhere else, but in the office? There's no way I can cope with seeing you every day and not fucking you. How will I look at you in your sexy little outfits—"

"I do not wear sexy little outfits."

"That, baby, is in the eye of the beholder—you always look sexy to me. I've been fantasizing about that wrap dress of yours for way too long. You, the dress, my desk. Me, balls-deep in your tight wet pussy. Choking you with those strings of pearls. Fuck, keeping this a secret is going to be impossible."

I'm feeling a little short of breath after that speech, and my pulse is pounding away in time with the throbbing in my core. His fantasies have become mine too.

"Unless you want to tell everyone?" he asks. "And not only because I want to fuck you over my desk, but because I want to make this work, mi rosa. So, whatever you need ..."

My heart almost explodes with happiness when he says he wants to make this work. "I don't think I'm ready for everyone to know yet, Drake. As much as you're worried about being known as the guy screwing his secretary, it's way worse to be known as the woman banging her new boss."

He sucks on his top lip and nods. "I get it. We'll keep it under wraps. It'll be a piece of cake, right?" He winks at me, and I almost melt into his lap.

"It can't be any more difficult than the last few months, can it? I swear, the amount of times I've imagined kneeling at your feet and unzipping your pants while you're dictating ..." I press my hand over my mouth to stifle a snigger.

"Miss Ryder." He gasps loudly before burying his lips against my neck. "I hope you know that is how all dictation is going to go from here on out."

He tickles me, and I burst into a fit of giggles, wondering how on earth my world got so big and bright so quickly.

THIRTY

DRAKE

Although I've already fucked her twice this morning, it kills me to leave her in bed. Looking at her as she lies there all drowsy and satisfied is enough to make me hard again. Even if I weren't, I'd still want to stay. I hate the thought of leaving her naked body while it's all warm and soft and so fucking ready for me.

"Are you sure you have to go?" she says lazily, rolling onto her belly and looking up at me. I eye her gorgeous round ass and growl. "Yes. Believe me, I'd rather stay here with you. And your ass. But we don't all have today off."

"I know," she says, stretching out. "Lucky me, eh? Or maybe just really great planning, who knows?"

I arch an eyebrow at her. "Maybe my secretary should organize my calendar a little more efficiently. I definitely need a day off soon." A day for me to spend every fucking hour with a part of me inside her.

Her lips twitch with a smirk. "But seriously, I know how important work is to you, and I know you've already taken the weekend off. But will I ... Will I see you later? Or at work tomorrow?"

I should say I'll see her at work tomorrow and give us both a little breathing room, but my dick is already telling me that's not going to happen. Still, I try to play it as casual as possible. "I'll call you tonight, mi rosa. We can make plans if you want to. And if you're lucky, maybe they'll be plans involving that beautiful ass. "

I lean down and kiss her, my tongue tangling with hers and her arms snaking around my neck. "Promises, promises," she says, winking at me. Fuck. Yeah. Definitely hard again. It's going to be an uncomfortable ride back to the penthouse.

I close the door behind me and walk straight into two teenage boys who are standing in the communal hallway. They look about sixteen and seventeen, all gangly limbs, peach fuzz, and low-hanging skater pants. They stare at me for a few seconds, then the taller one breaks out into a grin. "Dude!" he says. "Way to go!"

They disappear off into their apartment, laughing and pushing each other, and I can't help smiling. I guess the walls to her apartment are pretty damn thin.

Constantine is waiting outside for me, and he raises one eyebrow when he sees how I'm dressed. He knows this is her place and that I've been here since he dropped me off on Friday. "I can trust you, right?" I say simply.

"Of course, boss. My lips are sealed. And congrats. She's a great girl. Here's that number you asked me to find."

I murmur my thanks and climb inside, sinking into the soft black leather seat with a sigh. My temples throb with an impending headache. It's been a long time since I stayed up all night doing anything other than work. I wasn't at all tired while I was with her, but now the lack of sleep is threatening to catch up with me. I need a quick shower, fresh clothes, and coffee, not necessarily in that order.

I glance at the phone number on the folded piece of paper. It belongs to Trent McKenzie, owner of McKenzie Holdings and a number of apartment buildings across the state. He answers after a few rings, his voice thick with sleep.

"Trent McKenzie?" I ask.

"Yeah. Who the fuck's this?"

"Drake James, on behalf of the law firm James and James. I'm calling about the apartment building you own in Brooklyn."

He snorts. "It's six fucking a.m. Call the office."

"I'm aware of the time, which is precisely why I'm calling you and not your office. Specifically regarding the building violations at Geneva Place."

"That building is up to code," he snaps. "They're all up to code."

"I don't give a rat's ass about your other buildings, Trent, but the security measures at Geneva are nonexistent. I'll let you do a little research on my law firm when you get off this call. But know this, if you don't have a security system that prevents strangers from entering the building in place by the end of the week, I will take a very personal interest in you and all of your properties. If that happens, you and I will get to know each other really well, and I promise you that is not something you want to happen."

"Who the fuck do you—"

"Think I am? Like I said, look me up." I end the call and close my eyes, pressing my neck back against the headrest. That was satisfying, at least, and helped me blow off steam ahead of what I know will be a tough day. I have to talk to Nathan, for starters.

The thought of that fills me with dread, but I remind myself of why I need to speak to him. Amelia Ryder. Everything about her calls to me. Her deep, infectious laugh, the way her eyes sparkle when she smiles, her hands in my hair. My head between her thighs. Her scent. Her taste.

I stifle a groan. Today is going to be a long fucking day, made even worse by the fact that she won't be in it.

~

I JERK my head in the direction of my older brother's office door. "Is he free?"

Helen offers me a brief smile. "Well, he's not in a meeting." Her not-so-subtle way of telling me he's slammed and I shouldn't take up too much of his time. Probably sorting out the shit with the Ryans that he mentioned on Friday, which now feels like a different lifetime.

"I won't keep him long, Helen."

"He will always make time for you, Mr. James, you know that."

"Noted." I stride past her desk and knock once, then announce it's me before stepping inside.

He's just putting down his phone and raises an eyebrow when he sees me. "Hello, stranger," he says, looking marginally pissed. "Where the fuck have you been?"

"You mean over the weekend? Traditionally the time when people aren't in the office?"

"You're not *people* though, are you Drake? You're a workaholic who thinks weekends are fictional. And anyway, I wasn't talking about work. You disappeared from Dad's on Friday, and nobody's been able to get hold of you on the phone since. I ended up checking in with Constantine just to make sure you were alive." His right eye twitches, and he shoves his hands through his hair. I bite back my sarcastic retort. He already looks stressed as fuck, and I'm about to add to his woes.

"Message received and understood, brother. I was a selfish ass, and I apologize. You okay? You look like shit."

"Thanks, I appreciate the compliment." He scrubs his hand down his face and sighs. "Sorry I went off on you. You're a grown-up, you can do what you like with your spare time. I'm just in a crappy mood. Luke is teething, and sleep is a distant land. Plus, three of the Ryans' clubs got raided last week, so they've obviously pissed off somebody important. I feel like I'm wading through shit."

I drop into the seat opposite him, watching as he flicks his tongue over his bottom lip. For the Iceman, this is having a meltdown. "Anything I can help with?"

"You can take me out for a drink when this day from hell is over."

When this day from hell is over, I'll either be heading back to Brooklyn or I'll be in my penthouse wishing I was in Brooklyn. Every moment away from her feels wasted, and I already miss her. Still, this is my brother, and if he needs a drink and some company, I'll make sure he gets it.

"That I can do, bro. How's Mel?"

"She's fine, why?"

"Well, I'm guessing that Luke's teething and sleepless nights are probably affecting her too. And, you know, I like her more than I like you."

Eyes twinkling, he places his hand over his heart. "Ouch! You really know how to boost a guy's morale, don't you?"

I nod. "It's a gift. And everyone likes her more than you, so you better get used to it."

He laughs, then rests his forearms on the desk. "Did you come here to tell me how much you like my wife, or was there something else?"

Oh yeah. That. I wince. This is our firm. The clue's in the name—James and James. We built it together, but I can never escape the feeling that he's really the one in charge. Maybe it's because it was his idea or because he's a few years older than me. I don't know where it comes from, but right now I feel like I'm asking permission or apologizing, and I don't love it.

"Yeah. I do need to talk to you about something."

He nods, eyes narrowed as he regards me with suspicion. I loosen my tie. "Stop trying to read me, Nathan."

"Can't help it. It's my job. Stop fidgeting and talk to me. Then I won't need to read you, will I?"

I blow out a breath. I guess I better just rip off the Band-Aid. "I slept with Amelia."

He frowns. "This isn't new information."

"Again. This weekend. Several times."

He closes his eyes and leans back in his chair. "For fuck's sake, Drake," he mutters.

"Don't *for fuck's sake* me. Like you just said, I'm a grown-up."

His eyes snap open. "I take that back. You fucked your goddamn secretary. Do you have any idea of the Pandora's box you just opened? Of how many HR policies you're in breach of? You could get the whole firm sued or canceled."

Anger simmers beneath my skin. "Don't treat me like your fucking junior associate, Nathan. I—"

"A junior associate fucking your secretary wouldn't be half as bad as you doing it, numbnuts," he barks.

I know he's right, but still, I'm pissed and I'm not here for a lecture. I'm here to talk to my brother, my ally in life, and instead, I feel like I'm talking to my boss.

"I know that, dipshit. And I don't need to be reminded of our HR policies. I fucking wrote them."

He grinds his jaw like he wants to argue, but for whatever reason, he doesn't. We've had our fair share of fights, and we both know how easily it can escalate. "And don't call it fucking," I add. "It was more than that."

He sighs, leaning back in his chair. The anger seems to drain out of him, and he just looks tired. "What the fuck, Drake?"

"I know. I tried to stay away from her. I tried so fucking hard. But I couldn't. I can't stop thinking about her for more than a damn second." I screw my eyes closed and wait for a rebuke that never comes.

"So what the hell are you going to do now?" he asks instead, his tone a little softer.

I recall the way I left her, lying naked on her bed, her big hazel eyes looking up at me with such trust. She's taking a huge chance on me, and I won't let her down. "I like her, Nathan. And she really likes her job."

His frown turns to a scowl. "So?"

I suck in a deep breath. "So we're going to keep seeing each other in secret and see where this goes. For the time being, she's going to keep working for me. I was thinking of getting her moved over to work with Fred Darwin when Marla goes on maternity, but—"

"Fred announced his retirement. Yeah."

I was actually kind of glad when I got word. Having Amelia around was torture, at least before this weekend, but it was a torture I was addicted to. Now I'm addicted to everything about her, and I don't want anybody else as my secretary.

Nathan blinks at me. I loosen my tie again, and we stare at each other in silence like we're in some kind of standoff. What the fuck did I come in here for? Approval? No, I came for advice. Maybe even for congratulations, because this is a big fucking deal for me. Deep down, I was excited to tell him and thought he'd be happy for me. Instead, he seems more concerned with HR policies and our image.

Even if he thinks I'm a nutjob who's putting our entire firm at risk, he's still my big brother, and I want him to be that right now more than anything else. "I've never felt like this before, Nathan. Not about Tiff, and definitely not about anybody since then. My last relationship ended when I was twenty-three. I don't know what I'm doing, and I badly want this to work. How do I not fuck it up?"

"You haven't exactly given yourselves a fighting chance, Drake. The secrecy ..." He shakes his head and lets out a weary sigh. "It might be exciting for a while, but it'll get old real fucking quick. What about Dad and the others? Will you tell them? Will she tell her family, her friends? Will Emily Gregor gossip about it to Amber at some society lunch?"

"Amber already knows some of it, and she isn't likely to do anything to damage our firm, Nathan."

He looks surprised and a little upset. Maybe he thinks I should have confided more in him, but here we are, shooting daggers at each other. Is it any wonder I didn't?

"I don't find the secrecy exciting, by the way. I fucking hate it. But for now, there's no other way to do this. I can't force her out of her job. It wouldn't be fair. And I have no intentions of going back to Chicago."

He jerks back as though I've taken a swing at him. "Who even mentioned you going back to Chicago?"

"That would be the only way for me to not be her boss. I could transfer her, I guess, but I know she'd see it as a punishment, and ..." I drop my head into my hands. "Of all the fucking people I could fall for."

"She'll have to sign an NDA," he says, his legal brain kicking in and looking for solutions.

My head snaps up. "Fuck no," I say, my legal brain completely backfiring.

He rolls his eyes. "It's no big deal. We've had employees sign them before."

Is he fucking serious? I get to my feet, outraged. "Not about stuff like this. Not a please-don't-tell-anyone-your-boss-screws-you-on-his-desk-every-afternoon NDA."

Nathan's eyes flicker to his desk, and I swear that deviant

fucker smirks. I fold my arms and lean away. "You've fucked Mel on this desk, haven't you?"

"A gentleman never tells," he says smoothly, but the twinkle in his eyes says I'm right. Of course I'm right. What's the point of having your own office and a huge sturdy desk if not to fuck the woman you're obsessed with on it every chance you get?

I force images of Amelia naked and spread out on my desk from my head and sit back down. "I'm not having her sign an NDA. I trust her."

"You barely know her," he counters.

"I know her better than I know any other employee we have."

"Let's fucking hope she's the only one you know so intimately," he mutters.

I roll my eyes. "Get your head out of the gutter. I don't mean like that. I know when I can trust someone, Nathan, and I can trust Amelia."

He runs a hand over his jaw, staring past me at the painting hanging on his office wall. He does his best thinking staring at the painting of the beach in Spain that Mom finished before she got too sick to paint anymore. "If this gets out ..."

"It won't. At least not until we're ready for it to. Hey, maybe it'll just fizzle out and we're worrying for nothing." Even as I say that, I find myself thinking *like fuck it will*.

We sit in silence again, with nothing but the relentless ticking of his clock and my own heartbeat in my ears. Like always, it's me who cracks first. "Just please tell me you have my back. It's not like the way you and Mel started up was conventional."

"I always have your fucking back, dickwad. That doesn't mean I have to agree with everything you do or throw a fucking ticker tape parade at every stupid decision you make. You really, truly like this girl?"

I can't help but grin at him. "Yeah, I do."

"All right. Then I suppose you'd better find a way to make it work, hadn't you?"

I will find a way, I vow to myself. Amelia Ryder is mine, and there's not a chance in hell I'm ever letting her go. I'm going to make that woman happy if it's the last damn thing I do.

THIRTY-ONE

AMELIA

"Amelia, honey?" Mom says as soon as I answer my phone. She sounds different than usual—more excited, more like her old self.

"Hey, Mom! I was just on my way over. I'm in Mr. Aziz's place. Do you need anything?"

"No, I'm fine. Look, there's a man here who says he knows you."

I place the ice cream I was inspecting back in the freezer and give her my full attention. Mom has lived in New York all her life, but I still wouldn't call her streetwise. She's always been quick to see the good in people, and I usually think that's an admirable quality, but maybe not where strange men are concerned.

I quickly pay for my goods, give Mr. Aziz a little wave as I leave, and start to power-walk the five blocks to my childhood home. "What's his name, Mom? And you haven't let him in the house, have you? Look, I'll be there soon. Is the slugger still in the hallway?" Two women living alone need to take a few precautions, and we've always kept a baseball bat by the door.

"Amelia, sweetheart, stop worrying. Constantine is a

perfectly lovely man. He's been showing me photos of his baby girl."

I stop in my tracks, flooded first with relief, but then confusion hits. What the hell is Drake's driver doing at my mom's house?

It's been almost a week since we finally worked out that we wanted to be together, and I'm the happiest I've ever been. Sure, the secrecy thing is a drag, and our living arrangements leave a lot to be desired, but I'm not complaining. The man drives me crazy in bed, and added to that, he's great company. I know it's early days, but every time I think of him, I get this goofy grin that I can't quite wipe off my face.

"Right. Okay, well, I do know Constantine. Can you put him on for a moment?"

"Hi, Miss Ryder." His familiar deep voice sounds amused. Constantine is one of the few people who knows the truth about me and Drake, and I can't help but think it must be like watching a soap opera for him.

"Back at ya, Constantine. You mind telling me what you're doing in Brooklyn? Specifically at my mom's house, at night?"

"Uh, I could tell you, Miss Ryder, but then I'd have to kill you."

"Ha ha," I say, deadpan. "Spill."

"It's a surprise. Organized by our lord and master himself."

I have to laugh at that. He's a funny guy, Constantine. I sigh and tell him I'll be there soon. He gives the impression of being super laid-back, but he's a tough cookie. He won't crack over the phone.

When I arrive at Mom's, Drake's SUV is taking up most of the street and net curtains are twitching in every window. A few neighborhood kids stand a couple feet away, staring at it in amazement. Seeing a car like that in a place like this is pretty much akin to a spaceship landing and little green men walking down a gangplank.

"Moving up in the world, Amelia?" shouts Mrs. Katzberg from across the way. She's sitting out on her porch, doing a crossword puzzle and smoking a cigarette, which has been her nighttime routine for as long as I've known her.

"Doing my best, Mrs. K, doing my best."

The scene inside is hilarious. Constantine is a big man, and he overwhelms the small living space. My mom is next to him on the couch, wearing a dress I've never seen before. It's her kind of style but looks expensive, in a pretty shade of deep green that brings out the forest tones in her eyes. She's brushed her hair out into a big nimbus and is even wearing a flash of red lipstick. She used to love a red lip, but I haven't seen her like this in years.

"Amelia!" She jumps up and skips toward me. Her breathing pays the price, but she stands still and recovers quickly, her eyes sparkling from excitement. "We're going to the movies."

"What?" I look to Constantine for answers, and when none are forthcoming, I return my attention to her. "But I thought you didn't want to go to the movies anymore. You said you didn't feel comfortable being around all those people."

"I know, but tonight there won't be any other people. Constantine here tells me you've won some kind of prize at work, baby. Employee of the month? Why didn't you tell me?"

Uh, because it's a totally made-up thing? But she looks so happy that I can't possibly burst her bubble. I haven't seen her this excited in a long time, and it makes my heart sing.

"Thank you so much for choosing this as your reward, sweetie. I can't believe your Mr. James booked out the entire theater just for us. And he's screening *Witness*—you know that one where Harrison Ford is a detective and he has to hide out with an Amish family? You remember? The one with the really hot dance scene to that Sam Cooke song?"

"I remember, Mom," I say, smiling at how animated she is. "This is great. I'll just go and freshen up, if I have time?" I look to Constantine for an answer.

"Certainly, Miss Ryder. The show won't be starting without its guests of honor. The employee of the month is a big deal."

I shoot him a look and head upstairs. As soon as I'm alone, I dial Drake's number. "What the heck is going on? Since when am I employee of the month?"

"Mi rosa, you're employee of the month every month. That blowjob you gave me this morning at my desk? Sensational."

My body heats at the memory. I loved the feel of his huge cock in my mouth, teasing him with my tongue, making him groan, torturing him the same way he tortures me. And the delicious salty taste of him when he came ...

"Amelia, are you still there?"

"Uh, yes. But I'm still confused."

I hear noise in the background, the sound of a baby crying. "Is Luke still teething?" I ask. It's weird that we know so much about each other's families without being directly involved in them.

"He is, and it's turned him into a grouchy little F.U.C.K."

"I don't think you need to worry about him copying your words at his age, Drake."

"You never know. He's a bright kid. Anyway, I know her birthday is coming up, and I wanted to do something nice for your mom and, by extension, something nice for you. You've been worried about her, and I just thought this might be, you know, nice." He pauses, and I picture him sitting there with the baby on his lap. I always wanted kids with Chad, but every time I raised the subject, he said we weren't ready. That we'd do it next year. Next year never came, and I have no idea now if I'll ever be a mom. I'd love to meet Luke some time, though.

"I can't believe how many times I said the word 'nice' in that sentence," Drake says. "Between this baby and you, my brain is getting turned to mush."

"Aaah, that's nice," I say, giggling. "And thank you. Did you send the dress for her as well?"

"I did. I've seen pictures of her, so I knew what she liked. I told her it was all part of the prize package you chose."

"Wait, you spoke to my mom?" I ask, frowning. I mean, it's not exactly breaking the rules, but it's not something I expected either.

"Just briefly, on the phone. Don't worry, I didn't mention that I was also fucking your brains out every day."

I suppress another giggle. "Well, that's something. Will you be able to come to the movies with us?"

"Much as I'd like to sit in the back row and get up close and personal with you, Miss Ryder, I'm babysitting tonight. Constantine is at your service for the whole evening, though, and I've arranged for concessions to be open and free of charge, so go crazy with the popcorn. They also have two other Harrison Ford movies on hand if she's enjoying herself."

"Which ones?" I ask, curious.

"*Working Girl* and *Cowboys & Aliens*."

"Ooh, that's the one with Daniel Craig in it too!"

"Don't sound so excited, Miss Ryder, or I might get jealous." I think he's joking, but I'm not really sure. For all I know, he might threaten to break Daniel Craig's fingers and banish him to the Chicago office.

Mom's calling my name from downstairs, so I don't have time to find out. "Thank you again. This was incredibly thoughtful of you. I really do, um, like you, you know?"

Shit. That was close. I almost dropped an accidental "I love you" into the conversation. And neither of us are ready for that hand grenade to be tossed into our relationship just yet.

THIRTY-TWO

AMELIA

My mom had the absolute best time at the movies and stayed for all of *Witness* and *Working Girl*. I could see the change in her, the way she laughed and smiled as she was transported back to the eighties, a time when I guess her life was more carefree. Before she was a mother and had to work so hard to raise me.

I have always felt loved and cherished by my mom. I know she never regretted having me for a second, but I also know it's been tough. She doesn't talk about my father, but I always got the impression that he hurt her badly. The few things she let slip over the years suggested that he didn't want anything to do with her once she got pregnant and that he left her to deal with it all alone. I don't care who he is, and I have no desire to meet him. If he hurt my mom like that, he isn't worth shit and doesn't deserve to know me. Mom is enough for me, and I love seeing her happy.

Having the whole theater to ourselves was such a treat, and I spent as much time watching her as I did the giant screen. Seeing such simple joy on her face filled me with new hope, as well as love for Drake that he would organize something like that for her. She took her little oxygen tank with her, and because we were there alone, she didn't feel embarrassed about using it or her inhalers. Going to the bathroom wasn't an endurance test for her because they stopped the films when she left. She ate a hotdog, popcorn, and got through a huge container of Coke, so excited by it all that you'd think she'd never eaten from a concession stand before in her life. Money can't buy happiness, I know, but on nights like that, it sure can feel like it.

Since then, she's seemed much more upbeat. Her health hasn't changed and her blood oxygen levels are still unpredictable, but mentally, she seems much better. Today is her birthday, and she's actually agreed to come out for lunch with me to celebrate. We've booked a table at a cute little Italian place she likes in the neighborhood, and Emily and Kimmy are going to meet us there.

I know she's nervous, but at least she's willing to try, and that's really all I can ask. Looks like Drake James has worked his magic in more ways than one.

My body heats and my heart flutters when I think about him, which I seem to always be doing. Things are going so great that I'm actually anxious, which I know is completely messed up, but life has taught me a few harsh lessons. Everything about him thrills me, and I can't get enough. So far, the feeling seems entirely mutual, but part of me wonders how long that will last. How long a man like him will be interested in a woman like me. I mean, even Chad got fed up with me, and he wasn't a fraction of the man that Drake is.

As soon as I think about Drake, I miss him. I took the day off work, and although I'm excited about my day, I still wish he was in it. He hasn't been in touch this morning, but my phone has been giving me issues, so maybe that's why. The landlord of my building seems to have gone temporarily insane and has started an impromptu schedule of renovations. We've now got security cameras in the lobby and everyone is getting an individual intercom system so we can buzz our own guests up. He's even upgrading the Wi-Fi hub and introducing free cable. It's all pretty great, but the disruption is a little annoying, and I must admit that I'm worried about my rent when it comes time to renew my lease.

Men wearing Hi-Vis jackets and hard hats have been outside using their pneumatic drills since seven this morning. Whatever it is they're up to, my Wi-Fi has been out for hours, and my data service won't connect.

I'm sure it will all be back to normal soon, and until then, maybe I can have a little fun. Drake often messages me real early and asks what I'm wearing, even though he's going to see it in the office. It's a little joke between us. I decide to preempt it and type out a few lines, grinning as my fingers fly over the keyboard.

> Today I'm wearing a cute little sundress with a lace-up top. But not so long ago, I was wearing nothing at all. I was naked and thinking of you.

I'm getting better at this stuff, but I still occasionally feel embarrassed when I flirt with him so outrageously. He'll want photos, and I know exactly what he likes. Lying back on the bed, I untie the ribbon on the peasant-style top—just enough to let my breasts spill out a little—and take a quick snap. I know he's in meetings all day today, and I love the thought of him seeing this while he's in the middle of one. I know the effect it will have on him, that he will immediately go hard as he imagines untying the rest of that ribbon.

Maybe he's right, I think, as I press send. Maybe I am a vixen after all. I love the way he makes me feel about myself.

I tie myself back up so I look respectable and grab my jacket and purse. I want to stop by the florist on my way to the restaurant and buy Mom a huge bouquet of her favorite flowers.

I wave to the workmen as I pass and get an appreciative smile in return. No wolf whistles, though, and I laugh as I picture them sitting through workplace sensitivity training.

It's a gorgeous summer day, the sun bright and warm on my skin, so dazzling that I wish I'd brought shades. I love this time of year, when everything feels so bright and hopeful, the colorful flowers and bright blue skies making it difficult to remember the gloom from a few short months ago. New York can be hell in winter, but this always makes up for it. My optimism and joy are at an all-time high as I stroll through the neighborhood and exchange pleasantries with people I've known my whole life. The florist knows exactly what I'm there for and has already put together the most gorgeous bouquet of bright yellow sunflowers that emit a mildly sweet scent. I call out my thanks once more and bounce out the door, excited about having lunch with Mom and my best friends.

I haven't told any of them about Drake. The two of us made a deal to keep it a secret, and I intend to stick to it. It's there to protect us both. But I'm so damn happy and desperate to share the reason for that happiness with the three of them. They were all there for me when Chad broke my heart, and I can't wait until they can be there to see how well my heart has healed. That it's stronger than ever.

I duck into Wanda's, intending to get a box of cannoli for later. For Drake, when he comes over to untie this dress. I'm waiting in line, hoping there's some pistachio left, when my phone lets out a barrage of bleeps. Looks like it's back in action. Rolling my eyes, I fish it from my purse. A whole morning's worth of communication is probably all landing at once.

There is a whole load of messages and missed calls. Unease creeps in as I scroll through them. The unease turns to outright panic starts when I realize that most of the early ones are from Mom. After that are several from a number I don't recognize.

I click quickly through to my voicemails, and the first one is from my mom, telling me she maybe doesn't feel well enough to make lunch today, apologizing for being a "wet blanket." The next is also from her, saying that she definitely can't make it because she feels too rough. The third one asks if I can come by, and she sounds terrible—breathless, exhausted, her voice small and strained as she struggles to get the words out and breathe at the same time.

My heart is beating frantically in my chest. The line at Wanda's has moved on, and it's my turn to be served, but I stagger outside, tears filling my eyes. In spite of my shaking legs, I run toward Mom's house, pulling up the last voicemail as I do. It's from a nurse at the local hospital, telling me that she's looking for the next of kin of Edith Ryder and could I call her back as soon as possible.

My feet seem to stop working. I stumble before quickly righting myself and continuing toward her place despite knowing she's not there. It's fine. It will all be fine. My breathing is fast and shallow. Blood whooshes in my ears. Fear grips my chest, and I suck in deep, rasping breaths. What could have happened? Why didn't I check on her earlier? Why didn't I spend the night with her so I could wake up with her on the morning of her birthday? I'm the worst daughter in the whole damn world.

I reach my childhood home out of breath, my head spinning with questions and scenarios. Mrs. Katzberg shouts me over and lays a wrinkled hand on my arm. "Calm down, honey. Take a breath, won't you. It's not gonna help anyone if you pass out as well."

"I know, I know ... What happened, Mrs. K?"

"She left in an ambulance maybe an hour and a half ago,

dear. She didn't look great, I won't lie, but she was still kicking, and that's what matters, right? Now listen, I've been in the hospital so many times I've lost count, and she'll need some things. Go into the house now and put her a bag together. Her pajamas, her toothbrush, her favorite pillow—anything that will make her more comfortable while she's there. Then hightail it over there—I'll give you a ride."

I nod, grateful to have the older woman tell me what to do. I let myself into the house, and it all feels so normal. The TV is still on, and her half-empty coffee mug is on the table next to a romance novel she was reading. I stand still and force myself to breathe like Mrs. K said. I feel sick. Hot and sick. But I dash around my childhood home, grabbing the items Mrs. K suggested. I add the romance novel as well, hoping she gets the chance to finish it.

I'm stressed and distracted during the drive there, which is probably a good thing because Mrs. K is eighty-seven and really shouldn't be behind the wheel of a car anymore. I quickly message Emily and Kimmy, telling them what's happened and promising to be in touch later. I thank Mrs. K for the ride—and thank God for surviving it—and clamber out, telling her I'll let her know what's going on. She's parked in a taxi zone, and when one of the yellow cars beeps its horn at her, she leans out the window, gives him the finger, and swears at him in several different languages. Damn. Remind me to never mess with Mrs. Katzberg.

Within a few minutes, I'm at Mom's bedside, holding her hand and telling her I'm sorry. She's in and out of consciousness, a plastic oxygen mask on her face, the monitors she's hooked up to bleeping and flashing in a sickening chorus. She turns, sees me, and squeezes my fingers. She tries to pull off her mask, but I hold it in place.

"No, let's leave that exactly where it is, shall we? I'm sorry I didn't get here sooner, Mom. I love you so much. I can't believe this has happened."

She gestures me closer, and her voice is just above a whisper. "It's okay, honey. I'll be fine. But this birthday sucks ass."

I can't help laughing, probably way harder than the comment deserves, but I'm so damn relieved that she's talking. That she's still here. She's still her.

"Miss Ryder?" a nurse asks, approaching me from the doorway.

"Yes, that's me. I'm sorry it took me so long to get here. I didn't have cell reception, and then I had errands, and then I was in Wanda's, and ..."

"Hey," the nurse says as she guides me out into the hallway, her sneakered feet squeaking on the linoleum. "Slow down. It's okay. Some people take days to respond to us, so you're doing well." She waits for me to nod before continuing. "Your mom was brought in to us this morning with an acute exacerbation of her COPD. She had chest pains, wheezing, and she was having trouble breathing."

"What was her O2?" I ask, no stranger to this stuff.

"It was eighty-two when she arrived, but we've stabilized her. With the oxygen and the steroids, she's up to eighty-six now. Still not great, obviously, and we need to do some more tests to see what's going on with her, but please try not to worry too much."

That's easy for her to say, I think, glancing back at my mom. It's not her mother lying there.

"My dad has it too," she adds, smiling at me sympathetically. "And I see cases like this every day. It's a bad flare-up, but I think she'll be fine. She's in the best place."

"It's her birthday, you know. I bought her sunflowers, but I ... I don't know where they are." I could have dropped them in the bakery, in the house, or even in Mrs. K's car. I don't suppose it matters. I'll get her more flowers.

"It must be so hard to have your special plans derailed by all this. I'm really so sorry. Maybe she'll be feeling better later and you can bring her a cake."

The warmth and assurance in her tone lifts a small bit of the weight from my shoulders. "Thank you, Nurse. I really do appreciate your kindness."

"Of course. There is little worse than seeing our parents so vulnerable. I know it isn't the best time, Miss Ryder, but when you have a moment, I do need to get some information from you."

Of course she does. Thank goodness I have a good job with a fantastic healthcare package. I would have found the money we needed regardless, but it's one less thing to worry about, and I'm grateful.

I tell her I'll go with her now, and the mundane act helps to calm me down. Emily and Kimmy both send their love and ask me to keep them updated, and Drake has responded to the message I sent earlier.

> You are a shameless siren and I had to leave the board room as soon as I saw you in that dress. There will be consequences. And you will enjoy them. I'll call you later do discuss terms.

Normally, I'd be thrilled. I'd feel that familiar sense of warmth run through me, the delicious tingle between my legs, excitement about seeing him later. Now, though, I just feel … I feel empty.

I dial his number, not expecting him to answer but wanting to hear his voice on the recording. Even listening to him say "Hi, you've reached Drake James" might ground me. I will tell him about my mom tonight, obviously, but not while he's so busy. I know his schedule inside and out—I'm the one who set it for him —and today is an absolute doozy with back-to-back meetings.

I'm so surprised when he picks up that I don't speak.

"Cat got your tongue, vixen?" he says, his voice liquid chocolate. "In which case, lucky cat." I open my mouth to respond, but nothing comes out. "Amelia? Are you there? Is everything okay?"

"Um, no," I finally say. "Not really. My mom's in the hospital. I wasn't going to mention it ... What are you doing answering your phone anyway? Shouldn't you be in the Vickerson deposition right now?"

"It got pushed back so I was grabbing a coffee. What do you mean, your mom's in the hospital? What happened? Which hospital? I'll be right there."

"No, no. Please don't do that. There's no need. I know what today looks like for you, and there's nothing you can do here anyway. She's okay. She had a bad flare-up and got brought in by ambulance, but she's okay."

I don't tell him how I found out or how devastated I am knowing I let her down. I know he'll understand, but I don't want to cry on the phone. I don't want to be weak or to need him as much as I do. What if he lets me down?

"Amelia, have I ever given you reason to believe that I'm a heartless bastard?" he asks, raising his voice slightly to be heard over a blaring horn and muffled shouts.

"No, of course you haven't. I don't think that about you at all. I just know that your work is important, and I don't want to drag you away for nothing."

"You are not nothing, mi rosa. Now, where are you? I could get one of the other secretaries to call every hospital in New

CHAPTER THIRTY-TWO

York, starting with Brooklyn, but it would be far easier if you just told me."

Giving in, I tell him. He says he'll be here as soon as he can, then hangs up, probably to call Constantine.

So many emotions wrestle for dominance that I have no idea which to focus on. There's worry about Mom, guilt for not being there for her, fear that if I pull Drake into this part of my life, he'll see how dull my world actually is. And as I turn that one over and examine it, I realize it's the one that I'm least sure what to do with.

This thing between us is so new, so fragile. There are so many reasons for it not to work. Will it survive something like this? Can it survive it, given his own experiences? It's clear that he still struggles with his own demons when it comes to his mother's passing, although he hasn't shared them with me.

And what the hell is wrong with me? I'm sitting here, worrying about my not-quite boyfriend when my mom is upstairs in a hospital bed.

I head straight back up to her room, determined to push all thoughts of Drake from my mind. Whatever will be, will be.

I reach the doorway to her room and stop dead in my tracks. She's not alone, and the man holding her hand isn't a doctor or a nurse. He's someone I know much better than that. Someone who really shouldn't be anywhere near us.

"Chad? What are you doing here?"

THIRTY-THREE

DRAKE

The guy standing in front of my girl smiles, flashing a row of perfectly straight, dazzling white teeth that I'd quite happily punch down his throat. Then he holds out his hand. "Chad Poindexter."

I glance down at his hand but don't reciprocate. "Yeah, I know who you are."

Unbothered by my refusal to shake his hand, he smiles wider. "You do, huh? I'm honored to know you've heard of me."

Yeah, don't be, dickface. I only know who you are because I googled you when I started obsessively cyberstalking your ex-wife because I'm so into her that I had to see for myself what kind of prize jerkwad would let her slip away.

I'd like to say all of that out loud, but Amelia is hovering behind him, her brow lined with worry. She's all that matters right now, and getting into a pissing match with her ex wouldn't make things any better for her. She looks so forlorn and troubled, and it breaks my heart. All I want to do is get her away from here so I can wrap her in my arms.

On the journey over, I was pissed at her for not calling me straight away and for behaving like she thought she was bothering me. For even toying with the idea that I was the kind of man who would sit through business meetings while knowing the woman he loves is with her sick mom at the hospital.

Except, yeah, well ...

I haven't told her that I love her yet, have I? It scares me to even admit it to myself, never mind say it aloud to her. So maybe she has every right to doubt me. I managed to calm myself down before I got here, reminding myself that this was all about her, not my injured pride.

Arriving here and being greeted by this douchebag, though, has brought all that anger back up to the surface. What the fuck is Chad up to? She didn't mention him on the phone, so I have to assume she didn't know he'd be here.

I ignore him and turn my undivided attention to Amelia. Under normal circumstances, that cute little sundress would be enough to drive me wild, but the tears in her eyes keep my libido in check. "Amelia. How is your mom?"

We're in the corridor outside her room, and my own stress levels are through the roof. I still bear the scars of spending too much time in places like this during my mother's treatment. She died at home, but hallways like this one were a big part of our lives for way too long. Everything about hospitals—the smells, the sounds, the pervasive sense of desperation that bleeds from the walls—reminds of the most painful time of my life. I know exactly what Amelia is feeling right now.

She swats a tear from her cheek. "She's stable. Her oxygen levels are slowly rising, but she'll need to stay in the hospital overnight. Probably for a few days."

"I'm so glad I was here for you today, angel face," Chad says in a saccharine tone. Angel face? Who the fuck gave him permission to speak? Who the fuck gave him permission to *live*?

She offers him a halfhearted smile, and I once again resist

the urge to punch him in his smug face. "What exactly were you doing here, Chad?" I ask instead.

"I had a meeting in town with some really important investors," he says, announcing it like he was having coffee and bagels with Jesus fucking Christ. "I'm still on the emergency contact list for Edith, and when they couldn't initially get hold of Mimi, they tried me."

Mimi? I didn't think the prick could be any more annoying, but it looks like I was wrong. He looks at her with a fake-sad expression and pats her on the shoulder like the condescending fuckwit he is. "Good thing I was here, huh?"

I watch her every move. I'm so attuned to her now that I see it all. The slight drop of her shoulder as she subtly moves away from his touch, the nervous way she swallows.

"I think she still got here before you did, Chad, so let's not plan the medal ceremony just yet, pal."

She shoots me a quick look that feels like a warning, and I bite my tongue. She doesn't need any extra crap from me.

"I'm sorry, Chad," she says, her voice quiet. "I forgot to have you taken off the list. I'll make sure to get that taken care of."

"Shh, now. It's okay." He tries to pull her into a hug.

I'm going to wrap his fucking neck around a stethoscope if he's not careful. Yeah, I know what I said, and doing it that way would be infinitely more painful.

Amelia dodges his attempted embrace and takes a step closer to me. I can smell her sweet perfume and see the unshed tears in her hazel eyes. Fuck, her pain kills me.

"I was on my way to meet her," she says. "I was going to the house to take her flowers, and we were planning on walking together to the restaurant to meet the girls. She's been doing so well recently, and she was looking forward to it. My cell was on the fritz, and I had no signal at my apartment. She'd tried to call me ..."

A sob racks her body, and I can't hold back for a second longer. Without any thought for Chad and what he or anyone else might think, I fold her into my arms, pressing her close to my chest. Exactly where she belongs. She doesn't resist, sagging into me and resting her cheek against me. Her shoulders are trembling, and her tears moisten the fabric of my shirt.

"You're her *boss*?" he sneers.

I snarl back at him. "Yes, I'm her boss. I'm also a decent human being who gives a shit about the people I work with. And now that I'm here, I see no reason for you to hang around any longer."

His eyes narrow in suspicion. He's maybe only ninety-nine percent idiot, and the other one percent is jealous. That one percent suspects I'm much more than her employer but isn't confident enough to challenge me. Because it's entirely plausible that I'm simply comforting my secretary after her mom was rushed to the ER, like any caring boss would.

"Mimi?" Chad asks, like he doesn't quite believe me.

Untangling herself from my arms, she scrubs the tears from her cheeks. She glances at the stain she's left on my shirt and grimaces, although I obviously don't give a shit.

"Thank you for coming, Chad, but he's right. There's no reason for you to be here. I appreciate you coming, but it's fine for you to go now. And please don't call me Mimi."

His eyes dart between her and me, and a muscle tics in his clenched jaw. I bite on my cheek so I don't tell him to fuck off. He clears his throat. "If you say so."

He turns to leave, and I find myself wondering what his game is. Isn't he engaged to someone else now? Why is he sniffing around Amelia like the dog he is? Is he going to stay away from her, or am I going to have to put him down?

WE FINALLY LEAVE the hospital around ten, after the staff assures Amelia that her mom is doing better and Edith herself insists that it's time for us to leave.

"It was really nice to finally meet you, Edith," I say just before we head out. "I've heard so much about you."

She's no fool, this woman, and even from her hospital bed, her eyes glint with amusement. "Yeah? That's nice. You sure do take a keen interest in your employees' families, Mr. James." She winks at me while Amelia isn't looking, leaving me with no doubt that our secret isn't quite as much of a secret as it once was.

"I absolutely do," I reply, grinning.

"You just make sure you treat my daughter well, now, you hear me? At work, obviously."

I pat her hand. "I promise you I will."

"Okay. You look like a man of your word to me. Now scoot, both of you—I need to be alone with my oxygen mask and my romance novel. Nothing says sexy quite like a nasal canula."

Amelia leans down to hug her, and I turn away when I see how hard they cling to each other. I still miss my own mother so much it hurts.

She holds it together until we're in the parking garage. With a sigh, she crumples like all the air has been let out of her, and I gather her into my arms. "You're okay, baby. And she is too. She's tough, your mom."

"I know. She's tougher than me. I'm just ... I'm just so scared, Drake. Every time I think she's doing okay, something seems to happen. And I don't know what I'd do without her."

"I get that," I reply, stroking her hair and kissing her forehead. "I really do. And hopefully you won't need to find the answer to that question for many years. Come on, let's get out of here."

"Has Constantine been waiting all this time?" she says as we approach the SUV.

"No. I sent him home in a cab. Tonight, madam, I will be your driver. Where do you want to go? Straight home is fine. You probably want a hot shower and your bed."

She manages a weak smile as she climbs into the front seat, refusing to get in the back "because you're not my chauffeur."

"I'm actually not physically tired at all," she says as she fastens her seatbelt. "It's more psychological, you know? This day has not gone the way I expected. I pictured a cozy birthday lunch with Mom, catching up with the girls, then seeing you back at my place."

"Oh?" I glance at her out of the corner of my eye as I leave the parking garage. "And what did you think might happen there?"

Her wicked smile lifts my heart. After everything she's gone through today, she can still give me goosebumps. There are things we need to talk about, issues we need to address— including Chad—but now is not the time for issues. Now is the time for making my girl feel better.

"Well, I thought you might want to untie this dress, for a start," she says, running her hands over her breasts teasingly. "I know you always like to untie me."

I grit my teeth and keep my eyes on the road. It's a bad time to get turned on, but my cock doesn't seem to have gotten the memo.

"I do, Miss Ryder, I do. And believe me, I'm interested. But I don't want you to feel like we have to have sex."

"What? Don't you want to have sex with me?"

"Only when I'm awake. And when I'm asleep. Basically all the fucking time. You know I can't get enough of you, baby. All I'm saying is we don't have to. We could just, you know, cuddle and spoon."

"Cuddle and spoon?" she repeats, sounding shocked.

"Yeah. Cuddle and spoon. Or fuck each other's brains out, whichever you prefer."

She puts her hand on my thigh, and fuck, her fingers feel good. Concentrate, Drake, concentrate. She gazes out the window and leans back in the seat. "Thank you for coming, Drake. It means a lot to me. I think she knows, don't you?"

"About us? She definitely knows. How do you feel about that?"

She lets out a little laugh and shakes her head. "I feel good about it. I hated hiding things from her, and I hated hiding you away. I'd love for you two to get to know each other, and it's not like she's going to tell anyone."

"I don't know. From what you've said, that Mrs. Katzberg lady from across the street might be trouble."

"True, but she's on my side. Anyway. I'm glad. I'm proud of you, and I'm proud of my mom, and it's nice that two of my very favorite people will get the chance to be friends."

I don't react much on the surface, but I'm secretly thrilled at her reaction and to hear that she's proud of me. I've often felt second-best in my life, but never with Amelia.

"But now," she continues, sighing. "Now I just want to try to calm down from everything for a while, you know? Mom is in good hands, she's out of danger, and she's doing well. The nurses have my number in case anything happens, and I hope you don't mind, but I gave them yours as a backup."

I nod. "Of course, that's fine."

"Anyway. It's like the nurse said earlier, I won't be able to help her if I'm too strung out myself. It's like that oxygen mask on the plane thing. Mom was good when we left, and I'll be back there first thing tomorrow. But tonight? Tonight I need to recharge. I need to not obsess about it all for hours on end. I just wish my brain came with an off switch or that I knew how to distract myself."

I have an idea, but it seems selfish to even consider it. Suggesting it would almost certainly make me sound like an asshole.

"Where have you gone, Drake?" she asks, staring over at me.

"Nowhere, baby. I, uh ... I had a thought."

"You know I could hit a homerun with that sentence, don't you?"

I laugh. "Swing for the fences, mi rosa, swing for the fences."

She giggles, and the sound lights me up. "You still haven't told me what your thought was."

Fuck. Why shouldn't I suggest it? She can say always say no if she's not into it. "You know how I like untying stuff? Especially if you're wearing it?"

"I had noticed that."

I hum softly, thinking of the right way to make this proposition.

"You have that length of cord in your office too. You play around with it when you're stressed. Is it the same kind of thing?" she asks, and I feel the heat of her eyes on me.

"Kinda. Have you heard of Shibari?"

"I think Kimmy told me about it once. A girl she dated was into it. It's like tying people up, right?"

"It's more than that. It's a kind of Japanese bondage, but it's more than sex. If you do it with the right partner, it can be deeply sensual. Incredibly enjoyable. It's also very distracting."

She's silent, and I risk a glance at her face. I was worried she'd be cringing in horror, but instead, I see she's sucking on her plump lower lip, her head tilted to one side as she thinks it over.

"Can you tell me a little more?" she asks. "Like … does it hurt?"

"That depends on whether you want it to. You can use ropes made of different materials, some rough and some soft, and different thicknesses. The knots and patterns and positions, well, they're hugely varied. It's not merely a kink, it's an art form. Shibari masters spend years learning their craft."

"Are you a master, Drake?"

Her curious, sultry tone goes straight to my dick, exactly the same way it does when she calls me sir. Fuck, I couldn't want this woman more if she were dipped in chocolate.

"I'm pretty good. I know what I'm doing, and you'd be safe with me if you wanted to try it. It doesn't even have to be sexual. It can be just about the act itself. It can simply allow you to get out of your head for a while."

I'm getting close to her apartment now, and she puts a hand on my arm. "Can we go to your place instead? I want to try it with you, and if we stay at mine, we'll have to make do with my nylons and your necktie." She flashes me a smirk. "I'm guessing it won't be quite the same experience."

"Are you sure?" I ask. "It's not for everyone."

"I want to try all the things you like, Drake. And judging by that bulge in your pants after only talking about it, I'm figuring you like it a lot."

"Ignore my cock. He has a mind of his own."

She flutters her eyelashes. "I couldn't ignore it even if I wanted to. The only reason I haven't touched it is because I don't want to die in a fiery crash. But I would like to try Shibari. I'd love to forget all about today and my mom hooked up to all those machines. I'd like to just feel good. Do you think it will help with that?"

I nod, thrilled at the prospect of trying this with her. "And if

Shibari doesn't help, then I'll just make you come so hard you pass out."

Her infectious laughter fills the car. "Deal."

THIRTY-FOUR

AMELIA

"J esus fucking Christ, Amelia. You're exquisite, you know that?"

My entire body flames with desire at his praise. Nobody has ever made me feel as good about myself as this man does.

Like a lot of women, I suppose, I've occasionally thought I was a little overweight. I've never hated my body, but I've also never felt particularly beautiful or sexy, certainly not in recent years. The way Drake is looking at me now, though, his dark brown eyes so full of need and adoration, I feel ... not only beautiful, but invincible.

He crawls between my spread legs and presses a soft kiss at the top of my inner thigh, right above a thick twist of rope. A low growl rolls out of him, and my body recognizes that sound. My core clenches at it, the reaction oddly Pavlovian. He growls, I vibrate.

My arms are tied behind me, coils of hemp twisting like snakes from my wrists up to my shoulders. More lengths of rope are pulled across my breasts, one above and one below my nipple, the friction of them rubbing deliciously against the sensitive peaks. He's used yet more to create a crisscross pattern of rope and knots all along my legs, which kind of looks like super-thick fishnet. I am completely naked apart from the coils, and my center is throbbing with need.

It took a long time to get to this stage. He's a perfectionist and he wanted to make sure I was completely comfortable with everything as we progressed. Comfortable? That's not the right word. I always thought I'd enjoy being restrained by him, but this ... This really is a thing of beauty. I totally get why it helps him switch off his busy mind. The intricacy of the patterns, the complexity of the knots, choosing the right rope. It's engrossing, and it's also kinky as fuck. I absolutely love it, and I love the way he's looking at me like I'm the only person in the world who has what he needs.

"You have such beautiful skin," he says, his breath warm against my flesh. "You look incredible like this. When I take the ropes off, there will be marks for a while."

"Good," I sigh, rubbing my wrists together and enjoying the sensation. "I want there to be marks."

He looks up at me from between my thighs, his eyes on fire as he runs his hands up my legs, licking his lips when he touches the bumps and ridges of the rope. Slowly, he works his way up my body, and I suck in a desperate breath when he reaches my breasts.

"I've truly never seen anything so perfect as this, Amelia. You, tied up beneath me. The way your flesh is so soft around the knots. The way your perfect tits are spilling around that rope." He reaches out, a mesmerized expression on his face, and tugs on one of the knots. It immediately makes the rope around my nipples tighten, and I cry out. He leans forward and sucks one after the other into his mouth, flicking them with his tongue. The sensation is heightened to the point that I'm almost too stimulated. "Drake!"

"I know, baby. I know it's a lot, but you're doing so fucking well. Your nipples were made for this. Are you okay? Are you still comfortable?"

"Not exactly comfortable, but I love it."

"I thought you would, my dirty minx. And now that I know you love it, there's so much more for us to try. I can make you fly or have your ass in the air for me to lick or hog-tie you while I fuck every hole you have."

"I thought this wasn't about sex?" I say teasingly, even though I can feel my inner walls contract at the images he's put in my mind.

He lifts his head and smirks. "It's not, but having you naked and tied up, completely at my mercy ..." He sucks air between his teeth. "Well, I'm not gonna *not* fuck you. You're too gorgeous to resist."

I huff with fake indignation. "I feel hoodwinked, sir. Tied up under false pretenses. I'm all about the art."

He narrows his eyes, and the look he gives me makes heat snake a slow path up my spine. Without dropping his gaze from mine, he drags his forefinger through my center, which I'm acutely aware is dripping wet. Then he holds it up, the tip coated in a thick sheen of my arousal. "You sure about that, Miss Ryder? Because while you are definitely beautiful enough to belong in a gallery, you're also soaking wet, as usual. You don't want me to fuck you?"

I press my lips together to stifle a giggle. "I didn't say that, sir."

"Sir ... I like the sound of that word on your lips. I like how tying you up brings the brat out in you. And I really like the way you look, trussed up and ready for my cock."

He sinks the same finger inside me, all the way to the knuckle, his eyes on mine as he does it. If I ever had a doubt as to how much he wants me, the look on his face dispels it completely. After he rubs my clit, making me moan his name, he lifts me up, flips me around, and lays me face down. His hands run around my neck, along my shoulders, and down my rope-tied arms, as though he's savoring every moment of slow, sensual contact. Then he groans and positions me on my knees, my ass bare before him. There is something deeply sexy about the way he's handling me, moving me around like I'm a doll, figuring out which part of me to fuck. I have no control over any of it. I'm his plaything, and boy am I enjoying the game.

He palms my cheeks, and I gasp and lean into his touch, loving the way his fingers feel. He strokes my thighs and the curve of my ass, and his breathing comes faster as he spreads my legs a little wider. I'm completely exposed to him and I feel a flush of embarrassment, but also a rush of need.

"Drake ..."

"Yeah, baby?" he asks, his touch making me tremble against my restraints.

"What are you thinking of back there? Are you planning to, uh ..." I falter over the words.

"Fuck you in the ass?" he says, his voice low and dangerous. "Is that what you want, Miss Ryder?"

Is it? Do I want my first time to happen while I'm completely restrained and at his mercy? "Yes," I blurt.

"Jesus fuck," he mutters, spreading my cheeks apart, and I let out a little cry. I want this, but I'm also a little scared. What if it hurts too much? What if I'm not built to take him that way? He's huge, and I've never had anything there, not even the tip of a finger.

As though he's reading my mind, he leans over me, lips dusting over my shoulder blades. "I would never do anything to hurt you, baby. I'll take it real slow, and the minute you say stop, we stop, okay?"

I nod, my cheek brushing against the comforter. "Yes sir."

He growls, low and dangerous. "That's my good girl. Don't move. I'll be right back, okay?"

I manage a shaky laugh. "I'm tied up. It's not like I can go anywhere."

"True," he says, getting something from his drawer. "And maybe that's how I'll keep you. Tied up, ass open, pussy wet. Twenty-four hours a fucking day."

"I think it might make work a little awkward," I joke as he climbs back onto the bed behind me. I'm nervous, and in the few seconds Drake's hands weren't on me, I lost some of my bravado.

He slaps my ass a couple of times, and I squeal. That felt shockingly good. He slides a finger inside my pussy, and the wet sound it makes fills the room. "Good," he says, pulling it out again. "I just wanted to check you were still a deviant. Now, are you sure about this, mi rosa? Let me make it clear that I want nothing more than to take this virgin ass of yours and make it mine, but I can wait. We can get you some nice little jeweled toys before you work your way up to my cock."

"I don't want toys. Only you," I murmur, my face pressed against his pillows and my thighs quivering with excitement. The way this man can make me feel just by talking dirty to me is insane.

He leans his body over my back, curving himself entirely around me until his lips are next to my ear. "I'm not going to lie, baby. This is going to hurt a little. But I promise if it doesn't feel good for you, we'll stop. You have to keep talking to me, okay?"

He spreads my cheeks again and massages some cold lube over my puckered hole. It feels strange but delicious, having him touch me in that taboo place, and my heart starts to race as he rubs the crown of his cock over my opening. "Just relax, mi rosa. I'm going to fill you up, and you're going to love it."

He slides his finger, slick with cold lube, inside me first, and

I groan at the intrusion. It's strange and different but not unpleasant. "Good girl," he says soothingly as he slowly works his finger in and out.

My entire body shudders with pleasure, and I moan his name.

He rubs a soothing hand over my lower back while he pushes in deeper and twists his finger a little to stretch me. I gasp at the new sensation, but once again, the unfamiliar feeling quickly gives way to pleasure.

"How's that, mi rosa?"

"G-good."

My legs tremble as he goes on gently working his finger in a smooth, steady motion, and that deep, churning vortex of pleasure is swirling deep in my core.

"Drake!" I plead, unsure what I'm pleading for, but his slow ministrations are exquisite torture.

"You ready for more, baby? You think you can take my cock now?"

I'm ready for it all. "Yes! Please."

He withdraws his finger, and then more cold lube slides between my ass cheeks, making me gasp. "We need plenty of this. I want to fuck you pretty hard, and I don't want to hurt you."

Oh. My. God.

He pushes the tip of his dick inside me a couple of inches, and I cry out at the sharp burning sensation that explodes inside me.

"I know, baby. Just breathe," he says, sliding his hands over my back and ass.

I suck in a deep breath, and he pushes in a little deeper. Stars flicker behind my eyelids.

"Okay?" he asks with a grunt.

"Yes. More." I pant out the words, pushing my ass back as much as possible while I'm bound so tightly.

"Christ, you look amazing. I wish you could see this. Your arms in those ropes. Your beautiful ass split in two. My hard cock disappearing inside it. Fuck," he groans, slowly pushing farther and farther inside me.

He runs a hand up my inner thigh and dips two fingers inside my pussy, pushing them in all the way while he sinks even deeper into my ass. I yell, shocked at the delectable pain when he fills me in both places.

"That still okay, baby?"

"Oh god, yes. Yes, Drake!"

"Good. Because I'm not sure how much longer I can hold back."

"Then don't. Please."

He pushes deeper and twists his fingers at the same time, pushing me forward so the ropes scrape against my nipples and chafe on my wrists. Despite his claim that he can't hold back, I can feel him doing just that. His body vibrates with the effort of not nailing me into the mattress as I'm sure he must want to. Instead, he gives me as much as I can take, his steady thrusts shallow and mind-blowing. I'm so full of him I could burst, and it is the dirtiest, hottest sensation I have ever experienced.

"You're doing so well Amelia," he says, his voice low and intense. "You're taking me like such a good girl. Fuck, you feel unbelievable."

He speeds up his thrusts, and every part of me is stretched wide and tight to fit him in. But I'd still take more of him if he pushed. I can't get enough. Every cell in my being is lit up, and I start to wail as I feel my climax build. He uses his other hand to hold my hip steady and drives a little harder into me, his fingers hitting the sweet spot inside my pussy. He's growling like an animal behind me, my ropes are tightening from the movement, and I am so crammed with Drake that I can barely breathe.

My inner walls clench around his fingers, and my ears begin to buzz. My vision blurs, and when I come, it feels like a whole-body experience. Everything explodes. The pleasure and the pain and the primal sense of being totally possessed by this man overwhelm me, and I scream his name as he continues to fuck me all the way through my orgasm. "Yes! Fuck, yes!" he shouts, his body shuddering as he finds his own release.

When he's spent, he collapses on top of me, and we both lie panting on the bed.

"That," he murmurs, his body hot against mine, "was fucking mind-blowing."

I couldn't agree more. I wanted a distraction, and wow, did he deliver. I can barely remember my own name.

CHAPTER

THIRTY-FIVE

DRAKE

I didn't think it was possible to be more obsessed with Amelia Ryder, but it turns out I under-estimated my own abilities. Since the night she let me tie her up, I've wanted her even more. It takes a certain level of trust to let someone do that to you, to cede control to them, and she did it without question.

She gazed up at me with those big hazel eyes, nothing but curiosity and heat in her expression as I showed her the cords and explained how it could work. Fuck, the way she looked with the ropes digging into her skin. Her nipples rigid and proud, trapped between coils. Her arms tied flat against her back as I fucked her gorgeous round ass, the first and last man to ever fuck her there. Jesus. The woman is perfect for me.

She loved the whole thing too, and as a gift, I had a Shibari rope kit delivered to her apartment for us to use there. She was thrilled, and I suspect there will be many more hours of fun to be had as we explore it together. I always enjoyed it with my professional companions—but this? This is a whole different beast. This is with the most gorgeous woman alive.

And now here she is, in the delectable flesh, perched on the corner of my desk. She sashayed into the room wearing one of her tight black pencil skirts and a little bolero jacket, holding a notepad and pen as though she intended to do some work. She knows I'm on the phone—she put the damn call through. She licks her lower lip as she studies me, listening in to my end of a deadly dull business conversation.

She crosses her legs slowly, deliberately, flashing me her lace-topped stockings and a frilly garter belt. Fuck. I suck in a breath, momentarily losing track of what I was saying, and I swear to god, I can already smell her—that deliciously sweet aroma of her soaking-wet pussy. It's a scent I'm achingly familiar with by now.

"Yes, Mrs. Forster, of course. I'm looking forward to it too. Shall I get my secretary to put something on my schedule?"

Amelia's eyes go wide, and she mouths, *who, me?* I narrow my gaze, both amused and aroused at the sight of her. She stretches one leg out, runs a hand up the silky length of her stocking, and lets me have another glimpse of the creamy flesh at the top of her thighs. Then she tugs her skirt up, wriggling her ass as she does, exposing both the garter belt and her panties.

"What was that, Mrs. Forster?" I ask. "You were breaking up a little there."

I'm barely holding my shit together here, and when Amelia runs a finger over the flimsy fabric of her panties, making it very fucking clear how wet she is, I almost slam the phone down. "Yes. Great. Of course. Will do!"

I barely manage to stay civil until the end of the conversation. After I slam the phone down, I immediately stand. She squeals, delighted when I lift her into my arms and seal my lips over hers, claiming her with my tongue. I grind my rock-hard cock against her as she wraps her legs around my waist, and she groans into my mouth.

Laying her down on the desk, I send legal pads and pens flying and tug off her jacket. Then I tear her silky blouse right open, causing buttons to pop and scatter and revealing heaving breasts encased in black lace.

"Drake! I can't work the rest of the day with my bra on display."

"You should have thought of that before you started your little striptease, you minx. You locked the door?"

She nods, her cheeks flushed and her pupils blown as I scoop out her perfect tits and suck one of her rigid nipples into my mouth. I squeeze the other one, nice and hard, and she shudders beneath me. Pulling away, I shove that tight skirt of hers all the way up to her waist, then tug her panties off and throw them across the room. Then I stand back for a moment to admire the view: her stocking-clad legs spread for me, her cunt glistening with her juices. "In the name of all that's holy, Amelia, I don't think I've ever seen such a beautiful pussy."

With deliberate slow strokes, I run my hands up her stockings, placing one of her feet on my shoulder and kissing my way down her leg. When my tongue reaches the bare skin at the top, she moans, and I twang her garter with a satisfying snap.

"You," I growl as I explore her, "are a very bad secretary. How dare you come in here, flaunting this perfect body and making my cock harder than steel while I'm talking on the phone with important clients."

"I'm sorry, sir," she murmurs, her hips rising up off my desk to meet my hands. "I've been very naughty. You probably need to punish me."

"You'd like that, wouldn't you, Miss Ryder? You'd like me to bend you over this desk and spank you until your juicy ass is bright red. Or maybe I should make you kneel under the desk and fill your filthy mouth with my cock while I carry on with my work. How does that sound?"

I'm rubbing her clit, and I know the filthy talk is working just as much as my fingers. My girl loves it as much as I do.

"Yes, Mr. James, sir, I would like that. I'd like all of that ... Oh!" She comes with a rush of her juices all over my hand, and I hold her down and work her through every last tremor. Her head is rolling from side to side and she's biting her lips in an attempt not to scream. I can tell she's not going to manage it, so I clamp my hand down over her mouth. Her eyes fly wide, and she darts out her tongue and licks my palm while she shakes and trembles. Fucking hell, I want her so much.

She's just about stopped bucking her hips when her phone rings. I look around, trying to find the damn thing so I can smash it with a hammer, but she grabs my arm. "I need to see who it is. It could be the hospital. I'm sorry."

"There's nothing to be sorry about," I say, ignoring the killer ache in my cock. Edith has been in the hospital for three nights now, and although she's stable, she still needs to be monitored. Amelia visits her every morning before work, and I get Constantine to drive her there every evening. She is devoted to her mom, which is how it should be.

Her still-ringing phone is in the pocket of her discarded jacket, and I grab it, hating the anxious look on her face. My blood pressure skyrockets at the name displayed on the screen.

"Why is your piece of shit ex-husband calling you?" I demand, waving it in her face. "In fact, why do you even still have his number in your phone?"

"I have no idea why he's calling me." She sounds confused and a little annoyed, her hair in disarray and her lips swollen from our kisses. "And I have his number because I have his number." She leaves off the word *jackass*, but I can tell it was on the tip of her tongue. "I'll call him back."

My possessive streak—which only seems to exist with Amelia—ignites with a fervor. I shake my head, a wicked grin spreading over my lips. "No, baby. That would be rude. Answer the call."

I grab her hips and move her to the center of my desk, then inch my chair forward, spreading her thighs apart with my shoulders.

She stares at me, open-mouthed. "What? Right now?"

Answering her with a nod, I thrust the phone into her hands, grab her legs, and pull her toward me. Her ass slides along the desk, and I hoist her feet over my shoulders and look down at her pretty pink pussy, still shining from her orgasm.

"Drake," she protests, but it's halfhearted.

"Answer him, baby," I command. "Or would you like me to speak to him and tell him exactly what I'm doing to you?" I slide a finger inside her wet center, and her back bows.

"You wouldn't." Her face is a mask of shock.

My eyes narrow. "You really want to test me on that, mi rosa?"

She shakes her head. "N-no."

Her phone stops ringing but immediately starts up again. "Then answer it, Amelia. Now."

Her fingers tremble as she accepts the call, and I lower my face to her core. She smells like sin and tastes even better, and my mouth glides along her opening, licking and sucking and exploring in exactly the way I know she likes.

"Uh, yeah, h-hi Chad." She draws a raspy breath.

I smile to myself as I work her over, curling my tongue and sliding it inside her wet center, gripping her thighs with my palms and keeping her spread wide. She uses her free hand to try to silence herself, ramming her knuckles into her mouth, but her moans still creep out. I hear Chad's voice coming from the phone, his smarmy tone infuriating me and making me lash her clit even faster.

I hear him asking how Edith is and listen to her breathy

pants as she tries to answer him while I bring her to the edge of ecstasy. When the fucker asks if she'd like to get together for dinner while he's in town, I see red. I'm going to kill him.

I slide my hands underneath her ass, digging my fingers into her perfect cheeks and raising her higher. My whole face is buried in her, her slick folds all around me, the smell of her intoxicating.

"I don't think ... I don't ... Oh god!" Her voice cracks more with every word. She's so close her thighs are trembling. Any second now, she's going to explode for me. For me, not for Chad. Not for any other man ever again.

I look up from my position in paradise and lock eyes with her as I very deliberately lick her all the way to heaven.

"Oh, b-bye!" she yells, then drops the phone as she comes. I hold her still, keeping my mouth on her, keeping my eyes on her, keeping my hands on her. I will never let her go.

Her juices coat my tongue, and her entire body shakes. She's mine. One hundred percent, totally mine, but that doesn't quell the jealous need to claim every inch of her that burns through me. While she's still coming down from her second orgasm, I pull her up, spin her around, and bend her flat over my desk.

With more force and urgency than necessary, I tug her pencil skirt up until it's bunched around her waist and her perfect ass and dripping pussy are on full display for me. She heaves in stuttering breaths that rack her body, but she doesn't get any reprieve yet. I'm nowhere near done with her. My grip rough on the back of her neck, I hold her down with one hand while I unfasten my belt and pull down my zipper with the other. My cock aches to be inside her, and her eager whimpers tell me she feels exactly the same.

I lean over her, my mouth at her ear as I drive inside her in one smooth stroke, too far gone with the need to fuck her. And she must realize I'm taking her bare, but she doesn't protest and I'm not about to stop what I'm doing to get a condom.

"Do you have any idea what you do to me?" I pull out and drive into her again. Her thighs slam against my desk, and she cries out in pleasure and pain. I smack her ass and admire the red handprint left behind on her creamy flesh. I want to mark her everywhere. "You are addictive and distracting, and you drive me fucking crazy in every possible way there is."

"D-Drake, please," she mewls, her back arching as I go on holding her down.

"You are mine, Amelia," I say menacingly, my voice a low growl. "You are mine, and no man will ever touch you again. Do you understand me?"

I drive harder into her tight, wet heat, and she groans. "Who do you belong to, Amelia? Let me hear you say it."

"You, Drake, I belong to you."

Yeah she fucking does. I fuck her until we both find oblivion and then fill her full of my cum. As I catch my breath, I pull her onto my lap and stroke her hair while smothering her with kisses. And she melts into my arms, utterly destroyed. She walked in here full of sass, and now she's full of my cum. And if I have my way, that's how she'll remain every day for the rest of her life.

THIRTY-SIX

AMELIA

Today has been the day from hell, and of course it's pouring down rain when it's time for me to leave the office. I should be traveling home with Drake, warm and dry in the comfort of a plush SUV, but instead here I am, pulling my coat around my neck and cursing the cold droplets that have already snuck through.

I hate this rain. I hate my coat. And right now, I really hate Drake James.

The day started out okay. I was still in a good place because of Mom being released from the hospital three nights ago. Both of us were so relieved to escape those sterile walls. I used to volunteer at a busy hospital in Philadelphia, but I now know that it's totally different from being there with a loved one. It's strangely exhausting sitting by a bedside for hours on end, and she was desperate to get home.

She'll need more tests, but for now, she's back in her little house and loving it. I stayed with her the first night, but she chased me out the next day, saying I had to get back to work so I could be employee of the month again. She's a big fan of Drake's, of course. As am I. Or I *was*, anyway.

On my way into the office this morning, I was so looking forward to seeing him. We've spent more time apart the past few days because of my mom's release, and I miss him.

Problem number one on the day from hell occurred when my usual subway stop was closed due to a power outage. I ended up having to walk the rest of the way in highly unsuitable heels. Problem number two—more like a bad omen really—was when I saw my favorite coffee truck was closed, its shutters down. Okay, not a big deal, they have coffee inside the building, I told myself as my blistered feet carried me into the James and James lobby.

Problem three came in the form of Linda from HR. Our relationship has improved slightly since we performed a karaoke duet of "You're the One That I Want" on the night of the team-building event—she was the Sandy to my Danny. But today, she was very much in monster form, pulling me aside and telling me we needed to have a meeting because of my "unacceptable undocumented absence" last week. Shocked, I told her my mom had been in the hospital and that Mr. James had authorized the two measly afternoons I took off. I hated feeling like I was using his name to buy myself special treatment, and I felt even worse when she said he had done no such thing and that she needed his signature on the forms to clear the absence.

We left it at her telling me she would check with him, me telling her she should do just that, and then we went our separate ways. At my desk, I sat rubbing my sore feet and convincing myself it was a simple misunderstanding.

But problem number four—and by far the biggest—was Drake himself. He rolled up late, which he pretty much never does, and was in a bad mood from the get-go, giving me only a curt nod of greeting as he strode past my desk with his phone glued to his ear.

"Good morning," I said, popping my head into his office a few minutes later. "May I ask you a favor?"

He gestured me in and was scowling at his mortal enemy—the coffee machine. "Are you okay?" I asked, getting him an espresso before he killed the poor thing.

"Fine. Just family stuff."

"Oh. Right."

That shutdown hurt, I was forced to admit. I'm aware that I'm not part of his family and that most of them have no clue I even exist or what role I play in Drake's life, but he talks about them all the time. His stories have made me feel like I know them, and I care about them because he cares about them. Being closed out that way that felt like a slap in the face.

"What favor did you want?" he asked.

"Oh, I was wondering if you could speak to Linda for me. She's on my back about not having the proper forms for the time I took when my mom was in the hospital."

He rubbed the bridge of his nose with his fingers and looked pained. "Of course. I should have done that already. Anything else?"

"N-no. Shall I, uh, leave you to it?"

He nodded. "If you don't mind."

That little exchange played out over the course of maybe five minutes, but it remained lodged in my mind hours later when his father and brother arrived at the office. I've never officially met either Dalton or Mason James before, but I recognized them from the photos Drake had shown me. It was all I could do not to jump up and hug them, which would have been weird. Definitely not normal secretary behavior.

"Hi, would it be possible to see Drake, or is he in there brokering a deal to buy Saturn?" Mason said.

I smiled and kept the joke going. "He already has Saturn. He's working on Mars right now."

Mason laughed, and I was charmed. It didn't hurt that he was almost as easy on the eyes as his big brother. Dalton was sterner, but Emily was right—the man's a silver fox.

"Just let me check if he's finished with his last call," I said. "I'm sure he'll have time for you two."

"I wouldn't be so sure about that," his dad huffed.

An excited smile on my face, I entered Drake's office and got close enough to his desk that nobody else could hear me. "Your dad and Mason are here to see you. It's so nice to meet them at last. I feel like I know them already because of how much you talk about them." He shot me a furious look, and I stopped babbling, unable to tell whether he was angry with me or his family.

"You're not exactly meeting them, are you, Amelia? You're just doing your job and showing them in."

I was so shocked at his tone, even more so by his words, that I didn't respond. Hindsight is, of course, twenty-twenty, and I've since come up with a million zingers I could have thrown back at him. But in that moment, I was hurt and off-balance.

I showed Mason and Dalton through, offered them pastries and coffee, and ended up standing there awkwardly when they both declined.

"Thank you, Miss Ryder," Drake said in a mechanical tone. "We won't be needing you again."

Mason flashed me a sympathetic look, and I stumbled out, trying to keep as much dignity as possible. I fled to the ladies' room and had a strong word with myself. What had I expected? That I'd sit down with them and chat? That I'd ask Dalton how things were going with his new cook, Luz, or check in on Mason's crazy love life? Of course not.

So what if Drake spends most of his free time with a body part inside me. Apparently, I'm not good enough to meet his family. Apparently, my role is to be his secretary and his fuck buddy and nothing more.

That was over an hour ago, and the final nail in the coffin of my day was bumping into Jacob in the hallway. He looked embarrassed when he saw me, and we were forced to have a painfully awkward exchange about the weather. I still feel terrible about the way I treated him, and right then, I was starting to question whether I'd even made the correct choice. I bet Jacob would have introduced me to his family. He wouldn't be ashamed of me.

The rational side of my brain shouted at me, telling me that I was being silly. Drake and I had agreed together that we would keep this thing secret. He offered to go public if that's what I wanted. But it still hurt. Maybe if it weren't so all-or-nothing—if we were able to be public with our friends and families but keep things a secret at work.

Regardless of whether my feelings were appropriate, enough was enough, and it was time to go home. Drake clearly didn't want me around, Linda was still chasing me for a performance meeting, and the bigger-than-Texas blister on the back of my foot was ready to burst.

I knocked on the door and peeked my head in, and all three of them turned around to look.

"Uh, Mr. James, did you need anything else?"

"Does it look like we do? If I wanted something, Amelia, I would have asked."

I glared at him. If he was going to treat me like crap, he could at least not "Amelia" me while he did it.

Back at my desk, I sent him a quick email—formal in tone—informing him that I was leaving half an hour early and would make it up on Monday. And now here I am. In the goddamn rain.

I head off toward the subway and nearly burst into tears when I see a sign that says this stop is still closed. To calm myself down, I picture treating myself to a steaming hot bubble bath when I get home, but my fantasy is interrupted by Drake shouting my name.

Refusing to give him a second of my time, I start walking without a thought for where I'm going. Arrogant ass crack.

"Amelia, stop." His voice isn't exactly louder, but it's definitely dripping with that authoritative do-what-I-say-without-question-or-I'll-take-it-out-on-your-ass quality he does so well.

I stop in my tracks and spin to face him. His car, which was crawling along beside me, stops too. Car horns blare from behind it, and Drake shows zero sign of being the slightest bit perturbed about bringing the busy traffic to a standstill. He's a selfish ass crack as well as an arrogant one.

The window slides the rest of the way down. "Get in the car."

A muscle in his jaw pulses, and I scowl back at him, rainwater dripping down my face. "No."

"Get. In. The. Car."

I fold my arms across my chest and glare at him while pedestrians hurriedly circle around me. "I believe I'm off the clock, Mr. James, which means you don't get to tell me what to do."

His features darken. The car door swings open, and he jumps out and stands right in front of me. I stay fixed to the spot, though. He can glare at me all he likes; he doesn't intimidate me. What's he going to do? Fire me?

His powerful hand cups my jaw, and he squeezes hard enough to let me know that he's not playing around. We're still close to the office. Anyone could see us out here, but I refuse to back down. I don't see why I should. He's been a bastard all day long, and I've done nothing to deserve it.

I glare right back at him, defiant even though he has my face clasped in his hand, and I hope he can feel every ounce of rage I throw at him. For a few seconds, he doesn't speak. He simply stares at me, his dark eyes trying to pierce my soul. Rain quickly soaks his thick hair and the shoulders of his suit jacket.

Why does he have to be so infuriatingly hot? Fighting against my attraction to him is hard, but he's been a giant asshole. I'm entitled to be angry and hurt.

After what feels like an eternity, he finally speaks. "Get in this car right now, or I swear to god, I will put you over my knee and spank your ass in the middle of the street."

My cheeks flush hot, and my breath catches in my throat as I process his threat. Part of me wants to call his bluff, see if he'd really do it. But the rational part of my brain knows better. Drake James always follows through on his promises, especially the dangerous ones. "You wouldn't dare," I snap, aware my voice lacks any real conviction.

His grip on my jaw tightens slightly. "Try me."

We stand toe-to-toe, locked in a silent battle of wills as the rain pours down around us. Pedestrians continue to stream by, some openly staring at our confrontation. A particularly loud horn blares behind Drake's car. With a frustrated sigh, I wrench my face from his grip. "Fine," I spit out. "But only because I don't want to cause a scene."

A triumphant smirk plays at the corners of his mouth as he steps aside, gesturing toward the open car door. I stomp past him, my heels clicking angrily on the wet sidewalk and my blister burning like the surface of the sun. As I slide across the plush leather seat, I feel a mix of irritation at letting him win so easily and relief at being out of the rain and off my feet. Not that he's won. Getting in the car doesn't mean I forfeit.

Drake climbs in after me and presses the intercom button to tell Constantine to move. The car pulls smoothly into traffic as I sit rigidly, staring straight ahead so I can avoid looking at him. Thanks to the privacy screen between us and the front seat, I could stab him with my nail file and get away with it.

"You're soaked," he observes, his low, dangerous tone sending a shiver down my spine.

I refuse to look at him. "That's quite the deduction, Einstein. What gave it away?"

He chuckles, and I hate that he's amused. "Your sharp tongue is still intact, I see."

"My sharp tongue is the least of your concerns right now." I finally turn to face him and find his dark eyes fixed on me, intense and unreadable.

"Is that so?" he asks. "And what, pray tell, should be my primary concern, Miss Ryder?"

I narrow my eyes at him. "How about the fact that you just threatened to spank me in public? Or that you're essentially kidnapping me right now?"

Drake leans back in his seat, looking infuriatingly relaxed. I know how good he is at faking that, though. The man often comes across as being made of stone, no matter how much turmoil he's in underneath the surface. "Kidnapping? That's a bit dramatic, don't you think? I'm offering you a ride home."

"A ride I explicitly refused," I remind him.

He shrugs, a small smile playing on his lips. "I'm a persistent man, Amelia. You should know that by now."

Persistent? Is that another word for asshole?

I roll my eyes and turn away from him, focusing on the rain-streaked window. Right now, I'm not sure I know him at all. This thing between us has been an emotional rollercoaster, and I'm growing weary of being stuck on the crazy ride. Maybe I'm still dealing with some residual stress from the situation with my mom, but I'm tired of all the sneaking around. Of the power plays. Of him blowing so hot and cold. One day, he's fucking me on his desk and telling me I'm his; the next, he's blanking me in front of his family. I thought I could deal with it, but this is impossible.

The city lights blur as we drive through the streets, the silence in the car growing thicker with each passing moment. I am not going to crack, and I will not cry. I won't give him the satisfaction of telling him how I feel. I will treat this as a free Uber, and he will not be getting a five-star rating.

"My dad had another heart attack," he announces. I try to stay silent because, really, why should that matter to me? I'm only the secretary. I sneak a glance at him, see the pain on his handsome, rain-soaked face. Shit. I can't ignore that.

"But he looked fine earlier. When did it happen?"

He sighs and pinches the bridge of his nose. "It wasn't a full-blown attack. A cardiac event, he called it. But it was his heart, Amelia. His fucking heart *again*. He was in the hospital for two days, and the sneaky fucker didn't tell any of us. Mason picked him up yesterday, and neither of them bothered to tell the rest of us until today."

It doesn't excuse his top-tier ass-hattery today, but a swell of empathy has me taking his hand in mine. He's been worried about my mom while his dad has been ill. "I'm so sorry, Drake."

He nods, his throat working as he swallows. "I've warned him about his lifestyle and that he needs to take better care of himself, but Dalton James knows best and everyone else can get fucked, right? I mean, does he even give a shit about us if he won't take care of his health?"

"I'm sure he doesn't see it like that. Sometimes it's hard for people to change," I say, incapable of ignoring the rawness in his voice. That's what today has all been about—his little performance out there in the rain, his coldness this morning. He was attempting to hide this deep-seated anguish. "Did you argue with him?"

"Worse. I called him a selfish asshole and stormed out of the house. Then Nathan and Mad called me and told me I was being a prick, and I felt like nobody understood how bad this could have been. When Dad and Mase showed up earlier, I called them a pair of selfish assholes, and Dad's blood pressure shot through the roof. I thought he was going to have another *cardiac event* right there in my office."

He's been dealing with all of this on his own. Unnecessarily so, but still. "Oh, Drake."

He runs a hand over his face. "Yeah, I know." He fixes his dark eyes on mine. "But none of that excuses the way I behaved toward you today. As upset as I was with my dad and brother, I shouldn't have taken any of that out on you." He laces his fingers through mine. "It's not enough to simply say I'm sorry, but I am."

I chew on my lip and try to ignore the pull I feel toward him. I see now there are valid reasons for his bad mood, for the way he's behaved, but is this how it's going to be for us? Every time something happens in his life that he doesn't like, is he going to shut me out like that?

"You treated me like crap today, Drake. I understand why you were upset, but if you'd told me what was happening, I would have been there for you the way you've been there for me. To talk it through and support you."

He nods sheepishly. "I'm not used to having someone I can lean on like that, Amelia. At least outside of my brothers. It's no excuse, but I am sorry."

I shake my head. He doesn't get to be forgiven so easily. "It wasn't just that you shut me out. You embarrassed me in front of your family. You took your pain out on me. I'd do anything for you, Drake, but I won't be your emotional punching bag, no matter how much I love you."

The words slip out without warning. I've thought them so many times that I'm amazed it didn't happen sooner. I clasp my hand over my mouth as though trying to chase them back in. Is there any chance that he didn't hear? Can I backtrack? And failing that, maybe I could open the car door and do a tuck and roll into traffic like they do on TV.

He stares at me, a frown on his face, and a sense of dread settles over me. I've gone too far. It's too early for love—he's not ready. He may never be ready. I walked out of that building full of fire and fury, but if this really is the end, I don't know how I'll cope.

"You love me?" he says, his voice low and intense. I close my eyes and will myself to become invisible. He takes hold of my jaw again, like he did outside in the rain. "Amelia. I asked you a question. Do you love me?"

"Yes," I say, slapping his hand away and finally giving in to the tears that have been threatening all day. "Yes, I love you, you infuriating asshole! Believe me, right now I wish I didn't— but I love you, Drake James. With all my stupid, foolish heart."

A slow smile creeps across his face, and a rumble of laughter fills the back of the car. I tell him I love him, and he laughs at me? What the hell?

"Good," he says, dragging me into his arms and holding me there even as I struggle against him. "That's good to know, Miss Ryder." He cups my cheek much more tenderly than before while he stares into my eyes. "Because I love you too. More than I've ever loved anyone in my entire stupid, foolish life."

If he weren't staring at me the way he is, his eyes filled with so much longing and desire, I might think I misheard him. The man who didn't even do relationships only a few short months ago loves me? Drake James—billionaire sex god with a magical tongue, a smile that can melt my ovaries, and a laugh that can make me forget my own name—loves me?

"You do?"

"I do." He seals his lips over mine and kisses me so hard that I almost forget what we were arguing about.

THIRTY-SEVEN

DRAKE

I wake up in her bed with her back snuggled into my chest and my arm slung around her. My thigh is over her hip, like I was trying to hold onto her even in my sleep. Why wouldn't I want to keep this incredible woman as close as humanly possible?

I inhale the scent of her shampoo and rest my cheek against her bare shoulder. She's so soft. So warm. So *mine*.

I thought things were good between us before, but now that I know she loves me? They're un-fucking-believable. I think I said it to her a million times last night. That and how sorry I was for acting like a pathetic asshole. I said it while I was eating her pussy and while I was fucking her. I said it while she sucked my cock. I love her, and there's no going back from this.

My hand coasts down her arm and slides across to one of her perfect tits. I hold it in my palm, letting my fingers gently toy with her nipple. She's still asleep, but even now, her body responds to me, the sensitive skin puckering beneath my touch. She murmurs and wriggles slightly, her ass pressed up against me in a way that makes me feel a lot less gentle. Yeah, I love her, but I still want to rail into her like an animal.

I kiss her neck, my lips barely there, and work my way to her shoulders, listening to the small mewling sounds that she makes as she starts to wake up. Maybe I should have let her sleep, but I'm too much of a selfish asshole. I want her now.

She turns her face to mine, her eyes still half closed and a sweet, sleepy smile on her lips. "Well, good morning, man that I love," she says, and both my heart and my dick swell. "You seem happy to see me."

She rubs herself against me, and I growl under my breath. "I am, baby. I love you so much. But right now I want to fuck your brains out."

"How romantic," she says, fluttering her eyelashes and grinning at me. "And while the prospect is very interesting to me ... I'm a little, uh, sore, you know? From the sheer number of times you fucked my brains out last night, I don't think I have any gray matter left."

I nudge her legs open with my thigh and run my fingers across her opening. She's wet but also swollen, and she winces slightly at my touch.

"You won't need any brainpower for what I have planned, baby. And I know you're a little sore, but I don't think your sweet pussy got the memo because you're fucking soaked for me."

"I always am. Just be gentle, okay, sir?" She presses her lips together, trying to act coy. Vixen.

And it makes me want to do the exact opposite. I want to flip her over, drag her ass into the air, and nail her into next week.

I brush my knuckles over her cheek. "Sure, baby. I can be gentle. I can be anything you want."

She smiles and lets her head fall back to the pillow. She still has her back to me, and I grab the last condom and slide it on. I groan as I slip my stiff cock inside her tight center, gradually easing myself all the way in. God, she feels good. I take my time, building up a steady rhythm, using my fingers on her clit as I thrust slowly in and out of her. It feels incredible, the way my dick is held inside her, the way I can feel every quiver of her pussy walls around it. I want to go harder, to make her scream. I want to do it all—but I can give her this too. Show her this isn't just sex for me. This is so much more. When she comes, it's a slow, juddering climax that makes her whole body tremble. I find my own release seconds later, groaning her name as I do.

I wrap my arms around her, staying inside, never wanting to move again.

"I love you, Amelia," I say, my face sinking against the velvety skin of her back. "I can't imagine my life without you in it. And I can't imagine your cunt without my cock in it either."

She laughs, and the sound warms my heart. "Well, that was half romantic and half hot. What are your plans for today?"

I finally pull out of her and roll her over so she's lying in my arms with her head on my chest. I know I have a lot of making up to do for the way I behaved yesterday. All the signs point toward her having forgiven me, but that doesn't mean I've forgiven myself. While the old me would always work on a Saturday, I can think of a much better way to spend my weekend these days.

"Well, aside from the obvious, I thought we could swing by and check in with your mom first," I say. "And then maybe head over to my dad's, get everyone together and introduce you to them properly."

I feel her tense slightly in my embrace, and she looks up at me with shining eyes. "Are you sure? You don't have to do that."

"Yes, I want to do it. It's way overdue, mi rosa. I love you and you love me, and this stuff shouldn't need to be so complicated. I know there are work headaches, but we'll find a way around them. I want you involved in every aspect of my life. And I want to show you off to my family."

She wriggles up and kisses me softly, holding my face between her hands and looking deep into my eyes. "Plus," she says seriously, "if you distract them with your new girlfriend, maybe they'll forget what a dick you were."

I laugh and squeeze her ass. "You see right through me, don't you, Miss Ryder?"

She hums contentedly before lying on my chest once more and snuggling into me, and I smile as I imagine the looks of shock on my brothers' faces when I introduce her as my girlfriend later. She'll fit in so well with all of them, just like she fits with me. Like she's always meant to be right here.

CHAPTER

THIRTY-EIGHT

DRAKE

"Oh my goodness!" she says, her eyes huge and sugar coating her lips. "This is delicious! Have I died and gone to heaven?"

Luz smiles approvingly at my girl's reaction and nods. "Almost, chiquita—you have gone to Venezuela! This is bien-mesabe—you do the honors, Drake, if you remember your Spanish?"

"It means 'it tastes good to me,' if I'm correct?"

"Exactly! This cake is made all over Latin American countries, but in my homeland, the secret ingredient is coconut and a little rum."

"A little rum?" Mason pipes up from across the kitchen. "There's enough rum in here to give Captain Morgan a hangover."

Everyone laughs, and it eases the lingering tension in the air. Gathering together the whole of my clan for an impromptu brunch is never easy and usually has to be planned months in advance because we're all so busy. But given the strained atmosphere that's existed the past few days thanks to Pop's health scare, they were all happy to rearrange their schedules and head on over here.

The fact that I had Amelia with me caused a little confusion at first, and my father glowered at me when we got here. "What the hell, son? You get us all together just so you can do some work?"

I didn't quite understand what his problem was until Nathan piped up. "No, Dad, he won't be doing any work. Amelia isn't just his secretary." Melanie shot me a knowing look. Nathan obviously tells his wife everything.

Dad stared at Amelia and me, his expression gradually softening as he realized what was going on. I slipped my arm around her shoulders to make it a little easier for him.

"Bro!" Mason said, jumping up and high-fiving us both, our fight yesterday already forgotten. He's always been like that, never one to hold a grudge. But still, I'll give him a proper apology later. "Congrats. And Amelia? Condolences." He swept her up in a big hug, dancing her around the room in a way that I wouldn't let any other man do.

He winked at me over her shoulder. "Come on, let me show you our Hall of Shame. Unless you're not interested in seeing baby pictures of Drake?"

"Oh, I so am," she replied, casting a quick look back at me to check in. I nodded and the two of them disappeared.

"Dad," I said immediately after they left the room. "I want to apologize. You're the least selfish person I know. I was—"

He cuts me off by wrapping me in a hug. "It's okay, son. I know you were just worried."

"Scared shitless," I mumble into his shoulder.

"Me too," he admits quietly.

I step back, my hands on his shoulders. "Promise you'll at least try to eat a little more heart friendly? And ease off on the Scotch?" I'm aware of the irony of my last request given how hard I was hammering it when I was trying to distract myself from Amelia, but I haven't had a heart attack.

"I'll take better care of myself. Promise," he agrees with a nod. "Exercise is the key though. I'm thinking more sex is what I need, if I'm being honest."

I screw my eyes closed. I'm aware he dates plenty of women, rarely more than once, but still. "Fuck, Dad," I groan.

"Watch it, son. You're not too grown-up for an ass-whooping."

Dad never gave us a single ass-whooping in our lives, although we certainly deserved it more than a few times. "Just behave yourself, all right, old man?" I wink at him, and he smiles in response.

It came as a huge relief to everyone to have the situation resolved. The James brothers might scrap and fight like overgrown puppies sometimes, but we love each other deeply, and anything that adds tension to our dynamic sucks.

Now, we're all in the kitchen where Luz has prepared a feast for us. Maddox mixed the cocktails even though he doesn't drink, and Luke has woken up from his nap and is sitting contentedly on his mom's lap.

"Can I hold him?" Amelia asks nervously, looking at the squirming bundle of chunky baby in Mel's arms.

"God, yes, please do." She passes him over, and he immediately spits up on Amelia's shoulder. No sense of decorum, that child. Luz hands her a dish towel, and nobody comments. That's what you get with babies.

Mel chats away to my girlfriend, and Amelia laughs as the kid whacks her in the face with one of his chubby fists. I know she's always wanted children and that Chad kept stalling. I hate that he hurt her that way, but I'm also glad he did. If he hadn't been such an asshole, she wouldn't be mine now.

"You happy, brother?" Maddox says, passing me an old

fashioned. "Because you look pretty damn happy. In fact, I'm not sure I've ever seen that particular look on your face before."

"Oh? What look is that?"

"The look that says you've finally discovered what true love is."

I grin at him. Out of all of us James boys, he's probably the one who's fallen in love the most. Had his heart broken plenty of times too, not to mention the other demons he's conquered. He inspires me every single day, and I wish he could cut himself a little slack sometimes because he is fucking incredible. "Yeah, I think I have, Mad."

He raises his glass of club soda and we make a silent toast to love, in all its forms.

THIRTY-NINE

AMELIA

'm at James and James when the call arrives. In fact, I'm with Drake in his office, and we're going through some paperwork for a complicated set of contract negotiations. We're both in full-on work mode, and apart from some deeply flirtatious banter, we've both managed to keep our pants on for once.

I glance at the screen, checking who it is, and drop the stack of papers I'm holding. They scatter over the floor, and Drake looks up at me in surprise.

"This is the hospital's number," I say, my hands shaking.

"Okay. Well, it's not necessarily anything to worry about. They might just be calling about insurance or an appointment."

I nod, telling myself he's right. I spoke to Mom last night, and she sounded okay. She was tired after taking her daily walk around the block, but she was holding her own. She's been monitoring her oxygen levels and taking her meds, and everything seemed good.

"Answer it," he says, laying his own work down on the desk. "Or would you like me to deal with it?"

I flash him a small smile. "No, it's okay—I'm your secretary, not the other way around." I accept the call.

"Miss Ryder?" a familiar voice says. "This is Jenny Griffin, from Brooklyn Emergency?" I immediately remember the kind nurse with the strong Southern accent who looked after both of us so well.

"Hi, Jenny. Is, uh, is everything okay?" My voice cracks, dread curling in my stomach as I anticipate the bad news I can hear in her tone.

"I'm sorry, honey, but no. She was brought in by the paramedics an hour ago. She collapsed on her way to somewhere called Wanda's? She didn't have any ID with her, so she was brought in as a Jane Doe, but as soon as I saw her, I knew who she was. She's not doing great, Miss Ryder. I think you'd better head on over here as soon as you can."

I hang up, tears streaming down my cheeks, my heart sinking to my ankles. I can't breathe. My mom ... She's ... I gasp for air, but there's none in the room.

Drake swoops across the room and gathers me into his arms. "It's okay, baby, I've got you. Whatever it is, we'll handle it together."

WHEN WE'RE DROPPED off at the hospital by a concerned Constantine, Mom is already in full respiratory failure. She's wearing the horribly familiar oxygen mask, and her arms are punctured and bruised with needle marks from blood tests. A saline drip is hanging from a stand at her side, and her face is battered and scraped from where she fell onto the sidewalk.

I fly to her side and see that her lips are blue, her eyelids closed. Her hand feels tiny in mine and completely unresponsive. "Mom," I say, squeezing her fingers. "I'm here, Mom, it's all going to be okay."

I glance at the heart monitor, seeing it as proof of life. While her heart is still beating, there's still hope. Drake is standing at my side, his face set in grim lines when Nurse Jenny walks into the room.

"Isn't there anything more you can do?" he asks, his tone demanding, his body language screaming power. He's the kind of man who's used to being able to fix things, and right now, he's coming off as intimidating. None of that bothers Jenny, of course. She's undoubtedly dealt with far worse.

She smiles sadly at him and shakes her head. "She has a DNR in place, so we can't perform invasive treatments."

"A DNR?" he echoes.

"A do-not-resuscitate order," she explains.

"I know what it is," he replies, gazing down at me. "I just ... why?"

"It was what she wanted," I answer, blinking away tears as I speak. "We discussed it many times, and she was always adamant. She knew she was never going to get better from this, and she didn't want it dragged out. One of her worst night-mares was being kept alive on a ventilator."

"But she's so damn young," he explodes, looking like he's going to punch a wall. I know that some of this anger is on my behalf, but I also know that some of it is related to the grief he still feels about his own mom.

Jenny looks at him sternly. "Sir, keep your voice down. You're not helping anybody behaving like this. We all want what's best for Edith, and I'm sure you do too."

He runs his hands through his hair and nods. "I'm sorry. Of course. Amelia, what can I do?"

"Just be with me, Drake. Just be with us."

"I can do that, mi rosa," he says, pulling a chair over to sit next to me. He puts his arm around my shoulder and holds me close. I take comfort and strength from him and wish I could send both to my mom.

"Can she hear me?" I ask Jenny.

"We don't know," she replies, shaking her head. "It's one of the big mysteries of the end of life. But I always tell loved ones to assume that they can. To say whatever you need to say. In your mom's case, given her oxygen levels, I don't think you have an awful lot of time left together, so make the most of it, honey. I'll be just outside if you need me."

"Talk to her, baby," Drake says, wiping away my tears with gentle fingers. "Don't leave this room with anything left unsaid, or believe me, you'll regret it."

"I know, but I ... I don't know what to say. Isn't that so stupid?"

He strokes my hair back from my face and kisses me lightly, his eyes intense on mine. "No, Amelia, it's not stupid at all. She's your mom. She's the person who has loved you the most for the entirety of your life, and you're about to lose her. There are no rule books for this kind of situation. If she were awake right now, what would you say to her?"

"I'd ask her why the hell she was going all the way to Wanda's on her own, for a start! But ... But I'd also tell her how much I love her. How much she means to me."

He nods and gestures at my mom with his head. "Then tell her. I truly believe she can hear you."

I bite my lip so hard I taste blood and nod, then turn to my mom, this wonderful woman. This glorious creature who has raised me, cherished me, made me who I am today.

With Drake at my side, I talk. I tell her how much love I have in my heart for her. I thank her for everything she gave to me, everything she gave up for me. I promise her that I will be strong—that even though I will miss her, I will go on living, just as she would want me to. I tell her I will never forget her.

CHAPTER THIRTY-NINE

I tell her goodbye.

FORTY

DRAKE

Edith Elizabeth Ryder departed this world not long after we arrived at the hospital. It was almost as though she was waiting for us to get there, waiting for her daughter to say goodbye. I had fucking tears in my eyes as Amelia spoke her piece, as she poured her heart and soul into those last few moments. Into the last few words she will ever share with her mom.

She might not realize it now, but those words will mean something to her later. They will comfort and console her, and she'll know that her mom died with nothing but the sound of love in her ears. It's the one blessing of a cursed day.

Amelia cried uncontrollably when Edith slipped away, throwing herself across the bed, her head on her mom's chest as though expecting one final embrace. Still expected the comfort that her mother had always provided. It almost broke me seeing her like that, her grief so raw and brutal. I know that grief, that pain. I have felt the same unfathomable loss. Today, Amelia's world shifted on its axis and changed forever.

If I understand all of that, then why do I feel like I'm doing such a bad job of caring for her? Why do I feel like I can't communicate?

We dealt with the necessary paperwork and started the grim process that follows a loved one's death. The nurse hugged her, and even Constantine held her close when we emerged into the evening. He's fond of her, I know, and he lost his father last year. Something about grief is contagious; it infects those around you. Your sadness becomes their sadness, and even if you are mourning completely different people, those primal feelings are communal. Amelia's pain taps into my pain about my own mother, and undoubtedly into Constantine's about his father. We are united by a common thread of emotional agony.

I took her back to my penthouse and tucked her up in my bed. For once, neither of us is interested in sex, although I would give her that if she seemed to need it. Right now, though, I'm not sure what she needs.

She refused food, refused wine, and she continues to refuse to really talk to me. I'm at a loss as to how to help. How to fix this.

"Can you just hold me?" she asks, her eyes huge, her skin pale.

"Always," I say, climbing under the covers with her. Wrapping her in my arms, I gently kiss her hair.

Her body shakes as she starts to cry. "It just doesn't feel real."

"I know," I say quietly. "I know it doesn't. That will take a while, baby. There's a hard road ahead, but you'll survive it. And I'll be on that road with you, every step of the way."

She nods against my chest, and I feel so helpless. Useless. Less in every possible way. What can I do for her? What could anybody have done for me? When my mom died, I was devastated. The pain was like acid, burning away everything else around it. Whenever I was in pain, I wanted my mom—and she was gone.

"Is there anything else I can get for you, mi rosa? Anything at all that you need?"

"No. I wish there was. I just feel so empty, you know? And scared. I'm scared that if I close my eyes, I'll go to sleep, and then when I wake up, I'll think that all of this was just a bad dream and have to go through it all again. Do you ... Do you really think she heard me?"

"I absolutely do. And I think what you said was beautiful."

Unlike my final words with my mom. They weren't so beautiful. In fact, they've haunted me ever since. She doesn't need to know that—not right now, anyway. The next few weeks will be all about her.

"I suppose I have to tell people," she murmurs against my skin.

"Can I help with that? Is there anyone you'd like me to call for you?"

She's about to answer when her phone rings. She left it in her bag when we got back to my place, so I brought it in and set it on my nightstand in case she needed it later. I pass it over to her, my chest contracting with anger when I see that it's Chad, but I clamp down on my emotions. Not the time or the place, and I certainly don't want to remind her of what happened the last time he called.

She glances at me nervously, and I shake my head. "It's fine, mi rosa. Go ahead."

She nods but takes the call on speakerphone, maybe to reassure me. Jeez. Am I that much of an asshole? I suppose I am.

"Hi Mimi," he says, and I cringe inside. Now, this guy is a *real* asshole. "The hospital called me. I guess I'm still on that list."

"Oh, Chad! I'm so sorry. I really should have sorted that out."

"Angel face, don't give it a second thought. I'm just so sorry. How are you doing?"

She sniffles and swipes at her eyes. "I'm ... not so good. You know how it was between us."

"I do, Mimi. You were so close. Other people don't understand it, that bond—you had no siblings, and she raised you alone. You were each other's world. You must feel like yours has ended."

Fuck. He's right. I didn't consider that. At least when my mom passed, we all had each other. That might not have always helped, but we had our shared memories, our shared experiences. We can all stand in Nathan's office and look at that painting of the beach in Spain and all know what it means to us. Amelia, though? She must feel so alone in this. Like part of her past has died too.

"I do, Chad. I really do. I know you two didn't always see eye to eye—"

"Hey, let's be honest, she fucking hated me. And who can blame her after the way I treated you? She was always such a fierce mama bear. You remember, that's what you used to call her. You bought her that stuffed grizzly when we went on that trip to Vancouver our senior year."

Amelia smiles, which is a small miracle. "Yeah. She loved that bear. She still has it in her room, you know?"

The tears start again, and I have no clue what to do for her. She looks up at me, those huge wet eyes seeming to say something that I don't understand, and shakes her head. "Chad, I have to go, okay? I'll let you know about the funeral arrangements."

"Okay, Mimi. You know I'm always here for you, right?

Anything you want, even if it's just to talk about her, to share memories. Reach out anytime."

Well, fuck. I hate Chad. The asshole cheated on her, broke her heart, and made her feel worthless as shit. Added to that, he's a slimy motherfucker with an ego the size of a planet. But what he just said? That was perfect. It was exactly what she needed.

She curls back up into my arms, and I make soothing noises and hold her tight. I do my best to make her feel safe, to make her feel less alone. But part of me wonders if I'm man enough for the job. And that part seems to grow bigger with every moment that passes.

FORTY-ONE

AMELIA

I hold the stuffed bear close to my heart and wonder if I'll ever let it go. It's old and tattered now, one ear hanging off and her once shiny eyes dull with age. She's wearing a T-shirt, as all grizzlies do, of course, that's emblazoned with the words *#1 Mama Bear*. I lie on Mom's bed, hugging that bear and inhaling the scent of her that lurks on the pillowcases.

I look around at the room that's been hers for as long as I've been alive and see the layers of her life. The clothes in the closet. The brush on her dresser that still contains strands of her precious hair. The half-used bottle of Anais Anais perfume that she loved so much. I will always treasure it. The still-unfinished romance novel on her bedside table. She only had a few chapters left to go, and it makes me unbearably sad that she will never get to the happy ending.

There is so much to do, and I don't want to do any of it. I need to go through her wardrobe and bag things up for donation. I need to speak to the funeral director about music. I need to cancel her cable and empty her fridge and tie up all the loose ends of her life. All I have the energy to do, though, is lie here in this bed that still smells of Mom and cuddle this stupid bear.

It's been four days since she died, and it still doesn't feel real. Drake is helping me with the legal stuff, and he's been great—incredible, in fact. A safe haven in a terrible time. Every member of his family has reached out with messages of sympathy, and I appreciate it so much. I know he's here for me. I only have to ask if I need anything at all. The problem is that I have no idea what I need or what would help. Sometimes I struggle to even speak about it and simply huddle in his arms, crying. I'm not a whole lot of fun to be around right now, but he's been incredibly patient.

He offered to come here with me today, but I told him no. I needed a few hours here alone first. A little time to let myself feel all the feels, smell all the smells, and cuddle all the bears. To pretend for just a little while that she's still here—that I could walk downstairs right now and she'd be sitting there on the couch, laughing at some funny video on her phone.

My mom—my beautiful, irreplaceable mom—is gone. I don't know what I'll do without her. It was always the two of us against the world, and now ... Now it's just the one of us, all by myself, and I don't think the world has much to fear.

I hear someone knocking at the door and drag myself off the bed. Neighbors must have noticed me arriving earlier and spread the word because they've been stopping by all day to pay their respects and give me casseroles that I'll never eat. Mom was real popular around here, and it's nice, but I'm exhausted by all of it. I trudge down the stairs, trying to plaster on a fake smile. The minute I open the door, my smile becomes real. Kimmy waves a giant roll of trash bags and Emily waves a bag full of wine. My girls are here.

They both come at me for a hug, and I burst into tears. I held it together in front of the neighbors, even Mrs. Katzberg who gave me a crossword puzzle book "to keep me busy." But seeing my girlfriends undoes me. I sob onto their shoulders and let them hold me up when my legs give up on supporting me. By the time I pull away, I am a snotty mess.

"Wow, Amelia, you look so hot right now," Kimmy says, fishing a tissue from her purse and dabbing my face with it. "So chic."

"Thank you," I reply, blowing my nose. "What are you guys doing here?"

"We've come to help," Emily says. "We weren't sure what that would look like, so we thought we could help you clean and pack up, then maybe get you drunk."

"That sounds like the best idea ever. I've been lying upstairs sniffing her pillows. It's tragic."

"It's normal," Kimmy says firmly. "It's human. It's okay."

I feel so much better for seeing them, and I have no idea why I've been avoiding them and putting them off with excuses. I've noticed that grief is super sneaky, especially for an only child like me. It creeps up on you, ambushes you, and isolates you. It tells you nobody shared the same past as you, so nobody can understand what you've lost. But that's where grief is wrong, at least in my case. These women might not be blood relatives, but they really are like sisters. I realize how long it's been since I properly talked to them, how tied up in Drake I've been.

"I have so much to tell you guys." I usher them into the house, deciding that the secrecy can go fuck itself. His family knows, and now that my mom is gone, Emily and Kimmy are all the family I have left. I'm going to tell them all about Drake James and how much I love him.

"Is it that you're getting back with Chad?" Kimmy asks, wrinkling her nose.

"Uh, no, of course not—why would you say that?"

"Because he's walking right toward us."

I pop my head through the still-open door and look down

the street. He hesitates when he sees who I'm with, and I look back at Kimmy to see her eyes narrowed menacingly. "Play nice," I say quietly. "I don't want to have to visit Chad in the hospital."

She snorts and schools her face into neutral. Emily does the same, but it looks more natural on her. He eyes them both warily as he approaches and nods in greeting.

"Chad," I say, frowning. "What are you doing here?"

"I was still in town, visiting my parents in the neighborhood. I just ... Look, I know this is weird, but I just wanted to come by and pay my respects to the place. Whatever happened between us, I spent a lot of time in this house. I have a lot of happy memories of it, of you. Of Edith. Is that okay?"

He looks nervous but sounds sincere. He was a big part of my life for a very long time, and however badly things ended between us, I can't erase that. He, in a very strange way, is also part of my family.

I spread my arms wide. "It's your lucky day. I'm open for bear hugs."

FORTY-TWO

DRAKE

F uck. Why is she hugging him? Why is she letting him touch her?

More to the point, why am I skulking here across the street, hiding behind an old SUV and watching it happen? Why aren't I striding over there and punching the asshat in the face?

Because, I tell myself, that would make me the asshat. I left work early, knowing how hard this was going to be for her. Going through Mom's things was one of the hardest things I've ever had to do in my life—divvying them up between us as keepsakes, the unexpected kick in the nuts that came from the smell of her perfume lingering on her clothes. Things are just things, stuff is just stuff, until they become more. Until they are memories, precious reminders of what you've lost. Amelia said she wanted to do this alone, but I knew better. Or at least I thought I did.

Turns out she's not alone anyway. She's standing there on the front step, wrapped up in Chad and accompanied by Emily Gregor and a woman I assume is the famous Kimmy Park. All three of them knew Edith a lot better than I did. All three of them have been in Amelia's life a lot longer than I have. She doesn't need me at all, and I was stupid to think I was going to be some knight in shining Armani, riding to her emotional rescue.

I could still go over there. I don't have to punch Chad in the face, no matter how much I want to. Instead, I could do something normal, like introduce myself properly to the women and kiss my girlfriend and help them sort out the house.

Hey, maybe we could all go out to dinner and talk about the old times. Except my old times with Edith, even my old times with Amelia, only go back a few months. I'm the new kid on the block, and I don't like the feeling. It's selfish and fucked up and wrong, but I like having her all to myself.

An ancient crone of a woman gives me the evil eye from a few doors down, and I suspect that must be Mrs. Katzberg. Before she can give the game away, I turn on my heel and stride away. Constantine dropped me a couple blocks from here, and I went to Wanda's to get Amelia some cannoli, thinking the familiar food she always talked about might bring her some comfort. Now, the box hangs from my fingers, and I can't imagine wanting to eat it alone.

If she can find some solace and comfort with Emily and Kimmy, or even with Chad, so be it. She deserves it. I get out my phone to call Constantine back, but Amber's name flashes on the screen. She's pretty much as fucked up as I am, which makes her one of the few people I could tolerate being around right now.

"Darling," she purrs when I answer. "Can I talk to you about clowns?"

"No," I reply. "But you can talk to me about what a shit I am. Are you free for a drink?"

. . .

334

"I REMEMBER THAT DAY SO CLEARLY." I gaze off over her shoulder, clinking the ice in my Scotch glass. "I kind of wish I didn't."

"I know, Drake. I feel the same. I've gone over it so many times, spent so many hours wishing it had played out differently. That I hadn't gone into her room to check on her. That she hadn't been on so many head-fuck drugs. Most of all, that you hadn't overheard it all."

I stare at my Scotch, losing myself in the memory. It was about three nights before Mom died. With hindsight, I now know that she was on a lot of pain meds, doped up to the eyeballs to help her tolerate those final days. Days that counted down to hours, to minutes, to nothing, the pain getting worse and worse, her mind getting more and more messed up. As Amber puts it, head-fuck drugs. I think my parents hid a few home truths from us—like how long she actually had left and how much it was going to suck. Maybe they were protecting us, maybe they didn't even know themselves. Maddox was only sixteen at the time, and I'm pretty sure they still saw all of us as babies anyway, no matter how old we were.

Elijah was already married to Amber, and they'd discovered that she couldn't have kids a few years after their wedding, once they started trying. Both of them really wanted children, and Dad was keen on the whole family name being continued thing, so it came as a blow to everyone. We're close, the James boys, and we all felt Elijah and Amber's pain. Back then, she hadn't shut down, the rest of my brothers hadn't closed off from her, and she still felt like part of the family.

I was walking past Mom's room that night, on my way back to my room after getting a beer from the kitchen. I was in my second year of law school, still living at home, although I was considering getting a place with my girlfriend pretty soon. Her door was slightly ajar, and I couldn't help but hear her voice coming from inside.

"You're so beautiful, Amber," she was saying, her voice edged with a slight slur. Some of the meds made her sound like she was drunk. "We were so pleased when you and Elijah settled down—seeing your child married is a big moment. It's such a shame that you'll never get to experience it."

I heard Amber gulp and stutter out a half-assed reply. I mean, I was shocked that my mom had said that, never mind Amber herself. "You look so healthy on the outside," Mom continued. "Nobody could have guessed that you were barren."

Amber's gasp was loud enough for me to hear, and I was so shocked I dropped my beer. "I'm sorry, Verona. I know how much you wanted grandkids. I ... I wish I could have given them to you."

"It doesn't change anything, does it? We all feel like this way, you know. It's sad that poor Elijah has to pretend he doesn't mind. And maybe he doesn't mind right now. But he will. One day, he'll resent you for what he's had to give up. You shouldn't have married my boy, Amber, knowing that you were broken."

Amber was sobbing, and I couldn't listen to it anymore. I burst into the room and confronted my mom even though she was so frail, so tiny in that big bed, her eyes bruised and drowsy. "Mom! What's wrong with you? Why are you saying these things? None of that is true. Why would you even think that?"

She looked up at me, confused and groggy, and then back at Amber, as though she was seeing her for the first time. "Amber?" she said, sounding a bit more like her true self. "Why are you crying, darling?"

"She's crying, Mom, because you just tore her to pieces about not being able to give Elijah kids. He loves her!"

I'll never forget the look on Mom's face as she stared at me, her mouth open in horror. Her normally supple skin was dry and thin, stretched across the bones of her face like tissue paper. Her beautiful dark hair had never grown back properly after the last round of chemo and lay in thin strands across her head. She looked old and sick, and nothing at all like my mom. The things that I'd just heard coming out of her mouth were not things my mom would have ever said either—she was the kindest, sweetest soul, and I think that's one of the reasons Amber and I were so shocked.

"No, that can't be right," she muttered, her veined hands fluttering in the air. "I wouldn't do that. I love Amber too. Why are you making things up about me, Drake? Why are you trying to make me feel bad, mi hijo? Why do you want to hurt me?"

"I'm not trying to make you feel bad. I'm telling you what happened. Just because you're sick ..." I stopped talking then, because her being sick changed everything, and it made her say shit she didn't mean. But the damage was already done.

She fell back onto her pillow then, tiny and gray, an alien who had taken over my mother's mind and body. "Go away, Drake," she said. "Leave me in peace."

So I left. I turned around and took Amber with me.

"She doesn't mean it, Amber," I said, comforting her as she wept before me. "It's the pain talking. Or the drugs, or—"

"Or maybe she does mean it. Maybe it's what she thought all along, and the drugs have taken away her inhibitions and let her actually say it. Is it true, Drake? Do you all hate me? And do you think Elijah will resent me one day? I didn't know when we got married, I swear I didn't!"

I held her in my arms and patted her back awkwardly. I was only twenty-three, not mature enough to really know what to do. I knew my mom didn't mean those cruel things, that it wasn't the real her, but I was still angry.

"Nobody hates you. And I meant what I said. Elijah loves you, you know that, right?" She nodded, but there was something in her eyes that told me she wasn't convinced. My mom had planted a seed of doubt in her mind, but I had no idea how much it would continue to grow.

Present-day Amber is older and colder, and I truly believe something inside her snapped that night. Those harsh words from a drug-addled dying woman broke something precious, and my sister-in-law has never quite been the same since. That's when she started retreating from us, avoiding family brunches, not returning calls. It was like she started to freeze us out before we got the chance to do it to her, and that caused a huge amount of friction between her and Elijah.

A few days later, Mom was gone. I saw her after that night, of course, but she was never totally lucid again. A combination of the drugs and the illness taking its terrible course, shutting down her organs and closing down her life. She was like an animal at the end, dominated by pain and fury, not even recognizing us anymore. I suppose that process had already started when she was so brutal to Amber, but we didn't know it at the time. We didn't know how close we were to losing her forever, and to my own dying day, I will regret the fact that I never got to make it up to her. That I never got to talk to my real mom again. How the very last words we shared were ones of anger and reprimand. My mom—my wonderful, kind, giving mother —died believing that I was trying to hurt her.

Amelia doesn't know it yet, but in some ways, she's lucky. Her mom died peacefully, with her daughter at her side and nothing but love between them.

Amber puts her hand over mine on the table. "You'll be okay, Drake."

"You think? I wonder sometimes if I'll ever get over it, you know? I've lived with it for all these years, that guilt. I wonder if maybe it's just part of me now."

"It doesn't have to be." She sips her wine. "You're in love. That changes everything."

"Does it, Amber? Is being in love enough? You and Elijah were in love."

"True," she says, letting out a bitter laugh. "And look at us now. Happily in hate."

"He doesn't hate you, and I'm sure you don't hate him. Why don't you tell him? Tell him about that night. At least let him get a glimpse of why things started to change between you. Maybe it's not too late to change them back."

"Ah, darling. What a lovely thought. If only we had a time machine."

If I had a time machine, the first thing I'd do is go back to this morning and not let Amelia out of my sight.

FORTY-THREE

AMELIA

S eeing my mother's casket lowered into her grave is one of the most surreal moments of my life. How can someone that important, that precious, be contained in a wooden box? How can someone so full of life so suddenly be gone? How can the final page of the story of her life have been turned? I stare at the flower-draped pine, struggling to believe that she is actually inside it.

It didn't feel real until today. But seeing this, seeing her disappear into the ground, is starting to make it so, and that reality is brutal. It's like my emotional tendons and ligaments are being stretched and torn, and my mind might never recover. I will never be the same shape again.

The service was beautiful in its own way. So many people came to say goodbye to her. People she used to work with in her many jobs, friends from the neighborhood, the men and women who lived near her. Nurse Jenny. My mom touched a lot of lives, and it was moving to see them all there, paying tribute.

I cried as I delivered the eulogy, my hands trembling on the folded notes that I could barely see. I spoke of her beautiful spirit, her generosity, her wicked sense of humor. Of her love of the finer things in life, like pistachio cannoli and Harrison Ford. The gathered mourners listened to me talk about how much she meant to me and how she made me feel like the world was at my feet, mine for the taking. I spoke of everything and nothing, and even if I'd spoken for a month straight, I couldn't possibly have said enough.

Drake's eyes were on mine throughout, and I took comfort in that. My friends were all there, and Chad came with his parents too. Whatever our present, our past tied us all together.

Now, standing at the graveside in the drizzling rain as Drake shields me with a black umbrella, I wonder how I will move on from this. I wonder how people survive this pain, how they don't simply throw themselves on top of the casket as it slides into the earth, begging to stay with those they love.

I am not the first person to lose a parent, I know. But it is the first time it has happened to me, and I don't know what to do with all this pain. It's filling me, suffocating me, choking me. I know Drake is worried, but I don't seem able to tell him to stop. Last night, he cooked me a dinner that I couldn't eat and held me in his arms while neither of us slept. We were physically together, but emotionally, I felt a distance between us that added to my sadness.

He loves me, I know he does, but I'm still concerned that this is all too much for him. That his own grief is lurking directly beneath the surface, waiting to be triggered by my own. There isn't enough room in the world for all our suffering, and I feel like it's starting to define us.

Drake holds me steady as the pastor reads from Ecclesiastes, telling us that to everything, there is a season. A time to be born and a time to die.

I turn into his chest, burying my face in his rain-soaked

shirt. I hate this season. I hate this day. I hate the mom-shaped hole that now dominates my life.

The service draws to a close, and people head back to their cars. There will be a small gathering back at Mom's house, and I'm already dreading it.

"You okay?" Drake whispers.

I cling to him tighter. "I don't know."

"Just a few more hours to get through, mi rosa." He kisses the top of my head. "I know this is hard, but you're doing great."

Am I though? I feel as if I'm sleepwalking through this. Like I'm sedated. It's as though my mind has numbed my senses to help me survive.

Chad is one of the last to leave, and he strides toward us. My feelings about him are complicated, but I'm grateful to him for coming and for the huge funeral bouquet he had delivered.

"Thank you, Chad, for the flowers. They were beautiful."

His gaze flickers to Drake, and tension shoots through me as the two men look each other up and down. Drake looks away first, and I love him for it. I know how much it cost him and that he did it for me.

"You're welcome, Mimi. Sunflowers, right? They were always her favorite. I remember you filling the whole house with them for her fiftieth birthday. She looked so happy when she walked through the door—like a little girl. Then the year after, when it was your turn, she filled the place with your favorite, yellow roses."

I smile at the memory and am pleased that I still can. Sometimes I feel like I'll never smile easily again. But surely there will be a day when her memory won't hurt this much. There has to be.

I think of Drake and his brothers and their father and how

they all found a way to move past their loss. Drake. I look up into his handsome face. This is simply one season for us, a season that will pass. One day soon, we'll have sunflowers and roses again.

FORTY-FOUR

DRAKE

F uck, I needed a drink tonight. It's been a tough few days, and I'm relieved to be sitting alone at the stylish bar of the Grand Regent, enjoying a good Scotch. The bartender was kind enough to take a huge tip and leave the bottle.

Amelia has been whisked upstate for a night at a spa hotel by Emily. She's been sending me photos throughout the day, including one of her newly pedicured toes and another of her and Emily in white robes, waiting for their massage.

The thought of my girl getting oiled up and rubbed all over is hot, but then I start getting jealous of someone else laying hands on her.

> Please tell me the masseuse is a 92 yr old grandma.

> He's 24 and looks like a young Brad Pitt.

I start to fume and actually consider calling Constantine and telling him to get ready for a road trip, but my phone dings with a new message.

CHAPTER FORTY-FOUR

Just kidding. Put your coat back on, big guy.

She knows me so well, I think, smiling. It's nice to see her go for a little lighthearted banter.

Two weeks have passed since Edith's funeral, and I still feel like something is slightly off between us. It's nothing I can quite put my finger on, and our sex life shows no signs of suffering because of it. In fact, pretty much the only time I feel like I'm doing my job properly is when we're fucking. When my mouth is on her pussy and she's calling my name, when I suck her nipples until her back bows. When she's tied up and begging for mercy, desperate for me to finally let her come. Then, we are truly together.

But the rest of the time? I'm not sure what to do for her, and she's not sure how to behave. It's a transition, and it sucks. I hate not being able to control things, and I hate not being able to relax. Mainly, I hate the feeling that I'm letting her down. When my mom died and Tiff wasn't there for me, it hurt worse than if I'd been alone.

The fact that I feel even an ounce of relief to have a night to myself makes me feel like an asshole, but logically, it makes sense. Everything has been so intense as we're settling into this thing between us.

I'm pondering all this and idly googling the place where she's staying, just in case that Brad Pitt comment was true, when a shadow falls over me. I look up and my lip curls at the sight of Chad fucking Poindexter standing beside me.

I wanted to beat the shit out of him at the funeral, with his fake concern and cloyingly sweet memories of his time with Edith and Amelia. It was all an act. If he loved them so much, he wouldn't have cheated. Wouldn't have thrown Amelia away like trash. I was also secretly and childishly annoyed by the fact that he not only knew what Edith's favorite flowers were, but

Amelia's too. Why the fuck didn't I know that? I swear to god, the man smirked at how uncomfortable I looked right then.

I kept myself calm, at least on the surface, for her sake. But now? Now he has delivered himself to my doorstep, when she isn't here to restrain me. Looks like I can add poor judgment to his lengthy list of flaws.

"Chad," I say slowly, not standing up to greet him or offering a hand to shake or any of that other polite male-posturing bullshit. I see him eye my open bottle of Scotch, but he can go fuck himself. I'd rather pour it down the drain than let him get a taste. He's already proved that the good stuff in life is wasted on him. "What are you doing here?"

To give the man his due, he has balls. He's never once backed down from me, even though I'm much bigger than him. Even though I'm right now baring my teeth and growling at him in a way that most would find intimidating. He sits down opposite me, the cheeky fucker. I ponder breaking his fingers one at a time and wonder if that smarmy grin on his tan face would fade as I snapped them.

"I came to talk to you, Drake. About Amelia."

I narrow my eyes at him over my glass. "I don't like her name on your lips, you jerk. Say your piece and fuck off, or I'll smash those shiny veneers down your throat." I deliver this vicious speech in a calm and reasonable tone, presenting like I do in court. He flinches slightly but shows no sign of leaving.

"Okay—this is my piece. She's my wife, and I want her back."

My pulse shoots up into the stratosphere. Is this joker for real?

"She's your ex-wife, and if I recall correctly, you gave her away. You cheated on her, broke her heart, and you're now engaged to your mistress. Did I leave anything out?"

"A lot. For a start, I'm not engaged. We broke it off. It was ...

a mistake. A stupid mistake. You wouldn't understand this, but marriage is complicated."

"I might not have been married, Chad, but I'm not a simpleton. Try me."

"Right. Well, it's like this—Amelia and I are meant to be together. We've loved each other since we were sixteen. Yeah, I fucked up, but I'm human, and that's what humans do. This thing with Edith, it's made me realize how much I still love her. You might think I'm a dick, and I can't argue, but I mean it. I still love her, Drake. She's amazing."

I bite back a snarl, because I don't want him to see that he's getting to me. "You don't have to tell me that."

"You know she wants kids, right?" The sudden change of subject confuses me. I don't show it, though, and simply nod. I know she does, but Amelia and I haven't discussed it properly. We had sex without a condom that day on my desk, with Chad bleating in the background, but she's had her period since. Was that a lucky escape, or was she secretly disappointed? It's something we do need to discuss, because while I'd love nothing more than to see my baby growing inside her at some stage, I'm not sure we're quite there yet. At least I'm not. I think I'd like her all to myself for a little while longer. Hell, maybe forever. I guess you could say I'm conflicted.

"Are you ready for that?" he asks. He gestures around him. "Are you ready to give up all of this? To give up your fancy bachelor lifestyle and be a husband and father? You live in a hotel, for god's sake."

"That's got fuck all to do with you, Chad. Is there a point to any of this?"

"My point is that I *am* ready for that. I'm ready to love her the way she deserves. I'm ready to have kids, to give her what she wants. You don't just throw away the kind of history we have together, and I know that deep down, she still wants us to work. She'd be willing to give us another chance and become a mom, just like she always dreamed of. There's only one thing in the way."

I sip my Scotch and ignore the frantic beat of my heart inside my chest. The sense of panic that's rising in my throat. "Let me guess," I say, smoothly and calmly. "Me?"

"Yes, you—you'll never be able to give her what she needs because you can't ever know her like I do. You won't be able to make her happy. If you really love her, you'll let her go."

He stands up to leave, and I force myself to stay where I am. If I rise to my feet, I will kill him. I will beat his smug face bloody and choke the fucking life out of him. I will squeeze his throat so hard he will never be able to say her name again.

Instead, I stare at his back as he strides away, fighting down my anger and my anguish. My self-loathing and my doubt. The self-loathing is doing its usual thing, lurking around and telling me I'm not quite good enough. And the doubt? The doubt is eating me alive.

Because as much as I hate to admit it, part of me wonders whether motherfucking Chad Poindexter might actually be right. He's been a damn sight better than me at consoling her in her grief—could it be that he'll be better at all the rest too?

FORTY-FIVE

She stares at me like I've grown an extra head, the confusion on her face ranging from her uncertain eyes to her parted lips.

"What?" she says, finally able to form words. "I don't understand."

She came to see me as soon as she got home from her trip, and I haven't been able to stop thinking about Chad's visit last night. I hate that he's undermined us like this, but I also can't ignore the fact that he might have a point. I've felt like crap recently, like I haven't been able to give Amelia what she needs —fuck, I don't even know what she needs.

"Look, mi rosa, I don't want to hurt you, but I think we need to take some time. Really think things through."

Her lower lips wobbles, and tears fill her eyes. "You don't get to call me mi rosa and say you don't want to hurt me while you break up with me, Drake."

"I'm not breaking up with you, Amelia, I'm just ... Fuck! Can we be honest with each other?"

"I suppose we should be," she replies, a touch of snark in

her voice that is spoiled by the impending tears. "If you think you're up for that."

I suck in a deep breath and try to ignore how fucking edible she looks perched on the edge of my bed like that, her skin glowing from her spa and her hair flipped in a dark cloud over her shoulders. She's wearing a little pink T-shirt that shows the jut of her nipples, and under normal circumstances, it would be driving me wild. In fact, it still is, dammit.

I sit in a chair a few feet away, facing her. If I get too close, if my body touches hers, I won't be able to do this—and I need to do this. For her sake. I need to give her time to figure out if I'm right for her. If she can live with my imperfections and my fucked-up way of seeing the world. I need to let her see me outside the whirlwind of what has been an incredibly intense and fast-moving relationship. Maybe I won't look quite so good from a distance.

"Amelia, I love you. I really do. But we have to face facts— we don't know each other that well. This thing between us has happened hard and fast, and maybe we both need to just slow it down and make sure we're where we want to be." I know where my cock wants to be, I think, seeing the slight tremor of emotion run through her body, making her chest heave. Fuck. It's a regular old nipple party over there. I stare at my hands instead.

"Where is this coming from, Drake?" She's unable to hide the hurt in her voice. She's suffering, and I want to comfort her. But I can't because I'm the one causing it. "Is it because ... Because I've been such a pain in the ass recently? I know I've been a misery to be around, with all the crying and the complaining—"

I snap my head up. "Stop right there. No, it isn't because of any of that. You haven't been a misery at all. You just lost your mom. I'm not such a heartless bastard that I expect you to get over that in a few weeks. This isn't anything you've done wrong."

"Really? Because it sure feels like I'm being punished for something, Drake. Why ... Why are you making this decision alone? Is it nothing at all to do with me? Am I that unimportant to you?"

I bury my face in my hands, wanting to scream. "Amelia, I wish I could find a better way to express myself. I feel so fucking tongue-tied. Do you trust me?"

"I did," she murmurs, the words barely there. "Until I walked through the door today and you said we needed to talk."

"I need you to carry on trusting me. I need you to believe that I want what's best for you."

She bites her lip and finally lets the tears she's been fighting spill over her cheeks. I have seen a lot of tears recently, but this time I'm the cause of them, and I feel like the biggest fucking asshole on the planet.

"What's best for me?" she echoes. "And you get to decide that, do you? I don't get a say in the matter?"

I force myself to stay tough. To fight the urge to rush over there and take her in my arms and tell her everything will be okay. Because what if Chad is right? What if I'm holding her back? What if she could have an entirely different, better future without me? There's a reason I've been single for so long. A reason I'm married to my work. A reason I pay women to spend time with me to avoid complications. The reason is that I'm fucked up, and I don't want her to suffer for it.

"No, you don't," I say decisively, hating the pain shining in her eyes but hating myself more. "Because I need to know that we're right for each other before we take this any further. I told you a little about Tiff, right?"

She nods, and a spark of interest flares in her eyes.

"Well, when my mom died, Tiff wasn't there for me. She

couldn't handle the complexity, the grief. She couldn't find a way to make me feel better, or maybe she didn't even want to, I don't know. The point is, we weren't right for each other. And since your mom died, I've felt like maybe I'm not right for you. I haven't been able to take care of you or comfort you or be part of your emotional life in the way I want to. I'm not sure I'm even capable of it."

"Why do you think that?" she asks, her voice rising in desperation. "Why would you think you're not enough for me? Have I made you feel like that? I hope not, because you are enough, Drake—more than enough. I love you, and I know we haven't talked what happens long-term, but for me this is it. This is forever. I get that you're not perfect, but who is? I'm certainly not, and I don't expect you to be. Please don't do this. Please don't throw this away. I can't imagine my life without you anymore."

"And maybe that's one of the problems. When we first met, you had to pretend to be Scarlet before you could even sleep with me, and you've said numerous times that you're different when we're together. That sometimes you don't recognize yourself. I don't want you to have to be someone else. Maybe I'm too broken for all of this, Amelia. Maybe I'm too broken for marriage and kids and a house in the suburbs."

She frowns at me, confused, and swipes the tears from her face as she speaks. "Yes, I am different when I'm with you, but in a good way. I like the person I am when I'm with you. I'm brave and bold with you. As for the rest—kids, marriage ... Have I ever pressured you about those things? Have I even brought them up?"

"No," I say, my heart twisting in my chest. "You haven't. But I know you want them. You deserve them. What I don't know is if I'm the man who can give you that life. I don't want you to waste your time on me when I might not ever be what you need."

She jumps to her feet, indignant, her temper mixing with her sadness. Her legs are shaking, and she leans back against the bed to steady herself. She looks like she could faint at any moment. Her hazel eyes burn holes in my face, and I have never hated myself so much in my whole life.

"Is that what we've been doing, Drake? Wasting each other's time? And here's me, thinking we were loving each other. Thinking we had something special. What a goddamn fool I am." She grabs a paper bag from the floor, one she brought back with her from her trip upstate with Emily. She throws it at me, and I catch it.

"There. That's for you. Shove it up your ass for all I care. I'll leave now. I wouldn't want to waste any more of your precious time."

The door slams shut behind her, and I peer inside the bag. Fucking hell. The black stuffed bear is wearing a T-shirt that says *#1 Boyfriend Bear*. It's exactly like the one she gave her mom all those years ago, and it obliterates what's left of my heart.

What the hell have I done?

FORTY-SIX

AMELIA

I call in sick for the next three days. I actually feel sick. The pain of losing Drake is physical, not just emotional, and I am racked with a killer headache, an upside-down tummy, and extreme fatigue. I can't eat, can't sleep. I can't do anything other than cry. For me, for him, for my mom. For all the suffering in the whole damn world.

He messaged me to say he's getting me transferred to a different department at work, so at least I won't have to face him every day. He probably told himself he was being kind. He's not. He's being a coward. This whole thing is about cowardice.

He might say it's just a break, that we need to figure things out and be sure of each other, but all I see is a man running scared. And I get it—this is scary. Love is scary. Hell, life is scary. None of us can ever know what's going to happen next, but I was willing to take the chance. To take that leap of faith. I loved him enough to risk it all.

And now, of course, I'm paying the price. I feel like I'll never be right again. I have lost too many parts of myself in too short a time, and I'm not sure there's enough of me left to make a whole.

I hate him for what he's done to me, but I miss him like crazy as well. There are signs of him everywhere—the spare clothes he keeps at my place, his toothbrush in the bathroom, the damn Shibari ropes that brought us both so many hours of mutual pleasure. I should box it all up and send it over to the office. Leave his new secretary to go through it and let her try to figure out what her boss needs so much rope for. I certainly won't be going back into that building myself ever again. I'll find a new job, somewhere less toxic. Like a chemical waste plant.

He's contacted me a couple of times to check on me and left messages asking me to call back, but I haven't. He can't have it both ways. He either wants me or he doesn't, there are no half measures. The way I feel about Drake is all-consuming, and I won't do this whole "taking a break" dance. If he's not all in, then he's all out.

I have nothing left to say to him, and I'm angry as well as broken. I feel like I've been tricked into loving him, that maybe I loved a mirage—because he's not the man I thought he was.

I roll around on the bed, which I've been doing pretty much all day. It now feels strange to have this bed all to myself. I let myself get used to him being here and filling it with me. To him being here and filling *me*, in every way possible. Now, I am as empty as the bed, and I have no clue what to do about it. I wish my mom were around so I could talk to her. She would help me through this. She would take my tarnished crown, polish it up, pop it back on my head, and remind me that I am a queen. Or at the very least, her princess.

Thinking about my mom makes everything so much worse, and I'm lost in despair. I don't know what to do with myself anymore. I don't seem able to reach out to my friends, and I haven't even told them what happened with Drake. I feel too hurt and too tired to discuss it. And also a touch humiliated.

They helped me through everything when Chad cheated on me, and I hate the idea of them having to do it all over again. There really must be something very wrong with me for this to keep happening.

It's just after 6:00 p.m., and I have a whole long-ass night ahead of me. That's the other thing about this new version of my life that sucks—without my mom to care for or Drake in my world, every day seems to stretch into infinity.

A message comes in, and I pull a face when I see who it is. I'm not in the mood for Chad. I'm not in the mood for anyone.

> I've found some photos of your mom I thought you might like. I can make copies of them for you and mail them, or would you like to come out for a bite to eat and a catch up? No pressure either way.

I sit up and push greasy hair away from my face. My personal hygiene has taken a nosedive recently, and I've worn nothing but pajamas since I got back here. I haven't been outside at all and have kept the drapes closed because the sunlight is too damn cheerful. The only people I've interacted with in the flesh are the guys who delivered the takeout I ended up throwing in the trash.

Maybe I should go out. Maybe I need to. Whatever happens with me and Drake, I have to go on living. I have to be strong. Because that's what I promised my mom I would do, and I'm a woman who keeps her promises.

CHAPTER
FORTY-SEVEN
DRAKE

What is it with me and hanging around street corners in Brooklyn? I'm going to get a reputation if I keep this up. Drake James, neighborhood creep.

I don't feel like I have any other choice right now though. As soon as she left the other day, I started to miss her. Everything ached without her near—my heart, my head, my cock. Even at work, I couldn't function without her. Not only is she a great secretary, but it turns out she's essential to me keeping my head on straight.

I can't concentrate in meetings, I'm fucking up paperwork, and I missed a court date for the first time in my life. Work has always been my great solace, the one thing that has never let me down, but it isn't doing the trick anymore. There's simply no space in my mind for work. It's too full of Amelia.

How the fuck did I let things get this bad? I did what I did for her sake. It came from a place of love. Which, I realize as I even think those stupid words, sounds fucking ridiculous. How can you hurt someone as badly as I hurt her and then tell yourself it was because you love them? That it was all for their own good? That's some patronizing bullshit right there.

The truth? I did it because I was scared. There. I said it. I was scared shitless of how much I love her. How much I need her. How much I had to lose. Chad put the fear of god into me, leaving me half convinced that he was right—that he might be the man for her. Amelia is the marrying kind. She's the fill-a-house-with-kids kind. And me? Who the fuck knows what I am. I've never dreamed of those things before, but with her? Hell yeah. With her, I want everything she's willing to give.

It's taken me three days without her to come to this conclusion, which is testimony to what a dumbass I am despite my expensive and extensive education. She's ignored my messages and hasn't called back, and I don't suppose I can blame her. She lost her mom, and while she was still grieving, the man who should have been by her side had a self-indulgent meltdown. My self-doubt is what drove the train, and it's beyond unfair. That's my own baggage, and Amelia has never done or said anything to make me feel that way. But I felt less than perfect after Edith died, I felt like I was messing up, dropping the ball. And heaven forbid the mighty Drake James does anything less than perfectly, right? Basically, I behaved like a giant asshole, and I desperately need to talk to her.

The only way to do that seems to be in person. I considered getting Linda to call her in for a meeting or being really sneaky and getting Melanie to contact her on my behalf, but even I'm not that much of a coward. So here I am, lurking outside her apartment building, planning what to say. Searching for the right words to apologize. For a man who makes a living from talking persuasively, I sometimes totally suck at it.

I'm clutching a huge bunch of yellow roses to my chest and I've just decided that a pretty solid place to begin would be "I'm sorry. I was a jackass, and I can't live without you." I'm about to cross the road and ring her buzzer when a cab pulls up outside the building and my old pal Chad rolls out. He stands there looking at his phone with a shit-eating grin on his punchable face, and within seconds, I know why.

Amelia—*my* Amelia—emerges from her building looking like a ray of fucking sunshine in human form. Her hair is a glorious shining curtain down her back, and she's wearing a peach-colored dress that skims her ass and ends not much farther down. Chad does a comedic double take, then pulls her in for a hug. She doesn't slap him or knee him in the balls, so I assume she doesn't mind. They chat for a few moments, him obviously complimenting her, and then the two of them set off down the street toward the main drag of bars and restaurants.

Fuck. What's happening? Is it a date? It certainly fucking looks like one. If I expected her to be in her apartment, wallowing in her misery and missing me so much she hasn't eaten or slept for the last three days, I was very much mistaken. She looks fantastic and is clearly on her way to a night out. With her ex-husband. The one who wants her back.

Pain tears through me like a bullet, so fierce that I swear I should be bleeding. I have no right to feel this way. No right to be jealous or angry or hurt. I have no right to be anything other than sorry. Because this is on me. I pushed her away, straight back into the waiting arms of Chad. Will she be happy with him? Is he really the right man for her? I truly don't know. Fighting back tears, I walk away from her apartment building, dumping the roses in a trashcan as I go. I know this much: If he hurts her again, I will fucking kill him.

I stagger along the sidewalk, no clue where I'm going, my vision blurred with tears I'm determined not to shed. This is too hard. Too raw. I need help.

It's time to call in the big guns.

. . .

I sit with all my brothers in a plush private booth in one of Manhattan's most exclusive bars. They surround me, physically and emotionally, four big men with even bigger hearts. I haven't cried in front of anyone since my mom died, but I broke that rule tonight, and they were here for me.

The table is overflowing with empty glasses and a bottle of insanely rare Yamazaki single-malt whisky from Japan. That was Maddox's idea, even though he doesn't even fucking drink, and I suspect we're all going to have million-dollar hangovers in the morning. Apart from him, of course, unless there's more in his OJ than he's letting on.

"To Julia Roberts!" says Nathan, holding up his glass. "And her incredible smile!" We all cheer and hold up our own glasses to match him. And why not? Julia Roberts does indeed have an incredible smile, and it's totally worth celebrating.

There have been a lot of toasts tonight, and they started off a lot more personal. We toasted little baby Luke, our dad, the memory of our mom. Then we toasted each other and the city of New York and our childhood dog, a red setter named Rupert. Since then, though, things have gone a little off the rails. We've toasted our colleges, our favorite diner, Mason's new tattoo, and Russell Crowe's fucking fantastic husband-to-a-murdered-wife speech from *Gladiator*. We've toasted everything in the whole damn world, and now we've included Julia Roberts's incredible smile in that.

I fall back against the seat and realize that I am totally shit-faced. It hasn't made the pain of seeing Amelia with Chad go away, but it is anesthetizing it for the night. My brothers, emotional surgeons.

"You remember that New Year's after Mom died?" I ask, pouring myself another whisky and spilling about $50,000 on the table. "When Dad poured us all a Macallan, even Maddox when he was, like, sixteen, and gave us that advice?"

"Yeah," Elijah answers, eyes hazy. "He told us to never fall in love. Said that if we obeyed that one rule, we'd never know a day's heartache in our lives."

We all fall silent, the easy laughter lost for a moment. "That was fucked up, man," Mason says, shaking his head.

"Nah." I down my whisky in one gulp and savor the burn in my throat. "He was one hundred percent right. I shoulda listened to the old man."

Visions of Amelia pour into my mind. The first time I saw her in that bridesmaid's dress that made her grimace every time she moved. Her shocked face when she walked into my office on the first day of her new job. Her moans and whimpers as I made her come on that fire escape. Her perfect skin, crossed and shaded by my knots and ropes. The way she looked at me when she told me she loved me.

The bright smile she gave Chad earlier tonight.

Nathan clasps my shoulder, dragging me back to reality. "He wasn't right, bro. That was his grief speaking. Life is nothing without love. Don't ever give up on it."

My vision blurs with tears. How do I not give up on it when the only woman I've ever loved is currently falling back in love with her douchefuck ex-husband? How do I not give up when I've lost the other half of my fucking soul?

FORTY-EIGHT

I pause outside my apartment building, narrowly dodging Kris with a K's boys as they zoom past me on their skateboards. They give me a wave, and I laugh at the sight of their pants hanging down over their skinny asses.

Juggling my groceries, I search for my keys in my purse and almost drop the other bundle I'm carrying: a massive bunch of gorgeous yellow Grandiflora roses. I decided to take a leaf out of Miley Cyrus's book and buy my own damn flowers. It's a declaration of self-love and a pat on the back—because today, I went on a job interview. Technically, I haven't handed in my notice at James and James, but I am planning to. I started casting around for vacancies and saw a position at a law firm in Williamsburg, right here in Brooklyn. The pay isn't as good, and the place isn't as prestigious, but on the plus side, the commute is tiny. And the plusiest side? Drake James doesn't work there.

I feel hopeful about it, and it's nice to have hope about at least one aspect of my life. The rest? That still pretty much sucks. Drake abruptly stopped trying to contact me, so I guess he's decided that I'm not worth the effort. Our alleged break has now become a breakup, and I am devastated. I'm functioning, and on the outside I am doing fine. But inside, I'm in pieces. Everything feels wrong without him, and I still cry myself to sleep every single night. That's if I sleep at all. Sometimes, I prefer not to because my dreams are a horrible blend of Drake and my mom, and occasionally one of them chasing me down a long corridor wearing a *Scream* mask and brandishing a knife.

Still, I tell myself as I finally find my keys, at least I had a job interview. I dressed for the job I wanted, talked them through my resume, and answered all their questions in a way that portrayed me in a positive and professional light. In short, I completely faked my way through it. Go me.

I'm lost in thought as I walk up the stairs to my apartment, wondering when I might hear from the Williamsburg firm and what might happen if they approach Drake for a reference. I don't think he'd screw me over out of spite, but who knows. I've proven to be a pretty crappy judge of character more than once in my life.

I pause, looking around me. Something feels wrong. I can't put my finger on it, maybe an unfamiliar smell, but a warning bell goes off in my brain. Straight away, I turn to go back the way I came.

Before I can get to the stairwell, I'm grabbed from behind and thrown hard against the wall. Someone takes hold of my wrist and sharply bends my arm up behind my back, making me yelp in pain. The flowers and the groceries hit the floor, and I watch a tub of Ben and Jerry's Chocolate Chip Cookie Dough roll away along the rug.

"Don't be screaming now, girl, or I'll have to break this pretty little arm of yours in two. We don't want to hurt you, but it won't bother us if we have to either." The voice in my ear is Irish, and his breath stinks of cigarettes and cheap booze. I struggle, managing to slam my other elbow back as hard as I can. I connect with something that crunches, and when I whirl around, I see a short, slightly overweight man clutching his nose. Blood pours out from between his fingers, and I have to fight the urge to apologize. He glares at me, his piggy eyes mean, and I run back along the corridor.

I don't make it far. My hair gets snatched up and used to stop me, and the pain is unbelievable. The next thing I know, I'm slammed face-first onto the back of a door and then thrown to the floor. A second man kicks me hard in the ribs. I double up and retch, gasping for breath as bile fills my mouth.

"Who are you?" I manage to mutter, trying not to show how terrified I am. "What the hell do you want from me? My boyfriend will be home soon."

It's a bare-faced lie, and the second man grins at me. It's not a nice grin, revealing a row of crooked yellowing teeth.

"We don't want anything from you, darling," he says, looming over me. "It's actually the man in your life we're interested in. You'll be coming with us now, and the less fuss you make, the better it will be for us all."

The man in my life? Drake? What has he—

My attacker holds a white cloth over my face, and the last thing I remember thinking is that it smells like the hospital.

FORTY-NINE

DRAKE

I really need to get a new secretary. The current temp is driving me nuts. It's not only that she isn't Amelia—that's hardly her fault—it's that she's fucking terrible at her job. She's constantly messing up my schedule, she can't spell for shit, and she can't even work the stupid espresso machine. I told her I didn't want to be disturbed today, but here she is, knocking on the door and walking in anyway.

"Miss Daniels, what part of 'do not disturb' are you struggling with?"

I'm being a dick, and I know I am. The poor woman looks terrified. I take a deep, calming breath and try again. "Miss Daniels, is there a problem?"

"There is, sir, yes. I have a man outside to see you. He's very insistent, and he seems very upset, and ... and I don't know how to make him go away."

I can't help thinking that Amelia would have known. I nod curtly. "I see. And what would his name be, this insistent guest?"

"Oh! Yes, right—that would be Chad. Chad Poindexter. He

said to tell you it was about Amelia? Isn't that your former secretary? The one who left?"

Bristling, I manage to keep my face neutral. She hasn't damn well left, at least not officially. And what the fuck is Chad doing here? Are they back together? If he's come to gloat, he might find that he leaves my office through my eighteenth-floor window.

"Show him through, Miss Daniels."

She sags with relief, and I straighten my tie as Chad walks into my office. He looks disheveled and distressed, but he still takes in the large room, the expensive furnishings, the stunning view. If I had to guess, this is exactly the kind of office he wants for himself. I wonder if he knows I'd give it all up in a heartbeat if it meant getting Amelia back.

"Chad," I say coldly. "What can I do for you?"

As he gets closer, I see more clearly exactly how bad he looks. There's a wild cast in his eyes, his jacket is badly creased, and he smells of stale sweat. Much as I can't stand the man, he's typically well-groomed.

"I need your help," he says simply, dragging his hands through his hair.

"And why, exactly, would I be willing to help you, Chad?"

He meets my eyes, and his face crumples. "Because they've taken Amelia."

I jump to my feet, sending my chair spinning away behind me, and close the distance between us. I grab him around the throat and force him back to the wall, holding him up against it as he whimpers and slaps at my hand. "What the fuck are you talking about?" I snarl. "Who's taken Amelia?"

I realize he can't talk and snatch away my fingers. He slides down the wall but manages to stay on his feet, rubbing at his neck and glaring at me. "A guy named Declan Boyle and someone else he works with. His cousin, I think. They have her, and they want half a million dollars to get her back."

I step away from him as my brain kicks in. They want half a million. That means she's still alive and their motive is strictly financial. And that's good news because fuck knows money means nothing to me compared to my girl.

"How long have they had her?"

"Uh, a little over a day."

"How long is a little over a day, Chad?" My tone is dripping with venom.

He checks his watch. "Twenty-six hours."

Twenty-six hours. Twenty-six fucking hours? My fury threatens to swallow me whole, but I push it down. Killing Chad won't do Amelia any good right now. I don't ask why he took so long to come to me for help. I already know—pride. He was too arrogant to admit he needed me, and because of his ego, she's been alone and suffering God knows what for twenty-six fucking hours.

I stride back over to my desk, and he limps behind me, still caressing his throat, the fucking coward. Sitting down, I rub the bridge of my nose. "Sit the fuck down," I command, and he slumps into the chair opposite me. His tan face, fake white smile, and flashy shoes tell a story of success that he doesn't come close to living up to. "Now tell me what the fuck is going on. Leave nothing out. And I warn you, do not mess with me right now or I will kill you. That is not a bluff or a threat—it's a statement of fact."

Whatever he sees in my eyes makes him gulp, and he nods. "Yeah, okay. You know I run an investment firm? We specialize in finding innovative new start-ups across the States, businesses run by the brightest and the best who—"

"Chad," I interrupt, exasperated by this dickwad's ego. "Do I look like I'm in the mood for a sales pitch? I don't give a damn about your shitty company." I slam my fist down on my desk so hard he jumps. "I only care about Amelia."

"I took their money, and they want it back," he says, the words all running together. "She's collateral."

"You took their money as in stole it?"

"No! Of course not. They invested it. But, as I'm sure you know and as I tell all my clients, investments can go down as well as up and—"

"Spare me. How quickly did this Boyle guy's investment go down?"

Chad glances past me at the window, his Adam's apple bobbing beneath his collar. "Um, well, there were adverse conditions and the market was volatile and—"

"Shut the fuck up. I get the picture. You messed up. You took money from the wrong people, and now because of your mistake, Amelia is in danger. Why her? You're divorced."

"I might have ... uh, well, they're based in New York, that was one of the reasons I was back in town. And I might have mentioned her, told them we were getting back together."

"And are you?" I ask, blood pounding through my veins. Not that it matters. I'd still move heaven and earth to keep her safe. He shakes his head, a tight expression on his face. "No. I tried, but she wasn't interested."

I know he has more to say on that subject, that he probably blames me for the rejection rather than the fact that he's a cheating dickwad who treated her like crap. "She's a good judge of character," I say, narrowing my eyes at him, relief flooding through me. She's not only alive, she's not with him. "And Chad, remember this—she's your *ex*-wife. Once I get her back, she's my *future* wife. You understand?"

He wants to argue, but maybe the memory of my fingers around his larynx helps him stay silent. He nods once.

"Good. Am I right to assume that Declan Boyle is Irish?"

CHAPTER FORTY-NINE

"Yeah, I think so. He has the accent anyway."

"And I'm guessing from the fact that he's kidnapped an innocent woman that he's not an orthodontist looking to boost his retirement fund?"

He shakes his head. "No. He's, uh, a businessman."

Right. A businessman. I know exactly what that means. And exactly who to talk to. I pick up my cell and find his name. He answers straight away.

"Drake. What can I do for you?"

That's one of the things I like about Shane Ryan, the head of the Irish Mafia in New York. He's all business.

"You know a guy named Declan Boyle?" I ask. A pause, the sound of music in the background, the clanking of metal on metal telling me I've interrupted a workout session.

"I do. He's a fat fuck with a face like a bloated weasel. Why?"

"He's taken someone. Someone I love the way you love Jessie."

The music fades, and he's obviously walking away. The mention of his wife has ensured I have his full attention. "What do you need from us?"

"For now, information. He's asking for cash. Is he the kind who'll stick to the deal? Will he hand her over if he gets what he wants?"

"Yeah, he will. He has money, enough for a fancy car and some of the trappings, but not enough for any real power. He's also a squeamish coward, which is good for your girl. He'll probably be working with his cousin Evan Finnegan, who's more likely to be handling anything, uh, physical."

I suck in a breath. If either of these Irish fucks has touched a hair on her head, I'll make them wish they were never born. Shane obviously knows what I'm thinking and adds, "Try not to worry too much about that. Neither of them are heavy guys.

Boyle is involved in gambling, and we tolerate him—but he's not a violent dude. Talks a good game, but he's soft. He once attacked Mikey with a fucking butter knife."

What the fuck? His brother Mikey is the size of a fucking rhino, and you'd probably need a chainsaw to do any damage to him. "Why?" I ask, needing to know if I'm dealing with a psycho here. Amelia is not the size of a rhino, and the thought of even a butter knife touching her perfect skin makes my blood freeze.

"Mikey fucked his wife ... At their wedding reception. Liam knocked him cold and stole his Maserati."

I shake my head. That's how it goes with the fucking Ryans. "Right. Good to know. If I come across this guy, will I be able to handle him?"

He snorts down the line. "Fuck yeah. In your sleep, pal. But he can be slippery, so maybe take something with you—a knife, maybe a gun. You need help with that?"

"No, that's handled. Look, Shane, I'm going to pay the guy because I need to get her back safe, but you should know that once that's done, I will be seeing them again. On less friendly terms."

There's a pause at the other end of the phone, and I wonder if he's going to give me trouble. If I'm going to provoke some Mafia bullshit pissing contest by laying hands on someone from their macho world. If so, bring it on.

"I get it. I know I'd burn the fucking world down if anyone touched Jessie. Let me know if we can help. Now or when you pay him that second visit."

He hangs up, and I make a second call, arranging for half a million in cash to be delivered to me in large bills. In most people's worlds, it's a lot of dough, and I see Chad's eyes widen as I request it like it's pocket money. I don't live in most people's worlds.

Once that's done, I tell Chad to call them and set up the exchange. He obeys immediately and puts the call on speaker so I can hear both sides of the conversation. There's some bullshit about swapping the cash for a location. It takes every ounce of self-control I have not to snatch the phone out of his hands and do it myself. It wouldn't help. If this scumbag gets wind of the fact that Amelia means something to someone with my kind of money, the best-case scenario would be a price hike. I can't even bring myself to consider the worst-case. It's better if I keep my distance, at least for now.

Once it's all sorted, Chad stands up and looks to me. The stupid fuck actually looks pleased with himself, like he's played some vital role in rescuing her instead of being the crooked cunt who got her abducted in the first place.

"Done?" I ask. He nods and starts to talk, but I'm not really listening at this stage. All the rage, all my fear and frustration are rising to the surface. I stride around my desk and enjoy his confused look as I prowl toward him.

"You put Amelia in danger," I say quietly, close enough that I can see the whites of his eyes. "Your greed put Amelia in danger. Your arrogance left her there for over a day. You are nothing but scum."

He takes a step back from me and looks as though he's going to bolt for the door. He's not quick enough, and my left jab lands perfectly in the center of his smug face, sending him sprawling to the floor.

It's the fucking least he deserves. I might yet kill him. Then I might kill the men who took her. Maybe I'll even kill the guy who owns her apartment for not making it safe enough. And there's a good chance I'll kill anyone who goes anywhere near her.

But first, I'm going to get her back.

FIFTY

DRAKE

It plays out exactly as Shane Ryan predicted: Boyle is only interested in the money. He gives us a time and place to leave the cash, and in return, Chad gets a location. These guys aren't criminal masterminds, and their entire plan is full of holes. If I wanted to take them down there and then, I could have.

But that can wait. Amelia comes first.

The address they've given us is an abandoned repair shop on the edge of Hell's Kitchen. Constantine drives us there, and I feel the tension build as we make our way through the dimly lit building. It smells of piss and old motor oil, and I can hear rats scurrying around in the darkness. I can't stand the thought of her being trapped, alone and scared, and my fists clench so tight that my nails slice into my palms.

What if she's not here? What if something goes wrong? If anything has happened to her ...

I shut down that train of thought and cast my flashlight around the room. The light flickers over piles of rotting newspapers, a heap of tires, and I think I can hear something that isn't a rat. I stand still and listen more closely. Yes! It's a mumbled voice, and it's coming from the next room. I kick the door open and spot her in one dark corner. As the light hits her, she closes her eyes against the glare. Thank fucking Christ, it's Amelia. She's here. She's alive.

Chad and I race forward and drop to our knees beside her. My eyes scan her for injury as I tear the gag from her mouth. She has some bruising on her face, but she's in one piece. She's sitting in an old office chair, and I growl when I see she's been tied to it with thick ropes. Our ropes. They must have taken the Shibari gear from her apartment. It was only ever intended to bring pleasure and comfort, not to abuse her. Her ankles and wrists are bound to the sides, and bile surges up into my mouth at the sight of broken skin where she's struggled against the hemp. Blistering rage blurs my vision, narrowing my focus until all I see is her. My girl. My everything. Bound and beaten.

"Mimi, honey." Chad's cloying, saccharine voice drags me back into focus. He's pulling on the knotted ropes but only making it worse. Amelia shivers, her eyes darting around the room like she's waiting for her kidnappers to return. She hasn't said a single word, and I realize she's terrified, hurt, probably dehydrated. My fury momentarily paralyzes me, and I listen to Chad say, "It's okay, angel face. I've got you now." Like he was any fucking use in this whole shitshow.

I shove my anger aside. That's not what she needs. Finally able to move again, I step up and pull out the knife that I brought in case of trouble. I could untie those knots eventually, but I want to get her free quickly. As I slice through the ropes, I feel sick at the thought of her being violated like this. I want to find the men who did it and carve them into tiny fucking pieces. She rubs at her wrists, still eerily silent as I do the same at her ankles. Chad strokes her hair and talks to her like she's a fucking child, and I decide I'd like to carve him into tiny pieces as well.

When she's completely free, she sucks in a deep heaving breath that makes her whole body shudder. Her fingers grip the sides of the chair, and her eyes are fixed on the door. "Have they really left?"

Chad answers before I can. "They're really gone, angel face."

Still crouched on the floor before her, I fight my anger along with the desire to pick her up, crush her to my chest, and never let her go again. She turns her attention to Chad and blinks. "Th-thank you, Chad," she whispers.

He preens at her response, and I ponder cutting off his dick and shoving it down his throat, but then she turns to me, her hazel eyes huge and shining. I meet her gaze, and as we lock eyes, the control she was holding onto so tightly crumbles. *She* crumbles. I hold out my arms, and she falls into them, tears running down her face, heavy sobs racking her body.

"Drake!" She chokes out my name, and I press my lips against her hair as I stand, scooping her up with me and holding her close.

"Shh, baby. I've got you now."

She throws her arms around me, burying her face against my chest and curling her fingers in the hair at the nape of my neck. She's trembling and frail, and I tighten my grip on her. "I was so scared. But I knew you'd come for me."

My heart cracks in two, but I need to get her out of this hell-hole. I lift her up into my arms, cradling her to me like she's a little girl, and put one foot in front of another in the direction of the exit. She sighs and rests her head on my shoulder, her whole body sagging with relief as she finally feels safe.

Chad scowls at me like I just stole his woman, the prick. I never stole her. He was stupid enough to let her go, and she's been mine since the day I met her. She'll always be mine.

I glare back at him, and his hand goes up to the black eye I gave him earlier. I nod, putting a warning into my fierce gaze: come near her again, I'll kill you.

Amelia sniffs. "Will you stay with me?"

I hold her tighter, pressing my lips against her temple. "Yeah, baby. I'll stay with you forever."

AMELIA DIDN'T WANT to go back to her apartment, which was totally understandable after those sick fucks lay in wait for her there. I had no intention of letting her out of my sight anyway and had already told Constantine to take us back to my place. He frowned when he saw the state of her and laid a gentle hand against her cheek. "You okay, Miss Ryder?" he asked quietly.

"Better now, Constantine," she said, managing a weak smile. We left Chad there in Hell's Kitchen, and he was pissed about it. Like he expected a fucking ride home.

It doesn't take us long to get back to the penthouse, and I run her a bath as she sits on the toilet seat, sipping from a bottle of water and watching me. She's dirty and tired and battered, but she insists she doesn't need a doctor. I checked her over as best I could in the car, and apart from bruises and scrapes, she seems to be okay. At least physically—the trauma might take longer to heal, and I intend to be here every step of the way.

I dip my hand into the bath water and check the temperature. Shaking off the bubbles, I tell her it's perfect and turn off the taps.

As I help her undress, I notice that she was wearing one of the outfits she used to wear to the office. "I had a job interview," she says, looking down at the pile of soiled clothes. "I'll have to burn those now."

A job interview? Fuck. She really was thinking of leaving. But what could I expect after the way I behaved?

There's a purple mark on her ribs, and she's holding her hand to her side as though it's tender. "I think I broke his nose. Then the other guy slammed me into the door and kicked me when I was down. I thought ... Well, I thought it was going to be a lot worse, but after that, they drugged me. When I woke up, I was there, in that place. In the dark. They said it was something to do with you."

My fury burns hot once more. "Me? They said that?"

She swallows. "They said that it was the man in my life they were interested in." A shudder runs through her, and I pull her to me. My hands skim the bare skin of her shoulders, and her naked body melts into my embrace. I hate that for a single second she thought I'd ever allow anything like that to happen to her because of me, but her basically telling me I'm the only one who holds the title of "the man in her life" takes a little of the edge off. "It wasn't me, mi rosa. Chad owed them some money."

"Chad? But he's ... we're ..."

"I think he's been telling people you were getting back together."

She blinks up at me, her eyes wet with tears. "We're not. You know that, right?"

I press a kiss on her forehead. "Yeah, I know that, baby." Because you're fucking mine. I don't add that last part—for now. Her body's still trembling, and I need to get her into the hot bath and take care of her, but we'll get there.

"I was so scared, Drake," she whispers.

"I know, baby. So was I. But it's okay. You're here with me now. You're safe."

I take her hand and help her into the bathtub. She sinks into the bubbles with a sigh and then submerges herself in the water completely. A few seconds later, she pops back up with a gasp. "That felt good."

I perch on the edge of the tub. "You need anything else? I ordered some takeout, but it won't be here for a while. Has to come all the way from Brooklyn."

Her eyes light up. "You didn't! You ordered Mario's?" The childish gleam of delight on her face gives me hope.

"He's even sending me some uncooked donut balls that can be deep-fried piping hot for you."

Her mouth drops open. "He is not!"

"He sure is."

"But he never does that. I mean, I know. I've asked."

The sparkle in her eyes warms my heart. She's so fucking beautiful, inside and out. Kidnapped, tied up, and slapped around, but she's willing to accept that the world is a good place because of exploding donut balls.

I shrug. "I guess you just never asked him the right way." By the right way, I mean a five thousand buck tip. Mario drives a hard bargain, but I'd pay him five million to see the smile on Amelia's face right now. It would be worth every cent.

"Wow. Have I ever told you that I love you, Drake James?" She laughs, but then she freezes. She used to tell me that she loved me all the time. I never took it for granted and it always felt special, but our time apart taught me exactly how special it was. I hate the way she's looking at me now, as though she thinks she made a mistake.

"You have," I reply quickly. "But I can never hear it enough. I love you too, mi rosa, and whenever you're ready, we can talk things through."

She nods and casts her eyes down at the water. When she looks back up, her smile is back. "If we have an hour to wait until food, would you maybe like to get in here with me? It's big enough for two."

I tilt my head and study her features. Is she deflecting? Asking me to get in with her because she wants to avoid a difficult conversation? She knows that her naked body against mine is the surest way to distract me, even if we don't have sex.

"Please?" she whispers, her eyes shining with unshed tears.

Fuck, how could I have been so stupid? She wants to be held. She wants to be reassured. Of course she fucking does—she was just held hostage for a whole day.

"Whatever you need, baby." Hurriedly, I undress and slide into the space behind her. I drape her wet hair over her shoulder, wrap my arms around her, and let her settle. She sighs, her body relaxing into mine.

"How are you doing?" I ask.

"I'm okay, I think. Maybe it will hit me tomorrow or the next day, but for now, I'm just grateful and relieved. Is that weird?"

"No." I kiss the top of her head. "I feel grateful and relieved too." Among a whole host of other things. Mostly anger. But I can deal with that tomorrow. For now, she is my only concern. Fuck, she'll always be my only concern, and it's about time she knew that.

"When Chad told me someone had taken you—when I thought I'd never ..." I choke back a sob, unable to finish the sentence. Unable to put into words the dark places my mind took me.

"I know," she says softly, her hand resting over mine.

"No, you don't know, Amelia." I turn her around so she's sitting on my lap, her legs around me. I need to be looking into her eyes when I say this. I need her to know how much I mean it. "Baby, I have never been so fucking scared in my entire life. The thought that I might never see you again. God, I'm so sorry I pushed you away. I'm sorry that I thought for a single second that I wasn't what you needed, mi rosa. I was scared of how much I loved you. Scared of how much I needed you too."

She blinks at me, and a tear rolls down her cheek. I brush it away with the pad of my thumb and cup her jaw. "I will always be everything you ever need, Amelia. Whatever and whenever you need it. It will always be me. Your ride or die. The other half of your heart and soul. Forever."

Her bottom lip wobbles. "Drake ..."

"I love you, Amelia. With every fucking fiber of my being, I love you. I would give my last breath to make you happy. I promise never to give up on us again, and if you let me, I will spend every second of the rest of my life proving that to you."

Another tear leaks from the corner of her eye, and she swats it away. "Are you sure this isn't just—" Her throat constricts as she swallows. "Are you sure this isn't just a reaction to what happened? I know it was scary, and I—"

I press my mouth against hers and run my tongue across the seam of her lips until she allows me entry. My chest aches at the thought of her doubting what I just said, even if she has good reason to. So I show her instead, doing exactly what I wanted to do when I saw her tied to that chair earlier and pouring every ounce of regret and longing and love for her into this one kiss. I moan into her mouth and wrap my arms around her, pulling her as close to me as humanly possible. Her skin, coated with bubbles, slides so easily against mine. It's as though she was made to be molded to my body. Like we were carved from the same star.

She snakes an arm around my neck, kissing me back with equal passion. My cock aches painfully, desperate to take her, but now is not the fucking time. Only when my jaw is aching and the water is growing cool do I break our kiss. She blinks up at me, her lips red and swollen. I brush my fingertips across her bruised eye and swallow down the river of rage that wants to erupt out of me at the thought of anyone's hands on her.

Tomorrow. I'll deal with them tomorrow.

"What happened to you was the kick in the ass I needed,

Amelia. I might not be the best at expressing my feelings, but believe me, they've always been there. From the first time you smiled at me, I was done for."

She grins at me, her beautiful eyes brimming with tears. "I think I fell in love with you during our first dance. I love dancing."

"I know, baby. And from now on, we're going to dance together every fucking day."

She shifts on my lap, and my cock twitches against her. She glances down, eyelashes fluttering and a wicked smile playing on her lips.

Placing my forefinger under her chin, I tip her head back up until she's looking into my eyes. "Ignore that. All my cock can feel is your sexy naked body pressed against him. Cocks have no idea how to read a room."

Hurt flashes across her face. "Maybe it's you who doesn't know how to read a room. You don't have to treat me any differently, Drake. And it's been so long."

A growl rumbles in my throat. "I'm not going to treat you any differently, mi rosa. But for now, we're going to put some more hot water in this tub, and you're going to let me wash your hair along with every other part of your beautiful body." I trail kisses down the side of her throat. "And then you're going to have some food and let me take care of that eye."

She arches an eyebrow. "And then?"

"Then you'll probably fall asleep on the couch, drooling."

She swats me playfully on the chest, and I catch her wrists, my fingers running over the red dents left by the rope they used to tie her. I hate that they did that to her. I hate every single thing they did to her. I'm going to make her some new marks when she's ready, chase away those ghosts and start writing our own history.

I yank her closer, resting my lips on her forehead. "If, after you've eaten a dozen exploding donut balls, you're not asleep and you still want me to, I will fuck you hard and long and deep, Amelia."

Her breath catches in her throat. "Promise?"

"I promise."

FIFTY-ONE

AMELIA

" **D**rake," I murmur as he coaxes the last tremor of my orgasm from me. He's made me come so many times that I am now made entirely of liquid. My bones are fluid, my muscles weak, and I can barely form a word. In fact, the only word I seem able to remember is his name.

We ate Mario's exploding donut balls and we talked and cuddled. Then, as promised, he fucked me hard and long and deep. Afterward, he fucked me slow and soft. Then he made me come with his lips and tongue. He has kissed every part of my body, caressed every inch, and told me repeatedly how much he loves me. How he's never going to let me go again.

I feel safe. Adored. Cherished. Drake's love language has always been sensual, but now he has added to it with actual language, telling me in words how he feels as well as with his actions.

He crawls up the bed to be next to me, swiping his beard clean with his hand.

"God, I missed having you squirt your cum all over my face," he says, climbing under the covers and pulling my shaking body into his arms.

"Wow, you're such a romantic," I say, nuzzling into his chest. "But also, me too."

He laughs softly, and the sound vibrates through his chest and into me. How I have missed that sound. It's been far too long since I've heard it. This is the happiest I've felt since Mom died, but a wave of sadness washes over me. Our problems haven't gone anywhere; they're still lurking just beneath the surface.

The look on his face tells me he's deep in thought too. "What happens now?" I ask, my voice shaky.

He cocks an eyebrow. "This is probably the part where you fall asleep and drool."

"That's not what I meant, Drake."

"I know." He kisses the top of my head and sighs, and despite his previous declarations of love, I prepare myself for the worst. "I think that as soon as you feel up to it, we should go visit my family because they've missed you like crazy too. And then we go into the office and tell the whole damn world that we're together."

My heart rate kicks up a notch. "You think we should tell everyone at work too?"

He nods. "I own the fucking firm. If I can't fall madly, passionately in love with my sexy-as-fuck secretary, who can?"

"But what about Linda?"

He looks down at me, frowning. "Nope, Linda definitely isn't allowed to fall madly, passionately in love with you."

I pinch his side and laugh when he tries to squirm away. "Come on, be serious. I am terrified of that woman."

"Don't be, baby. I'll protect you. Although ... Yeah, maybe not from Linda. She scares the fuck out of me too." His dramatic shudder makes me laugh. But then his arms are squeezing me tighter, and he rests his lips on the top of my head. "Don't be scared of Linda or anyone else, mi rosa. Nobody will ever hurt you again. I promise you that."

I snuggle closer. There is nowhere in the world I feel safer than I do with Drake.

"Besides, Linda will find out anyway when we change your address on your personnel file." He throws it out so casually, and I wriggle until I can untangle myself enough to rest my chin on my hands and stare down at his handsome face.

"And why would I be changing my address, Mr. James?"

His eyes narrow. "Because there's no way in hell you're going back to that apartment building which clearly still has terrible security." I open my mouth to protest, but he presses a finger to my lips and carries on talking. "And there isn't a world where I'm spending a single night away from you ever again, Amelia. Well, barring girly trips with your friends or whatever." He shrugs.

"Are you suggesting I move in with you?"

"Not suggesting, Miss Ryder." He shakes his head. "Demanding. I am your employer, after all. If you check the fine print of your contract, I'm sure you'll see it's all there."

"And if it's not?" I arch an eyebrow.

He hums softly, his eyes twinkling with devious intent. "I'll tie you up in court for years." He winks.

Is he serious about moving in together? Of course he is. This man wouldn't joke about something like that. "But you live in a hotel, Drake. And even if I don't particularly want to go back to my apartment, I have my mom's house now. It's paid off."

"I know. But I won't be living in a hotel for much longer. The contracts have finally gone through on my loft in Tribeca. That's where we'd live, mi rosa. We'd be neighbors with Ryan Reynolds and Blake Lively."

I nudge him in the ribs and laugh. "Oh, well, that's sold it. But, seriously, Drake."

He nods, and I can tell he's ten steps ahead of me. That he's already considered every objection I can put forth. "And if you're not ready to sell your mom's place, don't. Take your time, think about this. But when you're ready, you could rent it out. It could be the start of your own property empire."

I ponder what he's saying, and I can see the merit of it. I have no desire to sell my childhood home, but I also don't want to leave it empty. It's a nice neighborhood, and it would be good to see a new family enjoy it. I can't expect Mrs. K to keep an eye on it forever. Amelia Ryder, property developer ... Huh. I kinda like the ring of that. Still, I have a niggling sense of doubt. "Maybe this isn't the right time to make such a big decision. Us moving in together is huge. Maybe it's a little ... too fast?"

He tips my chin up so I'm looking right at him. There's so much love in those deep brown eyes that I melt.

"Mi rosa, I have been waiting thirty-seven years for you. If anything, it's too damn slow."

FIFTY-TWO

DRAKE

"You need any help there?" Liam asks, looking at me hopefully. All the Ryan brothers are built like monster trucks, but Liam can be especially menacing.

His older brother Conor lays a hand on his massive shoulder. "Does the man look like he needs any help?"

Liam studies me as though he's taking the question seriously. "Nah. I suppose not. I just wanted in on the fun."

It's been two days since we rescued Amelia. Two days of me pampering her and cocooning her and fucking her senseless. Two days of us reconnecting and planning for a future together that I can't wait to start.

We have dinner at my dad's house tonight, which she and the rest of my family are incredibly excited about. And so am I. It feels even more important than when I introduced her to them before, back when a part of me was still wondering if I had it in me to do the whole commitment thing. But now I'm surer than I've ever been of anything in my life. Sure of her. Of us. Before any of that, though, I have some business to take care of.

We're back at the abandoned car repair shop in Hell's

Kitchen, the place where she was tied up and held hostage. The three of us walk toward the room at the back where I found her, our boots crunching on broken glass and fuck knows what else.

"Here you go, Drake," Conor says, holding the door open for me. He grimaces as it falls off its hinges. "A little gift for you, from my brothers and me."

Inside, portable lights have been rigged up to make the place a lot brighter than it was the last time I was here. In the center of the room, two men sit tied to chairs. Both of them have gags stuffed in their mouths, and they look completely fucking terrified. As they should.

"You want us to stay?" Conor asks. "Just in case. There are two of them."

I shoot him a look, and he holds his hands up in surrender. "No offense, pal."

"None taken. And feel free to stay. You might enjoy it."

"Shit," says Liam, grinning at me and leaning against the wall. "If I'd known, I woulda brought popcorn."

I stretch my shoulders and crack my neck. "You don't know me." I flex my hands and loom over the two men tied up. "But you took something from me. Something precious. And now you're going to pay. First, I'm going to beat the living shit out of you. Then I might slice your throats. I haven't made up my mind yet."

I tear the gag out of Declan Boyle's mouth, and he immediately starts bleating. "What the fuck, Conor! What the *fuck*! Does Shane know about this?"

"Sure," Conor replies, a vicious smile on his lips. "It was his idea, Declan. You've been a pain in our ass for too long, and this time you crossed a line."

"How the fuck was I supposed to know the stupid bitch was anything special?"

I slap him hard across the face, and the whole chair goes

sprawling to the floor. I kneel down and hold my knife beneath one of his pig-like eyes. He goes pale and starts to beg, but all I use the knife for is to cut his ropes. Then I do the same with the other prick, his cousin. Both of them stand up, looking around the room, their scared eyes darting from me to the Ryans.

"Don't worry about them," I say. "They're not getting involved. Worry about me."

I make a come-and-get-me gesture with my hands, and I can tell the precise moment they decide they can take me. The fucking fools both run at me at once, and I almost feel sorry for them. My rage makes me superhuman. They don't stand a chance.

WE LEAVE the building a couple hours later. It feels weird to step out into sunlight, back into the civilized world. My sweatpants and T-shirt are covered in blood, my knuckles are scarred and swollen, and I have a nasty cut over my left eye. But, to use an old saying, you should see the other guys.

The other guys are in rough shape. In fact, they're both barely conscious, and in Boyle's case, missing part of an ear. I broke ribs, fingers, jaws, and cheekbones. I spilled blood and busted lips and snapped tendons. And still, it didn't feel like enough. I wanted to kill them, and the Ryans wouldn't have blinked an eye at that. They might be tough clients from a legal perspective, but they're definitely guys who would help get rid of a body.

In the end, I didn't kill them. Or maybe I did. Maybe it'll just take a real long time for them to die. I tied them both back up and stuffed the gags back in their broken, gap-toothed mouths, ignoring their screams of agony.

"I'm going now," I said once they were both bound and bleeding, their eyes pleading for mercy. "I'm going to close the door on this building, and I'm going to pay someone to padlock the place. Maybe add some steel doors and window shutters to make it extra secure. Nobody is getting in or out for a very long time. The only living creatures in here will be you and the rats. I hear rats like the scent of blood, and I know they like eating rotting flesh. Maybe someone will find you before they chew out your eyes and bite through your dicks. But then again, maybe not."

Boyle managed to slam one of his feet down onto the ground, and I kicked his ankle repeatedly until I was sure the little bones down there were shattered. Then I stamped on his foot, just to make my point. Tears poured from his battered, swollen eyes, and he let out muffled screams around the gag. He really didn't look so good when I left him there. I wouldn't be surprised if a heart attack takes him out before the rats have a chance to get to him.

We walked out and left them there with no light, no water, no food, and no way to communicate or cry for help. The Ryans are silent as we make our way to our vehicles. Liam passes me a big plastic bottle of water and some alcohol wipes from the back of their truck. They're the kind of men who keep that shit on hand.

I clean myself up. "Thanks, guys. I appreciate the favor."

Liam looks at me and shakes his head. "Are you actually intending to leave them in there to get eaten alive by rats?"

"I don't have a problem with that. They hurt the person I love more than anything or anyone else in the world. Getting eaten by rats is too good for them. But if you want to go back in and get them out, I won't hold it against you."

Conor sucks on his teeth. "I don't think it's the kind of mess Shane would want being found, so we'll probably come back for them in the morning. But regardless of what we do with them, they won't bother you or your girl again."

"Yeah. And Drake," Liam says, giving me a look that communicates a newfound respect, "you know we spar with Nathan every Tuesday and Thursday morning, right? You should really think about joining us and working off a little of that aggression." He laughs, and I join him, amused at the irony of Liam Ryan, one of the most violent men in the country, insinuating that I have anger problems. I don't. Not as a rule, anyway. Only when it comes to anyone fucking with my girl.

Maybe I will join them though. If only to keep in shape for all the sex I'll be having.

CHAPTER

FIFTY-THREE

DRAKE

"I see now why you keep this here," I say to Nathan as I stare at Mom's painting of the beach.

He steps up beside me. "It's calming, right?"

I nod. "Mindful."

"Are you nervous? About today, I mean?" he asks, concern in his voice.

I shake my head. "Nope. I'm eager to get everything out in the open, actually. And more than a little ecstatic about having my secretary back." I don't add that I've already fucked her on my desk once this morning. I swear she wears those sexy little outfits just to fuck with me.

He clears his throat. "How's she doing?"

Obviously, he knows what happened to Amelia two weeks ago and that the Ryans were involved in the aftermath, but for legal reasons, I haven't told him the details of what went down. Plausible deniability is our friend when shit gets shady.

"She's doing well. Better than well. She's fucking incredible, Nathan."

He offers me a knowing smile. I've got that same sappy,

pussy-whipped tone to my voice that he has when he's talking about Mel.

"And you're sure she's okay to come back to work? Because she can take all the time she needs. Helen can even help you out if you don't want another temp."

"I'm sure. Her face has healed enough for her to cover the fading bruises with makeup, and she really wants to be back in the office. She said she's going crazy being stuck at home. I might go crazy too. She's already organized the loft to within an inch of its life."

"Yeah, your decorating plans have given my wife ideas about our penthouse. She and Amelia were on the phone for an hour last night talking color swatches. I am now painfully aware that there are infinite shades of blue, and I can name at least twenty of them." He rolls his eyes, but there's nothing but affection in his tone. Mel and Amelia have become fast friends these past few weeks.

"I believe only ten minutes of that conversation were actually about color swatches, though, and the other fifty were spent talking about us all going on vacation to the Bahamas next spring."

"Huh. I must have missed that part."

"You're picturing your wife in a bikini now, aren't you?" I nudge him in the arm.

"Fuck yeah, I am." We both laugh.

"Anyway, listening to their color swatch chatter is the least you can do, seeing as how we're watching Luke for you this weekend," I remind him.

He grins wickedly. "Yeah. Thanks for that, bro."

We stare at the painting for a few more minutes before he speaks up again. "So, no last-minute doubts about the meeting this afternoon?"

"Nope. I've had it with the sneaking-around bullshit. This

isn't some fling with my secretary. This is being in love with a woman who also happens to be my secretary."

He arches an eyebrow at me, and his lips quirk up with amusement. "Did I hear that correctly? Drake James is in love?"

"Yeah, well," I say, grinning at him. "It happens to the best of us, right? But are you sure you're okay with this? I mean, I never asked."

He meets my eyes, and something flashes between us. "You don't need to ask my permission, Drake. We started this firm together, and we run it together. We're equals."

"Just equals? Need I remind you that I scored three points higher than you on the bar exam?"

"Don't push your luck, numbnuts. I'll see you in the meeting. And yeah, before you ask, I've got your back."

An hour later, the great and the good of James and James are gathered in the boardroom, along with key executives from HR, office services, and even the fucking catering department. I don't want to have to do this twice or for us to be the subject of gossip. If we tell them all at once, it will be done.

Personally, I don't give a rat's ass what any of them think. But I know she does. She generally gives several rats' asses about other people in general. Her gaze flickers over the assembled group and she nervously licks her lips. Fuck, I wish I could lick her lips. She's wearing that wrap dress again, and even with Linda watching us, I'd like to bend her over the massive conference table and sink my dick into her. I meet her eyes and look at her sternly. Like I'm her boss and she's done something to piss me off. Once I have her attention, I mouth, *I love you*, and her face is suddenly suffused with a smile. It's like the sun's come out.

I wipe the stupid grin off my own face and turn to the room. The chatter stops as I stand before them.

"I'm sure you're all curious about why I've called you here today," I say, studying each of their faces. "And I won't take up too much of your time. I know we're all busy." I pause for just a moment and give them the opportunity to murmur their agreement. "Most of you know Miss Amelia Ryder, my secretary."

A few people nod, some give her a little finger wave, and others look nonplussed. Amelia looks petrified.

"Amelia and I are now officially a couple. To clarify, we are romantic partners. We are boyfriend and girlfriend. She is my bae, my boo, my old lady."

There are a couple shocked looks, some amused surprise, and quite a lot of smiles. "Is she your LOML?" pipes up Drew, the guy in charge of catering.

"Maybe," I reply. "But I'm not sure what that is."

Amelia stands up beside me, her hand creeping into mine, a shy smile on her gorgeous face. "It stands for love of my life," she explains.

I nod and lock eyes with her. It feels like we're the only two people in this crowded room. "In that case, yeah, she is very much the LOML. Now, I know there are policies in place and that technically, I'm her boss. So, Linda—and everyone else— please take this as my official notice that I am in a relationship with Miss Ryder. And if any of you object to that, I refer you to a policy that I've just decided to add. It's called 'My name is on the door and I can do what I like.' Does anyone have any questions?"

Nathan is standing at the back of the room, arms crossed over his chest. He shakes his head in mock despair, but I can tell he's amused.

"Yes, Mr. James." Linda stands up, and I can't tell if she's actually scowling or if it's just her normal expression. "Could I get a copy of that new policy in writing please?"

Amelia giggles, and I make the most unprofessional choice I've probably ever made in my life—at least with witnesses—and pull her into my arms. I seal my lips over hers to a chorus of wolf whistles and cheers.

"Put that in your policy packet, Linda," someone pipes up from the back, and that has my girl laughing against my lips.

"Love you," I murmur.

She pulls back, leaving me breathless and wanting more. "You'd better get to work, sir. Looks like you have a new policy to write."

I press my lips to her ear so nobody will hear. "I'll need you to take *dic*tation, Miss Ryder."

Her cheeks flush pink. "Of course, Mr. James."

CHAPTER
FIFTY-FOUR
AMELIA

"Are you sure?" Drake asks, frowning.

"Yes, I'm sure, Drake. And you don't fool me. I can see your hard-on from here. I know you want this as much as I do."

He gives me a huge, slow smile. The kind that turns my core to molten lava along with all my organs.

"Of course *I* want this. If it were up to me, I'd have you tied up all the damn time, mi rosa. I'd have permanent access to your cunt and your ass and your mouth, and I'd keep your gorgeous body strung up and ready for me to play with twenty-four hours a day. That I want this is not in question."

It's so hot when he talks to me like that, and there' would be a a definite damp spot on my panties now—if I were wearing any that is. I know why he's being cautious, and I love him for it.

I slowly tug on the string that holds my wrap dress together and let it slide to the floor where it pools around my feet. I already removed my underwear, and now I stand before him completely naked apart from my pearls and my smile.

His face darkens, and the tent in his suit pants gets even bigger. "Jesus fuck, Amelia."

"Drake, I want this," I say clearly. "A traumatic thing happened to me, and yes, it was terrible. But what would be truly terrible would be if it stopped me from enjoying life. Enjoying sex. Enjoying Shibari. What we do together is nothing like what those assholes did to me. Being tied up by you is nothing but pleasure—sweet, sexy pleasure. I'm not going to have some kind of flashback to what they did. This isn't going to make my trauma worse. It's going to help me. I want the last rope marks on my skin to be made by the man I love and trust more than anyone in this world."

His eyes rake over my body, hot and dark. He stands up and prowls toward me. "I'm sorry," he says. "Were you talking? I was distracted by imagining you tied up and begging for my cock." He winks and leads me toward the bedroom where he keeps his ropes. Then he stands me in the middle of the floor and runs his hands over my naked flesh, giving me goose-bumps. I shiver as he looks me up and down, his eyes assessing, biting his lower lip. My nipples pucker in response to his scrutiny.

"Are you planning what to do with me?" I ask, my voice small and breathless.

After removing several lengths of rope of all different thick-nesses from the large wooden chest that holds all his equip-ment, he wraps one of them around my neck, very gently, then tightens the coil until I gasp. He pulls my pearls around it and uses both to tug me toward him. His hand goes to my bare ass, and he slams me into his hips. "I am, my little vixen. And you are going to love every fucking minute of it, aren't you?"

I nod, my bottom lip caught between my teeth as I pant for breath, excitement and desire curling up my spine. "Yes sir."

He groans. "You know what those words do to me, don't you?"

"Yes sir."

"God, you're such a naughty fucking girl. Maybe I'll spank this beautiful ass while you're tied up for me. Shall I do that?" He slips his hand between my thighs, and his fingers toy with my sensitive flesh until I whimper.

"I asked you a question, Amelia." He circles the tip of his finger at my wet entrance, teasing me.

"Yes please," I gasp out, and he rewards me by sinking inside me. My knees buckle, and I would drop to the floor if he weren't holding me up.

"Always so damn wet for me, baby." His voice is a low, commanding growl.

I press my face against his chest and nod, my knees trembling as he finger-fucks me so slowly and skillfully that pleasure lights up every cell in my body.

"Drake," I whimper, fingernails digging into the taut muscles of his biceps.

"I know, baby. You're so fucking snug and wet. I'm gonna play with you all night."

Oh, holy hell. My orgasm builds quickly and fiercely, ignited further by his filthy talk. I hold onto him, my entire body trembling as he sends me over the edge, sinking deeper and harder while his thumb brushes over my needy clit.

Coming down from the highest of highs, I sag into his arms. He carries me to the bed and lays me down on it. His eyes are dark and fierce as they rake over my body. "That was all for you, baby." He licks his lips. "Now it's my turn."

FIFTY-FIVE

AMELIA—NEW YEAR'S EVE

Drake's childhood home is full of laughter tonight. All of his brothers are here, along with extended family members, and it's been an evening of fun, fine food, and even finer company. As an only child who recently lost her mom, being at the heart of something like this takes some getting used to—the noise, the banter, the way they all bounce off each other. I still feel a little shy around them sometimes, but I love every minute of it.

It's getting close to midnight, and Nathan and Mel have disappeared. Maybe they're tired, or maybe they're otherwise engaged. It's impossible not to notice that they can't keep their hands off each other.

Drake was deep in conversation with Nathan earlier, and they ended their chat with a hug. Everyone seems to be in a good mood, and I've enjoyed meeting a few new people and spending some time with the now-sleeping baby Luke. He's turning one in a couple of days, and I'm sure his parents will love the toddler drum set Drake and I picked out. I know I'm excited to attend his first concert.

I laugh as I watch Maddox demonstrate that he can in fact

do a full circuit of the room walking on his hands and as Mason hands him a $100 bill afterward. I wouldn't bet against Maddox when it comes to the wild and wacky, and I'm surprised Mason did. Elijah shakes his head at their antics and goes back to his cell phone. From the wicked smirk on his face, I'd bet my last dollar he's talking to a woman. But who?

"Having fun?" asks Drake as he sidles up behind me. He slides his hands around my waist and pulls me back into him.

I rub myself against his body and smile in satisfaction when I feel his cock immediately respond. "I am now." I'm wearing a dress that ties up the back, and his hands have been toying with it all night. I am indeed behaving like a vixen this evening. I knew exactly the reaction it would provoke in him.

"I'm looking forward to getting you out of this dress," he says, whispering against my neck and making my heart beat faster. "It's a very sexy dress, but not even half as sexy as the woman wearing it. You feeling naughty tonight, mi rosa?"

I glance up at him over my shoulder, my cheeks hot. "I guess I am, sir. I probably need to be punished."

His cock twitches against me, and he groans. "You are a wicked, wicked woman. Now, come outside with me."

Holding my hand, he pulls me with him toward the huge balcony that runs along the whole front of the house. He leads us both through the glass door and outside, where there's a magnificent view of the lights of Manhattan laid out before us in the distance.

Even though it's not quite midnight, there are already fireworks going off all over the city, multicolored explosions painting the inky black sky with glitter.

"It's beautiful isn't it?" I murmur, mesmerized.

"It is," he replies, turning me to face him. "But not even half as beautiful as you, Amelia."

He kisses me, his lips surprisingly gentle against mine. His breath is warm against my skin as he whispers, "I love you. So damn much. I don't know how I ever lived without you."

Before I can reply, he drops down to one knee in front of me. My hands fly to my mouth, and I stare in disbelief as he pulls a small black velvet box from his jacket pocket.

"Oh my god ..." My breath catches in my throat.

"Nora Amelia Ryder," he says seriously, opening the box. "You are my entire fucking world. My everything. On the night we met, I said nobody could ever promise forever. I was wrong, and that's what I'm promising you now—forever. Would you do me the honor of becoming my wife? Will you promise me forever?"

Tears spill from my eyes, and as the new year begins, the sky explodes around us. Cheers erupt from inside the house, and the sound of a whole city celebrating reaches my ears. None of it compares to what I see in Drake's eyes—love, devotion, and the promise of eternity.

I nod, my lips trembling. "Yes. Of course I will."

Another chorus of cheers, this time accompanied by wolf whistles, carries out of the house. "Put the ring on her finger before she changes her mind, bro," Mason calls.

Drake flashes me a sexy wink before he slides the almond-shaped diamond set in a platinum band onto my finger. I steal a quick glance at my new family. All of them are smiling widely, many of them holding champagne glasses in the air. I wave my hand, flashing my newest accessory, and then I pop my foot up for show like I'm the star of my own romantic comedy before I return my attention to Drake.

My fiancé. My everything. He's on his feet now, and he wastes no time at all wrapping me in his strong arms and sealing his lips over mine.

Cue more whistles and cheering.

"They're so fucking nosy. Can't a guy kiss his fiancée in

private?" Drake murmurs against my lips. But he's smiling, and so am I.

We're surrounded by a sea of hugs from Drake's brothers and Dalton, then Mel, Tyler, Ashley, and Luz join the pile. Drake is eventually pulled away by Maddox and Mason, and they hoist him into the air like he just scored the game-winning touchdown at the homecoming game.

Dalton wraps his arm around my shoulders. "Thank you, Amelia," he says softly, his gray eyes brimming with tears.

"For what?" I ask him, confused. Surely not for agreeing to marry his son. That is a dream come true.

He glances at his sons, all of them together now. Nathan and Elijah have stolen Drake and are parading him around like a trophy. "Out of all of them, I worried most about Drake being alone. I never thought anyone would make him smile like that."

Tears fill my own eyes as I look up at my husband-to-be, his head thrown back in laughter as he demands his brothers put him down so he can get back to his wife. "I love him more than anything in this world, Dalton. I would die to make him happy."

He takes my hand in his and presses a kiss to my knuckles. "I know that, sweetheart. And he would for you too. That's the kind of love my Verona wanted for all her boys, but especially for him. If you have more than two, the middle child is always the tricky one, just so you know." He winks.

Is he suggesting ...? A blush creeps over my cheeks, but I can't help the surge of hopeful excitement that rushes through me. These last few months together have been a whirlwind of fun and dates and hot sex, lots and lots of that, and Drake and I have skirted around the idea of kids. I know he's never imagined a life with kids before, but he's also not opposed to it now, so maybe ...

"Hey Pop, you putting the moves on my wife?" Drake's deep, sexy voice snaps me from my thoughts, and I realize I'm staring into Dalton's face, hypnotized at the thought of making him a grandfather again.

"She's not your wife yet, son. You'd better keep a tight hold on her." He plants a tender kiss on my cheek and allows his middle son to wrap me in his arms once more.

"Oh, I fucking intend to," Drake growls while squeezing me tightly. "Now, don't you all have some champagne to drink and some canapés to eat?" He jerks his head toward the open balcony doors.

Taking his hint, everyone files back into the house, leaving us alone once more. Drake dusts his lips over my forehead. "What were you and Dad talking about so intently?"

I hum while I think of a tactful way to tell him that his dad is expecting some more grandbabies. "Um, you and how incredible you are."

He laughs, and his warm breath washes over my skin. "Anything else?"

I bite down on my lip, a flutter of nerves dancing in my belly that I'm unaccustomed to feeling around this man. Not like this, anyway. He makes me feel so secure in every way, but this is a huge step, and he's already taken one of those tonight. Still, we promised each other honesty always. "He said that if we have more than two kids, the middle one is always the trickiest."

I hold my breath, waiting for his reaction. His dark eyes glisten as he gazes at me. "Ah, that figures." Before I can ask what that means, he kisses me, and my body melts into his. If he's trying to distract me from having *the talk*, then it's sure as hell working.

When he pulls back, he leaves us both panting. "And just for the record, Miss Ryder—soon to be Mrs. James ..." He presses his mouth to my ear. "I cannot fucking wait to fuck a baby into you."

My knees buckle, but his hold on me keeps me upright. "You can make absolutely anything sound filthy, can't you?"

He shrugs, the corner of his lips quirked upward. "It's a gift."

I hold onto him, my fingers sinking into the soft lapels of his tuxedo jacket. "So you do want kids?"

He clicks his tongue against the roof of his mouth and tilts his head to the side.

"Drake?"

He laughs, brushing my hair back from my face. "Yes, I want kids, Amelia. A whole fucking tribe of tiny humans who are part me and part you. I mean, hopefully mostly you, but I think a little of the James gene will be tolerable." He laughs again, and it makes his dark eyes twinkle.

"A whole tribe?" I try my best to frown and feign shock, but I can't quite manage it because I'm just about delirious with happiness.

"As many as you want, mi rosa. But I guess we'll start with one and see what happens."

I snake my arms around his neck and pull his mouth close to mine again. "Have I ever told you how much I love you?"

"Yes, but I much prefer it when you show me."

"I can do that." I purr the words and rub myself against him, smiling when I feel how hard he is already.

He groans and jerks his head toward the house. "That lot are going to want to stay up celebrating our engagement for hours, and I don't want to deny you or them the pleasure of that. But know that the minute I get you alone ..." He growls instead of finishing his sentence.

I brush my lips over his, taunting him with the promise of a kiss before we're interrupted by Dalton yelling for us to come inside so they can do a toast. Drake rolls his eyes dramatically.

I walk back into his childhood home in a different year as

his fiancée rather than his girlfriend, with the knowledge that there is nothing this world could throw at us that would make us falter.

It's me and him.

It's us.

Forever.

EPILOGUE

AMELIA—CHRISTMAS EVE

"Okay, so if it's a girl, Edith Verona?" he says, his brows knitted together as he sips his coffee.

My hand goes to my belly, the now noticeably swollen place where our baby lives. We chose to wait until the baby is born to find out the sex, but the closer it gets, the more we feel the pressure to have names picked out. "I like that," I say quietly. "And I think they would too."

"You don't think it's a bit ... I don't know. A bit maudlin?"

"No, absolutely not. They were our moms. We loved them, and this is our way of paying tribute to that love. I think they'd like it too, don't you?"

He nods and smiles a little sadly. He's told me all about his final conversation with his mother and the pain and guilt it's caused him for so many years. I was able to tell him about my time as a volunteer in the hospital and how I saw so many people lose their sense of self as they neared death. The way the drugs messed with their minds and the outrageous things they could say. But I was also able to tell him, sincerely, that a few harsh words at the end could never outweigh a lifetime of love.

That his mom wouldn't want him to torture himself for a minute longer.

"Yeah, I think our moms would love it." He squeezes my fingers. "It'll be like a little bit of them is still with us, won't it?"

"Exactly. I hope it is a girl. With Nathan and Mel's two boys, we could do with some girl energy to balance out all that testosterone. The James family needs a feminine touch."

His resulting laugh is the perfect balm for the undercurrent of sadness that often accompanies talking about our moms. "You're not wrong. We're all ruffians."

I can't argue with that, so I don't. "We should probably get ready to leave soon. Luz said dinner will be served at six on the dot, and she's not the kind of woman I want to get on the wrong side of."

Drake murmurs contentedly, his nose pressed against my hair. "I already packed the car. We have a little time yet before we have to decamp to the madhouse for Christmas."

I adore my extended family. I loved spending last Christmas with them, and I'm excited to see them all today too, but I get what he means. This is pure heaven right here. We're sitting out on the terrace of our new home in Tribeca, sheltered beneath a heated roof that is strung with fairy lights. New York is putting on a show for us: Pure white snow glistens on the rooftops and sidewalks, and the skies are a perfect dark blue despite the plummeting temperatures.

Drake has draped a blanket around our shoulders, and we had freshly fried Mario's donut balls for our lunch. Our very own Christmas Eve tradition.

"What if it's a boy?" he asks. "Nathan took my dad's and grandad's names, and I'd hate to saddle a kid with Jerónimo. It was old-fashioned even way back when my abuelito was born."

"No way." I shake my head. I'm not even worried about our little Jerónimo getting bullied. No kid deserves to face the full wrath of six James men simply for teasing a classmate about his name. "Personally, I think Drake is a fine name. Or maybe Charlie?"

He smiles at me wickedly. "Charlie," he says, "was a man of exquisite taste. Speaking of ... I think it's time to unwrap my Christmas gift. You know, tradition and all that."

I shake my head. "That's not our tradition. We do one tonight and then the rest in the morning, just like last year."

He pulls me onto his lap, already tugging at the belt on my red wrap dress. "I'm talking about the one that's just for us, mi rosa. Remember?"

A memory of him stripping me naked and fucking me beneath our huge Christmas tree immediately before we left for Dalton's house last year flashes into my mind. My cheeks flush with heat, as does the space between my thighs. "Oh, you're not talking about an actual gift."

He hums, his sinful lips dusting over the skin of my neck. "Yes, I am. The very best gift a man could have—you, Mrs. James."

He pulls the blanket all the way over us before he opens my dress and slips his hand into my panties. "We're doing this out here?" I arch into the pleasure his fingers are already bringing.

"Only this part. Gonna make you come out here on our balcony, and then I'll take you inside to fuck you. I want you fully unwrapped for that. And that's for my eyes only, right?"

I nod, my bottom lip caught between my teeth while his fingers brush expertly over my clit. He knows my body better than I do.

"You belong to me, Amelia," he growls possessively.

"Yes, Drake," I pant as he sinks a thick finger inside me. This right here is like every Christmas wish I ever had rolled into one. I belong to Drake James forever and then some.

EPILOGUE 2

DRAKE

Jesus fucking Christ, my wife is the sexiest, most incredible woman on the planet.

And she tastes like fucking heaven. I glance up at her from my favorite position in the world—my head between her thighs —and wink when I catch her eye. Of course, she has to push up onto her elbows for me to be able to do that now, given that she's seven months pregnant. Her cheeks are flushed pink from how hard I just made her come, and I swear my heart feels like it's about to burst. How the fuck did I get so goddamn lucky? Crashing Emily and Tucker's wedding was the best damn decision I've ever made in my life.

My cell phone vibrates on the nightstand—probably one of my brothers asking if we've left for Dad's house yet. We'll be there in time for dinner, but I want my wife to myself just a little while longer. She's become an integral part of the James family, but right now, she's mine and only mine. My possessive streak, already bordering on the psychotic where she's concerned, has only gotten more fervent since she became my wife and started growing our child. I would maim, kill, and die for her without a second thought.

"Drake." She moans out my name as her head drops back between her shoulder blades.

I crawl up her body, trailing kisses over her swollen belly before rolling her onto her side so that I can fuck her comfortably. Although I considered sticking more closely to our recent tradition and fucking her beside our Christmas tree, I carried her to bed instead. Nothing but luxury for my heavily pregnant queen. "You still okay there, mi rosa?"

She nods, her luscious bottom lip clamped between her teeth.

"You're so fucking perfect." I skim my hand across her abdomen. I'm constantly amazed by the fact that she's growing our child in there. While most men are probably awed by the miracle of pregnancy, it's not until you watch your partner actually grow a human being that it hits home how truly remarkable it is. I can't wait to meet our child. Boy or girl doesn't matter to me; I just want them to be here.

"You're pretty perfect yourself, sir." She purrs the last word, and my cock twitches against her juicy ass.

I nip her shoulder blade. "Any more of your sass, my little vixen, and I'll tie you up and punish you severely. And then we'll be late for dinner."

She giggles. "If I weren't so scared of Luz, I'd take you up on that offer, Daddy."

Sir? Daddy? This woman is trying to kill me, I swear.

I nuzzle her neck, inhaling her sweet scent and basking in everything that is her. "Behave yourself, mi rosa." I sink my cock inside her, and her soft whimpers fill the room.

"I love you, baby," I murmur, my lips against her ear. "So fucking much."

"I love you too, Drake."

I fuck her slowly, savoring the feeling of her tight heat squeezing my cock each time I sink back inside her. And I tell her over and over again how incredible she is, how much I love her. I promise to take care of her and our baby, and any more that might come along. I promise to be everything they ever need.

I promise her forever.

Have you read Nathan and Melanie's story yet? If not you can find out all about them in Broken

The rest of the James brothers' stories are available for preorder now

Elijah

Mason

Maddox

ALSO BY SADIE KINCAID

Have you tried Sadie's bestselling paranormal/ fantasy series yet? If you love possessive broody vampires, witches, wolves and all things magic, then try the Broken Bloodlines series here

Forged in Blood

Promised in Blood

Bound in Blood

The complete, bestselling Chicago Ruthless is available now. Following the lives of the notoriously ruthless Moretti siblings - this series will take you on a rollercoaster of emotions. Packed with angst, action and plenty of steam.

Dante

Joey

Lorenzo

Keres

If you haven't read the full New York Ruthless series yet, you can find them on Amazon and Kindle Unlimited

Ryan Rule

Ryan Redemption

Ryan Retribution

Ryan Reign

Ryan Renewed

And the complete short stories and novellas attached to this series are available in one collection

A Ryan Recollection

If you'd prefer to head to LA to meet Alejandro and Alana, and Jackson and Lucia, you can find out all about them in Sadie's internationally bestselling LA Ruthless series. Available on Amazon and FREE in Kindle Unlimited.

Fierce King

Fierce Queen

Fierce Betrayal

Fierce Obsession

If you'd like to read about London's hottest couple. Gabriel and Samantha, then check out Sadie's London Ruthless series on Amazon. FREE in Kindle Unlimited.

Dark Angel

Fallen Angel

Dark/ Fallen Angel Duet

If you enjoy super spicy short stories, Sadie also writes the Bound series feat Mack and Jenna, Books 1, 2, 3 and 4 are available now.

Bound and Tamed

Bound and Shared

Bound and Dominated

Bound and Deceived

ACKNOWLEDGMENTS

As always I would love to thank all of my incredible readers, and especially the members of Sadie's Ladies and Sizzling Alphas. My beloved belt whores! You are all superstars. To my amazing ARC and street teams, the love you have for these books continues to amaze and inspire me. I am so grateful for all of you.

But to all of the readers who have bought any of my books, everything I write is for you and you all make my dreams come true.

To all of my author friends who help make this journey all that more special.

Super special mention to my lovely PA's, Kate, Kate and Andrea, for their support and honesty and everything they do to make my life easier.

To the silent ninja, Bobby Kim. Thank you for continuing to push me to be better. And to my amazing editor, Jaime, who puts up with my insane writing process and helps me make each book better than the last.

To my incredible boys who inspire me to be better every single day. And last, but no means least, a huge thank you to Mr. Kincaid—all my book boyfriends rolled into one. I couldn't do this without you!

ABOUT THE AUTHOR

Sadie Kincaid is a dark and contemporary romance author who loves to read and write about hot alpha males and strong, feisty females.

Sadie loves to connect with readers so why not get in touch via social media?

Join Sadie's reader group for the latest news, book recommendations and plenty of fun. Sadie's ladies and Sizzling Alphas

Made in the USA
Monee, IL
16 January 2025

77013614R00246